The Nightingale

A Rufus Stone Detective Story

Book Four

by

K. J. Frost

GWL
PUBLISHING

First Published in 2021
by GWL Publishing
an imprint of Great War Literature Publishing LLP

Produced in United Kingdom

ISBN 978-1-910603-80-2 Paperback Edition

GWL Publishing
Forum House
Sterling Road
Chichester PO19 7DN

www.gwlpublishing.co.uk

Dedication

To S.L.

Chapter One

End of January 1940

"So, what do you think?"

He glances up at me, blinking a few times and doing his best to look innocent. He's still wearing his work clothes, although he's taken off his shoes, his slippered feet stretched out towards the roaring fire. And as I gaze at him, I can't help thinking to myself that there are two things wrong with this scene. Firstly, I really do wish he'd change when he comes home from work. Not only does he look really silly, sitting there in smart trousers and slippers, but I can't help thinking he's about to go out again, at any moment. And secondly? That's the fact that my husband is anything but innocent, no matter how much he might like to pretend.

"Hmm? What's that, dear?"

"I said, what do you think? Have you been listening to a word I've said?"

"Sorry, I was just reading this article about George Gershwin in the Radio Times. There's going to be a programme on about him next Tuesday evening, which looks like it might be quite interesting. A 'musical biography', they're calling it. We could try and listen to that, couldn't we? It doesn't finish until quarter past ten, but I think it'll be worth staying up for. I've always been quite partial to George Gershwin." His voice fades and he puts the magazine down on the arm of the chair beside him, raising his eyebrows at me, expectantly, and I sigh in exasperation.

"I know you've always liked George Gershwin, not that I can see the fascination myself, but can I assume that you haven't been listening to me at all, given your preoccupation?"

"Sorry, dear."

"Honestly, you really are very irritating sometimes. I've just spent the last ten minutes talking to you – or rather, talking to myself – about decorating the spare bedroom."

"The spare bedroom?" He frowns, as though I'm the one not making sense here, when in reality, he's got his head in the clouds, as usual.

"Yes. The one next to ours," I clarify, because we live in a four bedroomed house – well, five, if you count the attic room, which I don't – and I feel the need to be precise about this.

"Decorating it? Whatever for?" he yawns, which vexes me still further, being as it seems he can't take anything to do with me, or our marriage, seriously.

"Because it would make a good nursery," I snap, wondering why I have to explain everything in triplicate. Not only have I mentioned my reasons this evening, while his mind was evidently otherwise occupied – with George Gershwin, of all things – but we've discussed this before, several times in the last two years at least.

"Y—You're not pregnant, are you?" He sits forward, startled, which isn't that surprising, being as a conception at this point in time would be nothing short of a miracle, of Biblical proportions. He hasn't been near me in months, after all.

"No. Of course I'm not. But I'll be thirty in the summer, and we always said we'd have a child – or children – one day. We can't wait too much longer, can we? Especially if we want to have more than one…"

I notice his face fall, assuming that the prospect of impregnating me doesn't exactly inspire him, or fill him with any enthusiasm.

"Babies cost a lot of money, dear," he says, his eyes darting around the living room, as though he's looking for excuses in the floral wallpaper, or the oak sideboard, or the landscape paintings. "And I'm not sure we can afford any redecorations at the moment. And besides, with the war and everything, perhaps it would be better to wait…"

"I don't see how the war really affects us. It's not as though you're going to have to go and fight, is it?"

"Well, no. But there's still the financial consideration."

"Are we short of money then?" I ask him, because if we are, it's news to me.

"Not 'short' exactly," he replies. "But we're not overflowing either. We need to be careful and not rush into things."

He smiles, then picks up the Radio Times again, dismissing both me and the topic of conversation. I stare at him for a while, uncertain whether his lack of enthusiasm *is related to a genuine shortage of funds, about which he has chosen, for some reason, to keep me in the dark. Or whether he's truly so appalled at the prospect of physical intimacy with me, that he'll use any excuse to avoid it.*

I'm tempted to ask him whether his carnal appetites are being satisfied elsewhere, but I bite my tongue. Although I suppose it would explain his abstinence in the bedroom over the last few months, I can't believe he'd do that to me again. Not when he promised so faithfully that he wouldn't…

———•———

"Congratulations!"

"Good luck!"

"Don't do anything I wouldn't do!"

That last comment rings out from Harry Thompson, my sergeant, and oldest friend, his arm around his pregnant wife, Julia, and I smile in his direction, as the crowd of well-wishers gathers on the driveway. And then I climb into my car, beside my bride and turn to face her, unable to wipe away the smile that's adorned my face all day, from the moment I awoke at just after six this morning, and realised that today was the day I would become the happiest of men.

"Ready?" I ask Amelie and she nods her head in agreement as I start the engine and pull out onto the road, relieved that we're finally alone.

Don't get me wrong. It's been a magnificent day, filled with smiles, and laughter – and the odd tear, from my mother and Aunt Dotty – and plenty of good cheer all round. But in spite of all of that, this is the moment I've been waiting for all day… some quiet solitude with the woman I love. And the freedom to be ourselves, because we're married now, so no-one can tell us what to do… or, perhaps more importantly, what not to do.

"Are you sure you're going to be all right to drive?" Amelie asks, resting her hand gently on my leg.

"I'm positive."

"We can still catch the train, if you'd rather," she suggests, leaning closer to me.

"And risk having to share you with other people? I don't think so. Besides, we deliberately chose somewhere that wasn't too far away, so that we *could* drive." It's true. We chose our honeymoon destination entirely around the practicalities of petrol rationing and the fact that my arm has only been out of plaster for just under four weeks, making a long drive out of the question. Not if I want to be fit for anything when we reach our destination, which I most certainly do. Scenic views and romance didn't really enter into our decision making at all. But then, I think we were both in agreement that, providing we could have some time together, we didn't really mind where we were. Totnes, or Timbuktu, it matters not, providing we're alone, with each other. As it is, we've chosen an inn at Bury, in the South Downs, just over an hour away from home, and I've been driving as much as I can over the last couple of weeks, just to get ready for the journey and to acclimatise to my new vehicle; a beautiful British racing green, MG T drop head coupé, which my mother bought for me after I crashed my last car… breaking my arm in the process.

"You really don't mind?" Amelie asks.

"I really don't mind. There's no way I'm sharing you with anyone for the next seven days… not unless I absolutely have to. And at the moment, I don't absolutely have to."

She giggles, removes her hat, placing it on her lap, and rests her head on my shoulder. "It was a lovely reception, wasn't it?" she muses. "And I was so pleased Aunt Millicent came downstairs and joined in."

"She quite surprised me, actually," I reply, still paying attention to the road, although it feels very comfortable having Amelie nestling against me. "She didn't seem nearly as mad as the last time I spoke to her."

"She's not mad." Amelie slaps my knee playfully.

"Well, she's still convinced I'm Errol Flynn, so I wouldn't be too sure about that."

"You do bear a remarkable resemblance, Rufus… so it's not really her fault."

"It is when she actually starts calling me 'Mr Flynn'."

"She didn't, did she?"

"Yes. Twice. Still think she's not mad?"

"Let's say she's touched, shall we?"

I shrug and smile down at her briefly, before returning my gaze to the road ahead. "If you insist, darling… if you insist."

"I thought Julia looked much more pregnant than when I last saw her, and extremely beautiful with it, didn't you?" she asks.

"She looked lovely, but nowhere near as beautiful as you."

"Hmm…" she sighs wistfully, as she gazes out of the window, and a thought crosses my mind.

Instinctively I slow the car, my foot easing off the accelerator, and I turn to look at her.

"Are you trying to tell me something, darling?"

"Like what?"

"Like that maybe you'd rather not wait to start a family?" I voice my thoughts, wondering if she's had a change of heart since we first discussed this, a few weeks ago.

"No." She sounds surprised. "We agreed to wait."

"And you're still happy about that? Because if you've changed your mind…"

"I'm not ready for motherhood yet," she interrupts. "And besides, I think I'd like us to have some time to ourselves first…" Her voice fades.

"I couldn't have put that better myself. I mean, obviously, if you'd wanted to do things differently, I'd have…"

"Well, I don't," she says firmly. "This is our time, Rufus. And I think we've earned it."

She's not wrong. From the moment of our first meeting, which came about over the brutal murder of her sister – or at least the girl she'd grown up with as a sister – our brief relationship has been filled with incident, and no small amount of trauma… including a threat to her life and two attempts on mine. She's quite right. We need some time to ourselves… even if only to draw breath.

"That's about the best thing I've heard all day… apart from when you said, 'I do', of course."

She leans over and kisses me briefly on the cheek. "Well, I meant every word."

"I'm glad to hear it, Mrs Stone."

She giggles and I slowly accelerate again.

"Was everything all right with Harry?" she asks, after a brief pause. "He seemed a bit quieter than usual."

I glance across at her, feeling a cloud descending over us. "I wasn't going to say anything, but now you've mentioned it… his mother telephoned him last night, just before he and I were due to go out to the pub, to tell him that his youngest brother, Vic, has just shipped out to France. He'd been training up in Yorkshire, or somewhere, since before Christmas, but he sailed yesterday morning. They only gave him twenty-four hours' leave, so he had time to visit their mother, but not to come and see Harry. His other brother, Fred, is already out there, so…"

"Harry must be worried sick." Amelie finishes my sentence for me, showing her customary understanding.

"He is."

"Did you still go out?" she asks.

"I wasn't sure we should, but Julia said she thought it would take Harry's mind off things, and in the end she was probably right, although we didn't stay out late. I was tucked up in bed and sound asleep by ten-thirty."

"I'm glad to hear it," Amelie says, and I glance at her, noticing her smile.

"And would there be a reason that you want me well rested?" I ask, teasing her, because I can.

"N—No," she stutters, and even though I can't look at her, because I'm approaching a roundabout, I'd be willing to bet she's blushing. "Do you think your mother will have stopped crying yet?" she asks, once I've made the required turn and we're on a nice straight section of road again.

"I expect so. Aunt Dotty's probably plied her with alcohol. Between her and Aunt Issa, I dread to think what mischief they'll be getting up to, without me." My aunts and my mother living under one roof is a recipe for disaster at the best of times, and is something that's usually best handled in small doses. But with my mother having come to stay at Aunt Dotty's back in November, when I was injured and in need of her care, and Issa coming for Christmas, and then deciding to stay on for the wedding, it's beginning to feel like a permanent state of affairs. "I'm rather relieved to be absent for the next seven days. At least I won't have to pick up the pieces… or arrest any of them."

"They're not that bad," Amelie says, chuckling. "They've been really helpful with arranging the wedding, you know? Without them, I don't think we could have got everything done in time."

I take her hand in mine and give it a gentle squeeze, because I know she's not exaggerating. Amelie and I set ourselves a ludicrously tight schedule, by announcing our engagement just before Christmas, and then setting the date for our wedding just over five weeks later. Most of the pressure fell on Amelie though, and I know how deeply it affected her, being as she came to me at Aunt Dotty's one evening, just over two weeks ago, in floods of tears and told me we couldn't possibly get married. My initial reaction was fear – naturally – accompanied by confusion, because I thought I must have done something to upset her, but had no idea what that might be. She made her tearful announcement and then turned to leave, without so much as an explanation. But I wasn't having that, so I took her hand in mine and pulled her into the dining room, sat her down at the table, knelt before her, and begged her to tell me what was wrong. To start with, she just sat and cried, and every so often, looked up at me and just said, "Sorry." But then, between sobs and sighs, she revealed that, in her words, 'everything was going wrong'. In this instance, 'everything' turned out to include the flowers, because she'd heard from the florist, who couldn't get hold of the particular roses Amelie had asked for. Then there was her aunt, who was making a fuss about the decorations for the reception. And to top it all off, there was fact that she still hadn't found anything to wear. Once she'd finished telling me all of that, she broke down completely, falling into my arms and wailing that we may as well call the whole thing off. It took me a while to calm her, but when I did, and she was able to focus on me properly, without crying, I suggested that she ask Aunt Issa to speak to the florist, not because she's an expert on the matter, but because few people will dare to argue with her. I pointed out that Aunt Dotty could be relied upon to deal with Millicent Templeton, and the decorations. Not only does my aunt's natural artistic flare make her the perfect candidate for anything decorative, but she was married to a diplomat for years, and some of his capabilities definitely rubbed off. My aunt is a dab hand at knowing just what to say, and how to say it, in almost any situation. And as for something to wear… I was brave enough to suggest Amelie enlist my mother's help, because while Mother can be a bit fanciful and flighty, she'll always do what's right. Once Amelie had agreed to my suggestions, I kissed away her tears, and then I kissed her. Very thoroughly. And when I'd finished doing that, I asked her if she'd mind not scaring me like that again, for which she apologised, quite unnecessarily… and finally, we agreed that being married was more important than anything else. And we were right. We've got our whole lives to prove it, too. But first, we've got seven days of honeymoon to while away.

And I intend to make the most of them.

We arrive at the inn, a beautiful sixteenth century thatched building on the main road, at just before six o'clock, and the landlord welcomes us warmly, showing us to our room. Rotund and jovial, with a smattering of silver-grey hair, and a ruddy complexion, he points out the adjoining bathroom, and informs us that dinner is served in the restaurant downstairs until eight o'clock. I thank him profusely, depositing our small suitcases by the wardrobe, and informing him that we'll be down shortly, before he leaves, a beaming smile on his face.

Once we're alone, Amelie starts moving around the room, opening drawers and cupboard doors, peering inside, and I sense her uneasiness, taking pity on her.

"Shall we unpack?" I suggest to break the ice and she nods enthusiastically, coming back to the bed. I lift up the cases, putting them on the mattress and, lying them flat, she opens them, before we both unpack our own clothes, placing them in the chest of drawers, having first agreed on the division of space. As I'm squeezing my thick blue jumper into the bottom drawer, I notice that Amelie is laying a very appealing-looking white nightdress on the bed, straightening it out, and she catches my eye, flushing, as I smile at her.

"You're sleeping on that side, are you?" I ask, amused.

"I—I don't have to," she replies, snatching up her nightgown again and holding it to her chest.

I stand, walking around the bed and and take the soft, silky garment from her, before placing it back down on the mattress again. "It's fine, Amelie. I don't mind where I sleep, as long as you're beside me."

She blushes, biting her bottom lip, and I reach out, freeing it with my thumb and kissing her briefly, aware that if I intensify the moment, in the way that I usually would, the nightdress is likely to prove superfluous and we'll almost certainly miss dinner.

I pull away from her and return to my own unpacking, my final task being to unwrap my new pyjamas, leaving the bottoms on the bed, by the pillow, and placing the top on the chair in the corner of the room, next to the wardrobe.

"What are you doing?" Amelie asks, staring at me from her side of the bed.

"Unwrapping my pyjamas," I explain.

"But why have you put the top half over there?" She nods towards the chair.

"Because I won't be needing it."

"You won't?"

"No. I don't wear the top half of pyjamas… only the bottoms. Haven't I told you that before?"

She shakes her head. "No. When would you have told me that?"

I smile again. "Well, I suppose it's not something that comes up in everyday conversation. But I wouldn't worry about it… it's not as though you haven't seen me half naked before."

She lowers her head, embarrassed, I assume, perhaps recalling my times in hospital at the end of last year, when I was forced, due to my injuries, to remain bare chested. I suppose she might also be remembering her visits to me back then, when we got both rather got used to the feeling of her skin on mine whenever she touched me. Or maybe she's nervous, concerned about the other half of of my body, the half she hasn't seen yet, that remains a mystery to her. For now at least.

I move around the bed once more, hoping to put her at ease. "Have you finished unpacking?" I ask.

"Yes." She looks up, and leans over, closing her suitcase. I take it and, together with my own, I stack it on top of the wardrobe.

"Do you want to change, or shall we go down and have a drink before dinner?" I ask, turning back to her.

"Do I need to change?" She sounds uncertain, and I go back to her, taking her hands in mine and holding them between us.

"No. You look absolutely beautiful." She does. The result of her shopping expedition with my mother is the stunning pale blue dress she's now wearing, with a fitted jacket on top that shows off her slim waist to perfection. I can still remember the twinkle in my mother's eye when she and Amelie returned triumphant, and how, over dinner that night, Mother told me her lips were sealed as to what they'd bought, but that I wouldn't be disappointed. She wasn't wrong. "I'm not sure I've told you that today, have I?"

"Yes," Amelie replies, smiling. "About ten times, I think."

"Well, that's nowhere near enough." I lean down and kiss her gently. "You look beautiful, my darling. And you don't need to change. Ever. Not in any way."

After a very nice meal of local trout, we return to our room. The restaurant was busier than I'd expected it to be, and we both felt rather overdressed in the end, not that we minded. It didn't seem that our fellow diners minded either – not in Amelie's case anyway – being as she attracted a great many admiring glances from the men in the room. She failed to notice, and focused her own gaze entirely on me, which was very gratifying, and rather than embarrassing her by pointing out how much attention she was drawing, I revelled quietly in the fact that she's mine, and we spent the entire meal discussing our day and how perfect it's been, which it has. From the moment I first saw her in the Registry office and was simply dazzled by her beauty, to our first kiss as husband and wife; from my mother's rather unexpected tears, to the extremely emotional speech that Amelie's uncle gave before we departed, we couldn't have asked for more.

Throughout all of that, neither of us mentioned the part of the day that's yet to come, but as I open the bedroom door, flicking on the lights, and standing aside to let Amelie enter before me, I can sense her uneasiness and, while I'll admit I'm nervous myself, I know I have to do everything I can to make this easier for her.

"Would you like to go to the bathroom while I get undressed?" I suggest and she looks up at me and smiles gratefully, before going over to the bed and picking up her silky nightgown, folding it over her arm and retreating to the bathroom in the corner of the room, where she pulls the door closed quietly behind her.

Once she's gone, I switch on the lamps on either side of the bed and turn off the main one, which creates a much softer, more romantic atmosphere. Obviously, if she's feeling shy and wants me to switch the lights off altogether, then I will, but I have to admit, I'd rather not. I'd rather see her. Completely. And I think I'd rather she saw me too.

Realising that she might be back at any moment and that standing around daydreaming isn't achieving much, other than fuelling my imagination, I undress quickly, and pull on my pyjama bottoms, before climbing into bed.

I've just got comfortable when the bathroom door opens. Amelie turns off the light behind her, but even in the gentle glow from the bedside lamps, I can see her clearly, and what I see takes my breath away. I didn't have time to appreciate earlier, that the top half of her nightdress is made entirely of lace, and that it therefore hides absolutely nothing, but my body responds to her instantly and, leaning up on one elbow, I study her perfect form, the see-through bodice revealing her to me for the first time.

She's staring at me too, biting her bottom lip, apprehensive, although whether or not she's feeling shy is hard to tell. I'm about to ask whether she'd prefer to have the lights turned off – because I feel I should at least offer – when suddenly, she reaches up and starts to scratch her shoulder, beneath the lace strap.

"Are you all right?" I ask, and she shakes her head.

"Not really."

I smile. "What's wrong?"

"It's this lace… it's really itchy."

Pulling back the covers, I climb out of bed and walk over to her, even though I know my very natural reaction to her is going to be fairly obvious. I've got nothing to hide from her anymore, though, and I'm certainly not ashamed of my responses. "Well, you look absolutely stunning," I murmur, as I get close to her. "But I have a feeling that this nightgown was probably designed by a man… for men. And I doubt he had any consideration at all for the women who'd have to wear it."

She chuckles and nods her head, surprising me by how at ease she seems, considering her earlier nerves, until it dawns on me that with the light behind me, she probably can't see me that clearly, and in any case, she's kept her eyes resolutely fixed on mine the whole time. "I have no idea why on earth any woman would want to put themselves through wearing something like this."

I take the last step, standing right in front of her now, our bodies almost touching. "You don't have to," I whisper. And with that, I lean down, clasping the silky material in my hands, and pull the gown up and over her head, throwing it across the room. She gasps as I expose her, but I clasp her face with one hand, capturing her lips with mine, moving my other hand behind her, into the small of her back, and pulling her closer, letting her feel the effect she has on me, and relishing the soft moan that she breathes into my mouth and the glorious sensation of her delicate skin against my chest as I kiss her passionately, matching her fervent sighs with my own, before I turn us both around and start to walk her slowly backwards towards the bed.

We've been staring at each other for some time now, still slightly breathless… still very much in awe of what we've just done.

"I love you," I whisper, although I've lost count of how many times I've said that, since the backs of Amelie's legs hit the bed, causing her to squeal gently and break our kiss, and I lifted her into my arms and lowered her onto the soft mattress.

"I love you," she replies, the smile still etched on her lips.

"You're sure I didn't hurt you?"

"A little. But it was worth it." I smile back at her, sighing with satisfaction, and rest my hand on her naked hip. "There is one thing, though," she says, tracing small circles across my chest with the tip of her forefinger.

"What's that?"

"I thought we agreed – twice, if memory serves – that we were going to wait a while before starting a family…" Her voice fades.

"Ahh… yes. Well, what can I say?" I kiss her gently. "I got carried away. I'm sorry, darling. I won't make a habit of it."

She smiles. "I'm not complaining."

"No, but I should be more careful… more responsible. And I will be. Next time."

Her smile broadens and I kiss her more deeply, before moving us down the bed a little and pulling her close in my arms.

"So, being as we've established that you're not a huge fan of fancy nightgowns," I muse out loud, "I'm intrigued to know what you normally wear in bed?"

"A little more than I'm wearing now," she replies, glancing down at the narrow space between our naked bodies. We're lying, facing each other, my leg wrapped around her, and I have to chuckle.

"Well, I like you just as you are." I kiss her soft lips and she sighs gently, leaning into me.

"I wear pyjamas," she says, when I eventually pull away from her.

"Of course," I remark, a memory pricking at the back of my mind. "You told me once, when I telephoned you from work, that you were going to have a bath and get into your pyjamas."

"Yes, I did," she says, her eyes glistening into mine, and I wonder if she's remembering that, although I'd phoned her at the time, to tell her I was going to have to work late, once she'd revealed her plans to me, I'd suggested I could visit her anyway… later on. The case I'd been investigating had been a difficult one, and that moment had been a welcome, lighthearted break from the darkness. "But unfortunately, I didn't bring any pyjamas with me," she adds, "so I'll just have to put up with the scratchy nightdress." She lowers her eyes, as though she's embarrassed. "I—I only bought it because I thought it was more appropriate for our honeymoon than my pyjamas."

I lower my leg slightly and roll her onto her back, settling into the cradle she makes for me, my body craving more of her already. "No," I murmur, raising myself above her, "the way you are now is much more appropriate…"

I wake with a start.

It's pitch black, but I'm aware of movement in the room.

"Who's there?" I ask, flicking on the lamp beside the bed and sitting upright.

"It's just me," Amelie says and I turn to see her on the far side of the room, seemingly searching for something. She's looking behind the chair that's beside the window, anyway. She's also stark naked, and utterly beautiful.

"What are you doing?"

"I'm sorry I woke you," she mutters, still searching. "I'm just trying to find my nightdress. Do you know where you threw it?"

"No. I was a bit distracted at the time. Why do you need it?"

"Because I'm cold," she replies.

"Then come back to bed." I hold the covers back for her to climb in, but she shakes her head and I wonder what's wrong. "I'll keep you warm, I promise."

"I know, but also need the bathroom… and it's freezing in there."

I chuckle and clamber out of bed. "In which case, your flimsy nightgown isn't going to be of much use is it?" I point out.

"Well, no," she replies, "but it's all I've got."

"No, it isn't." I walk over to the other chair – the one by the by the wardrobe – and pick up my pyjama top, carrying it back to her. "Try this," I suggest and she takes it from me, slipping it on and wrapping it around her.

"Oh… that's much better," she says.

"Good… now go to the bathroom, and come back to bed. I miss you."

She smiles and turns to dart into the bathroom, although before she does, I pat her gently on the behind and she yelps, giggling, before she dashes away, and I go back and straighten the sheets, pulling up the blanket and eiderdown, and then I climb into bed, resting my head on my arm and think about how adorable my wife just looked. How adorable my wife always looks, actually.

After a few minutes, the bathroom door opens and she steps out. I notice that she's done up the buttons of my pyjama top, and that she doesn't take her eyes from mine as she walks across the room and slides into bed beside me.

"Better now?" I ask quietly.

"Much."

She snuggles down and I switch off the light and turn back to her, letting my lips brush against hers while I slowly undo the buttons again.

On the second to last day of our honeymoon, I wake to find Amelie staring at me. Normally I'm awake before her, so this is an unusual occurrence in itself.

"What's wrong?" I ask, rubbing my eyes.

"Nothing… I just don't want this to end, that's all."

She sounds unbearably sad, and I pull her closer, turning onto my back and cradling her in my arms as she rests her head on my chest.

"Who says it has to end?" I ask, kissing her forehead.

"We're going home tomorrow, remember?"

"I know, but that doesn't mean anything has to end, darling."

"Yes it does. You'll be going back to work on Monday, and…" Her voice cracks as she falls silent.

"I know." I turn to face her. "But we'll be home by tomorrow lunchtime, and we'll have the whole of Sunday to ourselves before work has to start getting in the way, and then our evenings will still be ours. I'm not going to stop loving you, or making love to you, at every opportunity, just because we're no longer on our honeymoon."

"I hope not," she says quietly, nestling into me. "I've got rather used to having your undivided attention."

"You've always had that." I run my hand across her soft skin and she shudders slightly.

"I think I have, haven't I?" she muses, almost to herself. "Although I think it'll make a pleasant change for us to just be able to sit and talk, and hold hands, and hug, and kiss, and..."

Her voice fades, and I fill in the gap. "And make love?" I suggest.

"Yes."

"As opposed to what?" I ask, feeling intrigued.

"As opposed to you constantly having to comfort me, and dry my tears. I feel like you've been doing that since the moment we first met."

I reach up and cup her cheek with my hand. "Well, I didn't dry your tears the first time we met, because I didn't know you well enough."

"No, but you've dried them every time since."

"I know. And I like drying your tears."

She looks at me, a furrow forming on her brow. "You do?"

"Well, no, obviously I don't *like* it. I don't want you to cry. But I think you've had plenty to cry about over the last few months, don't you?"

"Hmm... I suppose," she whispers.

"There's no 'suppose' about it, Amelie. You've been through a lot... including falling in love with me. And that's enough to make anyone weep."

She chuckles. "It most certainly is," she says and snuggles into me a little further.

"Was it worth it?" I ask her, still being playful.

"Yes... every single minute."

I smile and turn over onto my back again, letting her rest against me, and, as I hold her, I think about our time together, and how much we've been through, which is probably more than most couples would, in a lifetime. But more importantly, I think about our perfect week, and how much we've learned about each other. Like Amelie, I don't want it to end either, but it has to, I suppose, at least in terms of spending quite so much time together, and being able to do whatever we like, whenever we like, without work, or anything else getting in the way. It certainly has been 'our time', but if I don't start taking more care, we'll soon be sharing that time... with an unexpected addition, and I resolve to stick to my promise and be more responsible, once we get home, being as I've failed dismally while we've been here. My only excuse is that one of the things I've learned is that Amelie is, quite simply, too distracting for words... and that's not all I've discovered about her this week. I know now that she likes a cup of tea in bed in the morning, and that she takes ages doing her hair – which is surprising, considering it's quite short. I know that she hums show tunes when she's in the bath, even when I'm in there with her, and even though I refuse to join in, despite her teasing and cajoling. I have worked out a couple of ways of stopping her in her tracks, though; of turning her tune to a sigh, a moan, or a gasp – even mid-note, on occasion – and the memory of those moments is enough to make me smile whenever I think about it, which I imagine I'll probably be doing for some time to come. I've discovered that she feels incredibly soft and warm when she first wakes up in my arms; that her skin is pure and delicate, especially in that space between her breasts, and on the inside of her thighs, where just the slightest breath, or the flick of my tongue is enough to make her shudder. I know that she tastes sweet, like honey – only better – *and* that she was well worth the wait. I also realised on the Tuesday after our marriage, that she is the best birthday present a man could ever have; that she's an intoxicating combination of innocence and sensuality, learning and yet somehow instinctively knowing at the same time.

Like I said, she's too distracting.

And I love her more than I can ever hope to say... although that's not going to stop me telling her. And showing her. Every. Single. Day.

Chapter Two

How could he? How could he do this to me... again?

Just a few days ago, I lived in hope. I was planning our future, thinking about the child we're yet to have, contemplating the next stage of our lives together.

Admittedly, his reticence had thrown me, but the next morning, after our conversation about decorating the nursery, when I thought about it, remembering what he'd said and how he'd said it, his explanation did seem reasonable. And I spent a couple of days trying to work out how we could perhaps furnish the room on a tighter budget. It wasn't vital that we redecorate it. After all, babies don't care what colour the walls are, do they? And I felt certain we could find the money for a cot, and whatever else might be required. I reasoned to myself that it wasn't as though we'd have to buy everything at once. Babies take nine months... well, they do once they've been conceived.

I bite my lip, tears threatening again. What was I thinking? How could I have been so blind and so stupid? There isn't going to be a baby. Not now. Maybe not ever. Not for me.

"He swore to me," I mutter under my breath, gazing out of the living room window, my arms clasped around myself, in cold comfort. "He promised."

But it seems he's incapable of keeping his promises, or of telling the truth, about anything.

Turning back into the room, I stoke the fire, adding a small log from the basket, then I flop down on the sofa, letting my head roll back on the cushion behind me, and I recall the conversation I overheard last night; the conversation that has changed everything and flipped my whole life upside down.

I heard every word that little trollop said, and through my tears, had to listen while my own husband offered her money. Money! She turned him down, seemingly insulted... but the point is, he still offered. He didn't deny a single word of the filth that came out of her mouth, but he tried to buy her off instead. And that told me that not only had he cheated on me again, but he'd also lied to me. We're not hard up at all, not if he's got enough to pay that scheming little slut. We could have a child if he wanted... and that's just it. He doesn't want to. He'd rather sleep with conniving tarts than give me the only thing I've ever really asked of him.

Well, I'm damned if his mistakes are going to ruin my future. I'm damned if I'm going to let a little whore like her take away everything I've ever worked for...

It's just after midday when I park the car outside our home in School Road.

It seems strange to think of it as 'our home', even though that's exactly what it is, being as this is the house which Amelie's Uncle Gordon gave to us as a very generous wedding present.

He warned us that the place was in a bit of a state when he made the gift, on Christmas Eve, over a month before our wedding, and he wasn't joking. When he brought us to view the house a few days later, Amelie and I looked at each other and wondered what we'd let ourselves in for. Between the cracked windows, the broken back door and the missing roof tiles, there was plenty to do, and that didn't include the internal decorations, buying new furniture, and installing kitchen equipment.

I can still remember the worried expression on Amelie's face when she turned to me and asked whether I was sure I was still happy to pay for the refurbishments, which was what I'd agreed with her uncle, and my smile when I'd replied that, of course I was, even though I honestly had no idea how much it was likely to cost.

And so, my future bride set to work, with the help of my mother and my aunts, and between them and a few local tradesmen, they've managed to get it all done. And I know Amelie was extremely relieved that she'd decided to resign from her position at Hawker's Aviation in the first week of January, because it meant she could devote her time to the house... well, and the wedding preparations, of course.

Fortunately, my own work hasn't been too busy since Christmas, and I've been able to spend my weekends here too, the only problem then being keeping my hands to myself whenever Amelie and I have been alone, although I'm glad now that I managed it, and that we waited. I think the wait made our honeymoon even more special. If that were possible.

Climbing out of the car, I go around to Amelie's side and open the door, offering her my hand, which she takes with a smile, as I raise her to her feet.

She stands in front of me, my hands resting on her tiny waist. "Pleased to be home?" I ask.

"Yes." She tilts her head a little. "But only because you've got the weekend off. I've got used to having you around, Inspector Stone." She smiles up at me, squinting slightly into the pale sunshine, and biting her bottom lip as I grin back, and then I bend down and lift her into my arms. She yelps. "What are you doing?"

"Carrying you over the threshold, of course."

"Don't you think you should unlock the door first?"

She probably has a point, but I'm not about to be defeated and, crossing the narrow pavement, I nudge the gate open, remembering that I didn't get around to fixing the latch before the wedding, and mentally reminding myself that I'll try and get it done sometime next weekend. I won't worry about it today, or tomorrow, because I've got my hands full… with my wife.

"The keys are in my pocket," I tell her as I walk up the short path to the front door. "Can you reach?"

She leans back slightly, reaching behind her and into my jacket pocket, pulling out the keys and holding them up triumphantly.

"Lovely, darling, but you're going to have to open the door… My hands are otherwise occupied."

She giggles and I hold her still while she turns the key in the lock and I push the door open, letting us directly into the living room, the staircase right ahead of us.

"Who lit the fire?" she asks and I turn, closing the door in the process and notice the logs burning in the grate, the metal guard surrounding it.

"My mother, I assume."

She has a key, because we had to have the telephone connected in our absence and she agreed to let the engineer in and wait while the work was completed.

"That's kind of her," Amelie replies. "I've been dreading coming home to a cold house."

"Well, I'd have found a way to warm you up," I murmur and she giggles again as I lean down and kiss her, carrying her further into the room at the same time. She drops the keys onto the sofa and cups my face in her hands, kissing me back until we're both breathless.

"Gosh," she says, as I straighten and slowly lower her to the floor, unbuttoning her coat and throwing it over the back of the couch. "You really meant it, didn't you?"

"Meant what?"

"When you said that that coming home wouldn't make any difference... that the honeymoon wouldn't be over."

"The honeymoon will *never* be over," I whisper, pulling her close to me. "Not as far as I'm concerned." She smiles and pushes my jacket from my shoulders, letting it fall to the floor, before she tugs my shirt from my trousers, slowly undoing the buttons, her eyes fixed on mine.

I wait for her to finish, and then place my hands on the hem of her thin jumper, pulling it gently over her head, then reaching behind her, unfastening her skirt and allowing it to drop to her ankles. She's wearing a full-length slip which I lift over her head, throwing it onto the chair by the window and sucking in a breath, unable to believe that it was only this morning that I watched her dress; only this morning that I held her naked in my arms...

"Upstairs or down here?" I mutter, shrugging off my shirt completely and holding her close to me.

She's breathless, almost panting with desire, and looks up at me, her hands resting on my bare chest. "I don't mind... anywhere... everywhere."

I smile, because I love her enthusiasm, and I take her hand, leading her around the sofa and sitting her down, kneeling before her, just as the telephone rings, its shrill chime echoing around the room, making

Amelie jump. "Damn," I murmur under my breath, then mouth, "Sorry," to her, before I get up again and go across to the small shelf by the front door, picking up the receiver. "Hello. Stone here," I bark.

"Rufus?" I recognise the voice of Harry Thompson on the other end of the line.

"Yes."

"I'm so sorry," he says quickly, as I feel my shoulders drop. "I wasn't sure you'd be back yet, but I thought I'd give you a try."

"We've only just walked in the door. What's wrong?" I can tell from his tone that something is.

"We've got a dead body on our hands," he replies.

"A murder?" I ask, hoping I'm wrong in my assumption, just as I feel Amelie's hands on my back, right before she leans into me, and I turn and put my free arm around her, letting her nestle against my chest.

"I'm afraid so," he says.

"I thought the chief super was covering for me while I was on my honeymoon," I point out, adding, "which I still am, until Monday morning."

"I know," he replies, "but unfortunately the chief super has gone down with flu, along with half the station. We've got Tooley, myself, and about a dozen men left." He sighs. "But I can handle it myself for the time being…" His voice fades.

"No, it's fine." I glance down at Amelie and she looks up at me, then blinks a few times and sighs, but manages a smile – just – and I kiss her forehead. "Where do you need me to be?" I ask Thompson.

"The body is still in situ," he says. "It's in the graveyard of St Nicholas' Church in Thames Ditton."

"Okay. Get yourself over there and make sure no-one moves it, or touches anything, before I arrive… and that includes Doctor Wyatt. I'll be half an hour. I just need to… um…" I leave my sentence unfinished, unsure what to say next.

"Get dressed?" he suggests, with a chuckle.

I smile, but just respond with a, "No comment," before hanging up. "I'm so sorry," I say immediately, turning to Amelie and cupping her face in my hands.

"What's happened?" she asks, gazing up at me.

"That was Thompson. There's a dead body been found in the graveyard at the church in Thames Ditton."

"One that's not meant to be there, I presume?" she asks.

"I'm guessing so," I reply and she nods. "I'm sorry," I repeat, "but I'm going to have to go."

"Don't apologise. I knew there would be times like this when I married you."

"Yes, but my job wasn't supposed to interfere quite so early on… certainly not while we're still officially on our honeymoon."

"It can't be helped," she replies, although I can hear the emotion in her voice.

I lean down and kiss her, reminding myself to keep it brief, before leaning back. "We can carry on with this later," I whisper, running my thumb along her bottom lip.

"I hope so," she replies, her eyes sparkling, and we stare at each other for a long moment, before she blinks, the action seeming to bring us back to reality. "I suppose we'd better unload the car, so that I can unpack," she says.

"That's a good idea, but I think we should probably get dressed first, don't you?"

She giggles and I kiss her again, then release her and gather up our clothes, laying them on the back of the sofa, before I stop and look down at them.

"Actually, I should probably go upstairs and put on a suit. If I'm going to have to work, I'd rather be dressed for the part. I'll feel more comfortable."

Amelie smiles up at me as she pulls on her sweater and I lean down for one last kiss, before I go up the stairs, taking my shirt and grey tweed jacket with me.

Our bedroom is at the front of the house and, like all of the rooms, is painted plain white, with a few of Aunt Dotty's paintings dotted around to make it feel more homely. Mother has made us some lovely curtains to hang at the windows, which in here are white, with pale blue and pink flowers on them, and in the corner is a large walnut wardrobe, with two doors, either side of a full length mirror. My clothes hang on the right hand side, placed in here literally the day before the wedding, when Amelie and I moved our personal belonging in, despite the fact that we ourselves wouldn't be taking up residence until today, and I open the door, pulling out a grey pinstripe suit and white shirt, laying them on the bed and adding a blue tie.

I make short work of dressing, adding the cufflinks that Amelie bought me for Christmas, and a pair of black shoes, then I take my grey fedora from the shelf at the top of the wardrobe, before going back downstairs, where my bride is standing fully clothed now, over by the fire, waiting for me.

"You look lovely," she says, her eyes wandering over me.

"So do you." I drop my hat on the sofa and wander over to her, taking her in my arms. "Will you be all right by yourself?" She nods. "Make sure you eat something for lunch, won't you?"

"Yes. But I'll have to go shopping first. We don't have any food in the house, remember?"

"Oh, God… so we don't."

I take her hand and we wander together from the small sitting room, with its dark blue sofa, two occasional tables at either end, each supporting a shaded lamp, the matching chair by the window, and the small cabinet in the alcove by the fire, which houses the wireless, taking her through to the dining room, sparsely furnished at the moment, with just a rectangular dining table and four chairs – two on each side – and into the long, galley kitchen. In here, a cottage style window overlooks the side alleyway that eventually leads out to the small patch of lawn that qualifies as a back garden, the half-glazed door to which is covered with a black-out curtain. Down the left hand side of the narrow room there is a deep ceramic sink, beneath the window, and beyond that, are various cupboards, the tops of which provide some preparation space. On the right, a little further down from the sink, is the stove, and yet more cupboards. At the end of the room, is a closed door, which leads to the bathroom. The door to the larder, which is immediately to our right, is ajar, and I glance at Amelie, feeling curious, as I go over and open it completely.

"Well, I'll be…"

"What is it?" She joins me and together we look at the shelves, which we left empty, but which now contain a few basics, including some milk, eggs, bread and cheese. "It doesn't look like I'll starve, does it?" Amelie smiles up at me. "It seems that your mother's been at work again."

"Hmm, it looks that way, doesn't it?" I turn to face her. "You're sure you'll be okay?"

"I think even I can manage to boil an egg, or make some cheese on toast," she remarks, leaning into me. "But I'll pop out to the shops first and make sure we've got something nice for dinner."

I pull my wallet from my inside pocket and hand her a couple of folded notes. "That should be enough, unless you're planning a banquet."

She grins. "You should be so lucky."

"I am lucky," I reply, kissing her forehead. "I'm the luckiest man in the world… because you're my wife."

"I'll remind you of that when I'm serving you something inedible later," she replies, chuckling.

"I won't mind."

"I'll remind you of that too… when you've wasted away."

I chuckle myself now. "I won't waste away. And neither will you. Cooking really isn't that hard, my darling. I promise."

"I'll take your word for that."

We make our way back to the front of the house and I go outside, bringing in our cases, which I take upstairs, despite Amelie's protests that she could manage that by herself. I leave my coat in the car, though, because I'll need it later, and then pick up my hat from the sofa.

"I wish I didn't have to go," I murmur, pulling Amelie close to me again, holding her in my arms and looking down at her.

"So do I, but I've got plenty to do, and you'll be busy too. The time will soon pass." She sounds like she's trying to put on a brave face, but I don't remark on that for fear of upsetting her even more.

"And then I'll be home again," I say instead.

"And I can poison you with my cooking," she jokes.

"And I can take you to bed," I reply and she sighs, smiling.

"I think I prefer your idea to mine," she murmurs.

"On the whole… so do I."

I lean down and capture her lips with mine, leaving her breathless as I pull away and go out to the car. She stands on the doorstep, blowing me kisses and waving me goodbye and, while I'm still cursing the curtailing of our honeymoon, I'll admit, there is something marvellously domesticated about all of this, which makes me smile to myself as I drive off down the road.

I approach St Nicholas' Church down Church Lane, parking my car beside one of two Wolseleys and putting on my overcoat, before walking the rest of the way to the graveyard, where my route is almost immediately blocked by a police constable I don't recognise; a man probably ten or more years my senior, of medium height and build, with a scar on his chin.

"You can't come through here, son," he says, standing upright, his hands behind his back as he rocks on the balls of his feet with a slightly arrogant expression on his face.

"I think you'll find I can," I remark, and just before he starts to argue with me, I show him my warrant card.

He blanches and flusters, "Sorry, sir. I didn't realise."

"Don't worry about it, Constable. Just point me in the right direction, would you?"

"Yes, sir. The body was found around the back of the church, past the main entrance. You'll find your sergeant down there already." He points along the footpath and I nod my head, making my way past the multitude of lichen covered gravestones until I come upon another constable, standing by a yew tree, who, upon sight of my warrant card, directs me towards the rear of the ancient flint and stone church, where I find Detective Sergeant Harry Thompson and yet another constable, both of them standing a short distance away from what appears to be the body of a young woman, lying on a patch of grass between the outer wall of the building, and a large tombstone that's raised on a plinth and surrounded by wrought iron railings.

"Good afternoon." I announce myself and Thompson looks up, a smile forming on his lips.

"Hello, sir," he beams and I cringe slightly at his manner of address, although I understand why he's used it, given that we're not alone at present, even though we agreed that, whenever possible, he wouldn't refer to me as 'sir' at all. "This is Constable Fellowes," he adds, nodding to his companion. "He's from the local station, and he was first on the scene."

I smile at Fellowes, a youngster of probably no more than twenty years of age, who's holding his helmet under his arm, revealing very light blonde hair. His face is pale, but that's hardly surprising, in the circumstances, and he greets me by raising his eyebrows, seemingly nervous, and clearly keen to avoid looking at the body, which is lying on its side, facing the church wall.

"Who raised the alarm?" I ask as I approach them.

"It was a woman from the village," Fellowes replies, his voice deeper than I would have imagined for one so young. "The way she explained it to me was that she came here to lay some flowers on her husband's grave, being as today's his birthday… and she came round the back here to get some water from the tap to put into the vase." He indicates off to his right, where there's a standpipe by the back wall of the graveyard, then looks back at me. "And that's when she saw the body."

I nod towards the flowers scattered on the grass. "These are hers?" I ask.

"Yes, sir," he replies.

"And where is this woman now?"

"She's in the church, with Constable Newman," Thompson explains. "She was upset… understandably, so I thought it best to let her go somewhere quiet. But I assumed you'd want to speak to her."

"I will… in a minute," I muse, nodding my head, and then I turn and move towards the body. "Has she been touched or moved at all?"

"No," Thompson replies, leaving Fellowes where he is, and stepping closer to me. "We've just been waiting for you and the doctor to arrive."

"Wyatt's not here yet then?" I enquire, crouching down and studying the female form before me.

"No. He's on his way though."

I nod, removing my hat and taking in the position of the victim, which is that she's curled up, almost in the foetal position, although her lower leg is straightened beneath her. Her dark winter coat is unbuttoned at the front, her hands clenched over the top of her jade coloured dress, clutching her lower stomach. She's wearing a simple black felt hat, perched on top of her long, loose auburn hair, which hangs across her face, concealing it, and she has on sensible black shoes and skin-toned stockings.

About three inches above the place where her hands are clasped together, there's a very obvious red stain, which has leached out into an area of roughly eight or nine inches, across her abdomen, a small darker slash at the centre showing the point of the incision that killed her, and giving away the cause of death – unless I'm very much mistaken – to be a stabbing.

Feeling the softness of the earth beneath my feet, I glance up at Thompson. "You've had rain here recently?"

"Yes," he replies. "It poured for most of yesterday morning, but then it brightened up in the late afternoon, and turned frosty by nightfall."

"I see." Despite the circumstances, it's hard not to recall the fact that I've been completely oblivious to the weather for the last seven days, for the simple reason that I've had better things to do than look outside, or even listen for the sound of raindrops against the window pane.

"Inspector?" I turn at the sound of Doctor Wyatt's voice and get to my feet, stepping to one side, as he comes closer. He usually wears a suit beneath his overcoat, albeit a slightly dishevelled one, but today he's dressed down even more than normal, and has on a pair of dark brown corduroy trousers, with a thick checked shirt, and no tie, his hat hanging loosely in one hand, his medical bag in the other.

"Doctor," I reply. "Sorry to call you out on a Saturday."

He shrugs. "Gets me out of the gardening." His response, coupled with his attire, makes me realise that I know nothing of his domestic situation. But then, it dawns on me that he probably knows nothing of mine either. I doubt he's aware of the fact that I'm officially still on my honeymoon, for example.

He looks down at the girl before us, taking over my position, and puts his bag on the ground, his hat balanced on top, before crouching, studying her for a while, until he stands and shakes his head, sighing. "Shall we?" he asks and I nod, bending down, and between us, we turn her onto her back.

"Good Lord," Thompson says in a hoarse whisper, and Wyatt sucks in a loud breath. For myself, I simply close my eyes, and try to imagine how this incredibly beautiful young girl would have looked in life. It's difficult though, because her face shows the agony of her death, her lips contorted, her pale green eyes staring blindly at the sky above us.

Wyatt crouches again, examining her closely. "She was killed here," he says quietly, almost to himself. "There's a large quantity of blood beneath the body…" He points, indicating the staining on the grass, which is much more visible now that we've moved the body. "She'd have bled to death," he adds slowly, "and she'd have known about it."

"Any idea of time?" I ask, more in hope than expectation.

"No," he replies, getting to his feet and looking up at me. "But if you really want me to hazard a guess, I'd say she's been lying here all night. And before you say anything, I know that doesn't help you very much."

I hold up my hand. "It's better than nothing."

"I'll hopefully be able to tell you more after the post mortem," he adds, "but I'm not making any promises. Cases like this are notoriously difficult to pinpoint."

"I understand."

He raises an eyebrow, gazing at me. "You're being remarkably accommodating," he says, narrowing his eyes slightly.

"That's because he's not officially here," Thompson puts in, grinning, and I can almost hear myself groan out loud.

"He's not?" Wyatt remarks, glancing at me, then returning his gaze to Thompson again.

"No… he's still on his honeymoon."

Wyatt takes a half step back. "Honeymoon?" he says, clearly surprised.

"Yes," I reply.

"You've just got married?"

I frown. "Well, that's what normally happens immediately before a honeymoon… so yes."

"And you're choosing to be here, instead of with your bride?" He seems even more surprised now.

"I wouldn't say 'choosing', no. I think it would be more accurate to say that duty called."

"Well, I called, actually. If you want to be strictly accurate," Thompson quips, and I roll my eyes at him.

"And you answered?" Wyatt says, a smile beginning to form on his lips as I nod my head. "You must have a very understanding wife."

I smile myself now. "I do indeed, Doctor."

He holds out his right hand and, in spite of my initial surprise, I take it. "Congratulations," he says, with sincerity as we shake hands.

"Thank you."

He bends, picking up his bag and puts his hat back on his head. "I'll have the body removed, shall I?"

"Go ahead."

He turns, moving away, and calls over his shoulder, "I should have the preliminary report ready by Monday," before he disappears around the corner of the church.

Normal service has been resumed, it seems.

Turning to Thompson, I issue him with instructions to get Fellowes to stand guard by the body until Wyatt's men return to remove the girl, and ask him to arrange for a fingertip search to be started.

"Of the whole graveyard?" he asks.

"Yes."

"Looking for the murder weapon, I presume?"

I nod my head. "Obviously we won't know exactly what type of blade we're looking for, but generally speaking, I don't think knives are found in graveyards, so anything would be useful. And can you get hold of Prentice?" I ask, referring to our forensics expert.

"Yes. You want him over here?" he surmises.

"Yes, please. I'd like him to see if he can get any useful footprints. I know it's unlikely, given the amount of traffic there is around here, but you never know, we might get lucky." I glance around the area. "There's no handbag."

"No. Do you think it was a robbery, gone wrong?"

"Not necessarily." I crouch down again. "Let's have a quick look in her pockets."

I start with the right one, and discover a small purse, containing a few shillings, a house key on a silver coloured fob, crafted in the shape of a dove, and an identity card. The left pocket yields nothing but a plain white handkerchief, with a neat lace edging.

Keeping these items in my hand, I stand again, holding them out to Thompson, who looks at them, then raises his eyes to mine. "Not a robbery then," he muses.

"No."

I hand him the purse, the handkerchief, and the key, and then open the identity card. "Mildred Ryder," I say out loud, reading the name.

"And her address?" Thompson asks.

"She's local," I reply. "She lives in Station Road."

He nods, taking the identity card from me. "I'll get everything organised, and I'll make sure there are constables stationed at all the entrances to the churchyard," he says quietly. "Where will you be?"

"I'm going to talk to the woman who found the body first... and then I'll go to the vicarage."

"Okay. I'll catch up with you."

He moves away towards Constable Fellowes and I glance down at Mildred Ryder one last time, taking a deep breath, before I walk slowly around to the front of the church and in through the wide oak doors.

It's quite dark inside, despite the winter sunshine, and I pause for a moment to let my eyes acclimatise, taking in the high stone arches, the off-white walls, interspersed with brass plaques and name plates, the sturdy wooden pews, and ornate pulpit, and the impressive stained glass windows.

"Can I help?" A police constable in uniform walks over to me and I remove my warrant card, yet again, from the inside pocket of my jacket and show it to him. "Sorry, sir," he says.

"Don't be. You're Constable Newman, aren't you?" He nods. "Where's the witness?" I murmur, lowering my voice.

"This way." He turns and leads me into the main body of the church, to where there's a diminutive-looking lady sitting in one of the pews. I stand beside her and she startles, looking up, her face paling. "This is Mrs Bird," Newman says, helpfully, and I smile down at her. She's probably in her mid-sixties, with short silver-grey hair beneath a knitted green hat, and light blue eyes that give away her current anxiety.

"I'm Detective Inspector Stone," I tell her, softening my voice, and she relaxes noticeably, as I sit in the pew directly in front of her, making myself less threatening, and turning around to face her. "Do you think you could tell me what happened?"

She nods slowly, glancing down at her clasped hands, then looks up at me again. "I came to put some flowers on Edwin's grave," she begins and I hold up my hand, stopping her.

"Can you remember what time that was?" I ask.

"I suppose about ten o'clock," she replies. "It wouldn't have been before, because I went down to the greengrocers first thing, to get some carrots, and then when I got back, I had a cup of tea, and then I had get the flowers from the greenhouse, and cut some foliage from the garden, and then find a vase... I don't leave one here, in case it gets broken... or stolen." Her voice fades and she lowers her eyes again.

"So, about ten," I prompt and she nods. "And what happened when you got here?"

"I didn't even get to Edwin's grave," she replies, pulling a handkerchief from inside her sleeve, and dabbing at her nose. "I—I went to the tap to get some water... and that's when I saw her."

She starts to sniffle and I reach over, taking her free hand in mine. She's not wearing any gloves and her fingers are freezing, so I keep hold of her until she's calmed. "What did you do?" I ask softly.

"I dropped the flowers," she replies. "Although somehow I managed to hold onto the vase." She nods to the ornate, cut-glass container on the pew beside her. "And then I ran out onto Summer Road... what with that being the nearest entrance to the churchyard."

"And that was where you found Constable Fellowes?" I suggest.

"Yes. He was very kind," she adds, as though concerned I'm about to find fault with him in some way.

I smile to let her know I'm not. "You didn't see anyone else?" I ask, even though I know she probably won't have done.

"No." She sits forward slightly. "I don't suppose I could have my flowers back, could I?"

I think about her scattered buds and stems, strewn across the grass. "Probably not," I reply, noting the drop in her shoulders, before I turn to Newman. "Can you drive?" I ask him.

"Yes, sir." He stands upright.

"Good. There are a couple of Wolseleys parked in Church Lane. I'd like you to take Mrs Bird home in one of them, and help her to gather up some more flowers from her greenhouse…" I look at Mrs Bird. "Is that going to be possible?" I ask her and she nods.

"Yes, I grow them on especially for Edwin's birthday, every year," she explains. "I didn't pick them all this morning… I thought it would be nice to have some in the kitchen to brighten the place up a bit, but needs must…"

"Indeed," I reply, facing Newman again. "When you've done that, I want you to bring Mrs Bird back here, and make sure she gets to arrange the flowers on her husband's grave. I imagine by then there will be a search going on, but tell whoever's in charge that I gave you permission to use the tap behind the church, and to lay the flowers… all right?"

"Yes, sir."

"If there are any problems, I'll be at the vicarage."

He nods his head as Mrs Bird stands and I do likewise, stepping out into the aisle as she looks up at me. "Thank you," she murmurs as we walk together along the back of the church towards the door. "This is so kind of you."

"You don't have to thank us, Mrs Bird." I lead her from the church and out into the mid-afternoon sunshine, replacing my hat. "You've been very helpful."

She smiles and I watch as Newman escorts her down the path, passing Sergeant Thompson, who's coming the other way.

"Everything organised?" I ask him, as he approaches.

"Yes. I drove down to the local station and telephoned Prentice from there. He's on his way over, and reckons he'll be here in about twenty minutes. And the desk sergeant there said he'll get the search started straight away."

"Good."

He shrugs. "I'd have involved our own lads," he adds, "but we're so short staffed at the moment, I didn't like to offer anyone."

"It's just a search," I point out. "I'm sure the local uniform chaps can handle it."

"What next?" he asks, looking around.

"The vicarage."

"Okay… well, we can get to it through the churchyard, I believe. I think there's a gate over there somewhere." He points towards the far corner of the graveyard. "But being as it's a maze of pathways, I think it might be safer, and quicker, to use the less direct route."

He indicates down the pathway, in the opposite direction to that taken by Mrs Bird and Constable Newman, and we turn and start walking.

"Did you learn anything from the lady who found the body?" he asks.

"Mrs Bird?" I reply and he nods. "No, not much. She went to the tap as soon as she arrived, and that was when she discovered the body. So she didn't even enter the graveyard properly."

"Not that I think she'd have seen anything if she did," he remarks.

"No. I think Wyatt was right about the fact that Miss Ryder had been here all night." I bury my hands in my pockets. "Anyway, I've sent Constable Newman back to Mrs Bird's home with her, so she can collect some more flowers to lay on her husband's grave. It seemed like the least we could do in the circumstances."

We get to the end of the pathway and turn left onto Summer Road, going along a few yards, and turning into a driveway that leads up to a large red-brick Victorian house.

"Nice place," Thompson comments, and I can't fail to agree. It is an extremely grand property, with a magnificent arched doorway, the surrounding brickwork being fashioned in an alternating black and white pattern, which is matched on the window to the right. "That's impressive," he adds, nodding to our left, in the direction of the ornate first floor bay window that dominates the front elevation.

"I think they're called oriel windows," I reply and he turns, smirking.

"You would know something like that."

"Well, I suppose some of us have it…" I murmur, knocking on the door and taking a step back.

"And some of us don't care," he mutters, just managing to wipe the smile from his face as the door opens and we're faced with a man of medium height, in his mid-thirties, with sandy-coloured hair, deep blue eyes, and a friendly face, which I suppose makes sense, given that, immediately beneath his chin, he's wearing the dog-collar that symbolises his profession. The remainder of his clothing is less formal, however, consisting of grey flannel trousers and a dark red sweater.

"Can I help?" he asks, raising his eyebrows, his hand still on the door, as though he's quite prepared to close it again, at a moment's notice.

"I hope so." I reach for my warrant card, holding it out. "I'm Detective Inspector Stone, and this Detective Sergeant Thompson."

"Oh yes?" He remains where he is, looking inquisitive now and perhaps a little contemptuous, rather than friendly, and clearly still not about to let us into the house – not until he knows our business, anyway.

"What's going on?" The female voice that sounds from behind him is just slightly nasal and he steps aside for the first time, revealing an attractive woman with neat brown hair and a trim figure, currently displayed in a tweed skirt and plain white long-sleeved blouse, done right up to her neckline, with a bow at the collar. "Why haven't you invited these gentlemen in, Neville?" she asks, nudging him completely out of the way and ushering us into the house, with a prim, if insincere smile. We remove our hats, keeping hold of them, standing on ceremony.

"I was about to, dear," he says, with a tired voice, closing the front door, although I doubt he's telling the truth. "And they're policemen."

He makes it sound as though our profession in some way makes it impossible for us to also be considered 'gentlemen'.

"So?" she retorts, opening a door to her left. "Please, come in." She smiles, holding out her hand as we pass. "I'm Eileen Hodge, and you've already met my husband, Neville."

"Yes," I reply, not taking the trouble to point out that he hadn't bothered to introduce himself.

We follow her into a substantial drawing room, which overlooks the side of the house, two large, deep red sofas sitting either side of an impressive stone fireplace, with a few meagre logs crackling in its hearth, an intricately carved sideboard against the wall to my right, and a couple of low tables dotted around, with ornaments and lamps placed upon them. The walls are decorated with large landscapes, which are grand in scale, if not in content. It's not exactly a sparse room, but it couldn't be considered homely either. I would say 'unloved' would be a good way of describing this room.

"Please, take a seat," the vicar offers, commandeering the role of host from his wife, who has already sat herself down in the corner of one of the sofas, moving a book to the table beside her, making it clear that our arrival interrupted her reading.

We sit opposite her, although the vicar remains standing for the time being, his arms folded across his chest.

"We don't often get a visit from the police," he remarks.

"Well, I don't imagine you often have a body in your churchyard," I remark. "At least not one that hasn't been buried, anyway."

His arms drop to his sides and he startles, while Mrs Hodge sits forward, her hand clasped to her throat. "D—Did you say a body?" she whispers.

"Yes."

"A *dead* body?" the vicar echoes, rather unnecessarily.

"Yes. There have been officers in your churchyard for the last couple of hours. I'm surprised you haven't noticed them." I watch the couple closely.

"Well, because of the height of the hedges on that side, only our bedroom and the spare room next door, which we don't really use, actually overlook the churchyard, and in any case, we've both been busy today," the vicar says, glancing at his wife. "Eileen's been in the kitchen, and I've been sorting through some old papers on the dining room table."

"Who was it?" Mrs Hodge asks, lowering her hand at last, her eyes wide. "The body, I mean. Was it someone local?"

"Yes. A young lady by the name of Mildred Ryder."

The reverend suddenly flops down into the sofa, at the opposite end to his wife, as though his legs have simply ceased supporting him, his face pasty and pale. "Not Mildred," he mutters.

"You knew her?" I ask.

"Of course we did. Although I probably knew her better than my wife, being as she sung in the church choir."

"In that case, I'm sorry to have to tell you that it appears she was murdered."

They both gasp and Mrs Hodge says, "In the churchyard?" in a tone that makes me wonder if she thinks the whereabouts of the crime is the greatest matter of consideration in the case.

"Yes."

"How?" her husband asks. "How was she murdered?"

"She was stabbed."

"Stabbed?" he whispers, incredulous.

"But... she's such a lovely girl," Mrs Hodge adds, equally disbelieving. "I—I mean, she *was* a lovely girl. I—I don't think she was even twenty years old, was she?" She turns to her husband, but he's staring into space, as though in shock. "She worked for Norman and Lucy Wharton," Mrs Hodge continues, looking back at me again, when her husband doesn't respond.

"In what capacity?" I enquire, as Thompson starts to take notes.

"As their maid," she replies.

"And do they live in Station Road?" I ask, recalling the young woman's address from her identity card.

"Yes. That's right. The second house on the left, if you're going from the village to the station."

I nod my head. "Does she have family in the area?" I ask.

"Oh yes," she replies. "Her mother lives in Queen's Road."

"You wouldn't know the number, I suppose?"

"Yes. Number twelve. But she won't be there now… not just yet anyway. Since her husband died, she's been doing cleaning jobs… you know, charring." She raises her nose, looking down it. "She mainly works at local houses, where they don't have a live-in, but on Saturday mornings, she cleans the offices at Wharton's Electronics. She finishes there at about two, I think, but it takes her an hour or so to cycle home again and she often stops off to do some shopping on the way home." She finishes talking at last and I wonder about asking her what her neighbours had for breakfast this morning, feeling fairly certain she'd be able to furnish me with the correct answers.

"So, you think she'd be safely home by, say, half past three?" I ask, checking my watch and realising that Mrs Ryder will have left her place of employment about half an hour ago, and could therefore be anywhere on the road between West Molesey and her home in Thames Ditton… or in any of the shops in between.

"Yes, I would have thought so."

"Very well," I murmur. "We'll have to wait until she gets home before seeing her." I glance back up at Mrs Hodge. "And Wharton's Electronics? Would that have anything to do with Miss Ryder's employer?" I ask.

"Yes. Norman Wharton owns the factory," she replies. "It's over in West Molesey somewhere, I believe." She lets out a long sigh and sits back slightly.

"Poor Mildred… She sang a solo at the Christmas service," the vicar says wistfully, his mind still clearly fixed on the girl, as though he hasn't heard any of the interchange between his wife and myself. "She had the voice of a nightingale… absolutely beautiful."

"When did you last see her?" I ask, looking at him directly.

"At choir practice, yesterday evening." He focuses on me now, instead of some imaginary object in the distance. "Everyone left together at just after eight o'clock and then I locked the church."

"Did you actually see Miss Ryder leave?"

He frowns for a moment, thinking. "Well, I saw her leave the church, but I didn't see her leave the graveyard, if that's what you mean. She did tell me she'd arranged to meet someone though."

"She did?" I'm intrigued now.

"Yes. I offered to wait with her, as it was so dark, what with the blackout and everything, but she insisted she was perfectly fine by herself." He shakes his head, bringing his hand up to his neck, just above his dog collar, mirroring his wife's earlier action. "I should have waited, shouldn't I? She'd still be alive if I had…"

I can't answer that, because we all know it's probably the truth… unless, of course, he's the murderer.

"Did she say who she was intending to meet?" I ask instead.

"No, but I assumed it was her fiancé, given that she'd gone in the direction of Summer Road."

"Who is her fiancé?"

"Sam Higgs," Mrs Hodge supplies. "They've been walking out for years. He lives in Alexandra Road, which is just this side of Queen's Road." She points in the vague direction, over her shoulder.

"Thank you. I know where it is." I turn back to her husband. "Did you come straight home from the church then, Reverend?"

"No," he replies, without hesitation. "I started to, but then I realised I'd left my sermon in the vestry, so I went back for it. I'd been working on it before choir practice and I wanted to read it through before going to bed. So, I went back and collected it."

I nod my head and turn to Mrs Hodge, who is staring directly at me. "And were you with your husband?"

She smiles. "No, Inspector. I can't sing a note, so I doubt I'd be welcome in the choir. I stayed at home all evening, listening to the wireless and doing some knitting."

"My wife was here when I got back," the vicar confirms, without me asking him to – something which always makes me suspicious. "She was just pouring our cocoa, actually. I took mine to my study, so I could read over my sermon in peace."

"And I took mine up to bed with me," his wife adds. "I wanted to finish reading a book I'd borrowed from the library."

"You didn't hear a scream, or voices, or footsteps?" I ask.

"No, I'm afraid not," the vicar replies.

I get to my feet, with Thompson following suit, replacing his notebook in his pocket and picking up his hat from its place on the sofa beside him. "Is that it?" Mrs Hodge asks, and I recognise the familiar signs of a village gossip, who I have no doubt will be spreading rumours of Miss Ryder's demise before we've even made our way down their considerable driveway. If anyone ever accused her of being a tittle-tattle, she'd be mortally offended, but that doesn't make it any less true.

"Yes… for now."

Mrs Hodge gets up, clearing her throat to attract her husband's attention, being as he doesn't seem to have realised that we're about to leave.

"Sorry," he mumbles, standing at last. "I was elsewhere…"

"That's understandable," I reply, moving towards the door.

"Yes. This has all come as a terrible shock," Mrs Hodge says a little unnecessarily, smiling as she lets us out.

Thompson waits until we're at the end of their driveway before he turns to me.

"Well?"

"Unusual pair," I comment.

"That's putting it mildly. He was a strange one."

"Him?" I look at him. "I was thinking more of her, actually."

"Oh, she's just a typical vicar's wife," he says, shaking his head and smirking slightly. "Full of overbearing self-importance and too busy trying to run everyone else's life to notice the cracks in her own."

"Cracks?" I query, interested in hearing his opinion of the couple we've just left, even though I've formed a few of my own.

"Yes. I imagine those two either live in stony silence, or bicker incessantly."

I nod. "There didn't seem to be a huge amount of togetherness going on between them, did there?"

"That's one way of putting it," he says, shaking his head. "What did you think was wrong about him then?" He changes the subject to the reverend, and I let him, even though I think there's more to be said yet about Mrs Hodge.

"He seemed a bit too affected by the whole thing, if you ask me."

"Well, I suppose it's not the most pleasant situation to find yourself in, is it?" he reasons, as we turn into the churchyard again, noticing the many uniformed men, searching behind gravestones and under bushes. "It's not every day that a member of your choir is killed in your own churchyard, after all."

"I know. But there was just something about his reactions that didn't quite ring true."

"You think he was lying?" Thompson asks.

"No… but I don't think he was telling us everything. Not by a long chalk."

He chuckles quietly. "If everyone told us everything we needed to know at the first time of asking, Rufus, we'd never have anything to do, would we?"

"I suppose not."

"Where are we going next?" he asks.

"Mr and Mrs Wharton, I suppose. We can't go to see Mrs Ryder yet. There's no point if she won't be home from work."

He nods. "Mrs Hodge certainly seemed to know about her movements, didn't she?"

"Hmm… in minute detail. But then, Mrs Hodge struck me as the type who'd know about everyone's movements… while keeping her own very much to herself."

He opens his mouth to speak, but then closes it again as we reach the end of Church Lane, where there are even more cars parked than there were earlier, and the constable on duty seems to be in a heated discussion with a member of the public.

"What's going on?" Thompson asks, wading in, while I hang back a little.

"This gentleman is…" the constable begins, but before he can complete his sentence, the man interrupts him.

"Are you in charge?" he says, his leaning forward and jabbing Thompson in the chest with his forefinger.

"No," Thompson replies. "But I suggest you stop doing that."

"I don't care what you suggest. I want to speak to whoever is in charge."

"That would be me," I say, stepping forward.

The man, probably around sixty-five, with thick, iron grey hair, metal rimmed spectacles and a ruddy complexion, turns to face me, narrowing his eyes slightly.

"And you are?" he demands.

"Detective Inspector Stone," I reply. "And you are?"

"I'm Randolf Harding." He makes it sound as though I should know who he is, so I make an effort to look at him as blankly as possible. "I live here." He points to the house on the corner of the churchyard. "And I've had just about enough. You've completely blocked the lane with your cars; there are policemen coming and going all over the place, and the…"

"It can't be helped, Mr Harding," I interrupt, his face reddening with anger. "We're conducting a murder enquiry and I'm afraid there will be further disruptions over the coming days."

"A murder enquiry?"

"Yes."

"Who's been murdered?" he asks, his ire forgotten, his inquisitiveness rising to the fore.

"A young lady of this parish," I reply, moving away slightly, and dismissing him in the process. "And now, if you don't mind, we've got work to do."

He goes to speak and then thinks better of it, stepping back and allowing us to pass.

"Idiot," Thompson mutters under his breath, and I smile at him as we approach my car. "We're taking yours, are we?" he asks, eyeing the Wolseley that's parked alongside.

"Yes. We may as well be comfortable."

"I'm not sure I'd call your car comfortable," he replies, lowering himself into the seat, "but it definitely has style."

"I like to think so."

I turn the car with some difficulty, pondering that, despite his attitude problem, Mr Harding may have a point, considering the number of police vehicles that are currently blocking the narrow lane, but I manage to make my manoeuvre eventually, and we start on our way back towards the village, passing along the High Street and into Station Road. It's only a short journey – not long enough for us to enter into any conversation – and I suppose we could have walked it really, but we're going to need the car later, and I didn't want to cause any further antagonism towards Mr Harding and the other local residents by leaving my car there any longer than was strictly necessary.

I park a little further along the street, at a safe distance from the junction with Watts Road, and we walk back to the second house, which has a wrought iron gate. I pass through that, with Thompson behind me, and then lead the way up the long garden path, taking the five steep steps in my stride, before finally reaching the bright red door.

Thompson knocks, but then steps back, allowing me to take his place, just as the door opens, revealing a tall, dark haired man, probably in his early thirties. He's casually dressed, in dark brown trousers, with a paler coloured jumper on top, and rather worn looking brogues on his feet. I don't think there's anyone alive who wouldn't call him handsome, but has a slightly pompous look about his face, as though he thinks all men should want to be his best friend, and all women should fall at his feet and worship him.

"Yes?" he says, impatiently, looking over my shoulder, which strikes me as odd.

"I'm sorry to disturb you," I reply, being as it's clear we are. "I'm Detective Inspector Stone and this is my colleague…"

"You're from the police?" he interrupts, his eyes darting to mine. "Oh… do come in. We've been expecting you."

I glance at Thompson, who shrugs. "You have?" I ask, feeling confused.

"Yes." Mr Wharton stands back, letting us enter his house, and then closes the door. "Please come through." He barely gives us time to take in the rather smart hallway, with its parquet flooring and very fine grandfather clock, which seems to have pride of place at the bottom of the stairs, before he motions towards a door on the left and, taking off our hats, we follow him into a neatly furnished drawing room. The contrast between this room and the one we've just left is too great not to notice, for where the vicarage furniture was worn and a little old-fashioned, everything in here is pristine and stylish, from the understated oak sideboard that graces the wall opposite the wide french windows, to the much more refined paintings, and the three large sofas arranged in a 'U' shape around the blazing fire, on one of which is a very pretty young woman, who stands upon our entrance. She's in her late twenties, or possibly early thirties, I would say, with extremely light blonde hair, piercing blue eyes and an air of sophistication that exudes from every pore, and every stitch of stylish fabric that cleaves to her slim body. Her surroundings may be tasteful, but there's something about this woman, in the way that she holds herself, the manner of her standing, the grace of her pose, that makes her seem almost too elegant for the setting... and definitely too refined for her husband. "It's the police, Lucy," Mr Wharton says to her, and she smiles.

"Goodness, that was quick." Her voice is just as cultured as the rest of her, but I'm confused by her response and look from her to him, shaking my head.

"I feel as though we might be talking at crossed purposes. You said you were expecting us?"

"Of course," Mrs Wharton replies, before her husband can. "We telephoned the police station just ten minutes ago."

"May I ask why?"

"To report that our maid has gone missing," her husband says, moving further into the room and standing beside his wife, looking and sounding confused himself now. "Isn't that why you're here?" He tilts his head slightly.

"Well, yes... and no."

They both stare at me for a moment and then Mrs Wharton seems snap out of her trance, apologises profusely for forgetting her manners, and offers Thompson and myself a seat, indicating the sofa opposite to hers, where she perches again, her husband sitting beside her.

"I should probably explain that last statement," I say quietly.

"I wish you would," Mr Wharton replies.

"I'm sorry to have to tell you that we've just come from the graveyard at St Nicholas' Church, where the body of Mildred Ryder was discovered earlier this morning."

"Body?" Mrs Wharton says and reaches out, clutching at her husband's hand. "You mean she's…"

"She's dead?" Mr Wharton completes her sentence, forming the inevitable question.

"Yes. I'm afraid she was murdered." They both gasp. "I'm very sorry," I add as I sit forward. "The thing is… the thing that's confusing me at the moment is that the last time she was seen – that we know of – was at just after eight o'clock last night, when she left the church after choir practice. Her body was discovered not long after ten o'clock this morning… and yet you've just told me that you only reported her missing ten minutes ago. Can you tell me if there is a reason why it's taken you so long to notice that she wasn't here?" I let my eyes dart from one of them to the other, noticing the pallor of Mrs Wharton's complexion, and the confusion that continues to light her husband's eyes.

"We… We were out very late last night," Mr Wharton says, slowly coming to terms with the news, I think.

"Early this morning would be more accurate, Norman," his wife whispers.

"Yes, I suppose it would. We didn't get in until nearly three."

"I see… And where had you been?"

"We'd been at the home of some friends of ours, who were celebrating a birthday. They live in Ashley Road…" He glances at his wife and I notice she's frowning at him.

"Would this be the same Ashley Road that leads into Church Lane?" I ask, noting his confused expression and trying to get my bearings at the same time.

"Yes," she murmurs, blinking a few times.

"We walked home," Mr Wharton continues quickly, glossing over that minor detail, "because we'd had quite a lot to drink, and then we didn't get up until after eleven this morning."

"That was when we noticed Mildred wasn't here," his wife says helpfully. "But to start with, we thought she'd probably gone shopping... That's quite normal, you see, for a Saturday morning, especially if she's been busy on the Friday... which she was yesterday, because we were going through the linen together for most of the morning, and then she took the older things that we didn't want anymore, together with some clothes that I'd sorted out, down to the WVS shop in the village just before they closed up for the day... They'd dropped a leaflet through the door, asking for donations, you see."

"So you weren't overly surprised to find her absent this morning?" I ask, just to clarify, being as Mrs Wharton has rather gone off on a tangent, that speech of hers made in nervous, undulating waves, with frequent pauses and gaps, although none were long enough for anyone else to say anything, as though she was determined to keep talking in order to prevent me from asking questions. I've seen this before, usually in people who are guilty of something – or at least who have something to hide – and it always makes me suspicious.

"No," her husband replies. "But when she hadn't returned by lunchtime, we started to wonder."

"And that was when I went to check her room," Mrs Wharton says. "Her bed didn't seem to have been slept in. So, I called Norman and he came upstairs too."

"I did point out to my wife that it was perfectly possible that Mildred had got up and made her bed before leaving the house, but we talked it through and decided that her prolonged absence was out of character, and that we should really notify the police."

"You didn't think to contact her mother, perhaps? After all, something might have occurred to a member of her family, requiring her presence."

"Her mother isn't on the telephone," Mr Wharton points out a little huffily. "And, in any case, we decided that, if she'd been called away for some reason, she would have left a note."

"She was a very responsible girl," his wife adds.

"I see." I glance at Thompson, who's writing furiously in his notebook, trying to keep up with their changing conversation, it seems.

"Can you tell me the name of your friends?"

"Our friends?" Mrs Wharton seems confused.

"The people whose party you attended last night in Ashley Road," I explain and she nods her head, although it's her husband who responds to my question.

"Susan and Laurence Conroy," he says. "They live at number sixteen. I've been friends with them since we were all at the village school together… many, many years ago."

"Was it his birthday, or his wife's?" I ask.

"It was Laurence's," he replies.

"And you were there all evening?"

He frowns and I half expect him to object to my line of questioning, but instead he just nods his head.

"You didn't leave the party at all?"

"Well, we didn't leave exactly but we both popped out into the porch for a cigarette from time to time," Mrs Wharton says. "But that's only because Susan doesn't like people smoking in her house."

"And did you do that together?" I ask.

"Sometimes," she replies. "Although sometimes I went by myself. I'm sure Norman did the same." She glances at him quickly and then looks away and it's hard not to read something into that gesture… a sense of distrust, perhaps?

"I see. And other than that, you remained at the party?"

"My wife has already said so," Mr Wharton's voice takes on a frosty tone, his blue eyes matching it in their chilly gaze.

Part of me wants to point out that, in fact, she hasn't. She's merely told me that, on occasion, each of them left the party, both alone and with each other, but she hasn't actually told me what else they did. Even so, I don't see the value in antagonising him. Not yet, anyway. Instead, I ask, "Do you know who your maid might have been meeting after choir practice?"

"How do you know she was meeting anyone?" Mrs Wharton asks, while her husband continues to glare at me.

"Because she told Reverend Hodge about it."

She turns to her husband, and for a moment, I wonder at the troubled expression on her face, but it's gone within seconds, and she looks back at me. "She didn't really have that many friends, although she knew some of the people at church, I suppose, and in the choir, but I'm not aware of her socialising with any of them, and it wouldn't make sense for her to be meeting them *after* choir practice – because she'd have just seen them, wouldn't she?"

"Yes. You say she didn't have many friends?" I ask, picking up on her comment.

"No. She was a very quiet, reserved kind of girl," Mrs Wharton continues, her earlier uncertainty about her husband seemingly forgotten. "I think that's why she went into service, to be honest – or more likely, why she came to work in a small household, like ours, rather than in an office or a factory, where she'd probably have had to meet more people. And obviously, she wanted to stay close to her family as well."

"Her family?" I query. "I know she has a mother, but…"

"There's also a younger brother and a sister as well," she says. "They're very close, and Mildred used to go and visit them every other Sunday afternoon, without fail."

"I see."

"You know about her fiancé, I presume?" Mr Wharton says, speaking again at last.

"Yes. Mrs Hodge informed us about him."

"Well, I think he's the most likely candidate for Mildred's mystery meeting, don't you?" He sounds rather smug and is still put out by my earlier questions, that much is obvious from the sour expression on his face.

"Very possibly," I reply, turning back to his wife once more, although she's gazing at him again, with that same curious expression on her face. "Mrs Wharton?" She flips her head around, plastering a smile on her lips and focusing on me.

"Yes, Inspector?"

"Would it be possible for us to take a look at Miss Ryder's room?"

"Oh… yes, of course."

She gets to her feet at once, and Thompson and I follow, leaving Mr Wharton sitting in the corner of the sofa, his legs crossed, his eyes fixed in the middle distance, and the thought crossing my mind that these two are doing a fairly good job of looking guilty, even if they're not. Between his over-reactions and her peculiar glances, they're certainly giving me a lot to think about.

We follow Mrs Wharton from the room, back into the hallway, and up the stairs.

"What does your husband do?" I ask her when we get to the first landing, even though I already know the answer to that. I'd like some meat on the bones of the scant information Mrs Hodge has provided and I'm not sure I'll get it from Mr Wharton at the moment.

"He owns a small factory in West Molesey," she replies, repeating Mrs Hodge's information. "They make wireless parts," she adds, more usefully. "Well, they did before the war, anyway. I'm not exactly sure what they do now, and I'm not sure he'll tell you either."

"Why not?" I ask as we start up the next flight of stairs, which are narrower and uncarpeted.

"Because he's just been awarded a contract by the War Office, and it's all very top secret. Even I don't know what it's about, so I doubt he'll be forthcoming."

"I understand that Mrs Ryder works for your husband?" I ask and she turns at the top of the stairs, looking down at me.

"Yes, she does. But I'm afraid I know nothing about their arrangements. Even before he got this new contract, my husband kept his business dealings very much to himself, Inspector," she says, lowering her voice. "I do know he hadn't been doing very well before the war, and I believe the government contract came along at just the right time... There were some financial issues, not long after we were married, but I didn't ever ask him for details. I just accepted what Norman told me, even though my father tried to fill my head with nonsense about impending bankruptcy..." Her voice fades, but then she looks up at me, takes a deep breath and smiles. "None of it was true, of course. Norman was nowhere near bankruptcy. But my father didn't approve of my marriage, you see, and takes every opportunity to find fault. But then… you can't help who you fall in love with, can you?" There's a heartbreaking sadness to her voice, and for a moment, I wonder if her father isn't the only one who regrets her decisions. But then I see the look in her eyes and realise that her regrets almost certainly don't stem from her choice of husband, but probably from some hurt that's been caused between them, because it's clear to me that she still loves him very much indeed.

I nod my head, returning her smile, although mine is more genuine than hers, and she moves away, opening the right hand of two doors on the small landing, revealing a medium sized bedroom, the walls of which are painted white, with a couple of paintings of nondescript landscapes on the wall opposite the window to break up the monotony. The room is simply furnished, with a single bed against the far wall, a bedside table and a chest of drawers, and small wardrobe. There's also a bookshelf above the bed, with a few leather-bound volumes and some worn paperbacks along its length.

"We have to search her belongings, I'm afraid," I point out to Mrs Wharton. "It's entirely up to you whether you wish to remain present or not."

She blinks a couple of times, then says, "I'll stay, if that's all right with you."

"That's perfectly all right."

She nods. "It's just that they were her things, after all," she says softly. "It seems only right that someone should be here."

I smile at her again, appreciating the sentiment, and then, leaving her in the doorway, set about going through the maid's belongings.

She was a neat girl, her clothes folded tidily in place, within her drawers, her shoes stacked at the bottom of her wardrobe.

"How was she killed?" Mrs Wharton asks, interrupting my search of Miss Ryder's bedside table.

I look up, seeing her standing upright, her arms folded across her chest, taking in our movements. "She was stabbed," I reply and notice the grimace that briefly crosses her face, and I wait for her to ask the question which to me is inevitable – namely whether or not the girl suffered in death. Fortunately, Mrs Wharton lowers her eyes in silence and I continue my search, grateful that I didn't have to lie to her.

Tucked down the side of the drawer in her bedside table, I discover two small books, both leather bound, one red, the other blue, and both with the year embossed in gold numbers on the front. One says '1939', the other '1940'. Being as it's only early February, I'm not entirely surprised that she still has last year's diary and, rather than going through them now, I put them into my pocket.

"What's that?" Mrs Wharton asks, eyeing me suspiciously from the door.

"Her diaries," I reply. "I'll take them away for now, and if they don't prove useful, I'll return them to Miss Ryder's mother."

She hesitates, and I'd swear I notice a look of fear cross her face, before she nods slowly.

There is no doubt about it, Mrs Wharton is hiding something; or she's at least very troubled by something. I'm not sure whether it's related to Miss Ryder's murder, but as we leave the room, with just the diaries to show for our search, I determine to find out.

Chapter Three

As much as I detest having to cook and clean, and the kitchen really isn't my natural domain, I came straight out here as soon as the inspector and his sergeant left, unable to look my supposedly loving husband in the face for a moment longer, knowing what he's done, knowing that he's to blame, that his actions have caused all of this and that, because of him, I'm having to lie to the police, and pretend to be something I'm not.

The way he bluffed and blustered, and the guilty look on his face when the inspector was asking his questions was such a giveaway, I'm surprised they didn't just arrest him there and then, and I have to admit, I'm exhausted now, not only from having to put on an act myself – for obvious reasons – but from having to try and prevent him from giving himself away. Because if he did that, he'd give me away into the bargain. And I'm damned if I'm going to let him do that, not after everything else he's done. Not after the promises he made me, and then broke, without a second thought. Whatever happens, I have to protect myself, and unfortunately at the moment, that means I also have to protect him. I have to hide his role in all of this, and I have to lie to shield him… even though he doesn't deserve it.

The door opens behind me, but I remain focused on the sink and the untouched washing up, left over from lunchtime, that has lain in the tepid water since before the police arrived.

"That was all a bit shocking, wasn't it?" he says, stating the obvious.

"Yes, it was." I pick up a saucer, attacking the tea stain on it with the cloth, then rinsing it under the tap and placing it on the drainer.

"I certainly didn't expect that, when they knocked on the door."

"No."

"It must have been Sam she was meeting, don't you think?" he says, coming over and standing beside me, leaning back against the draining board, and getting in the way, rather than actually helping.

"Who else could it have been?" I avoid answering him, because I know perfectly well who she was meeting – and that it wasn't Sam at all.

He shrugs, folding his arms. "I don't know." I nudge him slightly and he moves aside, so I can put the teacup on the drainer. "It just seems so sad…"

I glance up at him, noting the regret in his eyes, which hardens my heart, even as I murmur, "Yes, doesn't it?" in reply.

"Well, I think I'll go out for a while," he says, lowering his arms and walking towards the door, as though he hasn't a care in the world, which I suppose he hasn't. Not any longer. In solving my problems, I've also solved his, no matter how inadvertently, and even if he does harbour some regret at Mildred's passing, that will be easily overshadowed by his relief that he's safe now… she can't hurt him anymore.

I want to call out after him, to ask where he's going, but I'm scared of hearing the answer, so instead I pick up the drinking glass in the bottom of the sink, gripping it tightly, my anger almost overwhelming me. How can he look me in the eye and lie in the way he does? And how can he be so blasé about everything? I jump out of my skin and yelp with pain when the glass shatters in my hand, unaware I'd been holding it quite so tight. A few drops of blood seep into the water, turning it pink, and I reach for a tea towel, holding it over the small cut on my finger, desperately trying not to cry. It's not the pain that hurts so much as the knowledge that I've killed to save my position and my marriage, and I'm not sure it was ever really worth saving.

———•———

The light is fading by the time we leave the Whartons' property and I glance up at the clear sky above, wondering if the men in the churchyard will have finished their search yet. A frost is already forming on the edges of the fir tree that overhangs the pavement, and I recall that last night was just as cold – at least according to Thompson, anyway – and that Mildred Ryder would have lain on the freezing ground behind the church, alone, cold and frightened, knowing that she was going to die, with no-one to comfort her.

"Another interesting couple," Thompson remarks, interrupting my thoughts, as we get into my car.

I turn to face him, switching on the engine and pulling away from the kerb. "What did you make of him?"

"He was hiding something," he replies. "But then, so was she."

I nod my head. "That's what I thought too. The question is, are they hiding the same thing, and is it connected to the case?"

"That's two questions, Rufus," he points out. "But I think the answer is the same to both."

"So do I."

"Namely that we don't know yet?" I can hear the smile in his voice, even though I'm concentrating on the road.

"Exactly."

"Did you think she was scared?" he asks.

"Yes, but more of us than of him."

"Why do you say that?"

"Because she didn't stop talking. It was a nervous response to my questions; an attempt to steer me off course."

"To protect herself?" He twists in his seat slightly as I turn right just before the railway bridge, into Speer Road.

"Or him. She clearly loves him very much… think about what she said when we got upstairs. She went against her father's wishes to marry him. That takes some courage, especially for someone of her background."

"What's her background then?" he asks.

"I don't know… not precisely."

"Then I don't understand."

"What I mean is, you can tell just from looking at her, at the way she dresses, and stands and talks, that she's a cut above him. She'd have been used to a certain way of life, I imagine, and in marrying Norman Wharton, she'd have given that up."

"I see," he muses, as I pull up behind a delivery van that's blocking the road.

"And with that in mind, how far do we think Mrs Wharton might go to protect her husband?" I ask.

"As far as murder?" he suggests.

"At least as far as lying for him, definitely."

"You think he's the murderer, then?" Thompson turns to face me.

"Not necessarily. But I do have to wonder what he's done to put that troubled look in his wife's eyes. Because he's definitely done something... mark my words."

He shakes his head, facing the front again, as the driver of the van comes out of a house to our left and gives me an apologetic wave for double parking. I wave back and he gets into his cab. "With a girl as beautiful as Mildred Ryder in the house, it wouldn't surprise me if he'd been tempted to stray." He sighs. "Although Mrs Wharton isn't exactly yesterday's news, is she?"

"Behave yourself... you're a happily married man, remember?"

He rolls his eyes as I pull away again, following the van down the road. "I'm perfectly well aware of that. And I'm not saying I'd be tempted myself. I'm just conjecturing. He wouldn't be the first man to have a fling with the hired help, would he?"

"No... and he won't be the last, either. But I'm not interested in Mr Wharton's extra marital affairs. What I am interested in is whether Mrs Wharton found out about them, and whether she decided to remove her rival... permanently."

"Assuming she had a rival, of course."

"Of course." I nod my head in acknowledgement. "We could be reading too much into the whole thing."

"Who are we going to see next? The mother?" Thompson enquires.

"I think we'll just pay a visit to the boyfriend first," I suggest. "Mrs Ryder will probably have only just got in from work, and I want to know whether it was the boyfriend that Mildred had arranged to meet last night."

He nods his head, and we drive on to the end of Speer Road, turning to the right and then taking the second on the left, by-passing Queen's Road and turning into Alexandra Road instead, pulling up outside a neat terraced house, with a small garden at the front, retained by a low brick wall.

We get out and walk in silence to the front door, which I knock upon.

"I don't think there's anyone at home," Thompson whispers, even though we haven't waited for very long.

"No." I'm inclined to agree. The house just has that empty feeling about it. "Let's go and see Mrs Ryder and then come back here later on."

He nods his agreement and we make our way back to the car.

"It's a shame we couldn't have told Mrs Ryder about her daughter's death before anyone else," Thompson says, as we both get in. He sounds thoughtful and I turn to look at him.

"I know. But we could hardly go chasing her around at her place of work, or looking for her up and down the high street…" I let my voice fade.

"No, we couldn't," he replies. "And I suppose, if I'm being honest, our time might well have been better spent interviewing the Hodges and the Whartons."

"Because you think one of them is our murderer?" I ask, just as I'm about to start the engine.

"Don't you?"

"Yes."

He nods. "Care to share your reasoning?" he asks.

I suck in a breath. "I don't have any. It's just a gut reaction."

He sighs. "Thank heavens for that," he murmurs. "I was starting to think I was losing my touch."

"Did you ever have a touch?" I ask, chuckling as I switch on the engine, and he grins.

"I think we both know the answer to that," he replies.

I drive us to the end of Alexandra Road, where I turn right, and then right again into Queen's Road.

Number twelve is on the right, a short way down; a brick-faced, terraced building with sash windows and a tiny but neat patch of front garden.

Knocking on the door, we hear footsteps almost immediately, but we're both flummoxed, when it's opened by none other than Reverend Hodge. He's replaced his red sweater with a more formal, dark jacket, as befits his role, I suppose, and has the decency to blush as he holds the door open for us, letting us pass directly into a small sitting room, furnished with a single sofa and chair, a low side table, with a potted plant on top, and a narrow bookcase in the alcove created by the chimney breast, its shelves filled with leather-bound tomes.

"Inspector," he says by way of greeting, as Thompson and I remove our hats.

"Reverend Hodge," I reply. "We've come to see Mrs Ryder."

"Of course." He closes the door again and holds out his arm, pointing in the direction of a door directly ahead of us. "Everyone is in the dining room."

"Everyone?" I query, following him as he takes the lead, which seems to be his forte.

"Mrs Ryder and her other children," he explains, opening the door.

We move through, past the stairs, which go up at a right angle in the centre of the house, to a slightly larger room, where a middle-aged woman with auburn hair, almost the same shade as her deceased daughter, barring the few strands of visible grey, is sitting at the head of a rectangular table, her elbows resting in front of her, a handkerchief clasped to her nose, as she sobs woefully. Despite her obvious distress, it's easy to see that Mildred Ryder's good looks were inherited from her mother, who's a very attractive woman, and I imagine in the flush of youth, would have been just as captivating as her daughter. By her side stands a boy of probably fourteen years of age, his arm resting on his mother's shoulders, his lips pursed tightly as he attempts to control his emotions. A girl, probably a year or so older, sits on the other side of her mother, her hands covering her face, her shoulders shaking, in obvious distress.

"Who... who are you?" Mrs Ryder asks, pulling the handkerchief from her face and looking up at me, her green eyes overflowing with tears.

"I'm Detective Inspector Stone," I reply, making every effort to control my voice, despite my raging anger that Reverend Hodge has clearly hot-footed it down here to break the news to the family. He may have meant well. He may even have had their best interests at heart, although having sat with him for the best part of half an hour earlier, I doubt both of those sentiments; but the point is, this situation is very far from ideal.

"You're looking into what happened to M—Mildred?" she asks, stumbling over her daughter's name.

"Yes," I reply, "and I apologise for not coming to see you earlier."

"Oh, I wouldn't have been here anyway," she replies, sniffing and dismissing my apology. "I've only been home for a few minutes. But luckily the vicar was already here with Joe and Shirley. He... he told us the news." She stutters her words, struggling not to cry again.

He was waiting for her? I glance at him, but he's currently pre-occupied, staring at the floor.

She puts her handkerchief down, taking her daughter's hand in hers and leaning slightly into her son, clearly wanting to offer her support to them, as much as to feel theirs in return, I imagine.

"The reverend assures me Mildred wouldn't have felt any pain," Mrs Ryder says, blinking back her tears. "So I suppose that's something."

I take a breath, reining in my temper and admitting to myself that I'd have told her the same thing, given the chance. I certainly wouldn't have told her that her daughter bled to death on a grass verge, alone, and no doubt terrified.

"Can you tell me when you last saw Mildred?" I ask.

"Not for a couple of weeks," she replies, her voice cracking. "She was kept very busy at work, but used to have Wednesday afternoons and every other Sunday off. She'd spend her Wednesdays with Sam... her fiancé, but she'd come here after church on Sundays, regular as clockwork, and have lunch with us, and then stay for the afternoon. She was due to come tomorrow..." She starts to cry again now, releasing her daughter's hand and picking up her handkerchief once more, dabbing at her eyes, while Thompson and I glance around the room, to give her time to compose herself.

The shelves in the alcoves on either side of the small fireplace are littered with religious artefacts; a postcard of the Madonna and child, propped up against a few books, a statue, which I presume to be of Christ, his arms outstretched, a couple of angelic figurines and two crosses – one wooden and one made of a shiny golden coloured metal of some kind. There are also several framed photographs. One is of

Mildred, perhaps from a couple of years ago, taken at Christmas, by the looks of things, and I'm struck once again by her beauty, which death did not diminish, it seems. There's another of a man, in his mid-forties, perhaps, who I assume to be Mrs Ryder's late husband. The others are of babies and children, but whether they're of a younger Mildred, or of Joe and Shirley, it's hard to say.

"Come now, Edna." Reverend Hodge steps forward, intervening between Mrs Ryder and her daughter, placing his hand on her shoulder. She looks up, a plaintive expression on her face, and seems to calm in an instant, and while a part of me is grateful, I still resent his intrusion, and simply glare at him myself, before returning my attention to the grieving mother.

"Did your daughter leave any of her possessions at home?" I ask. "After she moved out, I mean."

"Yes," Mrs Ryder replies. "There's a box upstairs with a few things in it. We've got a lodger now, who has Mildred's room."

"A lodger?" This sounds more interesting.

"Yes. The money comes in handy since my husband died…" She sniffles again. "George Buxton is his name. He's out at the moment, I'm afraid, and I can't tell you when he'll be back." I nod my head.

"Did your daughter know this Mr Buxton?"

"Yes, of course."

"I'll need to question him then." I pull a calling card from my inside pocket and hand it to Mrs Ryder. "Perhaps you could ask him to telephone the police station in Kingston when he returns, to make an appointment for me to come back."

"We don't have a telephone," she remarks, looking down at my card, and I remember Mr Wharton explaining that fact to us earlier.

"Don't worry about that," the vicar says, before I have the chance to reply, to explain to her that he can just pop into the local station and they'll help him. "You just send him down to the vicarage. He can use our telephone."

"Oh, you're so kind," Mrs Ryder says, looking up at him again, as yet more tears start falling onto her cheeks.

I wonder if it really is kindness, or a desire to know everything that's going on with regard to our investigation, which is driving the vicar's actions. Either way, I say nothing about his offer. "Would it be possible to see your daughter's belongings?" I ask.

She nods and turns to her son. "Joe, could you go and fetch the box? It's on top of the wardrobe in my room."

The boy beside her nods his head and silently leaves the room, returning just a few moments later with a cardboard box, which he deposits on the table, returning to his place beside his mother and giving his sister a sympathetic glance, being as her place has been rather usurped by the vicar.

"Do you mind?" I ask Mrs Ryder, before opening it and she bites her bottom lip.

"Go ahead." Her voice is a strangled whisper, and I decide to just get through the task in hand and leave them to their grief.

The box contains four more diaries, going back to 1935, together with some drawings, which were obviously done when she was young and which, for some reason either Mildred or her mother have decided to keep. There are a few birthday and Christmas cards, probably retained for sentimentality, and a couple of small, slightly worn teddy bears.

"Would you mind if we took your daughter's diaries away with us?" I ask, holding them in my hand.

"If you think it will help to find whoever did this, you can take whatever you like," Mrs Ryder replies, her voice a little stronger. "But you will bring them back, won't you?"

"Of course we will." I smile at her. "And I really am very sorry."

"She didn't deserve this," she says, choking up again. "Not Mildred…" She starts to sob as she says her daughter's name and I take this as our signal to leave. There's nothing more they can tell us, and we're not helping them.

"We'll keep you informed of our progress," I say quietly and Mrs Ryder nods her head, unable to speak now, although she nudges her son and waves her hand vaguely in our direction.

"I'll show you out," he murmurs, his voice deeper than I'd expected it to be.

"You don't have to," I reply.

"It's no trouble. And anyway, I'd better do the blackout at the front."

He comes around the table and escorts us from the room, closing the door firmly behind us and taking us into the living room once more. "Wait here a minute," he says and we stand by the door in the darkness, the room's only illumination coming from the moonlight filtering in through the window, while Joe makes his way across the room, pulling the curtains tight and then going to the front door and switching on the light.

"Will you be all right?" I ask as we join him.

"We'd be a lot better if the vicar would leave us alone," he replies, then glances up at me, a guilty expression on his face. "Sorry," he adds quickly. "I probably shouldn't have said that. It wasn't very generous of me."

"Don't be sorry. There's no need."

He takes a breath, running his fingers back through his thick hair, which is more of a reddish brown than his mother's or his older sister's. "I don't even know why he's here," he says, looking at the door to the dining room.

"He's just come to help your mother," I reply, trying to sound reasonable, even though I don't feel it.

"To interfere, more like," he says, resentfully. "Surely he knows that, when someone is killed…" His voice fades for a moment, but then he squares his narrow shoulders and continues, "When someone is killed, it's up to the police to inform the next of kin… not for busy-body vicars to barge their way in."

I smile, just lightly. "And how do you know so much about police procedures?" I ask him.

He smiles himself. "I like detective stories," he says, but then his smile drops. "And that's how I know he shouldn't be here… not like this. He should have waited."

It's hard not to agree with him, but I don't want to fuel the fires of his anger, just in case he goes back into the dining room and starts an argument with Reverend Hodge. He might feel better if he did that, but his mother wouldn't thank him.

"Well, sometimes things don't go to plan," I say instead and he sighs deeply, clearly dissatisfied.

He switches off the light again and opens the front door, stepping to one side, to let us exit into the now dark street.

"Before we go," I say, stopping on the threshold, "can you tell me how old your sister was?"

"She turned twenty last summer," he replies and it dawns on me that Mildred would have been very close in age to Amelie, being only six months or so older, which sends a shiver down my spine. "Mum wanted to have a party," he continues, unprompted, "but Mildred wouldn't hear of it. She said it was a waste of money… what with all the talk of war that was going on back then." He sniffs and wipes his nose on the back of his hand.

"Look after your mother and your sister, Joe," I say as I move onto the pathway.

"I will," he replies with determination, and Thompson and I make our way out onto the street, hearing the door close behind us.

"Nice lad that," Thompson says as we get to my car.

"Yes."

"And maybe a future copper in the making."

"Maybe."

He stalls. "You're not very happy are you?"

"That would be one way of putting it." We climb into the car and both face forwards. "I'm inclined to agree with Joe, only a little more forcefully." I turn to look at Thompson. "What the hell did Hodge think he was doing? I'd made it fairly clear that we were delaying our visit to Mrs Ryder until she got home from work. The man must have come straight down here almost as soon as we left the vicarage."

"It certainly looks that way," Thompson replies.

"The only thing we need to know, is why?"

"I suppose it's possible he just wanted to be helpful," he says and I stare at him for a moment. "Okay… so it's not very likely," he adds.

"No, it's not. It's infinitely more likely that he wanted to make sure he had some influence over the proceedings. Which means, either he's just plain nosy… or…"

"He's the murderer?"

I sigh. "Well, if he isn't, he might be very keen to protect the murderer… let's put it that way."

"You think it's his wife?"

"I'm not sure. But if I were a gambling man – which I'm not – I'd be willing to wager a week's salary that it's one or the other of them."

Thompson raises his eyebrows, but doesn't reply and I start the car. "Shall we just try Sam Higgs once more, before we call it a night?"

He agrees and settles back into his seat, although I'm not sure why he's getting comfortable, being as it takes me less than two minutes to get back to Alexandra Road again..

This time, the door is answered promptly by a middle-aged woman, who stares up at me in the darkness.

"Yes?" she says, perhaps a little abruptly.

"I'm sorry to trouble you. We're looking for Sam? Sam Higgs?"

"That's my son." She glances over her shoulder. "You'd better come in."

She moves aside and we enter her living room, waiting while she closes the door and flicks on the light. "I'm sorry," she continues, "I've got some milk boiling on the stove… would you excuse me?"

"Of course."

She disappears at speed, and I glance around, taking in the sofa and chair, crammed into the small space, along with a small cupboard and a coffee table, all of which are dark brown in colour, sucking the light from the room. Mrs Higgs returns within just a couple of moments, a little out of breath but much more relaxed.

"It didn't boil over," she says, relieved. "Now… you wanted to see Sam, you say?"

"Yes."

"I'm sorry, but I'm afraid he's not here," she says. "He's been called up, you see." I feel my heart sink at the prospect of having to try and trace him.

"He's gone already?" I ask, and she smiles, offering some hope.

"No… but today was his last day at work, and he's gone out for a drink with his friends, and his father's gone with them too, because Sam's going off on training next Tuesday morning."

He might not be… "When are you expecting him home?" I ask and her smile broadens.

"Well, his father said he was only going to stop for one pint, and then come home for his dinner. But as for Sam… you know what young men are like," she says, rolling her eyes. "It could be anytime."

"He'll be home tomorrow?" I suggest.

"Yes." Her face falls. "Can… can I ask what this is about." It's as though she's only just remembered that she's got no idea who we are.

"Of course. I do apologise. I should have introduced myself. I'm Detective Inspector Stone and this is Detective Sergeant Thompson." I turn towards him, but not before I've noticed Mrs Higgs' face paling in the harsh electric light.

"He… he's not in any trouble, is he?" she asks, clearly worried.

"Not at all," I reply. "It's a purely routine matter relating to one of his friends." I feel Thompson's eyes on me, but ignore him. I've already decided that, unlike with Mrs Ryder, I'd prefer to break the news of Mildred's death myself on this occasion.

"I see," she says, mollified. "Well, he'll be here all day tomorrow. He's got packing to do."

"We'll come round in the morning, if that's all right?"

She nods her head. "That's fine with me." She smiles again. "Whether Sam will thank you is another matter."

Knowing what we have to tell him, I doubt that he'll thank us at all.

Back in the car, Thompson turns to me.

"What next?" he asks.

"There's not a great deal more we can do tonight, especially as we don't have the doctor's report, or any sign of the murder weapon, and they'll have called the search off ages ago. Did you drive over here?"

"Yes, my car's at the church," he explains.

I smirk. "The happy Mr Harding has probably let the air out of your tyres by now."

"He'd better not have done," he replies, as I reach into my pocket and pull out all of Mildred Ryder's diaries.

"Can you do me a favour and drop those off on my desk on your way home?"

He takes them from me. "Of course. We'll go through them tomorrow, shall we?"

"Yes, after we've been to see Sam Higgs." I start the engine. "I thought you could come and pick me up in the morning… does nine o'clock sound all right? It's Sunday and I doubt Mr Higgs will surface too early, bearing in mine that he's out drinking."

"Nine o'clock sounds fine, but why can't you drive yourself?"

"Because I've been driving all day," I point out. "And I'd like to remind you that I'm still officially on my honeymoon until Monday morning, so you can do the driving for tomorrow."

"Speaking of honeymoons, how did it go?" he asks. "I've been meaning to ask, but we barely seem to have had ten minutes to ourselves all afternoon."

"We had a lovely week, thank you," I reply, giving away as little information as I can, because I know from experience that Harry Thompson will make hay with any straw of knowledge he can glean.

"Well, there's a cagey reply, if ever I heard one," he jokes.

"It's the only reply you're going to get from me. And, by the way, I've been meaning to ask you all afternoon, has there been any word about your brothers?" I change the subject as adroitly as I can.

"No. But in this situation, I think no news is probably good news."

"Almost certainly."

"I'm sorry I was so quiet during your wedding… well, and the evening before. I wasn't on my usual form at all," he says, sounding genuinely contrite.

"I think you had good reason," I reply, shaking my head. "And in a way I'm grateful. At least you were too preoccupied to get me into any trouble."

"Me? Get you into trouble?" He does his best to sound innocent.

"Yes."

"The thought of it." Now he's making an effort to sound scandalised, although he's trying not to laugh at the same time, so the effect is slightly spoiled. "And don't think I didn't notice that rather speedy change of subject back then," he adds.

"I didn't for one second think you would have done."

He chuckles. "So... about your honeymoon... did you get out much? You know, for walks on the Downs?" he asks, still grinning.

"No comment."

He nods his head, sagely. "Was the weather too bad then?"

I glare at him. "No comment."

"Okay... I'll rephrase my original question. Did you actually leave your hotel room at all?"

"Still, no comment."

"Did anyone ever tell you, you're no fun?" he replies.

"Not in the last seven days, no."

Chapter Four

I pull the brush through my hair, keeping an eye on him in the mirror as he sits on the end of the bed, the sage green eiderdown beneath him, the sheets turned down ready for the night, and he unbuttons his shirt, shrugging it off, and leaving it on the bed while he removes his vest. Then he gets up and places both items into the laundry basket, which is over by the window, and without turning, unfastens his trousers, letting them fall to his ankles. These he folds and puts over the back of the chair in the corner of the room, his movements measured and predictable, like a man twenty years his senior, who's been performing this ritual for decades, rather than for the eight years of our marriage.

He moves back across to the bed and I remember to brush my hair once more, to at least give the impression of being occupied, even though my eyes are fixed on him, as he pulls on his pyjama top, buttoning it up, and then he removes his underpants, throwing them into the laundry basket and, although I can't see without turning around, probably missing. He usually does, and I'll pick them up myself in the morning. He turns then and bends, giving me a view of his behind as he pulls on his pyjama bottoms, concealing himself in an instant. That brief glimpse of his backside is as intimate as he and I get these days, and a week ago, I regretted that. Now, I don't. But then, everything has changed now. I know what he is, and because of what he is, I've become a murderer.

"Just off to the bathroom," he announces, using exactly the same tone of voice and turn of phrase that he does every other night.

I don't reply, but once he's gone, I put down my brush and let my head fall into my hands.

We lead separate lives nowadays, at least in private, and have done for a long while; although in public, we do our best to maintain the façade of a perfect marriage, for appearance's sake. But when we're alone, I'm always reminded that I'm not enough for him. I'm not sure that I ever was. And he does nothing to make me think any differently. Judging from the things he says, and the way he behaves, I think I've been a constant source of disappointment to him since the moment of our marriage. Although what he fails to take into consideration, and always did, is that when we married, I was young and extremely innocent. I knew he was more experienced than me, more worldly wise, but I honestly had no idea what was expected of me as a wife, especially when it came to the physical aspects of our union. And it never seems to occur to him that, if he'd been kinder, more gentle, less demanding, less critical… I might have been able to learn from him. I was certainly willing to try, at the beginning at least, and if he'd been more considerate, I might, in time, have developed more expansive tastes, and I could have learned to satisfy him. Instead of which, he looked elsewhere, and when I found out, he told me his infidelity was my own fault, because I was 'boring'.

I blink back my tears, clenching my fists and rubbing my eyes. "I will not cry," I whisper, as I listen to him whistling something unintelligible and slightly out of tune.

He's carrying on with his life, behaving as though he hasn't a worry in the world, which he hasn't now, because I've taken care of his problem for him. After all, Mildred had threatened to report him to the police for what he'd done to her. That's why he offered her the money. So, the fact that she's dead, and can't reveal his violation must feel like he's had a huge weight lifted from his shoulders.

I glance up at myself in the mirror and try to imagine how my life would be if I hadn't killed her; if she'd been allowed to report him instead. I picture the police coming and knocking on the door, rather like they did today, only this time, they'd have been taking my husband away, in handcuffs, I should think, most probably arresting him. There would have been newspaper reporters, a court case… and of course, there would have been the looks of pity on the faces of the villagers as they whispered about me behind my back, wondering if I'd known what he'd done, whether I was guilty by association. I'm not a native of these parts and I'd have had to leave, naturally. I'd have had to start again somewhere else, because I couldn't have gone back to my family… I can't even go back to them now. It would have been hard enough before all of this… but now…

I want to scream. It's so unfair…

Why do I have to be the one to suffer? I didn't do anything wrong. It's is all his fault. He's a cheat… a philanderer.

"No," I whisper under my breath, "call him what he really is…"
He's a rapist.

———•———

I walk into the house, grateful that Amelie has thought to leave the lights off in the living room, which means I can open the door with impunity.

Once inside, I pull across the blackout curtain – one of several made by my mother – and switch on the main light, before taking off my coat and hanging it up on one of the hooks behind the door. I place my hat on the end of the stairs, and remove my jacket, leaving it over the back of the sofa, but then change my mind about the lighting and turn on the two side lamps instead, extinguishing the central light, in favour of a more gentle glow. The fire is almost out, so I add a log from the basket and wander through into the dining room, smiling as I note that it's been laid for two, and then follow my nose into the kitchen, where I find my beautiful wife, standing at the stove. I have no idea what she's prepared for our supper, but there's a medium sized saucepan belching steam, and I can smell something else cooking as well… something familiar…

She's intent on whatever it is she's doing, blissfully unaware of me, it seems, and I walk over, placing my hands on her waist, whereupon she yelps and jumps, turning in my arms and slapping me gently on the chest.

"You scared me to death…"

I swallow the rest of her words with a kiss, endeavouring to make up for all the hours we've lost today, although I doubt that's possible with just a single kiss.

When I pull back, she smiles up at me, her hands now resting on my arms. "You're forgiven," she remarks and I smile, leading her away from the stove, further into the room, before reaching behind her and unfastening the button of her skirt. "What are you doing?" she asks, raising her eyebrows.

"I'm picking up where we left off at lunchtime." I kiss her again. "I've been thinking about you… and this… all afternoon." I let my hands rest on her backside and she nestles into me invitingly.

"And would it be possible to think about me… and this… for a bit longer?" she asks, with a tease in her voice.

"I intend thinking about you for the rest of my life, so I suppose so… why?"

"Because dinner's ready," she replies.

"And you think I can wait that long… for this?" I gently pat her behind.

She grins. "Being as it's taken me most of the afternoon to prepare and cook our dinner, yes I do."

"And what are we eating?" I ask, glancing over her shoulder at the stove.

"The saucepan contains carrots," she replies, "but as for what's in the oven… that's a surprise."

"Very well," I say softly, doing up her skirt again, with a great deal of reluctance. "But after dinner, you're all mine."

She leans up and kisses me on the lips. "I'm all yours now."

"Don't tempt me."

She chuckles, then claps her hands together, gleefully. "Go and sit at the table," she says, "and I'll bring the dinner through."

She's like a child with a new toy and, as much as I'd rather just stay out here with her, I don't want to spoil her obvious enjoyment of having cooked our first meal in our home together. So, rather enjoying my own role of obedient husband, I go back into the dining room and around the table, sitting facing the kitchen door. She's found a lace tablecloth that I didn't know we possessed, and laid out our new cutlery, together with two cups and saucers, and the breadboard in the centre, topped with the bread, which has already had a couple of slices taken off of it, for Amelie's lunch, I presume. I'm about to pick up the bread knife to start cutting us a slice or two each, when I hear a startled cry from the kitchen and leap to my feet, running back out through the door, to find her crouched by the oven, a folded cloth in one hand.

"What's wrong, darling?" I step up behind her. "You haven't burned yourself, have you?"

She shakes her head. "No... but look." She points into the oven and, although it's a tight squeeze to fit both of us into the narrow space, I bend, my face level with hers, and look inside to the enamel dish that's sitting on the middle shelf, containing a pale, rather congealed mess.

"What is it?" I ask and she stands, glaring at me.

"Rufus!"

"I'm sorry... but what's it supposed to be?" I'm trying so hard not to laugh.

"It's supposed to be toad in the hole," she says, turning back around and, using the cloth she's holding to remove the dish from the oven, placing it on top of the stove, while we both stand and examine its contents.

"Well, I can see those are sausages," I remark, pointing to the four, clearly undercooked sausages which are lying neatly in the centre of the container, surrounded by a coagulating mass of what I presume is meant to be batter, and she hits me around the arm with the tea towel.

"So help me God, if you say one more word, I'm going to tip the whole lot over your head."

She turns to face me as she's speaking and I can't help it, I burst out laughing, and so does she.

"What happened?" I ask, looking back at the dish and scratching my head.

"I've got no idea. But then I can't cook, remember?" She lets out a long sigh, her hands resting on her hips. "What are we going to do?" she says. "There's half a pound of sausages in there, not to mention the flour and milk... and an egg." She starts listing the ingredients and I have to smile, because although she's got everything right, somehow it's still gone completely wrong.

"Would you like me to come to the rescue?" I ask, putting my arms around her and pulling her close to me.

"I'd love you to... this cooking malarky is a lot more challenging than it looks."

I smile and lean down, kissing her, just briefly.

"In that case… remind me… do we own a frying pan?"

"Of course we do. We've got the one that used to be yours, from your flat."

"Oh yes. Why didn't I think of that?" She goes to move away, presumably to fetch it, but I pull her back, holding her close to me, and looking down into her eyes. "If I'm going to come to the rescue, I need sustenance first."

"Sustenance?" She looks up at me, her eyes sparkling.

"Yes." I pull her body tight against mine and kiss her, very hard indeed, as she sighs into me.

When we break away from each other, we're both breathless and I'm almost tempted to forget dinner and take Amelie straight to bed, but I feel as though it's important we try to make something out of the meal she worked so hard to create, so while she fetches the frying pan, I retrieve the sausages from the uncooked batter, scraping off the worst of the congealed mess with a knife.

"What are you going to do?" she asks, coming back to the stove.

"Well, first you're going to tell me if we've got any potatoes," I reply, "and then *we* are going to cook these sausages."

"We do have potatoes… but I'm not sure it's safe to let me anywhere near food. I'm dangerous."

I smile down at her. "No you're not. It just takes time to learn, that's all."

I add some fat to the frying pan, turning on the gas, and then put in the sausages, letting them sizzle while I cut the potatoes into thin slices, before adding them to the pan as well.

"How do you know what to do?" she asks, watching my every move, as I check on the carrots, making sure they're not boiling dry. They're going to be overcooked, but it doesn't matter; not in the grand scheme of things.

"Because I fended for myself for years," I reply, leaning down and kissing her forehead. "Now, why don't you turn the sausages?"

I hand her a fork and she nudges the sausages around the pan a little. "Like that?" she asks.

"Perfect."

She looks up at me as I put my arm around her. "Do you regret marrying me?" she says, taking me by surprise. She's not teasing now. In fact, there's a disarming candour to her question which makes my breath catch in my throat.

"Never. I love you with all my heart, and marrying you is the best decision I've ever made," I reply with equal honesty and she gazes up at me, unblinking.

"Promise?"

"I promise."

She nods, letting out a sigh. "Then would you mind if I just watched you cook for tonight. I'm suddenly really tired. I don't know what's…"

"You're not feeling unwell are you?" I put my hands on her shoulders and turn her to face me, looking down into her eyes.

"No. I'm just exhausted, that's all."

"I probably should have let you get more sleep during our week away," I point out, and she reaches up, touching my cheek with her fingertips.

"I liked our week away," she whispers.

"I noticed. And I meant what I said when we got back here this morning." She looks up, her brow furrowing in confusion. "As far as I'm concerned, our honeymoon will never be over."

She smiles and I kiss her, only stopping when I smell the sausages starting to burn.

"Tell me about your day?" I say, flipping them over and turning the potatoes at the same time.

She leans back against the cupboard beside the stove, folding her arms and looking up at me. "Well, the first thing I did was to walk down to Walton Road before the shops closed, and I went to the butcher's for the sausages, the greengrocer's for the carrots…"

"And potatoes?"

"Yes," she says. "Although it wasn't until later on that I realised we wouldn't need them if we were having toad in the hole… except we did, evidently. Because I can't cook."

"You'll learn. And look on the bright side, at least you thought to buy potatoes, which means we're definitely not going to starve tonight."

She manages a smile, then continues, "And after that, I came back here and made myself some cheese on toast for lunch, and then I went to see Mary." She's referring to the cook who's employed by her uncle and aunt, who promised to teach Amelie some culinary basics before we were married. Unfortunately, because the house needed so much work, she didn't have time to take Mary up on her offer, but she's clearly been there today for some advice, I presume. "I asked her how to make the toad in the hole," she says, lowering her eyes, "but to be honest, I couldn't quite follow it, which I suppose is obvious now."

I move over and stand in front of her. "It doesn't matter, darling... honestly." I cup her face with one hand, kissing her gently.

"Mary had to let me have some flour," she adds, "because I'd forgotten to buy any, but I got confused about the timings and the oven temperature... at least I think that must have been the problem, anyway. I probably should have written down the recipe, but Mary was quite busy, being as Uncle Gordon is at home and has someone going round for dinner this evening, so there wasn't really time, and she said it was such an easy thing to cook... unless you're me, of course."

"Personally, I'd say it's not the easiest thing for a novice cook to start off with. Yorkshire pudding batter can be very tricky."

"But it's your favourite, and I so wanted to make it for you."

I smile down at her. "And it means a great deal to me that you tried."

I kiss her forehead, as she lets out a long yawn.

"Goodness me, you are tired." I say, returning to the frying pan to turn the potatoes again. "I think perhaps I should let you get an early night..."

She grabs my arm, spinning me around, and steps in front of me, putting her arms around my waist. "That's the very last thing I want, Rufus," she says softly, looking up at me very temptingly through her eyelashes. "I need you."

"Hmm... I need you too." She stands up on her tiptoes and plants a kiss on my lips.

"Then can you stop all this silly talk about leaving me alone, and letting me rest... because after dinner, I fully expect you to take me to bed… where I'd like you to spend a great deal of time reminding me that we're still officially on our honeymoon."

"With pleasure, Mrs Stone… with pleasure."

I pull her closer, holding her against me, and despite my words, I resolve to myself that I need to keep an eye on Amelie. And I need to make less demands of her, not that I've 'demanded' anything, but I need to allow her to sleep, or to rest, at least for some of the time, when we get to bed, and I need to help out more around the house too… which means this case couldn't have come at a worse time. "Shall I dish up the dinner?" I suggest. "And we'll do our best to forget this afternoon, and enjoy a lovely evening together?"

"I think I'd like that," she whispers.

Over dinner, Amelie asks about my day, and I tell her about the discovery of Mildred Ryder's body, about our visit to the vicarage, and to Mr and Mrs Wharton. She immediately picks up on a change in me and stops eating, putting down her knife and fork and looking up at me.

"You suspect someone already, don't you?" she asks.

"Yes. But how did you know?"

"Because of the way you're talking," she remarks. "I've heard you speak like that before, but only at the end of a case, once you've worked out who's guilty."

"Well, maybe a week away has done me some good." I reach over, taking her hand in mine. "Because my brain is obviously working a lot more quickly than usual."

"Assuming you're right," she replies, pursing her lips and trying not to smile.

I squeeze her hand. "You mean you doubt it?"

"No," she says. "I never doubt you." I appreciate her confidence in me and lean over, raising her hand to my lips to kiss her fingers. "I'm not going to ask who you think it might be, because I'm going to assume you're not supposed to tell me."

I shake my head. "It's probably best if I don't. Not just yet."

"In case you're wrong?"

"Well, I suppose it's always possible. But in reality, I really ought to gather some evidence first."

She chuckles, and the sound warms my heart, before I release her hand and we continue eating.

"I assume you'll have to work tomorrow?" she asks, after a short pause.

"Yes. I'm sorry."

She shakes her head. "You don't have to be sorry, Rufus."

"It won't be like this all the time. I promise."

She attempts a smile and almost gets there. "I know," she says, and I seriously wish we could have come home to a modicum of peace and quiet. I never expected to walk straight into a murder case, and although Amelie's aware of how busy they can keep me, she's never had to live it full-time, like she's going to have to now… it's a baptism of fire for her. One she could probably have done without.

We finish our meal, then clear away and I wash up, while Amelie dries – because she refuses to sit down, even though I've asked her to – and between us, we put everything away, before I send Amelie into the living room, with very firm instructions to switch on the wireless and put her feet up, while I make us a cup of tea.

Joining her, she tells me that we're listening to something called *Saturday At Nine-thirty*, which evidently features songs and music from current and forthcoming films. She tells me this with a smile on her face, and as I sit down, our cups of tea placed on the side tables at either end of the sofa, I ask her if she'll be humming these tunes in the bath anytime soon.

"I expect so," she replies, shifting along the sofa and nestling in my arms.

"Comfy?" I ask, and she nods her head, as we settle down, the fire warming us nicely, and listen to the music, to which Amelie either taps her foot, or drums her fingers, in perfect time. We drink our tea, and I steal the occasional kiss, in between musical numbers, while Hugh Morton, the compère for the evening, announces each piece.

The programme finishes at ten-fifteen and I take our cups out to the kitchen, where Amelie joins me, taking me by surprise.

"I just need the bathroom before we go to bed," she says, looking far more shy than she did during the week of our honeymoon.

"Okay. I'll switch everything off and lock up… and I'll wait for you in the living room."

She shakes her head. "No, it's all right. You go on up."

"Are you sure?"

"Yes. I won't be long."

I decide against insisting, and bend down, kissing her cheek instead, before going back into the living room, extinguishing the lights, and checking that the front door is locked. After that, I go upstairs and into our bedroom, where I make sure the blackout is in place before turning on the bedside lamps.

Since my departure at lunchtime, Amelie has obviously been at work up here. There's no sign of our cases, although I assume she'll have put them in the spare room for now. But she has laid out a clean pair of pyjama bottoms on the bed, which makes me smile, as I pick them up and deposit them on the wicker chair in the corner of the room, and then start undressing. I wonder to myself what Amelie's pyjamas will look like, being as I've never seen them before, but I don't have long to wait, and I've just climbed into bed and pulled up the covers, when I hear her footsteps running up the stairs.

She comes in through the door and I can't help the grin that forms on my lips, being as she's not wearing her own nightclothes at all, but is wearing the pyjama top that matches the bottoms she'd laid out on the bed for me to wear. She glances at me and I notice a slight blush creep up her cheeks before my eyes settle on the armful of clothes she's carrying.

"I—I'll just put these away," she murmurs and starts moving around the room, opening drawers.

"Leave them," I tell her and she turns to face me, pausing for a moment, before she goes over to the chair and stops, about to put the rest of her clothes down, right as she notices my pyjama bottoms lying there. She doesn't say a word, but puts her own clothes on the seat of the chair, picking up my pyjama bottoms and turning back around again, holding them up, her head tilted to one side, and a look of mild

77

confusion etched on her face. "Come to bed," I whisper, pulling back the covers, and she takes a moment, her eyes widening slightly, before she drops the garment she's holding to the floor, and walks slowly across the bedroom.

"Are you all right?" I ask Amelie as she finishes her cup of tea.

I got up about half an hour ago and went down to the bathroom, after which I made a cup of tea for my wife and brought it up to bed. Then I opened the curtains, removing the blackout at the same time, and I'll admit, I was sorely tempted to let her sleep on. She looked so beautiful. But I know how much she appreciates that first cup of tea, so I woke her with a kiss, which she returned, smiling up at me, and we lay together for a while.

We didn't talk much, because Amelie isn't a great one for conversation before she's finished her cup of tea, and I was feeling guilty for what I'd done to her last night. I'd resolved to take more care of her, to be more attentive, less demanding, and I'd failed at the first hurdle; too easily distracted by her. Again.

"Yes, thank you." She smiles up at me, puts her cup down on the bedside table and turns towards me again, a satisfied look on her face.

I lean down and kiss her gently. "I've just realised how inconsiderate I was last night."

"You were?" Her brow furrows, like she's struggling to reconcile my words with her recollections. "I don't remember you being inconsiderate. If anything you were the exact opposite." She reaches up, caressing my cheek with her fingertips. "But then you're always considerate."

"Am I?" I query. "I'm not sure how considerate it was of me to forget my promise to be more responsible. I've made a fairly shocking job of that, so far."

She smiles. "Hmm… I'd noticed. But I'm still not complaining."

"I know. But aside from that, I'm not sure I should have made love to you for quite so long, not when you'd already explained how tired you're feeling at the moment."

"Of course you should have made love to me," she says firmly. "It was exactly what I needed."

"Sure?" I ask, still feeling a little uncertain.

"Absolutely positive." She pushes me onto my back and lies on top of me, her soft naked body along the length of mine. "Please don't worry. I'm sure the tiredness will go, once I get used to this new way of life… And please don't stop all those magical things you do to me. I couldn't bear it if you did. I need you so much… it's like a basic instinct, deep inside me."

I put my arms around her, holding her close. "I'm here, my darling… and I'm yours." She smiles again, and lets her head rest on my chest. "I'm also intrigued," I add.

"What about?" She looks up.

"About why you didn't change up here last night. I've seen you naked. I know every inch of your body. Intimately. You don't need to feel shy, or embarrassed around me. And if you do…"

She blushes. "I don't. I—I just wanted to surprise you. That's all."

"Surprise me?"

"Yes. When I was laying out our night clothes earlier in the evening, before you came home, I decided I… well, I'd rather wear your pyjamas than my own. You know… like I did when we were away."

I smile. "And why would that be?"

"Because I like your pyjamas," she says softly and I pull her up my body slightly, so her face is right above mine, that slight blush evident on her cheeks again, and I know that, in spite of her words, she was a little shy last night, and she still is now… and that's one of the most intoxicating things about her, as I already established during our week away, because even lying on top of me, naked, and warm and very, very alluring, she's still kind of innocent.

"So do I…" I run my hands down her back and she shudders, rather proving my point. "At least I do when you're wearing them. Although I'm not sure I want to wear them ever again."

"Well, I don't have a problem with that," she whispers, our lips almost touching. "I'm not sure I like you being covered up anyway." I'm about to roll her onto her back when she starts to squirm downwards, kissing my neck first, and then my chest. "I like being able to see all of you. That's been one of the best things about our week away together… spending time discovering which parts of you I like best…"

"And?" I tease, even as my breath hitches in my throat.

"And I've established that I especially like this," she says, looking back up at me, her fingers trailing through the hair on my chest, before she moves further down. "And this." She kisses my stomach, then looks up at me, our eyes locking and holding firm, as she slides lower still, coming to rest between my parted legs. "Although," she adds, her voice dropping a note or two, "I have to say, *this* is my favourite."

We make breakfast together, because it gives us a chance to spend some more time alone, in a confined space, and I don't think either of us is going to decline such an opportunity, not after the manner of our waking, which was deeply intimate, utterly exhilarating, and after Amelie had finished showing me how much she liked her favourite part of my body, mutually fulfilling. I made sure of that. It was also absolute proof, as if I needed it, of my bride's ability to be all things at all times. It was a reminder of why I find her so distracting, so tantalising… and so completely impossible to resist.

We're just sitting down in the dining room, unable to stop touching, or to take our eyes from each other, when the telephone rings, breaking the spell.

"Will it always be like this?" Amelie asks, sounding despondent.

"No," I reply, getting to my feet and walking around to her, kissing her lips just briefly before I go through to the living room, beginning to regret having the telephone installed at all. I recall the many conversations that were required in order to have it laid in before the wedding, with me having to explain repeatedly, that my job means that I need access to a phone at all times, which may not be a war priority, but is a necessity nonetheless. At one stage, it even looked like I might have to involve the Chief Constable, to get him to pull some strings, but it was finally arranged that the phone would be laid in while Amelie and I were away, and Mother agreed to be on hand to make sure things ran smoothly.

"Stone," I say into the receiver, sounding perhaps a little gruffer than I might otherwise have done, thanks to the interruption to an otherwise perfect morning.

"Good morning, dear." It's my mother and I immediately regret my tone of voice – mainly because I have no doubt she'll ask what's wrong. "Is everything all right?" She doesn't disappoint.

"Yes. Everything's fine. It's just that I'm having to work today."

"You are?" I can tell she's surprised. "I thought you weren't due back at work until tomorrow."

"I'm not… not officially, anyway. But there's been a murder at Thames Ditton, and the chief super's got flu, so I've been drafted back in."

"Oh dear," she replies. "I won't keep you. I was only calling to see if you and Amelie would like to come for lunch today, but as you're working, I'm assuming your answer will be 'no'."

"Mine will be, but Amelie might like to come for a visit," I suggest, it occurring to me that she'd probably enjoy the company.

"Well, she'll be more than welcome," Mother says. "And we can always have a light lunch, and then have something more substantial this evening, when you get back. You'll be home in time for dinner won't you?"

"I should be, yes." I realise, all of a sudden that I shouldn't be making plans on my wife's behalf, without asking her opinion. "Just hang on a minute, Mother," I say into the receiver. "I'll check that Amelie doesn't have anything else in mind for today."

"Okay, dear."

I place my hand over the mouthpiece and call to Amelie, who appears within moments. "Is something wrong?" she asks, looking concerned.

"No." I hold out my hand to her, and she comes over, but doesn't take it. Instead, she nestles into me and I put my arm around her, explaining Mother's idea. "How does that sound?" I ask, looking down at her.

"It sounds marvellous," Amelie replies, "especially as I've just realised that I didn't remember to buy anything for us to eat today." She looks up at me guiltily, biting her lip.

"In which case you'd definitely better come here," my mother says, chuckling in my other ear.

"And do you promise not to lead my wife astray?" I ask, knowing my mother's and my aunts' capacity for mischief.

"We'll have a lovely day together," Mother replies evasively, and I shake my head. "Now, put Amelie on the phone so we can make the arrangements."

I do as I'm told, returning to the dining room to pour the tea.

"Well, that's all settled," Amelie announces, coming back in a few minutes later, and sitting down beside me, instead of opposite me, although she doesn't look as pleased as I'd expected her to. In fact, she looks positively miserable.

"Is something wrong?" I ask. "You are happy with the plans, aren't you?"

"Yes. It'll be lovely to see your mother and your aunts." She smiles, but it doesn't touch her eyes and I know something is wrong.

"And you'll be all right walking down there?" I wonder if that might be the problem, although I can't really see why it would be. It's not that far, and she called on Mary yesterday, who's just opposite, at her guardian's house.

"Yes, of course. We've arranged that I'll go at around eleven."

"So, why the sad face?" I turn in my chair, facing her, then take hold of her legs, just above the knee, and twist her around in hers, looking into her eyes.

"It's nothing." She sighs. "I—It's just that I feel so stupid. I can't believe I forgot to buy us any meat at the butchers… I was so intent on getting the sausages and making the toad in the hole, I didn't think about anything else. It didn't even dawn on me that it was the weekend…"

"It doesn't matter, darling."

"Well, it doesn't I suppose. But that's thanks to your mother inviting us for dinner, not to me being an efficient housewife," she replies.

"We'd have worked something out."

"We might still have to," she mutters. "Your mother's just told me that the butcher's don't open on Mondays either."

"No, they don't."

She stares at me. "You were aware of this?"

"Yes." I nod my head, buttering a slice of toast very thinly, before offering it to Amelie, aware of the rationing that's just come in. It didn't affect us at the inn while we were on our honeymoon, but now we're back, we'll have to be much more restrained.

"Why wasn't I?" She shakes her head, staring at the plate before her, but not eating anything.

"Because you've never needed to be. It's my fault. I should have told you."

She looks at me for a moment, then tips her head to one side. "Why did you marry me?" she asks.

I put down my knife and shift closer to her, perching on the edge of my seat, so our legs are touching. "After everything we did and said this morning, you really need me to answer that?"

"No, probably not," she mumbles and I reach out, cupping her face with both of my hands now.

"Oh, I think perhaps you do," I reply and she looks up at me. "I married you because I love you. And I love you because you're beautiful, inside and out. You're loving and giving; you're kind and caring, and generous, and you restore my faith in humanity, every single time I look at you."

"Even if I'm absolutely useless at just about everything," she murmurs.

"You're not," I reply, pulling her a little closer still. "I don't care about any of that anyway."

"You will when we've got nothing to eat tomorrow night."

"It won't come to that." I stand, pulling her up with me, and into my arms, because I need to hold her, not just sit and look at her. "You're still tired, that's all."

She rests against me and nods her head. "I am," she whispers. "I don't know why. I slept quite well. But I still feel absolutely drained."

"Then let my mother and my aunts run around after you this afternoon. They'll enjoy. it. And I'll join you as soon as I can."

"Promise?" she asks, looking up at me.

"I promise."

We kiss briefly and then I sit, lowering Amelie down onto my lap this time, and reaching over to pull the plate of buttered toast back in front of her, before preparing a second slice for myself, while keeping half an eye on the clock.

"Can we eat breakfast like this every day?" she asks, chewing on her toast and leaning back into me, crumbs dropping onto her blouse.

"If you want to."

"You don't think it's a little impractical?"

"Not in the slightest, darling. Not in the slightest."

She drops the toast onto the plate, then twists on my lap and throws her arms around my neck, clinging to me. "In that case, I want to," she whispers as I snake my arms around her.

"I wish I didn't have to work today," I murmur.

"So do I."

"And I wish I could take you back to bed and spend the whole day there, pretending the rest of the world doesn't even exist. Because it doesn't, not when I'm with you."

She sighs deeply, as though imagining that perfection. "It doesn't, does it?" she says, her voice a mere whisper, and I lean back, pulling away and looking into her eyes.

"I promise, things will get better," I say firmly.

"I know."

She rests her forehead against mine and we sit for a moment, until the clock ticks around to ten to nine, and I realise I need to eat something, because I doubt I'll get another chance today.

A slice and a half of toast later, I hear the sound of a horn being tooted outside.

"That'll be Harry," I remark and Amelie immediately shoots to her feet, as though struck by lightning.

"Hey… you didn't have to stand up so quickly."

"But he's waiting for you."

"And? He's good at waiting. It's one of his better qualities." A smile touches her lips and I stand myself, pushing my chair under the table. "Will you be all right?" I ask, holding her in my arms again.

"I'll be fine." She sounds stronger now, more resolute, and she rests her hands on my chest as she's speaking. "Now, go and be a policeman. Catch whoever killed that poor girl, Inspector."

"Yes, Mrs Stone."

She smiles properly now. "I like it when you call me that."

"So do I."

I take her hand in mine, reluctant to let go of her, and even more reluctant to leave her, because this tiredness of hers has me worried. She's almost listless with it, and that's not like Amelie... not at all. I lead her into the living room, where I put on my jacket, standing still while Amelie picks a strand of cotton from my lapel. Then I shrug on my coat, holding my hat in my hand, as she opens the door.

"I'll see you later," she says, stepping to one side.

I look down at her and, impulsively, put my arm around her waist, my hat hanging loose behind her, pulling her close to me and kissing her very thoroughly, my free hand clasping her head, holding her, as I swallow down her gentle sighs.

"See you later," I whisper, finally releasing her, noticing her slightly swollen lips, and the sparkle in her eyes, before I step outside.

"Take care," she calls and I turn, blowing her a kiss.

"You too, darling."

Thompson has parked immediately behind my car, which means he'll have seen everything that's just gone on. But I don't care. In fact, I don't take my eyes from Amelie's as I walk around the car and open the door, settling into the seat.

"You're clearly still on your honeymoon," Thompson quips.

I reply without looking at him, without glancing away from Amelie, who is still standing on the doorstep. "Just drive, will you?"

"Certainly," he says, sounding confused. "To Sam Higgs' house, I take it?"

"No... to my mother's."

Chapter Five

I've attended church every Sunday since I was a child. It was what my parents did. And probably their parents before them. My mother always went to both services; the early one, and Matins, to which my father and I accompanied her. And for a while, after my marriage, I followed in her footsteps, enjoying the solitude of those early morning observances of tradition, the community of spirit and the sense of belonging. In recent months though, while I've continued to attend Matins regularly, I've given up with the eight o'clock service. I'm not really sure why. Perhaps it's just that the thought of getting up so early on a Sunday, especially in winter, has started to wear a little thin. However, it seems important today to make the effort, so I get up in plenty of time, making sure I'm bathed and dressed before seven.

"You're up early." His voice makes me jump when he comes downstairs at just after twenty past, but then I am rather preoccupied, staring out of the kitchen window and wondering whether I'm doing the right thing, or whether I'd be better off staying away from the church altogether. Except I can't help wondering whether my absence would attract even more attention, in the circumstances…

"I thought I'd put in an appearance at Holy Communion," I reply, gathering myself together and putting the hot toast on the breakfast table, as he sits down.

"Really?" He looks up at me, putting the milk into his cup, before pouring a cup of tea.

It always annoys me that he puts the milk in first, but then he doesn't pour me any, so at least it's only his own tea that he's spoiling, and I glance over at him as he takes a sip.

"Well, it seemed appropriate, given what happened to Mildred…"

He puts down his cup again. "Yes," he murmurs. "Yes, I suppose so…"

He butters his toast. "Don't use too much," I point out. "It's rationed now, remember?"

He glances at me, but continues with his spreading, regardless, muttering about it, *"Only being a bit of butter."*

I manage to avoid telling him that the 'bit of butter' currently on the kitchen table is meant to last us the week, but only because I don't need to have an argument with him. I swear he has no comprehension about food, or housekeeping, and as for rationing, he seems to think it applies to everyone except him.

"Does that mean you'll skip the later service?" he asks, taking a bite out of his toast.

"No. I'll go to that as well." I don't bother with butter on my slice of toast, and just have a little marmalade instead. "I think people will expect it after what's happened, and more people go to Matins."

"And it matters what people think, does it?"

I stare at him. "Yes, I think it does, don't you?"

He doesn't reply, but gets up from the table, his chair scraping on the quarry tiled floor, leaving his half eaten toast on the plate, and taking his tea with him.

I decide to ignore his abrupt departure, although the wasted butter does annoy me. But what's the point in saying anything? He won't listen anyway, so instead I swallow down my own breakfast, quickly wash up, leaving the crockery to dry on the draining board, and then get ready for the short walk to church, putting on my new hat and coat, my leather gloves and my black patent shoes, before going out of the front door and down the path.

I don't pass many people on the way, but then checking my watch, I see that I'm running a little late and I pick up my pace, not wanting to draw too much attention to myself by arriving after the service has started.

Upon my arrival, I note that there are no more people in the congregation than usual; their numbers amounting to less than fifteen, and I notice Mrs Higgs sitting on the far side of the church. She hasn't spotted me and I'm relieved. The last thing I need is to get into a discussion with her about Mildred. As I walk forward on tiptoes, always aware of my heels echoing throughout the ancient building, I nod my head to Mrs Shepherd, whose husband owns the pharmacy, and Miss Robson from the greengrocer's, going down the central aisle, before settling into my usual seat in the third row back on the left hand side, kneeling and bowing my head in silent prayer. After what I've done, I'm not sure God will be listening to me anymore, but then I reason that I need His forgiveness more than most, and screw my eyes closed, clasping my hands together so tightly, they hurt.

*

After the service, most people leave quickly, presumably keen to return home to perhaps a late breakfast, or to begin their Sunday chores, maybe doing some work in the garden, or starting to get the lunch ready. However, at the door, Mrs Shepherd is waiting, talking to Miss Robson and Mr Osborne, an elderly gentleman, who's lived in the village for longer than anyone can remember.

"We heard about Mildred Ryder," Mrs Shepherd says, stepping closer as I exit the church, and regretfully drawing me into their small group, just as I'd hoped to escape.

"Really? I didn't think it was public knowledge."

"Well, I don't think it is," she replies, "but young Joe came into the chemists last night to get some aspirin for his mother, and he told me about it. Fair cut up, he was."

"That's hardly surprising," Mr Osborne retorts, a little angrily. I want to point out that, if he's as averse to gossip as his attitude implies, then he doesn't have to stand around participating, but I hold my tongue.

"Indeed," Miss Robson adds, "that family don't have much luck, do they? First there was Bill having that heart attack… what was it? Two years ago?"

"Yes, it was," Mrs Shepherd confirms. "It was just after Christmas, if you remember. Terrible for Edna, of course, what with the two younger ones still to think about."

"She'll be grateful to have them now," Miss Robson says, as though Mrs Ryder might not have appreciated her children before, which I'm sure isn't the case at all.

"She'll miss Mildred though," Mrs Shepherd chimes in.

"I think we all will, won't we? In our own way, I mean," Mr Osborne remarks and we turn in his direction. "She was such a lovely girl," he adds and the other two women nod their heads, smiling.

I join in with their collective consensus, and then say, "I really must be going. I can't stand around gossiping all day."

"No," Mrs Shepherd replies. "Neither can I. If I don't get back and get the joint in the oven, it'll never be ready by the time George gets back from the allotments."

We all bid each other farewell and I make my way down the path, fortunately in the opposite direction to the three of them, pondering over our conversation, and especially over Mr Osborne's last comment. Obviously, most of the village thought of Mildred as a 'lovely girl', and I suppose on the outside, she may well have been.

But she was also scheming and conniving, and if I hadn't acted when I did, she'd have ruined everything I've spent the last eight years working for.

And, as much as I know it's my husband's fault, I was damned if I was going to let her do that.

———— • ————

Thompson obviously understood, without me having to say so, that when I asked him to take me to my mother's, what I actually meant was that I needed to go to Aunt Dotty's house, and that's where he parks the car, just a few minutes later. And while I know my aunts are both likely to be at home, Dotty probably painting, and Issa almost certainly working on the plot of her latest novel, I hope I'll be able to catch my mother alone. I don't have time for histrionics. Not today.

"Wait here, will you?" I say to Thompson as I get out of the car.

He doesn't reply, but switches off the engine and leans back in the seat, while I close the door behind me and open the gate, knocking on the front door and taking a half step back, looking down the road rather vacantly.

I hope I'm doing the right thing here, and that I won't regret enlisting my mother's help. Or, more importantly perhaps, that Amelie doesn't find out I've done this, and take offence, assuming as I think she might, that I'm interfering. I'm not. I just care about her. Deeply.

"Hello, dear." My mother's voice breaks into my thoughts and I turn to face her.

"Hello."

"What's wrong?" she asks, frowning and stepping back from the door to let me inside.

"I can't stop," I reply to the unspoken invitation. "I've got to go and interview someone."

"I see… then why are you here?" She moves closer again, lowering her voice, as though she knows I have something to tell her. But then, my mother always has had a sixth sense when it comes to me.

"It's Amelie."

"She's not ill, is she?" Mother asks, sounding concerned. "You're not here to tell us she can't come round today? We've been looking forward to seeing her so much." She stops talking, and blushes just slightly, reaching out and putting her hand on my arm. "And you as well, of course."

I smile, or I do my best to. "No, it's nothing like that. She's looking forward to seeing you all as well." I know that's true, just from her reaction when I told her of mother's invitation.

"Then what is it? Spit it out, Rufus, for heaven's sake."

"I want your help."

"You do?" She's surprised now, rather than concerned. "What with?"

"With Amelie." I realise I'm going to have to explain, at least in part. "She's tired… and I think she's a little run-down." Mother raises her eyebrows and tilts her head to one side, a slight smile forming on her lips. "What's amusing you?" I ask.

"Nothing, dear."

Somehow I don't believe her, but I don't have time to play games. Not this morning. "She's worrying about the smallest things," I continue, "including the fact that she only realised after she'd spoken to you this morning that she'd forgotten to buy us anything to eat today, and that the butcher's also won't be open tomorrow either."

"Well, that's not the end of the world," Mother reasons.

"I know it's not. I explained that we wouldn't starve; that I'm used to conjuring a meal out of whatever's in the larder, but she blamed herself, even though it wasn't her fault… like she did with last night's dinner."

"Why? What happened with last night's dinner?" Mother asks.

I describe Amelie's efforts with the toad in the hole, and my subsequent intervention, when it became apparent that something had gone badly wrong with the recipe.

"It sounds like rather good fun," she says at the end of my story, smiling once more.

"Hmm... I suppose it was. But she was so tired, and put out by the whole thing, it was difficult to enjoy it at the time."

She steps closer to me, becoming more serious. "You're worried about her, aren't you?" she murmurs.

"Yes. To be honest, I think she's been overdoing it... what with getting the house ready, and planning the wedding. I think she's exhausted herself. She's worn out."

Mother opens her mouth, then quickly snaps it shut again, two pink dots appearing on her cheeks and I instinctively know she was about to throw caution to the winds and ask if I was wearing Amelie out myself. I'm grateful she didn't though, because I'm not sure how I would have replied. Well, I do. I'd have lied, and denied it, because she's my mother.

"You need to stop worrying," she says calmly, nodding her head, as though she's just made a momentous decision.

"I do?" I'd like to know how she thinks that's even possible.

"Yes. For one thing, you can stop fretting over the food situation."

"I wasn't," I tell her. "That was the last thing on my mind. As I've already said, I'm quite accustomed to forgetting to buy anything for dinner, and having to make do."

"That's all well and good, Rufus, but you've got other people to think about now."

I frown at her turn of phrase. "Other people?" I repeat. "You mean my wife?"

"Yes..." She hesitates. "But you're missing the point."

"I am?" I've forgotten what the point was. But then, conversations with my mother tend to have that effect.

"Yes. Neither you, nor Amelie needs to worry about what you're going to eat tomorrow, because there will be plenty of left over meat from the roast beef we're going to have this evening." She shakes her head. "We all got rather pre-occupied yesterday, and forgot to go shopping ourselves, and when we did remember, we made the mistake of letting Issa go to the butcher's by herself, while Dotty went to the greengrocer's and I dealt with the groceries and visited the chemist's." She rolls her eyes now. "Issa met us in Walton Road, looking rather pleased with herself, and showed us the most enormous rib of beef, and when Dotty queried why she didn't get the butcher to just cut off a piece for us, she simply shrugged her shoulders and pointed out that she'd paid for it, and that we'd planned to invite you and Amelie anyway, so it wouldn't go to waste."

"I suppose it's lucky that meat isn't rationed," I point out.

"And that there aren't any shortages yet," she replies, smiling. "Still, the point is, that it means we'll have lots of left overs, even with five of us having dinner. We can explain to Amelie how to make cottage pie. She'll like that." Mother beams at me. "And it'll give us something to do this afternoon."

"Just don't overdo the explanations," I remind her. "She got confused about Mary's instructions for toad in the hole. So try and keep it simple, will you?"

"Yes, dear." She pats me on the arm. "Now, unless I'm much mistaken, you've got work to do. So, stop worrying and let us take care of your wife for the day."

"All right, but don't tire her out. And let her get some rest, will you?"

"What do you take us for?" she says, sounding scandalised... or trying to.

I roll my own eyes now, wondering if I've done the right thing, but knowing, deep down, that I have. Despite my frequent misgivings about my mother, and my aunts, I know they only have mine and Amelie's best interests at heart.

I kiss Mother on the cheek and then depart, returning to the car, where Thompson awaits, trying to pretend he hasn't been watching our conversation, even if he hasn't been able to hear it.

"Sam Higgs?" he says, starting the engine, as I settle in beside him, waving goodbye to my mother.

"Yes," I reply.

He turns the car and sets off along Spencer Road. "Do you want to talk about it?" he asks.

"Talk about what?"

"Whatever it is that's wrong."

I glance over at him, but he's concentrating on driving, or at least that's the impression he's giving. "Who says anything's wrong?"

"I do," he replies. "You were like love's young dream yesterday, and today, although you're still clearly very enamoured with your wife, it's as though you've got the worries of the world on your shoulders. Has something happened?"

He's not digging for gossip. In fact, he sounds genuinely concerned, and while I'm not about to reveal anything too personal, I do need to talk to someone… someone who'll hopefully understand, better than my mother, that this isn't just about undercooked toad in the hole, and Amelie not knowing about the butcher's opening hours. There's more to it than that.

"It's Amelie," I say quietly.

"I'd rather assumed that," he replies. "Is she all right?"

"I don't know. She says she's tired… and she certainly looks it."

"Tired?" He glances in my direction and it's hard not to notice the slight smile that crosses his lips, which reminds me of my mother's expression just now, when I told her how Amelie was feeling.

"Yes… tired. What's so strange about that?"

"Nothing," he says. "Except for the fact that you've just come back from your honeymoon."

I can't help smiling myself now. "Okay… so we might not have had much sleep for the last seven days—"

"I knew it!" He slaps his hand on the steering wheel.

"Oh, be quiet, will you?"

He chuckles and then turns to glance at me. "If she's feeling tired," he says, more seriously now, "then there could be all sorts of reasons… aside from the lack of sleep."

"I know she was really busy before the wedding… what with the house and the planning, and everything." I give him the same reasoning I gave to my mother.

"There is that," he muses. "But there's also the fact that she's trying to adjust to a new way of life. Julia found it quite hard, I know that. I used to come home from work and find her in tears most of the time."

"Good Lord… what did you do?"

"I talked to her… and I listened to her. I don't think I'd realised how much of a change her life had gone through until then." He looks at me again. "For us, marriage doesn't really alter our lives too much… other than in good ways." He smirks. "But for Julia, and for Amelie, the change is huge. And for Amelie, I imagine this case isn't helping much either…"

"No, it's not. Neither of us expected to come back to this."

"At least she's got your mother, and your aunts on hand," he says.

"That's why I wanted to call in there," I explain. "Mother had invited us for lunch, which we obviously couldn't attend, but Amelie's going there for the day instead, and I'm joining them later on. I just wanted to make sure they're aware of how fragile Amelie is at the moment, that's all."

"I'm sure they'll take care of her," he says, reassuringly.

"Oh, they will… providing they don't start involving too much gin in the proceedings."

"I don't know, it might do her good to get a bit tipsy."

"She'd probably be better off having a snooze on the sofa."

"I'm sure she would… but a little bit of gin never hurt anyone."

He's still smiling as he parks the car outside Sam Higgs' house, but before I can get out, he places his hand on my forearm, stopping me.

"Don't worry too much," he says.

"You might as well tell me stop breathing." I shake my head.

"I know, but what I'm trying to say is, things do settle down. The first few weeks of being married are a little bit like the first few weeks after you've had a baby. There's a lot of adjusting to do. But you get there in the end."

"And what do you do in the meantime?" I ask, surprising myself by asking Harry for advice, and then the thought occurs that this is exactly the sort of conversation I'd have had with my father, if he'd still been here… and I realise, not for the first time, how much I miss him.

"Help out as much as possible," he replies. "Make sure you spend as much time together as you can – which is difficult at the moment, I know – and just generally be reassuring, especially when things go wrong… which they will."

"And you didn't worry about Julia, when you first got married?"

He smiles. "Of course I did. Every minute of the day. Because worrying is part of our job, isn't it?"

"Then why are you telling me not to?"

"Because worrying is only *part* of our job," he says, looking out of the windscreen. "And if you spend too long doing that, you'll forget about all the other things that matter so much more…" His voice fades and he looks back at me, just for a moment, before he opens the car door and climbs out.

I suck in a long breath, composing myself and then follow, joining him at the gate.

"Thank you for that," I mutter and he shrugs, opening the gate and letting me pass through ahead of him, before we both take the two steps required to bring us to the front door, Thompson being the one to knock.

"Anytime," he whispers back, and we turn as the door is opened by a handsome man who's probably in his mid to late forties, with salt and pepper hair, receding at the temples, and dark blue eyes, set in a tanned face. He looks from myself to Thompson.

"You're the police?" he enquires.

"Yes, sir," I reply. "I'm Detective Inspector Stone and this is Detective Sergeant Thompson."

He nods, stepping aside and bidding us to enter. "Marjory told me about your visit," he explains. "Something to do with our Sam, is it?"

"Yes, sir. Is he here?"

He closes the door and turns to face us as I remark to myself that the dark brown furniture doesn't fare much better in daylight, still absorbing every ounce of brightness from the room.

"Yes, he is," Mr Higgs replies. "I'll fetch him for you."

He moves away, passing through the door which I assume leads to the dining room and kitchen, and I hear his footsteps on the stairs, then muffled voices, before he returns, with a younger man behind him.

"This is Sam," he says, introducing his son, who is very much a reflection of his father, with the same handsome features and blue eyes, although his hair remains dark brown, as yet untouched by the grey of age.

"You're from the police?" Sam enquires.

"Yes." I tell him our names, and we both show our warrant cards this time, before Mr Higgs steps forward.

"I'll leave you to it, shall I?" he suggests.

It dawns on me that I'm about to break the worst possible news to his son, and that having his father there might be helpful to this young man, whose age is probably no more than twenty, or twenty-one. "You can stay, if you want," I reply, giving Mr Higgs a meaningful look.

He frowns and nods his head.

"Why did you want to see me?" Sam asks, clearly inquisitive about our visit, and I wish I could prolong my announcement, give him a little longer to live in innocence of Mildred's fate.

"We've come about Mildred Ryder," I say, because I know I can't delay. The next few words that leave my mouth are going to change this young man's life forever, but they have to be said. "I'm afraid I have some very bad news." How inadequate does that sound?

"Has something happened to her?" he asks, his face paling.

"Yes."

Sam Higgs sits, flopping onto the arm of the chair that is fortunately right behind him.

"What is it?" his father asks. "What's happened?"

Not taking my eyes from Sam, I continue, "I'm terribly sorry, but I'm afraid she's dead." It doesn't matter how many times I have to say that, it doesn't get any easier.

Sam doesn't look at me. Instead he shakes his head, then lets it drop into his hands and, after a few moments of silence, he sobs like a child, a heart-wrenching cry emitting from deep inside him, filling the room; the shocking reality of grief manifesting itself before our eyes, as this young man literally disintegrates, falling forwards onto his knees, clutching his arms around him, throwing back his head and howling.

His father moves quickly, and with my help, we lift the boy and move him to the sofa, setting him down. Then I step away and let Mr Higgs sit beside his son, cradling him, rocking him gently, as though he were still an infant, not a grown man.

"Tea," I whisper to Thompson and he nods his head, disappearing through the door to the rear of the house. I've made the assumption that Mrs Higgs isn't here, being as I'm certain she would have come running at the sound of her son in such distress, a fact which is confirmed when Mr Higgs turns to look at me.

"My wife's gone to church," he says. "And she said was going to call in on her mother on the way home. She… she's not been well, you see." I can tell from the tone of his voice that he'd rather have his wife here with him, to help their son.

I move forward again and stand in front of Sam, in his line of sight and, as he becomes aware of me, he slowly starts to calm, to breathe more easily, his sobs subsiding.

"W—What happened to her?" he mumbles, stuttering over his words.

I crouch before him, taking a deep breath, noting the fear that forms in his eyes, my actions telling him that what I'm about to say won't be easy to hear. "I'm sorry," I say clearly. "She was murdered."

His eyes widen with shock, his mouth flopping open at the same time, although no sound comes out.

"Murdered?" His father speaks for him.

"Yes, sir."

At that moment, Thompson comes back in, carrying two steaming cups of tea, which he places on the low table just behind me.

"Thank you," I say, looking up at him as he steps back, removing his notebook and standing, poised.

I pick up one of the cups and hand it to Sam Higgs, whose father releases him. "Drink this," I tell him and he obeys me, automatically, drinking from the cup and wincing slightly.

"It's sweet," he says.

"It'll help," I reply and he takes another sip, as though he hopes I might be right.

"How was she killed?" he asks, after a few moments' silence.

"She was stabbed."

He closes his eyes, pain etched on his features and I remove the cup from his shaking hands, placing it back on the table again. "Stabbed?" he whispers.

"Yes. Do you think you could answer some questions?" I stand again, keen to forestall the inevitable enquiry about whether she'd have suffered, because I'm not sure I can lie to him, so I get straight to the point.

"If it'll help catch whoever did this to my Milly, I'll answer anything you want," he says, with renewed strength in his voice.

"Milly?" I query, being as he's the first person to use that name.

"Yes." He blushes. "It's what I called her. Just me… no-one else."

He glances at his father, who shifts slightly on the sofa, giving his son some room.

"What can you tell me about her?" I ask.

"What do you want to know?"

"What was she like?"

"Quiet," he replies, simply. "And shy. But also caring and kind. She never hurt anyone and she always tried to help people, if she could." He looks up at me. "Why would anyone want to do this to her?"

"I don't know." I sigh deeply. "I'm sorry, but I have to ask everyone connected with the case… can you tell me where you were on Friday evening?"

He blinks a few times and swallows. "I was here," he says.

"Alone?" I glance at his father.

"Yes," Sam replies. "Mum and Dad had gone out, and Mildred and I didn't normally see each other on Fridays anyway, because she had choir practice, so I spent the evening here."

"You didn't arrange to meet her after choir practice?" I ask.

"No. Wednesday afternoons and evenings were our regular times. We'd sometimes be able to meet up on Saturdays too, if Mr and Mrs Wharton were going out somewhere and Milly wasn't needed. They were good to her, like that…" He narrows his eyes. "I'd never have harmed her, Inspector, if that's what you're thinking. I—I loved her."

I nod my head. "How long had you been engaged?" I ask.

"Nearly a year," he replies. "We were supposed to get married just before Christmas last year, but… but Milly came and saw me towards the end of November and said maybe we should wait."

"Did she give you a reason?"

"She said it was to do with me being called up," he mumbles.

"Had you been called up back then?" I'm surprised. It seems like a long time ago to me, considering that he's only just received his orders to report for training.

"No," he replies. "But we knew it was only a matter of time. I—I told her it didn't matter; that being called up didn't make a difference. But she said it did. She said she'd have to leave her position if we were married, and then if I went away, what would become of her?" He shakes his head. "I didn't want to wait, but she was adamant, and in the end, I agreed with her."

"Would the Whartons have let her go, just because she was married?" I ask, intrigued. They seemed like an odd couple, but Sam's just painted a picture of them as reasonably kind employers, allowing her to go out of an evening, if her services weren't required. And their problems seem to be with each other, if anything. I doubt they'd be so heartless.

"I don't know." He shrugs. "But Milly thought they might." He looks up at me now, staring right into my eyes. "I got it wrong, didn't I? I made a mistake. We should have got married when we had the chance… then she'd have been safe with me, wouldn't she?" He covers his face with his hands, his shoulders shaking as he sobs again, and his father puts an arm around him.

I give them a moment, then step back, my movement attracting Mr Higgs' attention.

"We'll show ourselves out," I say quietly and he nods his head.

"Thank you, Inspector," he replies, which is a rather humbling sentiment, considering I've just turned their lives upside down.

I don't have a reply, so I turn and Thompson opens the door, letting us out and closing it behind him.

We both get back into the car before either of us speaks.

"What are you thinking?" he asks.

"Just about a conversation I had with Amelie once," I reply, honestly.

"A repeatable one?"

"Yes. I was just remembering a time when I told her that war tends to make people rush into marriage."

"Was that by way of explaining why you wanted to whisk her down the aisle yourself?" he jokes.

"No." I glare at him, although I'm smiling and shaking my head at the same time. "It was by way of explaining that war can make people do impetuous things. You know perfectly well that the war had nothing to do with my marriage to Amelie, or our very brief engagement."

"No…" he replies thoughtfully.

"Which is rather the point."

"It is?" He turns, looking at me.

"Yes. Amelie and I got married quickly because we were waiting for each other… and… well, it wasn't easy."

He smirks. "I remember," he says.

"And I'm fairly sure that if she'd come to me and asked me to postpone our wedding indefinitely, after nearly a year's engagement, I'd have had something to say about it… and it probably wouldn't have been a meek acceptance of the situation."

He shakes his head now, and then sighs and starts the engine, before looking back at me again. "You're forgetting something though, Rufus."

"I am?"

"Yes… you're forgetting the fact that Mildred Ryder and Sam Higgs may not have been waiting, like you were. And that makes a good deal of difference when you come to think about it."

I sit back in my seat. "Yes, I suppose it does," I whisper and he pulls the car away from the kerb.

"Where am I driving us?" he asks, looking across at me as we get to the end of the road.

I cease my musings and turn to face him. "I think we'll pay a quick visit to Susan and Laurence Conroy."

"Yes, sir," he replies, giving me a mock salute before turning left.

"Don't call me 'sir'," I growl at him.

He chuckles. "Sorry, guv'nor."

"Oh God… I think that's worse."

"It is, isn't it?" he grins.

"Which is why you said it."

"Absolutely."

He turns the car into the High Street and, after a short distance, goes right into Ashley Road.

"It was number sixteen, wasn't it?" I ask.

"Yes." He slows the car, and we find the house in question on the right hand side a short way down the road.

The properties down here are of many and varied styles, but the one we're looking at is substantial and semi-detached, with large bay windows at the front, and ornate gables. There's a low wall dividing the front garden from the footpath, and Thompson parks in front of this, both of us climbing from the car.

There's a rather flamboyant brass door knocker, in the shape of a lion's head, placed in the centre of the panelled door, and I use it, rapping hard, then stepping back and waiting long enough for me to think about knocking again, whereupon a young woman suddenly opens the door. She's of medium height, quite slim, and reasonably attractive, although there's something about her grey eyes that sends a shiver down my spine; something cold and calculating. Her dark blonde hair is styled away from her face, showing her long neck, accentuated by what seems to me to be an inappropriately low cut dress for not long after ten o'clock on a Sunday morning. Although on second glance, it appears that, while her hair may be styled to perfection, the dress has literally been thrown on, the buttons not properly fastened and the belt left untied.

"Mrs Conroy?" I ask, when she doesn't say anything.

"Yes?"

"My name is Detective Inspector Stone." I show her my warrant card, which she actually takes from me and scrutinises closely, before handing it back. "And this is Detective Sergeant Thompson." He offers her his, but she just nods at him, presumably because he's less worthy of her acute analysis. It's a trait I've come across before in people of a certain class, and one I despise. "May we come in?" I add.

"Why?" she asks.

"Because we need to ask you and your husband some questions," I explain.

"What about?"

She seems determined not to grant us admittance, which I find interesting in itself. "About the death of Mildred Ryder."

She frowns. "I don't know anyone called Mildred Ryder, and I doubt my husband does either."

She goes to shut the door, but I hold up my hand, preventing her and she glares at me.

"She's the maid who worked for your friends, Mr and Mrs Wharton," I say firmly.

Her face clears slightly, but now she tilts her head to one side, as though confused. "I see," she remarks. "I wasn't aware that was her name. And in any case, I fail to see what her death could possibly have to do with us."

"She was killed on Friday evening, when Mr and Mrs Wharton were here at your husband's party," I reply. "We just need to ask you a few questions about that evening, that's all."

"Did you say killed?" she asks, her eyes widening now.

"Yes." I let out a sigh. "I'm sorry, Mrs Conroy, but I'm afraid these questions do need to be asked, and it's entirely up to you whether we do so here, or whether you and your husband would prefer to accompany us to the police station and make your statements there."

I raise my eyebrows and stare at her, letting her know that, either way, she's going to talk to us, and I'm not backing down.

"Very well," she says, after a short pause. "Come in."

She steps back and we enter the hallway, with its black and white tiled floor, the stairs ahead of us and three closed doors, barring the way to various reception rooms, no doubt.

"Come through to the drawing room," she says, as we remove our hats and she leads the way, opening the first door on the left, which gives onto a large room, overlooking the front of the house, with the squared bay window. There are two cream coloured sofas and a separate chair, with a couple of low tables, and a drinks cabinet. The mirror above the wide fireplace is framed in a very shiny gold finish, as are all of the pictures on the walls and, in my view, they lower the tone of what would otherwise be a perfectly attractive room.

"Is your husband at home?" I ask, standing next to one of the sofas, being as we haven't been invited to sit.

"He's upstairs," she replies.

"Could you fetch him?"

She hesitates for a moment and then leaves the room, pulling the door closed behind her.

I turn to Thompson, who rolls his eyes, and then smirks. "What?" I whisper.

"Do you get the feeling we interrupted something?"

I think for a moment about the state of Mrs Conroy's clothing and then smile myself. "Her hair was a bit too neat though, don't you think?" I think about how beautifully dishevelled Amelie looked this morning when we finally got out of bed, even though her hair is significantly shorter than Mrs Conroy's.

"Well, maybe we didn't come in until the end," Thompson says, and then shakes his head, grinning. "And I'm aware I worded that very badly."

"Very badly indeed," I whisper, smiling at him as we hear the sound of footsteps coming down the stairs.

The door opens and Mrs Conroy reappears, followed closely by her husband, who to my surprise, is wearing the uniform of a pilot officer in the RAF. He's a handsome man, without perhaps the flair, or the arrogance of Norman Wharton, but with a kindliness to his eyes, which the other man lacks. His hair is a light brown, and he's of a slim build, roughly thirty years old, or thereabouts.

"I do apologise," he says, holding out his hand for me to shake, which I do. "I'm afraid you've caught us a little… um… off guard, this morning." As he's speaking, he looks down at his wife and smiles, before turning back to me. "I've just come to the end of my leave and I'm going back to base in about an hour, you see."

I nod my head, and realise that, if the rumours I've heard are true, he'll almost certainly be going overseas very soon and that, if I were in his shoes, with just an hour or so before my departure to an uncertain future, I'd have been spending my time in exactly the same way that he and his wife clearly have been.

"No need to apologise." I hold up my hand. "We just have a few routine questions and then we'll be out of your hair."

He nods. "My wife says this is about Norman and Lucy's maid?" He sounds intrigued, enquiring; not impatient, like his wife.

"Yes. I'm afraid she was murdered on Friday evening in the churchyard."

"The one just around the corner?" he asks, pointing over his shoulder.

"Yes."

"How awful." He lets out a sigh. "The poor girl... the thing is, I'm not sure how we can help."

"I understand that you had a party on Friday night," I say and his face lights up, just for a moment.

"We did," he replies. "It was a stroke of luck really that my leave coincided with my birthday, but that meant the party was very last-minute, and we literally just called a few friends and invited them round."

"And Mr and Mrs Wharton were among those friends?" I ask.

"Yes. Norman's never been one to miss out on a party, has he, Susie?" He turns to his wife and she smiles up at him, shaking her head.

"Can you confirm whether either Mr or Mrs Wharton left the party at any time?" I ask and Mr Conroy's face falls, becoming more serious.

"Well... no," he says. "I mean... I went out onto the front porch with Lucy for a cigarette at one stage, if that counts."

"You did?" His wife steps away from him, looking up into his face and frowning, her eyes narrowing slightly. I recognise the jealousy written on her features.

"We were outside for less than ten minutes," he replies, sighing.

"Did you see Mr Wharton leave the house?" I ask, getting their attention back to the point in hand, although I notice that Mrs Conroy continues to stare at her husband.

"No, but knowing Norman's capacity for smoking, he probably left several times during the evening," Mr Conroy replies.

"Well, I didn't see him leave at all," his wife puts in, a little too quickly for my liking, especially as the man himself has already admitted to taking time outside for cigarettes on several occasions during the evening, both with and without his wife.

Her husband turns to her, frowning, but then adds, "You have to understand, we had a houseful of guests, Inspector. It would have been impossible to keep track of everyone's movements."

"I see," I reply.

Mr Conroy glances at his wife, giving her an entreating look, which she ignores. "I'm sure Norman was here all evening," she continues, stubbornly, "but there were several times when Lucy wasn't with him." She smiles up at her husband. "But that's Lucy for you… always off with someone or other."

"How long have you known Mr and Mrs Wharton?" I ask, steering them away from their cat and mouse games.

"The friendship is really with Norman," Mr Conroy explains. "We all went to school together, Norman, Susan and myself. Lucy came along later."

I sense a dislike for Mrs Wharton in his tone, although I wonder if that's for his wife's benefit, given her jealous reaction to him having spent ten minutes alone in the woman's company.

"And did you know their maid at all?"

Susan Conroy finally turns to face me, a look of incredulity on her face. "Their maid?" she scoffs. "Of course not. I mean, she opened the door and served us at table. Why on earth would we *know* her?"

"She was a friendly, polite girl," her husband adds, a little more generously than his wife, making sure not to be too effusive in his praise, I notice.

"And she was always exhausted," puts in Mrs Conroy. "But then that's hardly surprising, is it?"

She folds her arms, looking a little too self satisfied for my liking.

"Why is that?" I ask and she tilts her head at me as though I'm being dense.

"Because she was one of those 'maids' who was expected to do everything, from the cooking and cleaning, to the laundry and shopping. She was literally a dogsbody… Lucy saw to that."

Her husband shifts from one foot to the other, looking uncomfortable, but says nothing.

"Miss Ryder was unhappy in her work?" I ask and Mrs Conroy shrugs.

"I wouldn't know. I didn't speak to the girl, but I know what Lucy's like. She was brought up with certain airs and graces."

"She was?" She mentioned her father having had expectations of her marriage, but I didn't get the impression of any haughtiness about her myself.

"Yes, of course," Mrs Conroy huffs, with a degree of impatience, as though I should know this story for myself, and she wonders why I don't. "She's Sir Edwin Phelps' daughter." I recognise the name of the well-known newspaper man. "She was born to better things than a little house in Thames Ditton."

"She made her choice," Mr Conroy says through gritted teeth. "And so did Norman."

"Yes, and she's made sure that Norman has regretted it ever since," his wife snaps at him, although she's still looking at me. "It's all about appearances with Lucy, I'm afraid," she remarks, and I try desperately not to look at the gilded mirror to my left, or to show any reaction on my face as I recall the Whartons' much more simple, and plain – and tasteful – decor.

"Is it?" I remark, not bothering to disguise my confusion. "Surely he can't be that badly off. He owns a factory in West Molesey, doesn't he?"

"He does," Mr Conroy replies. "Norman's father died just a few weeks before his marriage to Lucy, and he inherited the factory, together with a much larger house in Weston Green. Unfortunately, it became clear within a couple of months, that the factory wasn't doing as well as Norman had expected, so the house had to be sold, and he bought the place in Station Road. It was the sensible thing to do."

"It might well have been, but Lucy resented it, right form the word 'go'," Mrs Conroy says, interrupting her husband's flow. "Moving from Norman's nine bedroomed house to their pokey little four bedroomed place in Station Road was a real come-down for Lucy, even though she still insisted on keeping a housemaid, for heaven's sake. Do you know, it wouldn't surprise me if she only married him for his money…" She smiles, but it's an ugly smile. "I'd have loved to see her face when she discovered there wasn't any."

"There was still some money," her husband corrects her, earning a scowl. "But not as much as there had been. Their lives had to become quite modest, by comparison."

"It doesn't need to be so modest," Mrs Conroy says, raising her voice, almost angry, it seems. "Not any more. And I'm sure if Lucy didn't have such ridiculously expensive tastes, Norman could be doing a lot better for himself, especially now he's got this government contract. It's Lucy who's holding him back, you mark my words." She stops talking, breathing quite hard, her eyes alight.

I pause for a moment, asking myself whether perhaps there's more to Mrs Conroy's reactions than just a large hint of jealousy. It doesn't take a huge leap of my imagination to wonder whether, despite her suspicions over her husband's behaviour, she's actually attracted to Mr Wharton herself. I'm not clear whether her admiration is reciprocated; I didn't notice anything in Mr Wharton's responses about Mrs Conroy when we questioned him, but then I wasn't thinking along these lines at the time.

"Is there anything else, Inspector?" Mr Conroy's voice interrupts my train of thought.

"No, I don't think so."

He smiles. "I just have a few things to finish packing and then Susie's going to run me to the station."

"I see."

He moves towards the door, taking his wife's hand in his as he does so. She smiles up at him, her earlier jealousy seemingly forgotten, and I silently chastise myself for being so cynical about them. It's possible that the last few cases I've worked on have made me see infidelity at every turn, but as I look at Mr and Mrs Conroy, it occurs to me that I'm probably being uncharitable and that it's possible that Lucy Wharton and Susan Conroy simply don't get on with each other, and that Mrs Conroy is merely being loyal to her old school friend.

We move out into the hallway and Mr Conroy opens the door, standing to one side and putting his arm around his wife, who looks up at him affectionately. "Good luck to you," I say, shaking his hand as we leave.

He smiles, and says, "Thank you, Inspector," as he closes the door behind us.

On the way back to the station, we drive in silence for a while, but then Thompson breaks it eventually, as we're driving down the Portsmouth Road, alongside the river.

"I don't think I've ever seen anyone more obviously jealous, do you?" he remarks.

"No."

"It was hard to tell what she was more jealous of though, wasn't it?"

"Yes… she seemed to covet Mrs Wharton's husband, but also her lifestyle and possessions, I thought, didn't you?"

"I got that impression, yes," he replies. "She was one of those women who'll put someone down, rather than compliment them." He smiles. "She may have criticised Mrs Wharton for having a maid, but I imagine she'd give her eye teeth to be able to afford to employ one herself."

"Precisely," I muse.

"And she certainly didn't like the idea of her husband spending a few minutes alone with Mrs Wharton," he adds. "That seemed a bit pathetic to me."

"She didn't seem to trust him… which makes you wonder if she has cause for that."

He shakes his head. "No… I don't think that was it. I think it was pure dislike of Mrs Wharton, not distrust of her own husband."

"Either way, we seem to be looking at a series of unhappy, unfulfilled marriages in this case, don't we?"

He glances at me quickly before focusing on the road again. "Yes," he comments, "but at least they're only in the case and not in our lives."

"Absolutely." I smile at him and we fall back into our considered silence again.

Back at the station, I'm surprised by how deserted the office is, but remind myself that Thompson informed me yesterday how many men have gone down with flu in the last few days.

"It's like the Mary Celeste in here," I remark, removing my coat and carrying it through to my office, where I hang it on one of the hooks behind my door, adding my hat and turning around. My room looks exactly the same as it did just over a week ago, when I walked out of here on the Friday before my wedding, looking forward to marrying Amelie and spending a week alone with her. Now that's all behind us, reality is biting hard, and I let out a sigh, moving around my desk and sitting in my comfortable chair.

There's a message in front of me, saying that George Buxton, the lodger from the Ryder household, has called this morning, and will be coming here at two o'clock this afternoon, which suits me fine, being as we have no-one else to go and speak to at the moment, and I want to spend some time going over Mildred Ryder's diaries, which are stacked in a neat pile to one side of my desk.

"I thought you might like a cup of tea," Thompson says, coming into my office, bearing two cups and saucers.

"If it wasn't for the fact that you'd arrest me, I think I'd kill for one," I joke, and he smiles, placing one of the cups before me. "Shall we go through these?" I suggest, pulling the pile of diaries in front of me and looking up at him.

"We might as well make a start."

I toss the 1935 diary at him and he sits back, crossing his legs as he starts to flip through it, taking the occasional sip of tea.

For myself, I look at the most recent diary, the one dated 1940, which only features a few weeks' of entries and, finding very little of interest, I put it aside and pick up the one for last year. Sam Higgs' name crops up on various dates, making it clear they generally saw quite a bit of each other, but otherwise, the only things she seems to have noted down are appointments with her doctor, church events and weddings, at which I assume she may well have been singing in the choir. Every so often, however, there is simply a name marked alongside a date. Some are male and some female, but they are only Christian names and there's nothing else to signify what these entries mean. I'm just about to ask Thompson whether he's found any similar names in the earlier diary, when my eye alights on a tiny cross immediately next to the number '12' for the twelfth of September, which makes me smile as I recall seeing exactly the same symbol in Amelie's sister's diary after she was killed. Beth Templeton wasn't really Amelie's sister, of course, being as Beth was adopted by the Templetons and Amelie was taken in by them, following her own parents' deaths, but the two girls were brought up as siblings and were really close, and I have to remind myself constantly that, despite everything that's happened since, Beth only died approximately three months ago, and that, in reality, that's another reason for me to keep an eye on Amelie. She's still in mourning, although I know she tries to hide it most of the time, even though I wish she wouldn't.

Thompson puts down his cup, along with the diary he's been perusing, and picks up the one for 1936, while I drag my mind back to the point at hand.

"Did that diary have any names listed against various dates?" I ask him, holding my copy open and turning it around to show him.

"No," he remarks, leaning forward. "Do you think they're appointments?"

"There are no times by any of them," I point out. "And when she's marked down things like doctor's appointments, or church events, she's put a time as well." He shrugs and I pick up the diary for 1938, discovering that there are no names entered in that one either. Whatever these entries signify, it was obviously something new to Mildred. "What about this cross symbol?" I ask, putting down the 1938 diary, picking up last year's again, flipping over the page and showing that to him as well.

"Yes, I've got one of those every month, but we all know what that means…" He looks up at me. "Don't we?"

I smile. "Yes," I reply slowly, not telling him that I didn't, until Amelie pointed it out to me, after I'd asked her to explain its significance while perusing Beth's diary. That embarrassing situation occurred during our first meeting and I'm surprised she ever wanted to see me again after that. But she did… thank goodness.

"Is there anything in last year's diary about her meeting with Sam?" Thompson asks me picking up his cup again and draining it.

"What meeting with Sam?"

"The one where she broke off their engagement," he replies, shaking his head at me. "Remember? He told us about it? She might have noted something down, perhaps giving a more reasonable explanation."

"She might have done," I remark, flipping forward through the diary to November, then slowing down and turning the pages one at a time. "No," I reply, shaking my head, as I get to the end of the month, "there's nothing." I get into December, and then stop suddenly, flipping my way back to November again, where I notice the cross marked against the sixth of the month. Moving forward again, I go page by page all the way through December, sitting forward and placing the diary on my desk.

"What is it?" Thompson asks, mirroring my actions, his elbows resting on the surface of the table.

"Hang on," I reply, holding up my hand, before picking up the 1940 diary and searching all the way through January and into the beginning of February, right up to the day of her death. "Well… I wonder…" I muse out loud and then without responding to Thompson, I pick up the telephone and ask the operator for Aunt Dotty's number. I have to wait a while and I can sense Thompson's impatience to know what's going on, but eventually Aunt Dotty herself replies.

"Hello, Aunty Dotty." I'm surprised that her maid Ethel hasn't answered the telephone, but I don't comment. I've got more important things on my mind.

"Rufus!" She sounds delighted to hear from me. "How are you?"

"I'm fine, thank you. Do you think I could speak with Amelie, please?"

"Missing her already?" she teases.

"Yes," I reply and she coughs, which tells me she's surprised by my answer.

"Hold on a moment, I'll go and get her," she says, once she's recovered, and I hear the clunk of the telephone receiver being placed on the hall table.

A short while elapses and then I hear a rustling, before Amelie's voice sounds in my ear, making me smile instinctively.

"Hello?" she says, sounding doubtful. "Rufus?"

"Yes, darling." I couldn't care less that Thompson's in the room, and I sit back in my chair, crossing my legs.

"Is everything all right?" she asks.

"Yes. Everything's fine. I just have a question for you."

"You do?"

"Yes. It's to do with the case."

"Oh?" She sounds intrigued.

"We've been going through the victim's diaries," I begin, "and we've discovered that she used the same system as Beth did for noting down the beginning of her menstrual cycle." I fall silent for a second.

"Right," Amelie says, filling the gap I've left for her.

"And the thing is, the crosses that she used every other month suddenly seem to have stopped in December of last year. And what I want to know is, if a woman kept a note like that, religiously, every month, for what appears to be at least the last five years, do you think there's a reason why she might suddenly stop… other than the obvious one?"

There's a short pause, then Amelie replies, "I can't think why she would, no, unless of course she was unwell for some reason."

"Might that cause a… temporary interruption in the normal… um… cycle of things?" I ask, struggling to phrase my sentence and wishing we could have this conversation face-to-face, without my sergeant being present.

"It might," she replies. "But other than that, it's not something you'd just forget to do… I mean, it's like a habit, isn't it?"

"I don't know, darling, is it?" I answer, smiling again.

"Not for me, it's not," she says. "I've never done that myself, but then I've always been as regular as clockwork, to the point where you could literally set your watch by me…" She falls silent and I realise it's the first time she's ever discussed anything like this with me, and that I rather like the thought that she is.

"Where are you?" I ask her, lowering my voice slightly, although I'm not sure why, being as Thompson is sitting directly opposite me and can hear every word I'm saying.

"In the hall," she replies.

"Look in the mirror," I tell her.

"Why?"

"Because I want you to tell me if you're blushing."

I hear her very slight giggle. "Yes, I am."

I chuckle myself. "Well, there's no need to."

"I can't believe I just said that to you," she whispers, conspiratorially.

"I can… and I like that you did," I reply. "And now I'm afraid I have to get on, if I'm going to get back in time for dinner."

"In that case, I'll let you go," she says. "Was that all you needed to know?"

"Yes, thank you, darling. You've been extremely helpful."

"I'm sure I haven't."

"Well, I'll prove you wrong later," I reply and she giggles again. "Goodbye, sweetheart."

"Goodbye, Rufus. I love you."

I don't hesitate for a second before saying, "I love you too," and then I put down the receiver, and finally look up at Thompson, who's gone back to perusing the diary he's holding.

"You're sickeningly in love, aren't you?" he remarks, turning over a page.

"Yes."

He looks up now and smiles. "Care to enlighten me?"

"About love?" I tease.

"No, about the reason for that telephone conversation."

I hand him the diary for 1939, open in October. "Look for yourself," I tell him. "Pay attention to the crosses. There's one noted down in every month of her diaries. See? There's one on the ninth of the month."

"Yes," he says, flipping forward to November. "There's another one here, on the sixth."

"Keep going…"

He does, and then looks up at me. "They've stopped," he says.

"Precisely."

"So you think she was pregnant?"

"I think it's a possibility."

"Do you think Sam Higgs knew about it?" he asks.

"No." I genuinely don't.

"Do you think we should go and ask him?"

"No. We're speculating at the moment, and we could be wrong."

"Why did you call Amelie, then?" he asks.

"Because pregnancy seemed the most likely reason to me and I wanted her to confirm it. But as my wife has just pointed out, Miss Ryder might have had some kind of medical problem." I remember an entry in the 1940 diary and open it, double checking. "Look," I say, turning it around for Thompson to see, "there's an appointment here for her to see her doctor on the Wednesday before her death."

"That doesn't prove she had a medical problem," Thompson points out reasonably. "On the contrary, it could be the evidence that she was pregnant, and this was the appointment she made with her doctor to confirm it." He sits forward, right on the edge of his seat. "What's the doctor's name?"

"Absolutely no idea. There's no name. It just says 'Doctor – 12.30'."

"Well, that's singularly unhelpful." He flops back into his chair again, despondent.

"Hopefully Wyatt will get us his preliminary report tomorrow," I remind him, "and then we'll know, one way or the other."

George Buxton arrives on time and I arrange to have him shown into one of the interview rooms. It's not that I'm treating him as a suspect, but I'd rather keep things formal at this stage.

Entering the room, I size up the man before me, noting that he appears to be around forty-five years of age, with greying hair, a ruddy complexion, and an expanded waistline. He's wearing a suit and tie, but the hems are frayed and his shirt collar has seen better days. Still, he stands upon our entry and offers his hand across the table, which I accept, before suggesting we all sit.

"You wanted to see me?" he asks expectantly.

"Yes," I reply. "It's about Mildred Ryder."

"Her mother told me," he says, sounding sad now. "I was very upset to hear about what happened. She… she was a lovely girl. Always so kind and helpful, she was…"

I'm struck by his expression and the tone of his voice, how similar his words are to those employed by Sam Higgs, and also by the fact that he seems to have a caring, avuncular attitude towards the victim, rather than a lecherous one.

"Did you know her well?" I ask and he nods, then stops.

"I suppose so," he replies, "although I haven't really known her for very long. I've only been living with the Ryders for about a year, or just over, but…" he pauses and looks up at me, biting his lip and looking self-conscious.

"What is it, Mr Buxton?"

"I have trouble," he says cryptically.

"What with?"

"Reading… and writing." I nod my head. "I tend to move about quite a bit, because it's hard getting work in my situation, but since I've been here, I've managed to earn my keep doing odd jobs, and Mildred's been helping me."

"What with?"

"My reading and writing," he replies, frowning slightly, his answer obvious to him at least. "On Sundays when she came to visit her family, she'd spend a couple of hours at the dining table with me, after lunch, helping me with my words and letters. Numbers too… We were doing quite well… at least Mildred said we were, anyway."

"You got on well with her?"

"Yes," he says, nodding his head slowly.

"And had you noticed any change in her lately?" I ask.

"Change?" he queries. "Like what?"

"Well, was she quieter than usual, or more thoughtful, perhaps?"

"Not particularly," he replies, "but then I hadn't seen her for a fortnight." He stops and thinks for a moment. "There was that time before Christmas though," he remarks.

"What time before Christmas?"

"I think it was November," he muses, tilting his head to one side, "but it might have been October... I get muddled, you see..."

"And what was different about her then?" I ask.

"She was upset," he says. "She tried to hide it from her mother, and from Joe and Shirley, but when we were alone, working on my letters, and she thought I wasn't watching her, I noticed tears in her eyes. I wanted to ask what was wrong, but I was scared she might start crying, so I left it..." He sighs. "Of course, it wasn't long after that she called off the wedding, so I suppose that makes sense, really."

"And how was she after that?"

"Well, now I come to think about it, she had been quieter than she was before, but then that makes sense too, doesn't it, given that she and Sam weren't getting married anymore."

I nod my head, smiling, but deep down, I'm not so sure.

Chapter Six

I've spent the whole day watching him, trying to interpret his expressions, his actions and the few words he's bothered to speak to me.

Over lunch, he was much quieter than usual; thoughtful and distant, it seemed to me. I wondered for a while, whether he was thinking about Mildred, and about his child... the child I've killed. The idea that he could have been sitting at our dining table, thinking about his lover, made me angrier than I can put into words. But I had to maintain the impression of normality, so I talked about the morning church service, and who had been there, and who hadn't, and the weather, and my plans for doing some more work in the garden during the week, if the rain holds off. Gardening may not be exactly my 'thing', but we all have to do our bit for the war effort, and I've surprised myself by being quite good at it. He didn't seem that interested in my ideas, but nodded occasionally and tried to make all the right noises, even though I could tell he wasn't concentrating on a word I said.

As he carved our small joint of beef, which I bought because I refuse to eat mutton, even if he does claim money is scarce, I had to smile to myself, recalling that the knife he was using to hack indelicately into the meat, was the same one I'd employed to murder his lover and their unborn child. I'd washed it thoroughly, of course, but the thought that he was now using it to carve our Sunday roast gave me a great deal of satisfaction.

After lunch, we retired to the sitting room, and he promptly fell asleep, his face a picture of innocence as his head rested back on the chair behind him, his eyes closed and his cheeks puffing out with every breath he took. There was a part of me that wanted to step over to him, place a cushion over his face and smother the life out of him, but that would be giving myself away, wouldn't it? And I've done a good job of covering my tracks thus far, so why spoil it now?

*As I sat reading and keeping half an eye on him, I started to wonder though...
I may have covered my tracks, but what about him? Obviously he's not going to
advertise his involvement with Mildred, but has he left any tell-tale signs of his
misdemeanours? Anything that might link him to the girl, in a way that might make
the police suspicious? I started to panic at that point and wondered about searching
his study, almost immediately scolding myself for my stupidity. How can I search his
room when he's in the house? I can't, can I? I'll have to wait until I know he's going
to be out of the house for a long enough period of time to get the job done. In the
meantime, I'll just have to check elsewhere, starting with the bedroom...*

"What's for tea?" he asks, startling me. I've been concentrating so hard on my
plans, I hadn't realised he'd woken up.

"I can make some sandwiches, I suppose," I reply. "Do you want me to do it
now?"

He looks up at the clock on the mantelpiece. "I am quite peckish," he says and
I put down my book, just as he picks up the newspaper.

"Very well," I sigh. "I'll make you a sandwich, but then I'm going up to bed."

He glances up from the paper, which he's just opened. "You're going to bed?"

"Yes. I have a shocking headache." I don't, but I need an excuse to go upstairs
and be alone for a while.

"Oh... sorry to hear that, dear," he replies, with no feeling whatsoever.

I ignore his comment and take myself out to the kitchen, putting up the blackout
at the window, before switching on the light.

As I'm buttering the bread and slicing some cheese, I wonder how difficult it would
be to get hold of some kind of poison. I've read in books that you have to sign a register
or something, so I'm not sure that would work... and it would have to be a tasteless,
odourless poison, if there is such a thing. He's so very fussy about his food, so anything
out of the ordinary would be bound to attract his attention.

I shake my head. "Don't be silly," I whisper to myself. I don't need to kill him.
I just need to ensure he hasn't done anything stupid, like leave any trace of his
involvement with Mildred lying around, and then everything will be fine. We can go
back to how we were before and, in a few months this will all be forgotten. At least
it will by everyone else. I'm never going to forget what he's done. Not ever.

*Upstairs, I close the curtains and the blackout, and switch on the bedside lamp,
pulling back the covers so I can at least jump into bed quickly should I hear him coming*

up the stairs; not that I think he will. He couldn't care less about me, or about us. I'm the only one who cares...

Opening the wardrobe, I carefully and quietly go through the pockets of his jackets, finding them all empty, before starting on his trousers, which likewise divulge nothing of importance, other than a couple of handkerchiefs that should have been put into the laundry. I take great care to put everything back exactly as I found it, and then tiptoe across the room to his chest of drawers, which I search with equal caution, making sure to pull the drawers out slowly, so as not to make a noise.

I don't really know what I'm looking for, but as I close the bottom drawer and turn around empty handed, I know I'll have to take my chances tomorrow and search his study. I can't afford to leave any stone unturned... not now.

———— • ————

Thompson drops me off at Aunt Dotty's at a little after six and I knock on the door. I do actually still have a key from when I lived here – a time that in reality was just over a week ago – but it seems cheeky to use it now, when I'm no longer a resident.

Dotty herself answers the door, the hallway in darkness behind her.

"Rufus!" she cries, throwing her arms around me with enthusiasm.

"Aunt Dotty." She leans back, holding onto my face and looking me in the eyes, in the gloom.

"Marriage suits you," she chuckles and lets me go, stepping aside so I can enter the house.

"I like to think so," I reply and remove my coat, placing it over the end of the stairs, my hat on top.

"You look happier," she adds, adjusting the blackout again, now she's closed the door, the two of us managing to see by the dim light coming from the open sitting room door.

"I *am* happier. Happier than I've ever been."

She grins and links her arm through mine. "Come through," she offers, leading me to the sitting room, and we walk to the door together, where I step back and let her pass through ahead of me. Inside, the room is warm, the fire blazing, and Amelie is sitting by herself in the corner of one of the sofas. As I enter, she gets to her feet and comes over, standing before me, a little uncertain, until I put my arms around her and she reciprocates, her hands sneaking around my waist, beneath my jacket, clinging to me.

"Hello," I murmur.

"Hello," she replies and I lean back, looking down at her. She still looks tired, but there's a sparkle in her eyes that makes me smile, and her lips twitch upwards in response.

"Are you all right?"

She nods and takes my hand, pulling me back to the sofa with her, where we sit together, our fingers entwined. Aunt Dotty has already sat herself down opposite, and is smiling at us, benignly.

"Where is everyone?" I ask.

"Your mother and Issa are in charge of cooking tonight," Dotty replies.

"Oh? Is it Ethel's night off?" I enquire. "That was bad timing."

I notice the expression on Dotty's face as she shakes her head. "It's not Ethel's night off," she responds, putting her feet up. "She's left us, I'm afraid."

"Ethel's left you?"

"Hmm…" Dotty nods now. "While you two were away on your honeymoon, Ethel announced that she was leaving, and going to work in one of the factories in West Molesey, doing war work. She'd seen an advertisement in the local paper, evidently, and had applied."

"Without telling you?"

"Well, I presume she couldn't be sure they'd take her on," Dotty reasons. "She had no experience, after all."

"No, I suppose not."

"And we could hardly argue, could we? After all, everyone wants to do their bit, and cooking for three old ladies hardly qualifies as helping the war effort."

"Three old ladies?" I query, smiling.

"Well, we're not in our dotage," she says, smiling back, "but we're not in the first flush of youth either."

"I was questioning the number of you, not your age," I point out. "The fact that you said 'three' suggests Mother and Aunt Issa intend staying?"

Dotty smiles. "Oh, yes… you don't know about that, do you?"

"Clearly not," I reply.

"Well, they've decided to remain here, at least for the time being. Issa closed up the house in Somerset before she came up at Christmas, because she expected to be away for a few weeks at least, and then the wedding happened, and she says she's having such a good time here, she doesn't want to go back yet."

"Where is she working?" I ask. "Or isn't she?"

"Oh, she's working," Dotty replies, with a knowing look. "She's commandeered the room you were using to store your books. She loves it in there. She says there are no distractions and she can lose herself in her plots. And, of course, she can easily walk to the library from here to borrow any reference materials she might need."

"And what about the house?" I ask. "Can she just leave it closed up?"

"Well, she telephoned to her neighbour… Betty Robbins, I think her name is… and she's agreed to keep an eye on the place until Issa and your mother return."

"I assume Mother is thoroughly enjoying all of this?"

Dotty smiles once more. "Of course she is."

I roll my eyes. "Should I be scared?"

Dotty laughs now. "Of course you should."

At that, Amelie chuckles too and the sound warms my heart. I turn to her and lean down, kissing the tip of her nose. "And you can behave yourself," I tease.

"Why would she want to do that?" Dotty remarks, before Amelie can reply and I turn to face her. "She's having far too much fun misbehaving with us."

I look back at Amelie, who's still gazing at me. "I hope so," I reply and she lets her head rest on my shoulder.

Despite my misgivings about my mother remaining in the village for a prolonged period of time, and the mischief she might try and cause

– even if well-intentioned – I'm not going to worry too much, not if Amelie continues to be as relaxed as she seems to be right now, anyway.

"How's the case going?" Mother asks, once I've carved the rib of beef and we've all helped ourselves to vegetables.

"Not too bad," I reply.

"It's in Thames Ditton, isn't it?" Issa asks, passing the gravy.

"Yes. A housemaid was stabbed in the churchyard."

"Oh dear." Dotty grimaces.

"And I think we should change the subject, rather than discussing such gruesome things over dinner, don't you?" I say quickly, because I'm not really in the mood for talking about Mildred Ryder, or what happened to her, especially now I think she may have been pregnant at the time she was murdered.

"Probably," my mother replies. "Why don't you tell us about your honeymoon instead."

"Really, Mother?" I look up at her and see her blush.

"You don't have to give us too much detail, dear." She's almost stammering.

"Don't worry. I wasn't going to." Dotty laughs out loud, and we all follow.

"The inn was lovely," Amelie says, glancing at me and frowning, presumably because she's surprised by my reluctance to discuss the case. I shake my head just once and she nods hers. And I have to smile at that lovely little moment of understanding between us. "Although the food was a little limited," she continues. "It was basically trout, or trout."

"Yes, but you weren't there for the food, were you?" Mother says and then coughs, embarrassed once more.

"Shall we change the subject again?" I suggest and everyone agrees.

"Do you think your mother was deliberately trying to embarrass us?" Amelie asks as we walk home, arm in arm.

"No. I think she just sometimes forgets to engage her brain before she opens her mouth."

Amelie chuckles and rests her head on my shoulder, tightening her grip on my arm. In my other hand, I'm carrying a bag which contains some left-over beef, together with some carrots and potatoes.

"Did you have a good day?" I ask her.

"Yes." She looks up, smiling. "And I know how to make cottage pie now, if nothing else."

"Well, that's a start. And they didn't confuse you too much with their instructions?"

She shakes her head. "No, they kept it very simple. Your mother took charge and she even wrote out the recipe for me. She said she'd put it in the bag with the meat and vegetables."

I nod my head, feeling grateful… and perhaps a little pleased with myself that I took the trouble to call in and talk to my mother this morning. It would seem my journey wasn't wasted, and that she took my visit to heart.

"I just hope I don't mess it up," Amelie adds wistfully.

"I don't think you could," I reply. "I love cottage pie, shepherd's pie… anything like that."

"What's the difference between the two?" she asks.

"I think it's to do with one being made of beef and the other of lamb, but don't ask me which way round it is."

"I suppose it makes sense that the shepherd's pie would be lamb, doesn't it?" she asks and I nod my head.

"Yes, it does."

She glances up at me, looking rather pleased with herself now, and I smile to myself.

I open the garden gate, letting Amelie in ahead of me, and then follow her up the path to our front door, opening it with my key and allowing her to enter the house first.

"Do you want to bother switching on the lights?" she asks.

"Not particularly." I lean down and kiss her gently. "I think I'd rather just go to bed."

She smiles. "So would I."

"In that case, I'll put these things away in the larder, and I'll see you upstairs?"

She nods her head and makes her way up, while I quickly go through to the kitchen, emptying the bag of produce into the larder, and then I join Amelie.

She's standing beside our bed, the curtains drawn, and the bedside lamps glowing dimly.

"You look beautiful," I tell her, as I approach and she gazes up at me, while I slowly unbutton her blouse.

"I don't think I'll ever get enough of you," I murmur into her ear as she snuggles down beside me, her breathing finally returning to normal.

Her naked skin feels soft against mine and I pull her just a little closer, turning slightly so we're facing each other, making sure she's covered with the eiderdown. "Good," she whispers, her voice thick with satisfaction, a smile touching the corners of her slightly swollen lips. "Now," she adds, more seriously, "do you want to tell me about your day?"

"My day?" I query, moving down the bed, so our faces are at the same level.

"Yes. I noticed how you changed the subject earlier. You didn't want to talk about the case in front of your mother and your aunts, did you?"

"No."

"Do you want to talk to me now?" she asks, sounding concerned.

"I don't know." It's the truth. I'm not sure how she'll react to my theories about Mildred Ryder's condition, and while talking to Amelie always helps, I don't want to upset her.

"Is this to do with your phone call earlier?" She touches my cheek with her fingertips, brushing them downwards to my chin and holding them there.

"Yes."

"You think the victim was pregnant, don't you?"

I sigh, realising that I might as well tell her everything, being as she's guessed the worst of it anyway. "Yes."

"Tell me about her," she says softly, moving her hand down to my chest.

"Her name was Mildred," I reply, fixing my eyes on hers. "She worked as a maid in a house in Thames Ditton, and – you're quite right – I have reason to believe she was pregnant."

"She wasn't married?" Amelie queries.

"No. She was engaged to a young man, who she'd been walking out with for years. But she postponed their wedding last November, less than a month before it was due to take place."

Amelie frowns. "Did she give a reason?"

"She said it was because her young man might be called up, and being in domestic service, she'd be likely to lose her position when they got married, and be left to fend for herself."

Amelie tilts her head now, her frown deepening. "Really?" She sounds as sceptical as I feel.

"That's what she said." I nod my head.

"You don't believe that though, do you?"

"No… and from the look on your face, my darling, neither do you."

She sighs. "It doesn't ring true to me, that's all," she replies. "Surely, she'd have checked with her employers, asked if she would definitely lose her place, not called off the wedding on the off-chance." She bites her bottom lip for a moment. "Did she ask her employers, do you know?"

"No. But I can check with them the next time I see them." I should have done that already and could kick myself for not having remembered. Perhaps I'm as tired as Amelie…

She nods her head. "Would she have been pregnant at the time?" she asks.

"I don't think so," I reply. "There was a cross in her diary against the sixth of November, and she spoke to her fiancé about postponing the wedding a couple of weeks after that…"

"So that's not likely to have been the reason," she remarks. "And, in any case, that would be a reason to bring it forward, not put it back," she adds.

"Assuming he's the father," I point out and her mouth opens, her eyes widening.

"Oh… I see."

I run my fingertips gently down her spine and she shivers. "I can't be sure, but assuming she was pregnant, I don't think her fiancé knew about it. He didn't mention it…"

"Would he have done though?" she asks.

"If he was innocent of her murder, I don't see why not. He'd have been grieving even more, not just for her, but for their unborn child."

"Yes, I see what you mean. But what about if he *is* guilty of her murder?" she says, lowering her voice to a whisper.

I shake my head. "I don't believe he is. But once the doctor has confirmed the pregnancy – one way or the other – I'll have to question everyone again, and then I'll find out whether he knew or not and, depending on how the other suspects react, I might find out who is responsible."

"For the murder, or her condition?" she asks.

"Both."

"You think they're one and the same person?"

"No… I didn't say that."

"This is complicated, Rufus," she murmurs, resting her head against my chest now.

"I know… and you're tired."

"I am." She yawns.

"Then go to sleep, my darling. And thank you for listening."

"You're welcome," she mumbles, half asleep already.

"What have you got planned for today?" I ask Amelie over breakfast.

She was clearly feeling a little more refreshed after a good night's sleep and woke me over an hour ago, rather beautifully, I have to say. And now, she's seated on my lap, having evidently decided this really is the way to eat breakfast, and made the suggestion herself when she brought in the teapot and placed it on the table. And I was never likely to decline, was I?

"First thing's first, I'll make the bed," she replies, twisting on my lap and looking up at me, smiling, "being as the sheets are all over the place after this morning."

"Well you did get rather carried away," I tease.

"You helped," she murmurs.

"Just a little bit."

She smiles. "And then I'll tidy up down here. But after that I'm not sure what I'll do. I've got the cottage pie to make, but that's hardly going to take all day, is it?"

She sounds rather melancholy now and I tighten my grip on her. "You'll be all right, won't you?" I ask.

"I'll be fine, Rufus." She leans back, attempting a smile. "I'm sure I'll find plenty to do once you've gone."

"Well, just don't over-do it, will you? You're still tired…"

"And?"

"And I don't want to come home from work and find you've exhausted yourself."

"Why? Do you have something planned?" she asks, with a teasing note in her voice now.

"Yes." I reach around, clasping her chin and turning her face to mine, so I can kiss her. "Once you've fed me cottage pie, I want to take you to bed."

"Again?"

"Yes… again. I told you last night, I can't get enough of you."

She smiles. "The feeling is entirely mutual."

"I'm glad to hear it. But for now, it looks like a kiss is going to have to suffice to get me through the day." I lower my lips to hers and put my words into actions.

Doctor Wyatt is waiting in my office, together with Thompson, the two of them sitting on the chairs in front of my desk and talking quietly until my arrival, at which point they stop and turn, looking at me expectantly.

"What?" I say, taking off my hat and coat and hanging them on the hook behind the door.

"Nothing," Wyatt says, smiling.

"What is it?"

"The doctor here was just remarking on the fact that your timekeeping isn't what it used to be," Thompson says, pursing his lips and trying not to smirk.

"I'm not late." I check my watch just to be sure. It's eight forty-five, which I suppose is a little later than usual, but nothing to write home about.

Thompson raises his eyebrows, but doesn't say anything.

"I've been here for half an hour." Wyatt's voice is mirthful.

"As have I," Thompson adds. "Actually, I've been here since eight."

"And? Are you both looking for a commendation, or something?"

"No, but normally, I'd have expected to find you behind your desk," Wyatt says.

"Well, that was before I realised there's more to life than work," I point out, sitting down at my desk and facing them.

"You mean, that was before you got married," Wyatt replies, nodding to the photograph of Amelie on my desk, which reminds me that I'll need to replace it with one of our wedding photographs, once they're developed. "You're a lucky man."

"I know I am." I smile across at the two of them. "Now, enough of this. What have you got for us?"

Wyatt's expression changes from one of good cheer, to one of misery. "I don't like your cases, Stone," he says, more sourly. "They always have something 'off' about them."

"Don't I know it."

"In this instance," he says, opening the pale brown file that he's carrying, but continuing to look at me, "I can tell you that Mildred Ryder was stabbed twice with a long thin bladed knife – possibly a carving knife, or a kitchen knife... something like that, anyway."

"I hadn't realised there were two wounds," I remark, sitting forward and resting my hands on the desk.

"Yes." Wyatt puts down his file, and stands, demonstrating on himself that the first wound, the visible one, was high up on the girl's stomach, while the second one was hidden beneath her clenched hands, much lower down on her abdomen. "At the time," he adds, sitting again and reclaiming his file, "it looked as though she'd perhaps touched the upper wound, getting blood on her hands, but had then moved her hands lower down, when in reality, she was hiding the other puncture site."

"Does that mean she'd have died instantly?" I ask, even though I know it's highly unlikely.

"No." He shakes his head forlornly. "As I told you at the time, she'd have bled to death over a period of probably at least half an hour, but maybe longer."

"And she was definitely killed at the scene?"

"Yes. That much was obvious, just based on the amount of blood there was beneath the body."

I nod my head. "Do you have anything further to add regarding the timings?" I ask.

He pauses, seemingly reticent. "It's hard to be precise, Stone," he says eventually, looking down at his file. "I can't tell you exactly when the wound was inflicted, which I know is what you're really after. I'll need to do further tests as to the time of death even, but if you want me to hazard a guess, I'd say you're looking at somewhere between seven pm and midnight."

"A five hour window?" I remark, frowning.

"Yes. I'm sorry, but that's the best I can do at this stage. The temperature on Friday night was freezing, or just below and it doesn't help matters."

"Is there anything else?" I ask, wondering if my theory about the diary is correct.

Wyatt closes the file and puts it back on the table again. "Do you mean something like the fact that Mildred Ryder was approximately three months pregnant at the time of her death?"

"Yes, that's exactly what I mean," I reply and he stares at me.

"How did you know?" he asks.

I reach out to the side of my desk and pick up the diary for 1939, thumbing through to November and showing Wyatt the cross beside the sixth of the month. "Miss Ryder used this system to mark the beginning of her menstrual cycle," I tell him. "But, although she'd used the same routine for the previous five years or so, there are no such marks anywhere in December or January."

He smiles. "Anyone would think you were a detective," he says.

"They might. But in this instance, I can't claim the credit. My wife helped me to work this one out," I explain, and then smile, for the simple reason that I just said the words 'my wife', and I can't help smiling whenever I do that.

Wyatt shakes his head and then says his goodbyes, having nothing further to impart. He leaves us with his file and tells me that he'll do his best to get a more precise time for the stabbing, although he can't make any promises.

Once he's gone, Thompson turns to me, still smiling. "I'm sure you're not going to give me a reason for your late arrival, but I do have another message for you."

"Oh yes?" I ignore the first part of his statement and look at him, my eyebrows raised.

"Edgar Prentice came by earlier, looking for you. He said to tell you that he went over to the churchyard on Saturday afternoon, as requested, but that there's nothing doing with the footprints."

I sit back, sighing. "I didn't think there would be. There had been far too much traffic over the site, and the rain probably hadn't helped."

"Oddly enough that was exactly what he said... almost word for word. It's easy to tell that you two worked together at Scotland Yard for years."

He's not wrong. Edgar Prentice I worked at the Yard for a long time, before I moved back to Molesey to be with Amelie, and he followed suit; not out of any loyalty to me, but because he was looking for a quieter life, away from the hustle and bustle of London.

"He knows me too well," I remark. "Or perhaps it's the other way around. Not that I think it matters... not in this case. Not as far as the footprints are concerned, anyway."

"You don't?"

"No. I think we're going to find the solution to this one is within the personalities of the people involved, and their circumstances. I don't think hard evidence is going to have much to do with it."

"That should make it really easy to prove then, shouldn't it?" Thompson replies, letting out a deep sigh.

As I said to Amelie last night, I honestly don't believe that Sam Higgs is guilty of Mildred's murder, but now we know for sure that she was pregnant before her death, he has to be our first port of call, and Thompson drives us over to his parents' house, once we've had a cup of tea and gone through Mildred's diaries again, just in case there's anything we might have missed. We did get rather waylaid by discovering her pregnancy, after all.

"I suppose there's a chance he might be out," Thompson muses as we walk through the garden gate and up to the front door of the neat terraced house, which he knocks upon loudly.

"There is, but we have to try," I reply, just as the door opens and we gaze upon the young man himself. His eyes are red-rimmed, as though he's spent the last twenty-four hours crying, which I suppose isn't that surprising, and I wonder how he's going to react to our latest piece of information.

"Inspector," he says, his voice more monotone than I remember it.

"Mr Higgs. May we come inside?"

He steps aside, without responding, and we pass through, removing our hats as we do so, and going into the living room.

"Are your parents here?" I ask him.

"No." He shakes his head at the same time. "Dad's at work still…"

"Still?" I query, given the time of day.

"Yes, he's a postman." I nod my head and he continues, "And Mum's gone to the shops." He frowns slightly. "Did you want to see them?"

"No. I wanted to see you." I had hoped that one of them would be here though, because I think the young man in front of us might find today's conversation even harder than yesterday's – if that were possible.

"I assume this is about Milly?" he says, looking slightly more animated now. "Have you found out who did it? Do you know who killed her?"

"Not yet, no," I reply. "Can we sit down, do you think?"

His face falls again as he perhaps realises that I'm not the bearer of good news. Even so, he indicates the sofa against the wall, standing in front of the chair and waiting for Thompson and I to take a seat before sitting himself, staring across at me expectantly.

"What's this about, Inspector?" he asks.

I pause, just for a second, wondering how to phrase my question, but then decide there's no point in beating about the bush. "I have to ask, Mr Higgs… were you aware of the fact that Miss Ryder was expecting a baby?"

For a few moments, Sam continues to stare, but then his mouth drops open, his eyes widen and his face contorts, not in pain or grief like yesterday, but in anger… in overwhelming rage, as he leaps to his feet again.

"She was pregnant?" he shouts.

Thompson stands as well, holding out his hands. "Calm down," he says soothingly.

"Calm down?" Sam repeats. "Are you kidding?" He turns to me again. "He's just told me that my dead fiancée was pregnant, and you want me to calm down?"

I get up myself now, wondering why any of us bothered to sit in the first place.

"Mr Higgs," I say, trying to keep my voice as placid as possible, "this isn't helping."

He takes a step closer, standing just an inch or so from me, breathing heavily, and I'm aware of Thompson moving nearer, even as I hold out my hand to keep him back. "You think I care?" Sam says, tears welling in his eyes now. "You think I care about what helps and what doesn't?"

"Probably not, no."

He sucks in a deep breath, runs his fingers through his hair and moves away, going over to the window now, staring out at goodness knows what, while his shoulders heave up and down as he tries to regain control of his emotions. "How… how far gone was she?" he asks, not turning around.

"Three months," I reply.

He lowers his head, then turns back to face us, his eyes narrowed. "Three months?" I nod my head. "Three months… so that would make it November?"

"Yes."

"Around the time she postponed our wedding…" His voice fades and he covers his face with his hands, a picture of agony. "How could she?" he says eventually, lowering his hands and raising his face to the ceiling, his voice loud, and yet strangled at the same time. "How could she do something like that?"

"Can I take it the baby wasn't yours, then?" I query, even though I already know the answer.

"Of course it bloody well wasn't," he replies, lowering his head again, his eyes dark with barely contained fury.

"I'm sorry," I say softly. "I have to ask."

"Do you?" he says. "Do you really?" He glares at me. "I may not be sophisticated, or worldly-wise," he says, coming back into the centre of the room again, "but I know how things work. I'm not stupid." He stops talking and shakes his head. "Except, it seems I am. Because I fell for her lies… the little slut." I startle at his words, but before I can comment, he continues, "We were waiting. W—We agreed to wait until we were married, before we slept together… or at least I did, because that's what *she* wanted, for God's sake. And when she asked me to postpone the wedding, that was a bloody hard decision to make, because I really didn't want to have to wait any longer. But she begged me, and in the end, I went along with it, rather than upset her." He pauses, taking a breath. "Only now it seems the little tart was lying to me. She was sleeping with someone else the whole time, wasn't she?"

"You shouldn't jump to conclusions," I point out, but he sneers at me, his face an ugly contortion.

"Grow up, Inspector," he says. "My fiancée was pregnant by another man… and however you want to try and dress it up, there's only one conclusion any man can draw from that. She wasn't the woman I thought she was. She was a filthy lying whore, and I'm well rid of her." His voice breaks as he finishes his sentence and he turns away. "I'd like you to go now," he manages to say.

I put on my hat, stunned by the change in this young man, and Thompson does likewise, making his way over to the door, although I remain standing where I am.

"You're leaving tomorrow evening, I understand?" I say, surprised by the harshness of my own voice now.

"Yes." Sam Higgs turns around and faces me. "What of it?"

"I need to know how I can contact you."

"Well, I'm afraid I can't tell you that." He has a supercilious look on his face that just raises my anger another notch and I take a step closer to him, using my height to full advantage.

"You can… and you will," I say, sternly. "I'm not asking for anything confidential, I just need to know the name of your regiment, and your vague whereabouts for the next few weeks."

"And if I refuse to tell you?" he says, childishly.

"Then I'll waste valuable police time finding out the information for myself. And once I have, I'll apply to your CO to have you kept here until my enquiries have been completed. It's entirely up to you, Mr Higgs."

He sighs and murmurs, "Fine," under his breath. "I don't want to say here any longer than I have to. I'm joining the East Surreys and I've been ordered to report to Kingston. No-one's actually told us where we're going for our training. Not yet." He's suddenly a little more reasonable and I nod my head.

"Very well. I'll be able to trace you through the barracks in Kingston, should I need to."

"Do you think you'll need to?" he asks.

"I don't know."

I touch the brim of my hat in farewell, and join Thompson, who holds the door open, letting me pass outside, where he joins me, closing the door behind us.

"You're not being at your most understanding today, are you?" he says, a little gruffly as he gets into the car beside me, slamming the door and starting the engine.

"Excuse me?" I turn to face him, noting the sour expression on his face.

"Well, how would you have felt if you'd discovered Amelie was pregnant by another man right before your wedding?"

"How do you think I'd have felt?" I huff back at him. "Are you forgetting that I have a better understanding than most of how Sam Higgs feels? You slept with my fiancée, if you remember?"

It may have been more than six years ago, and I may have realised, after I met Amelie and fell in love with her, that I actually had a lucky escape as far as my previous fiancée was concerned, but I do at least have some knowledge of how it feels to be cheated on and lied to, and I'm not in the mood for being criticised by the man who was responsible.

He turns and glares at me. "Yes, but I didn't know who she was at the time, and I didn't get her pregnant, and in any case, I thought we'd put that behind us," he replies.

"We did."

"Then why are you bringing it up?"

"Because you're judging me; you're judging my opinions and my reactions when – quite frankly – you don't have the right."

"Are you honestly telling me that you can't sympathise with how Sam Higgs feels?" he says, still surprised, evidently.

"Yes, I am." I raise my voice and he stares at me, then shakes his head and pulls the car away from the kerb.

I sit in silence for a moment and then turn to face the front of the car.

"Based on Sam's response to the news of Mildred's death, I think he loved her very deeply, and that's why I don't understand his reaction now. He's behaving like I did when Victoria cheated... all anger and bluster... and I didn't love her at all. He's making it about him, just like I did. But I know now how different it is, when you're really in love... so, in answer to your question, if I'd discovered that Amelie was pregnant by another man right before our wedding, I would have been devastated. But, I would have wanted to know why she'd done it. I would have wanted to know what had caused her to cheat on me. I would have wanted to understand. And I would never – ever – have called her names. I'm not saying that I'd be able to just forgive and forget, because I wouldn't. But I know I wouldn't be able to cut her out of my life either, like I did with Victoria, or like Sam seems to want to do with Mildred. Can't you see?" I turn and look at him, but he's concentrating on driving – or at least he's pretending to – so I continue, "Can't you see that it doesn't fit? The descriptions we've been given of Mildred, even by Sam Higgs, don't tie in with someone who'd lie and cheat, and sleep around. Everyone we've spoken to has told us how kind and generous she was, that she was a sweet, lovely girl, that she'd do anything for anyone, and was always putting herself out for other people. It doesn't add up, Harry. Okay, so Sam might be willing to think that Mildred was a slut, but that's just his ego talking and, when he's calmed down, I hope he'll think differently about her, because I don't think she deserves this." I pause for a second and take a breath. "And in the meantime," I say more softly, "I'm going to do everything I can to prove him wrong."

Without any warning, Thompson pulls the car over to the side of the road, parking alongside a bare, gnarled oak tree.

"I'm sorry," he says, applying the handbrake and turning to look at me. "I had no right…"

"You don't have to apologise," I interrupt, smiling at him now. "And I'm sorry I raised the subject of Victoria."

He grimaces. "I hate my past mistakes coming between us."

"She was my mistake too." He smiles as I let out a sigh and stare out of the windscreen. "It's this case," I mutter. "It… it just feels more personal than usual."

"Why?" he asks, and then sits forward, staring at me. "Amelie's not pregnant already, is she?"

I turn back to him. "No, you idiot. You know perfectly well we've only been back from our honeymoon for two days… so I think it's a bit early for that. And, in any case, we've agreed we're going to wait a while before we have children."

"I don't blame you," he chuckles, shaking his head.

"Oh? Is there a reason for that?" I consider the fact that he already has a young son, with another baby on the way and wonder why he'd make that remark.

"Not really. I mean, I love Christopher, and I can't wait for the new baby to be born, but I'm glad Julia and I had a few years to ourselves first. Our courtship wasn't that long – although it was longer than yours, but then most people's are…" He smirks. "I think it just helped having a couple of years to really get to know each other before Christopher came along, especially given the job we do."

He turns to me and I nod my head, feeling vindicated in the decision Amelie and I took before our wedding.

"So, is there another reason why the case feels so personal?" he asks.

I shrug my shoulders. "I suppose it's just that Mildred seems to have been such a lovely person. No-one's had a bad word to say about her, and I know deep down that even Sam didn't mean all the things he's just said about her. He's hurt at the moment, and still in shock probably, and in time, he'll realise that he was wrong to say what he did. But that still leaves us with the fact that someone killed her, and her unborn child, quite deliberately, and then they left her to bleed to death in a freezing cold churchyard, frightened and all alone, with not even a crumb of comfort as she left this world…" I turn to him. "And I want to know why. I want to know what would drive a person to do that… and then I want to see them hang, whoever they are."

Chapter Seven

I wait until he's been gone for ten minutes, the house echoing with silence, my heart racing in my chest as I pace the living room floor, too scared to make a move yet, just in case he's forgotten something… just in case he should return unexpectedly.

The house remains silent though, the only sound being the ticking of various clocks, the one here in the living room, the grandfather clock in the hallway, and in the distance, the one in the dining room… all slightly out of time with each other and grating on my nerves. It's clear he's not going to come back though, so I turn and leave the room, going across the hall to his study.

I stand in the doorway for a moment and hesitate, staring at his desk, the green leather inlay cleared of papers, which are stacked in two neat piles on either side, his chair pushed underneath, the clock ticking on the mantelpiece and my mind filled with memories of that evening, five years ago…

I'd been to a WI meeting, but came home earlier than expected that night due to a poor turnout, almost certainly a result of some truly atrocious weather, and I let myself in through the back door as we usually do when it's wet, taking off my outer clothes and hooking them up, before coming through to the front of the house and going into the sitting room, where I'd expected to find my husband, reading, or listening to the wireless. He wasn't there though, and the room felt distinctly chilly, the embers of the fire dying in the grate.

Assuming he'd probably be in his study, catching up on work, I wandered across the hallway, opening the door and standing on the threshold, exactly where I am now, stilled in shock as I watched Annie Jennings, a seventeen year-old factory worker, sprawled completely naked on his desk, on top of the green leather inlay, her legs spread wide, his papers scattered to the floor, and my husband grunting and groaning as he penetrated her, over and over, harder and harder, sweat forming on his brow. His trousers were pooled around his ankles and his shirt was undone, swaying back and forth in time with each thrust. I can't recall how long I stood there, mesmerised, but eventually Annie noticed me. He didn't. He was in raptures until the moment when Annie screamed and sat up, trying to cover herself, at the same time as she attempted to reach for her clothes, which were on the chair behind him.

I shake my head and try to banish the memory, although it lingers. It always lingers. I can still see Annie pulling on her blouse and skirt, forgetting her underwear in her haste, while my husband stared at me for a moment, his face a picture of shock and confusion, before he turned away and pulled up his trousers, trying to tuck in his unbuttoned shirt, all the while maintaining, over his shoulder, that it wasn't what it seemed to be. I remember laughing about that, despite the pain. How could it be anything other than what it seemed to be?

Annie left, her head bowed, showing herself out of our home, and once she'd gone, I turned my attentions back to my husband; the man who had promised to love, comfort, honour and protect me, forsaking all others. He'd promised to worship me with his body too, and yet just three years into our marriage, he was doing a pretty good job of 'worshipping' someone else… someone much younger.

I yelled. I screamed. I raved at him. He stood, and didn't answer back. He didn't say a word. He had no defence for his actions and when I'd worn myself out, I went to bed, telling him to sleep in the spare bedroom. Not the one next door to ours, but the one further along the landing, at the back of the house. Away from me.

For weeks and months, we lived in stony silence, punctuated only by bitter accusations and angry arguments. I'll admit that, if I'd been able to face the ignominy of accepting that my marriage had been a mistake, I'd have left him and gone home to my parents. But I couldn't do that. I wasn't actually sure they'd have me back. And, in any case, I couldn't bear being told that I'd been wrong all along, especially not by my father, who'd made no secret of his disapproval when we'd announced our engagement. He thought I could have done better… he made no secret of that. And I think he thought his permission should have been sought, even if only so he could decline it. And maybe that's why we didn't bother, and instead made a simple announcement of our intentions over Sunday tea, telling both him and ourselves that I was over twenty-one – just – and the tradition of asking parental consent really was terribly old fashioned.

And so I stayed, rather than admit the error or my ways, and eventually, about eight or nine months after that scene took place, he came to me one evening while I was getting ready for bed. He knocked on the door and entered, asking if we could talk. I agreed, and he sat down on the edge of the bed, facing me, and then he begged for my forgiveness, his tearful pleas touching even my hardened heart. He said he'd missed me. He'd missed us, and he didn't want to keep living the life we were. He promised me never to stray again, claiming the girl had led him on, that she'd been the one to instigate things, and that he'd been weak. I couldn't deny that, but at the time, I believed him, and I wanted our marriage to work. So, I agreed to try. It was the best I could offer him. I knew forgiving him would be hard; trusting him again would be harder still. But, that night, I let him sleep in our bed for the first time since it had happened. It was the first of many steps on a long road, and as the years went on, without a single sign of him cheating again, I honestly thought I'd got my husband and my marriage back... until I found out about Mildred...

I sit down at his desk, trying to forget the past and remember why I'm here; that I need to make sure he hasn't left any evidence lying around, carelessly linking him to Mildred in any way, other than the obvious one. We can't afford for the police to discover what he's done... either of us. Although I deeply resent even the idea of having to protect him, let alone the practicalities of it.

I try the drawers of his desk, hoping he hasn't locked them and heave a sigh of relief when they all open. Going through them methodically, I check each document in turn, looking for clues or signs, but finding nothing until I get to the top right hand drawer, at the front of which, there's a thick brown envelope, which I pull out and place on the desk in front of me. It's unsealed and, holding my breath, I open it and glance inside, gasping when I see that it contains money. A lot of money. I pull it out and count the notes... "Fifty pounds," I mutter to myself, under my breath. What on earth is he doing with fifty pounds? And where did he get it from, considering that, just a few days ago, he told me money was tight?

Mildred... My mind leaps back to her and the conversation I overheard. Is this the money he was going to give her?

"It must be," I whisper out loud, my blood boiling, my hand shaking, even as I carefully replace the notes in the envelope and put it back in the drawer. I can't take it, as much as I want to, because if I do, he'll know I've been through his desk.

As I'm tucking the envelope away, I notice the corner of a blue envelope nestling between some papers and I pull it out, opening it, my heart pounding about what I'm going to discover next.

In my hand, I'm holding a single sheet of notepaper, with small handwriting covering both sides. It's dated six months ago, and is addressed to 'Dear Poochy', which makes me want to be sick. Turning the page over, I see it's signed 'your little teddy bear', and I feel my stomach churn, bile rising in my throat.

"How could he?" I cry, tears welling in my eyes.

How dare he? Annie was bad enough… and as for Mildred… but this as well? He vowed that he'd never betray me again, and he's done so, not once, but twice – because I know this letter has nothing to do with Mildred. Not only is the timing wrong, but also, based on the conversation I overheard between her and my husband, I can't imagine she'd ever have referred to him as 'Poochy'.

My hands are shaking, as I try to make sense of the depth of his deception… and just think… to protect him, and our marriage, I've killed a young girl… and his unborn child. For a man who's shown no more loyalty to me than an alley cat.

The grandfather clock in the hall strikes eleven and I come to my senses, wiping away my tears with the back of my hand and shoving the letter and its envelope into my cardigan pocket to be read later. I can't risk him coming back and finding me in here, but I'm going to discover what he's been doing behind my back… and then I'm going to decide what to do about it… and about him.

———◆———

"Where to next?" Thompson asks.

"Well, now we know Sam Higgs definitely wasn't the father of Mildred's unborn child, I think we need to take a good, long hard look at the other men who are involved in the case," I reply, glancing out of the windscreen. "And while I know we've got a fairly substantial list of names in her diary, I think we should deal with the more obvious suspects first, don't you?"

"Naturally."

"In which case, being as we're just a few yards away from it, why don't we start with the vicarage?"

"You want to ask the vicar whether he's been having extra marital relations with one of his choir members?" Thompson says, looking at me, and tilting his head to one side.

"Not in so many words, but yes."

He shakes his head and pulls the car away from the kerb again, driving the short distance to the vicarage and parking up on the driveway.

We're just climbing out of the car, when I hear footsteps and turn to see the vicar himself approaching from the direction of the graveyard, down one of the narrow pathways. He's wearing his dog collar, which is visible above a dark blue jumper that he's wearing underneath his jacket. He hasn't got a coat on, although he looks warm enough, having seemingly been walking, his complexion somewhat flushed from the exertion.

"Good afternoon," he says and I check my watch quickly, seeing that it's just gone noon – literally by a minute.

"Good afternoon," I respond.

"Have you come to see us?" he asks, smiling and evidently more cheerful than he was on our last visit.

"Yes, we have."

"Well, you're lucky to have caught me. I've just popped home for some lunch."

"I see."

He shrugs his shoulders, putting his hands in his trouser pockets. "It's rather pot luck here at mealtimes," he remarks, in a conspiratorial manner, lowering his voice and leaning towards me. "I'm afraid Eileen isn't exactly blessed in the culinary department, but she does her best, poor thing. She's always saying she'd like for us to have some domestic help, but I don't really approve of such things... even if the diocesan purse strings would stretch that far."

"Did you approve of Miss Ryder?" I ask, watching him closely to gauge his reaction, which is a startled confusion that interests me more than I'm willing to show.

"That's not for me to say," he replies, loosening his collar with his forefinger. "If others choose to employ servants, that's up to them."

That wasn't entirely what I'd meant by my question, but I let it stand and, after a couple of seconds, he turns towards the house.

"Do you want to come in?" he offers, opening the front door with his key and going in ahead of us. We enter, both removing our hats and, as he closes the door, Reverend Hodge, calls out, "I'm home, Eileen," in a loud voice.

From the back of the house, his wife appears, an apron tied around her waist, hiding a rather frumpy looking tweed skirt, above which she's wearing a pale yellow blouse, and a brown cardigan, a tea towel held in her hands. "Oh," she says, looking embarrassed, "I didn't know we had company. Why didn't you say, Neville?" She glares at her husband.

"It's just the police, dear," he replies, rolling his eyes through his implied insult.

"How was Mrs Ives?" Mrs Hodge asks of him.

"No better," he says forlornly. "I doubt she'll last the night." He turns to us. "I've just been visiting a dying parishioner," he explains. "She's in her nineties though, so she's had a good innings." He looks back at his wife again. "What's for lunch?"

"I'm going to try and make a cobbler for tonight's supper, with the left-overs from yesterday's roast. I've found a recipe and it doesn't look too difficult... so I thought we'd just have soup for lunch. It's easy and takes care of itself. It'll be ready in about half an hour."

"Good," he says, rubbing his tummy. "I'm famished."

I feel as though Thompson and I might as well be invisible and clear my throat to make our presence felt.

"I am sorry, Inspector," Mrs Hodge says, stepping forward and depositing her tea towel on the hall table. "Do please come into the drawing room. I'm sure you're not here to listen to us discussing our domestic arrangements, are you?"

I smile at her, but don't bother to answer, and we all traipse into the living room, which feels just as sparse and cold as it did yesterday, despite the fire crackling in the hearth, and I wonder if that lack of warmth actually emanates from the occupiers of the house, rather than from the room itself.

"How can we help?" the vicar asks, neither of them offering us a seat, nor taking one themselves.

"I was wondering if either of you was aware that Mildred Ryder was pregnant." I say, keeping my eyes on the reverend as I speak. He stares at me, deliberately I think, his eyes fixed, not wavering. His reaction feels like a challenge, and although I've got no intention of doing anything about it, I do find his response quite unusual.

"Good Lord," his wife says. "We had no idea, did we, Neville?" She turns to face him and he shakes his head, coming out of his trance.

"No, dear."

"And I must say I'm surprised at Sam," his wife continues before I can put either of them straight. "I thought he was brought up better than that... and as for Mildred." She folds her arms across her chest, shaking her head and pursing her lips in very obvious disapproval.

"We mustn't judge too harshly, dear," the vicar says, surprising me. Based on his comments, it seems he disapproves of domestic servants, but has a much more liberal attitude towards pre-marital sex. In my limited experience of the clergy, that's an unusual stance, to put it mildly.

"Sam Higgs denies that the baby is his," I say, again watching for their reactions. The vicar remains stoney faced, but his wife scoffs, rolling her eyes.

"Well, he would say that, wouldn't he?" she huffs.

"Did Mildred ever socialise with any other young men in the church, do you know?" I ask.

"What makes you think it was someone associated with the church?" Mrs Hodge seems very offended by my inference.

"Because, from what we've learned of her, it appears to have been her only source of meeting people."

"Well, I'm sorry to inform of you of this, Inspector," Mrs Hodge says, her hackles seriously raised now, "but I'm afraid that Christians don't generally approve of fornication."

I take a deep breath, giving her time to calm – hopefully. "And I hate to disillusion you, Mrs Hodge, but adultery is just as alive and well in the Church of England as it is everywhere else. I'm assuming you're suggesting adultery, in your use of the word 'fornication'. That is its usual definition, isn't it?" She glares at me, a blush creeping up her neck. "Although I'd dearly love to know why it is that you are assuming that the man involved was married. Perhaps you'd like to explain?"

She opens her mouth, then closes it again in despair.

"We didn't know her well enough to form an opinion," the vicar replies before his wife can get her lips around her response. "And I'm afraid that, outside of choir practice, I don't know of anyone with whom she met regularly, other than Sam. I didn't meet up with her myself, you see."

"You must have done, surely?" I suggest.

"Excuse me?" He raises his voice and takes a step closer, his face reddening. "What are you implying."

"I'm not implying anything. I'm merely pointing out that you must have seen something of Mildred outside of choir practice."

"I've just told you, I didn't," he says, affronted by my conjecture. "And perhaps you'd do me the courtesy of believing me when I tell you something."

"So you didn't have anything to do with the planning of her wedding?"

He stills, to the point where I actually think he's stopped breathing for a moment, and then lets out a long, slow breath.

"Well, of course I did... what I meant was, that I didn't see Mildred outside of the church, and my duties... but I don't see what her wedding plans have to do with anything. That was ages ago."

"Not that long ago," I remark. "She postponed it in November, I believe?"

"Yes," he replies. "She and Sam came to see me together."

"Did they?"

"Yes. They explained that they were worried about what would happen to Mildred if Sam was called up."

"Did you try and talk them out of their decision?" I ask.

"No." He seems surprised by my question. "I didn't see that as my role, Inspector. And, in any case, they'd already made up their minds."

"So you left them to it?"

"Yes. It wasn't a cancellation; merely a postponement."

"And did they set another date?" I ask.

"Well, no. No they didn't, as it happens."

"Why would they?" Mrs Hodge asks, cutting into the conversation having rediscovered her voice. "The whole point of the postponement was because of the war and Sam being called up… and in case you haven't noticed, Inspector, the war hasn't finished yet."

I stare at her for a moment, her eyes sparking with anger and wonder how much it would take for her to really lose control… and how far she'd go if she did.

"We'll leave you to get on with your lunch," I say, turning to the door.

"Yes, I'll say goodbye," Mrs Hodge replies. "I'd better go and check on the soup."

She scuttles away towards the back of the house, leaving her husband to see us out.

As we get to the door, he hesitates, holding it open. "Don't take Eileen too seriously," he says quietly as we stand on the threshold. I turn back and he twists around, looking down the hallway, presumably to check the coast is clear. "We've been trying for a baby, if you must know," he murmurs. "Only things aren't working out. This news about Mildred…" He lets his voice fade.

"I see," I reply, with as much sympathy as I can manufacture.

"She's taking it to heart," he says, giving me a knowing look.

"Well, I'm sorry to hear that."

He nods his thanks and we depart, getting into the car. Thompson reverses out of the driveway and onto the road, waiting for a truck to pass, and then pulling away.

"Did you believe that?" he asks, driving down Summer Road and back towards the village.

"Which part?"

"That last bit… about them trying for a baby."

"No."

"No, neither did I," he says. "Where am I going, by the way?"

"Mr and Mrs Wharton," I reply, then add, "Why didn't you believe him, just out of interest?"

"A couple of reasons," he says, stopping to let another car pass through a narrow part of the High Street. "Firstly, I don't think it's something people talk about, not really... not to a complete stranger, anyway."

"Well, not unless they were the guilty party, and they were trying to throw suspicion elsewhere."

"There is that," he replies.

"And secondly?"

"Secondly, I got the feeling they were both covering for each other."

I smile. "So did I. There was something odd about their reactions... even odder than yesterday. If you want me to be honest, I think they both believe the other one did it, and they're doing their best to protect each other... and ultimately putting their foot in it. Quite spectacularly, as it happens."

"They are both behaving like they're as guilty as sin, aren't they?" he says, grinning and parking a few houses down from Mr and Mrs Wharton's property, just like he did on Saturday, when we were last here. "The question is, which one of them actually did it?"

I turn to him. "You think it's only one of them?"

He frowns. "Well, I don't think they're in it together, not based on the hash they just made of trying to cover for each other, anyway. If they were working together, they'd have prepared their stories a lot better than that."

"I know... and I'm not suggesting they are working together."

His frown deepens, his brow furrowing. "Then what are you suggesting?"

"At the moment, I don't know. They're both behaving so oddly, it's hard to tell. And we really need to keep an open mind, because it's still perfectly possible that we're not looking at either the vicar or his wife. We've got a few other suspects still to consider."

"I know, but if it isn't them, then that would mean you're wrong... because let's face it, you've thought it was one of them almost since the beginning, haven't you?"

"I have. But I've been known to be wrong before, Harry. I've made mistakes in the past, you know that."

I get out of the car, and he follows suit, looking at me over the top of it. "Can you name the date that last happened?" he asks, smiling.

"Well, whatever date I proposed to Victoria… I can't remember exactly when that was, but it was a huge mistake."

"Yes, but it's one you got to rectify," he says, coming around to the pavement and falling into step beside me.

"Thanks to you I did, yes," I remark, leaning into him.

He shakes his head. "I did you a favour, sleeping with your fiancée, did I?"

"Well, you didn't sleep with the only fiancée who mattered, so yes."

He chuckles and I go in through the garden gate ahead of him, walking up the path and knocking on the bright red door.

Mrs Wharton answers herself, dressed in a very smart, very fitted navy blue dress, with matching cardigan and a string of pearls hanging from her neck, her light blonde hair styled away from her perfectly made-up face. The contrast between her sophisticated elegance and Mrs Hodge's old-fashioned dowdiness is too marked not to notice.

"Oh… Inspector," she says, sounding both surprised and disappointed at the same time. It's a response I've become accustomed to over the years and I smile at her.

"Yes. I'm sorry to intrude. We were hoping to speak with you and your husband again, if that's not inconvenient?"

"Well, I'm afraid Norman's at work," she replies, "but you're welcome to come in."

She opens the door wider, letting us enter, and then closes it behind us, before indicating the drawing room, holding out her hand in invitation. "Please come in," she says.

"Thank you."

We follow her and enter the stylish room, and I'm reminded of Susan Conroy's comments, and the difference in taste, style and gentility between the two women.

"I'm sorry my husband isn't here," Mrs Wharton says, sitting down on one of the sofas, and nodding to the other, where Thompson and I sit, side by side, our hats held in our hands. "He sometimes comes home for lunch, but he's in meetings today, I believe…" Her voice fades, as though she's uncertain about what she's saying, but then she looks up suddenly. "I do apologise… would you like some coffee?" She smiles, just slightly. "I can't guarantee it'll taste very nice. I've placed an advertisement for a new maid, but I doubt I'll be able to find one, not at the moment. Young girls don't seem to want to go into domestic service anymore… and I'm completely out of my depth in the kitchen. As Norman is discovering." Her smile fades and she lowers her eyes.

"We don't need coffee, thank you," I reply and she looks up, blinking but grateful, I think.

"How can I help?" she asks. "Or was it Norman you wanted to see?"

"It was both of you," I reply. "We need to ask if you were aware of the fact that Miss Ryder was pregnant when she was killed?"

Mrs Wharton pales significantly, her skin becoming almost the same shade as the pearls around her neck, despite her make-up.

"Pregnant?" she whispers, clasping her hands tightly together, her knuckles whitening. "Do… do you know who the father was? Was it Sam?"

"Sam denies it," I reply.

"Well, I suppose he probably would, in the circumstances," she says, shaking her head. "Mildred was such a quiet girl though… I can't see how…" She looks up, her eyes filled with tears, which seems like a very odd reaction to me. "It would have to be have been someone she knew, wouldn't it? I mean, someone she knew well?"

That seems fairly obvious to me, but I don't comment.

"Were you aware of any other men in Mildred's life?" I ask her instead, noting that she's only just managing not to cry, not to break down completely in front of us.

She shakes her head, seemingly unable to speak.

"Are you all right, Mrs Wharton?" I have to ask. She seems so genuinely upset.

"It's just… the unborn child…" she blurts out, but then her voice fades and she looks completely distraught and utterly hopeless. After a moment, she coughs and adds, "My husband and I have been talking about starting a family, you see…" The cracks in her voice become even more apparent, and she stutters in a breath, struggling for control.

I give her a moment, not saying a word, being as this has clearly become very personal to her, and eventually, she squares her shoulders and looks across at me, managing a slight smile.

"I'm sorry, Inspector," she says.

"Please, don't apologise. I do understand. And we can come back later on, if you'd prefer…?"

"No, please…"

She waves her hand, which I take as a signal to continue. So I do, clearing my throat first. "You knew that Mildred and Sam had postponed their wedding, didn't you?" I sit forward slightly, gauging her reactions again.

"Yes. Mildred informed my husband of that, in November, after she and Sam had been to see Reverend Hodge about it."

"Your husband?" I query because that strikes me as a little odd.

"Yes. I was out that evening… at a WI meeting, if memory serves. I remember, my husband wasn't best pleased that she'd interrupted his radio programme to bother him with her domestic problems, but I suppose she must have forgotten that I wasn't going to be at home."

"Did you speak to her about the situation at all?" I ask.

"Yes. The next day."

"And how did she seem to you?"

"Upset, obviously, which is understandable, although I did try and get her to see reason. Sam was only doing what was best for them, after all."

I feel my skin tingle slightly and take a breath. "Can you explain that?" I ask, not wanting her to suspect that she might just have revealed the first real anomaly in our evidence.

"Well, Mildred told my husband that Sam had wanted to postpone the wedding because he was worried about being called up and leaving her by herself… and what might happen to her if he was injured… or killed." She whispers the last word and turns away, staring at the fireplace, but then looks back at me. "I told her I thought it was sweet, and really quite sensible of him to be so concerned for her."

I nod my head. "And can I ask whether Mildred getting married would have meant her losing her job here? Was that something she spoke to you about?"

She stares at me for a moment, confused. "No, she didn't. And of course it wouldn't, especially not at the moment."

"Is that because domestic servants are so hard to come by?" I ask, feeling cynical.

"No," she says, outraged now. "Things are different in war, Inspector, and I'm not talking about the difficulty with finding household staff. What I mean is that, if they had got married last December, as they'd planned, Mildred would have needed to keep her place. Sam would have still been called up, and she'd have needed the security of her income and the stability of her job and her home here with us to keep her going. In peacetime, things would have been different, of course, and I imagine that if we hadn't been at war and they'd got married, Mildred would have handed in her notice straight away, so that she could set up home with Sam instead. They'd have wanted to live together and he'd have been working and would have been able to provide for her. It would have been a different thing entirely. I don't know what kind of woman you think I am, Inspector, but I can assure you…" She falls silent and I feel a little ashamed of having judged her, but then she smiles, quite unexpectedly. "Of course," she says, her voice softening, "you've spoken with Susan Conroy, haven't you?"

"Yes. We visited her and Mr Conroy yesterday."

"Well, that makes sense." She coughs, raising her hand to her mouth. "I can assure you, whatever Susan may have told you, I am not heartless, nor am I money-grubbing, or feckless. Susan is a very bitter woman, I'm afraid."

"She is?" I query, even though I've seen evidence of the woman's jealousy with my own eyes. I want to see what Mrs Wharton has to say on the matter, without any influence from me.

"Yes," she replies, letting out a long sigh and running her fingers along her pearls. "Norman, Laurence and Susan all went to school together," she explains. "But then Laurence went to university, while Norman went to work for his father at the factory, and Susan stayed here in the village. Norman and Susan started seeing each other some time after that – I'm not sure when – and before long, they were in a relationship. I have no idea whether it was physical and, quite frankly, I don't care. I'm not the sort of woman who's interested in the things that happened in my husband's life before he met me. The past is the past, as far as I'm concerned. It's what he's done *during* our marriage that matters so much more…" She stops talking and seems to choke on her emotions, her bottom lip trembling noticeably, but then she remembers where she is, and our presence, and gathers herself together again. "I do know that Norman was the one who broke it off," she continues, with some effort, "and shortly afterwards, he and I met, and we were married within a few months… for better or worse…" Her voice fades, but then she looks up again and says, "Susan has always resented me, no matter how hard I've tried to be friendly with her. So now, I'm afraid I don't really try anymore."

I nod my head, making sense in my own mind of Susan Conroy's attitude, her jealousy, not only of her own husband, but also of Norman Wharton, adding a new angle to the case, as I wonder what she might do to protect the man she so clearly still loves… or what she may be willing to do to incriminate the woman who – in her mind at least – stole him from her.

Outside, once we've taken our leave, we make our way back to the car, walking slowly.

"I think that confirms our thoughts about Susan Conroy and her jealousy, don't you?" Thompson says, pulling the car keys from his coat pocket.

"I do indeed. Not that they really needed confirming, but it's interesting to know the background." I fasten the buttons of my coat to stop it catching in the brisk wind. "I think it also confirms that Norman Wharton isn't entirely faithful in his marriage, and that his wife knows about it. That comment she made about the things he's done during their marriage mattering more… that was very telling, I thought."

"Yes, so did I," Thompson replies.

"Of course, that doesn't mean he's still being unfaithful, but I think she suspects as much, don't you?"

"Yes. And what we have to ask ourselves is whether he was being unfaithful with Mildred Ryder. She was their maid, after all."

"Exactly." I stop and turn to face him. "This is what I meant about the personalities of the people involved being so important to the case," I explain. "Between their jealousies and obsessions, their personal frailties, and people assuming guilt in others, we've got ourselves a tangled web here. All we have to do is to work out who's telling the truth, and who's lying – and why – and then it should all untangle."

"You make it sound easy," Thompson scoffs.

"No... if it was easy, anyone could do it... even you."

Chapter Eight

I wait until after lunch before taking myself off to my bedroom, lying down on the bed and pulling the letter from my cardigan pocket, where it's lain since I discovered it earlier this morning. I've felt it burning a hole there, especially during the visit from Inspector Stone, but I did my best to keep up appearances, despite my nerves and heightened emotions. It's not surprising that I got so upset, and struggled to maintain my composure, considering that I've just found out my husband has lied, cheated and deceived me… repeatedly. But I can't think about that now. I need to concentrate…

'Dear Poochy,' *I read and try to control the bile that rises in my throat.*

'It's been three interminably dull days since our last snatched half hour together and I'm going insane without you. I'm desperate to feel your lips all over my body again, and for the comfort of your arms around me. I ache for your touch and long for your whispered words of passion while you make love to me. I lie in bed at night, touching myself and dreaming of you… God, I need you, Poochy, more than you'll ever know. But I know from the things you say to me and the words you write to me that you need me as much as I need you, my love. And in a way I find that comforting. It's that thought that keeps me going, when I miss you most, like at night, when I'm alone in my bed, longing for you. Please write to me soon and tell me when we can next be together again. Or better still, come round and see me… and tell me that you've finally plucked up the courage to tell your wife about us, and that you've left her, so we can be together always. You know you don't love her any more – not that I can see how you ever could have done, not like you love me, anyway. She's too stuck up and boring, and I'll bet she doesn't please you like I do, does she? I'll bet she doesn't let you do all those wicked things you like doing with me, that I can't wait for you to do again.

Please call soon,

Your little teddy bear'

I read it through again, just to make sure I've completely understood, and then I crumple the pale blue paper into a tight ball in my hand.

"How dare he?" *I whisper under my breath.*

How many other women have there been? I ask myself. How many times has he made a fool of me? I knew about Annie, and about Mildred, but who on earth is his 'little teddy bear'?

I unfurl the page again and, laying it as flat as I can, read the date through the creases. It says '10th August 1939'… which seems so long ago now, before the war even started. Another lifetime. There are no clues there, but I suppose it at least eliminates Mildred. She made it clear in their conversation that her encounter with my husband had been a one-off. That means this letter is from someone else… some other little tart, evidently with ideas of replacing me. And it seems he was planning on letting her.

I've killed for him. I've lied for him… and all the while, not only has he been sleeping around behind my back, but he's been planning to leave me? To divorce me? Well, we'll see about that…

———◆———

Mr Wharton is just leaving his factory premises when we arrive, his coat slung over his arm and his hat perched on his head. As Thompson parks the car in one of about half a dozen parking spaces in front of the single storey brick building, Mr Wharton can be seen propping open one half of the double doors that form the main entrance to the property, talking to someone, and completely oblivious to our arrival.

"I wonder where he's off to," Thompson comments, glancing over at the man, who's laughing now, throwing his head back.

"Lunch, probably. But to be honest, I'm more interested in who he's talking to," I reply.

"Why?" he asks, turning to face me.

"Because of the way he's behaving. Look at him. It's obviously a woman on the other side of the door. You can tell a mile off."

Thompson looks back at Mr Wharton and lets out a sigh, shaking his head, as we both get out of the car and slowly stroll over, unobserved.

As we approach, I hear a giggle, a female giggle, and I cough loudly enough to interrupt the very obviously flirtatious conversation that appears to be going on between Mr Wharton and whoever is standing just out of our sight. Even if *he* has trouble remembering that he's married, the memory of his wife's sadness is something that's going to haunt me for some time to come.

Mr Wharton jumps, then turns to face us. "Inspector?" he says, frowning. "What are you doing here?"

"Looking for you," I reply a little facetiously.

"I see," he says, and he blushes as his eyes dart momentarily to the woman just inside the door. "I'll discuss that matter with you after work, shall I, Miss Taylor?" he says, sounding official and businesslike all of a sudden.

I step closer; close enough to hear a voice reply, "Yes, Mr Wharton, sir," in a familiar, coquettish tone, and without hesitating for a second, I yank open the other door, taking both Wharton and the woman on the other side by surprise.

"Ethel?" I stare down at the wide-eyed girl before me, dressed in mid-blue overalls, her hair hidden beneath a scarf, with just a few stray tendrils poking through.

"Why… Mr Stone. I mean, Inspector Stone," she stammers, her face flushed with embarrassment.

"What are you doing here?" I ask, repeating Wharton's earlier question, as I step into the small foyer.

"I work here now," she replies, blinking rapidly and biting her lip, her hands clenched in front of her. I think it's hard for both of us to forget the number of times she almost swooned in front of me at my aunt's house, simply because I bear a slight resemblance to her favourite film star. Even so, her presence here, and the fact that

Wharton seems to be taking a very keen interest in her, gives me cause for concern.

"Do you know Miss Taylor?" Wharton asks, coming to stand beside me, allowing the door to close, although Thompson opens it and joins us, all four of us filling the small space between the front entrance and the offices which are ahead of us.

"Yes, I do." I turn to look at him and see a smirk forming on his face.

"Really?" he says, and with that single word, he manages to imply a multitude of misdemeanours on my part – in mind, if not in deed.

"Yes. Before she came to work here, Ethel was the maid at my aunt's house." I narrow my eyes, daring him to insinuate anything improper, even though I know that's the direction his mind is taking.

"Oh, was she now," he says, nodding his head in a knowing way, that smirk still settled on his lips. "I see."

"Yes, I'm sure you do," I reply. "And it's fortuitous us meeting like this, Ethel," I add, turning back to her, "because I have a message for you from my aunt."

"You do?" She looks surprised, which isn't as unexpected as it might be, considering that I just made that up.

"Yes." I look over at Wharton again. "Perhaps you could take my sergeant into your office and wait for me there? I won't be a moment with Ethel, and then I'll join you."

He glances at his watch. "Well, I was just going to lunch," he says.

"We won't keep you long." I smile at him as pleasantly as I can manage and he huffs out a sigh, before moving towards another set of double doors ahead of us and holding the right hand one open to allow Sergeant Thompson to move through, which he does, glancing back at me and raising his eyebrows, before the two of them disappear.

"What's going on, Ethel?" I say, the moment the door closes.

"I—I don't know what you mean," she replies, raising her chin defiantly.

"Yes you do." I glare at her and eventually she lowers her eyes.

"Well… it doesn't hurt, does it?" she murmurs. "He's a nice man, and he's been very kind to me."

"I'm sure he has, but you need to understand that men like Mr Wharton generally have an ulterior motive in their kindness."

She looks up, frowning. "Ulterior motive?" she says.

"Yes." I take a deep breath, wondering why I started this conversation and how on earth I'm going to finish it. "I've just spent the last half hour or so with his wife…" Ethel's eyes widen. "She's a very nice woman too, and I'm fairly sure, based on something she said, that her husband has been unfaithful before during their marriage." Ethel's mouth drops open now.

"We haven't… I mean, we're not…" She stumbles over her words, her cheeks flushing bright red.

"Good. I'm glad to hear it," I reply, stepping forward. "Did you not know he was married, Ethel?" I ask.

"No, sir," she whispers.

"He didn't tell you?" She shakes her head.

"No. Today's my first day and he's been just… just so kind, showing me round personally, and taking such an interest, and everything…" Her voice cracks and tears well in her eyes as she looks up at me. "I've been rather foolish, haven't I?" she says.

I hand her a clean handkerchief from my jacket pocket. "Not yet, no," I reply.

"But what if I lose my job?" she wails, her despair obvious.

"You won't," I say firmly and she seems to pull herself together, staring up at me.

"I won't? But surely…"

"Just leave everything to me," I sigh, knowing full well that Mr Wharton is just the kind of man who'd sack an employee for refusing his advances, and that I'm going to have to handle this situation carefully if Ethel's going to retain her position.

"You'll… you'll speak to him?" she stutters.

"Yes. I think it's probably safest if I inform Mr Wharton that you're already spoken for, don't you?"

"W—With you, you mean?" She looks flustered, but her eyes are sparkling with excitement at the same time. *Good Lord.*

"No, Ethel," I say patiently. "Especially not as I'm also a married man."

"Oh yes, sir… of course. I was forgetting about that."

I wonder how that's even possible, considering that my wedding to Amelie was so recent, but I don't question her comment. Instead, I suggest to her that, should Mr Wharton raise the topic, she should go along with the story that she already has a young man in her life, just to put him off.

"I'll invent you someone suitable," I add.

"I—I'm ever so grateful for your help, sir, and I promise I won't be so foolish again." She flutters her eyelashes at me, smiling broadly and I wonder to myself whether she really will be more careful in future, or whether the next vaguely attractive and half-decent man she comes across will turn her head just as easily as Wharton has.

"Now, you get back to work," I tell her and she goes to turn away, but then hesitates, stops and looks up at me.

"There wasn't really a message from Mrs Lytle, was there?" she asks.

"No." I don't bother to pick her up on the fact that my aunt's official title is actually 'Lady Lytle', being as Aunt Dotty doesn't bother too much about it herself. "I just wanted to make sure you were all right, that's all… preferably without Mr Wharton being present."

"Mrs Lytle's okay though, isn't she?" She sounds concerned.

"Yes, she's fine. My mother and aunt are staying with her for the time being."

"Oh, that's nice," she sounds wistful, perhaps regretting her decision to leave my aunt's employment, especially given her current predicament. "Well, tell her I said hello, when you next see her."

"I will."

She gives me a slight bob curtsey, as was always her way, and darts through the double doors. I wait for a couple of seconds, and then follow her, finding myself in a narrow corridor, that's filled with the noise of machinery and an underlying general chatter, all of which is coming from the large room on my right, hidden behind a partition wall, half glazed from waist height up. To my left there is a series of offices, the first of which bears Mr Wharton's name, with the word

'Manager' beneath, and I knock once and then enter, without waiting to be asked.

Inside, Wharton is sitting behind a wide, rather old fashioned oak desk, leaning back in his chair, while Thompson is standing beside a filing cabinet on the far side of the room, pretending to look at the large, framed painting of Hampton Court Palace that is hanging on the wall to his right.

"Mr Wharton," I say, sounding a lot more jolly than I feel, as I take the seat he offers in front of his desk and Thompson moves around the room, so he's standing just behind me, "I do apologise for that. I wasn't expecting to see Ethel here."

He smiles. "You didn't realise she worked for me?"

"No. I've obviously known Ethel for some time," I lie nonchalantly, "but I've been away recently and didn't realise she'd left my aunt's employ until I returned."

"Lovely girl," he murmurs, as though to himself, a smile settling on his lips. "And very accommodating."

I chuckle. "Yes, she is, isn't she? Her young man certainly thinks so…" I leave my sentence hanging, quite deliberately.

"Young man?" He looks up sharply.

"Oh yes," I say, shaking my head. "Unfortunately, he also has quite a volatile temperament."

"He doesn't hurt her, does he?" he asks, pretending a concern I'm fairly sure he doesn't feel.

"Good Lord, no. He'd wouldn't touch a hair on Ethel's head. He positively dotes on her… but the last man who tried to interfere with her… well, let's just say it took all my influence to keep Ethel's young man out of prison." I roll my eyes. "He's a bit hot headed, and handy with his fists," I add, chuckling again, as though the situation would have amused me. It wouldn't, of course. But then this whole thing is a fiction, so what does it matter?

"I see," Wharton says, paling and swallowing hard, before he leans forward, his elbows on his desk. "I can't imagine you came here to discuss the private lives of my employees, Inspector?"

"No, I didn't."

He stares at me for a moment, seemingly unsure of himself now, but then says, "And I have better things to do myself… As I just explained, I was about to leave for lunch, and I've got to go through the accounts this afternoon…" He glances at the door. "Although I might go home and work from there… there are too many interruptions here."

Most of those are of his own creation, from what I've seen, but I don't comment, and sit back in my chair, instead. "You're busy at the moment?" I ask, sounding interested.

"Yes, we are. We've just been awarded a contract by the War Office, which I'm afraid I can't talk about, but I have to say, it's come at a very opportune time."

"Financially?" I suggest, when he doesn't clarify his comment.

"Yes," he replies, nodding his head slowly. "Things have been quite tough over the last few years. The business was in a pretty poor state when I inherited it from my father, which I hadn't expected, and I had a lot of debts to settle… so I took the decision to sell the family home, rather than lose the business." He holds my gaze. "My family's name means a lot around here and, as Lucy pointed out to me at the time, we employ nearly forty people, and they depend on us for their livelihoods." I'm interested to note that it was his wife who had the altruistic attitude, while Mr Wharton himself was more concerned with his own family's reputation. "Lucy and I had only just got married when I had to sell up, but she encouraged me in my decision, even though there have been plenty of times since then, when I've questioned my own sanity." He pauses and sighs.

"It's been hard work?" I suggest, surprised by this insight into his life, which is most unexpected.

"Bloody hard work." He rolls his eyes. "So, I have to say, this contract is just what we needed… not that money doesn't continue to be something of an issue, you understand? Although I'd rather you kept that to yourself, if you don't mind… just for appearance's sake."

"Naturally," I remark, recalling the comments made by Mr and Mrs Conroy, and the fact that, while they may have known the bare facts of their friend's financial situation and its consequences, they clearly have no knowledge or understanding of the details. But then I imagine

Mr Wharton likes it that way…

He eyes me closely. "Even so, Inspector, I'm sure you're not that interested in my personal finances, are you? You must have had another reason for coming here?"

"Yes, we did," I reply. "We came to ask whether you were aware that Mildred Ryder was pregnant at the time of her death."

His expression changes, a look of surprise settling across his handsome features. "Pregnant?" he murmurs.

"Yes… three months pregnant."

"I see." He leans back, tilting his head. "And what does Sam have to say about this?"

"He denies responsibility."

"Oh… does he now? Crafty little sod," Wharton scoffs.

"And I believe him," I add, which halts Wharton in his tracks.

"You do?" he whispers.

"Yes."

"But that must mean Mildred was seeing someone else," he says, clearly astonished by the prospect. "Who'd have thought… Mildred, of all people…" He seems amused now, which I find distasteful, like everything else about the man.

"Do you know of anyone else who Mildred Ryder might have associated with, outside of your household?" I ask him.

"No. As my wife informed you the other day, she mainly associated with her fellow choristers, and other members of the congregation."

"Anyone in particularly?" I'm finding his supercilious attitude annoying now.

"How would I know? Unlike Lucy, I don't attend church myself. Haven't done since I was a lad, and was forced to sit through the whole tedious rigmarole by my parents."

"So you've got no idea who Mildred might have known then?"

"None whatsoever. I'd always thought she was a quiet, innocent type… but now I'm starting to wonder." There's a lewd expression on his face, which is particularly unpleasant and I get to my feet, leaning over him.

"Do you know anything about the postponement of Mildred and Sam's wedding?" I ask.

"Only what she told me. Although why the girl thought I'd be interested in her personal problems, God knows. That's the sort of thing my wife should be dealing with, and I told Lucy that when she got home that evening. Still, looking back, I suppose it's not surprising Sam wanted to postpone the wedding is, is it? If he'd found out what she'd been up to."

"We don't believe he did."

He shrugs. "Well, maybe her conscience got the better of her, and she didn't want to admit that to us, so she said the postponement was Sam's idea," he muses. "Or perhaps she found she preferred the other man. Sam's a bit on the dull side, you know… wouldn't surprise me if he wasn't a little disappointing in the bedroom department."

His tone and attitude don't compare well with those of his wife, and make me wonder even more about his old school friends' interpretation of both himself and Lucy Wharton, who seems by far the nicest person of the group.

"Do you have any idea why Miss Ryder chose to talk to you about her wedding plans being postponed, rather than waiting for your wife?" I ask.

"No." He waves his hand as though he couldn't care less. "It was bloody annoying though. I missed the end of a really good detective play on the wireless, so I never did find out who did the murder." I'm starting to know how he feels. "And in any case, I don't have time for domestic issues. That's meant to be Lucy's department. I'm very busy with this new contract now. Even when I've finished here, my evenings and weekends are mostly spent in my study, catching up."

I nod my head, replacing my hat and wondering to myself why his wife puts up with him. But, as we take our leave, I remember her saying that you can't help who you fall in love with, and I'm overwhelmed with pity for the woman.

"That was quite impressive," Thompson says once we're back in the car. "Even I believed you for a while."

"I assume we're talking about Ethel's make-believe boyfriend?" I enquire, just to make sure we're both on the same topic.

"Of course." He smiles across at me.

"I've never liked lying, as you well know," I explain, "but Ethel told me that, even though today is her first day there, Mr Wharton has been rather fulsome with his attentions."

"So his wife's suspicions were justified?"

"It looks that ways, yes."

"And you decided to create a fake boyfriend for Ethel to throw Romeo off the scent, did you?"

"Yes. It seemed like a good idea at the time."

"Until she lets slip that he doesn't exist," he remarks.

"Oh, she won't do that." I shake my head. "I told her what I was going to do… after I'd explained why she didn't want to get involved with the likes of Norman Wharton."

"I'm surprised she needed telling," he points out.

"She's young and impressionable, and I suppose he's a handsome enough chap."

"In a creepy, overbearing kind of way, yes. What do these girls see in men like that?"

"God knows, but then we're not women, so their charms are probably wasted on us."

"Thank heavens for that," he replies, laughing, with a mock shudder, and I join in.

Mildred's diaries are still lying on my desk and, as I sit down, I pick up the one on top, which is for 1939, and thumb through it.

"We need to find out who all these people are," I say aloud to Thompson, who has followed me into my office, having left his hat and coat on his desk in the main office, which is deserted, partly because of the fact that so many men are still off sick, and also because it's now lunchtime, when the station always quieter anyway.

"Which people?" He sits down, leaning back and crossing his legs.

"The people Mildred Ryder listed in her diary." I turn the opened book around and he leans forward again, squinting at the page, then nods his head.

"Oh yes… we'd rather forgotten about them, hadn't we?"

I hand him the book, pushing the others across the desk as well. "Yes, we had, but we still need to know if they're significant… especially the men."

"The men?" He glances up at me.

"Well, we are looking for someone who may have fathered Mildred's unborn child, so at the moment, I'm more interested in the men than the women."

"There are a lot of them," Thompson replies, flipping through the pages himself now. "And and they're all just listed by Christian name. Where on earth do I start?"

"Mrs Wharton didn't seem to think Mildred had many interests outside of the church, so I'd suggest starting there. You could try the parish office, or the church warden, perhaps, being as the parish office might be a little too closely connected to the vicar."

"And that's a problem, is it? I mean, wouldn't it just be easier for me to pop back to the vicarage and ask the reverend himself?" he asks, settling back in his seat, but still thumbing through the diary, his face darkening as the enormity of his task seems to dawn on him.

"It might, but I'd really rather you didn't."

"Because you suspect him?" He looks up.

"Yes."

He puts the diary down on top of the pile and folds his arms across his chest. "Hang on a minute," he says calmly. "I know you've been saying you think it's either the vicar or his wife almost since the beginning, but you need to remember that he's a man of God…" His voice fades, presumably at the look on my face, which I imagine to be one of pity, bordering on incredulity.

"So? You think vicars don't commit adultery, don't get their mistresses pregnant, and then murder them to cover it up?"

He stares at me, then shakes his head. "It would be a first in my experience, but is that the way your mind is going?"

I shrug my shoulders. "I don't know. As you said, I'm fairly convinced that it's one or other of them, even if I can't put my finger on exactly how or why at the moment. The point at present is that I don't want you to ask him about those names… because I don't trust him, and I don't like him."

"And is there anyone else you don't like in this case?" he asks. "Just so I know who else I shouldn't be talking to?"

"The vicar's wife, obviously," I reply seriously, even though Thompson's trying not to smile.

"I suppose I should have expected that, especially given her attitude earlier on."

"Hmm… and then there's Mr Wharton."

"I can understand that," he says thoughtfully. "So, is there anyone you *do* like? I think at the current rate of knots, it might be quicker to start there."

"I feel sorry for Mrs Wharton, if that counts."

"I suppose it does. Why do you feel sorry for her?" he asks.

"Because she obviously loves her husband very much, and I'm not sure he even notices her. We know from what happened with Ethel that he's open to having an affair, if he isn't already having one, and I don't think Mrs Wharton deserves that."

"I suppose it's difficult to know what goes on in someone else's marriage. She might be completely different with her husband to how she is with us."

"I hope she is," I reply. "And I agree with you about marriage being private, but at the same time, I think we both know Mr Wharton isn't faithful, don't we?"

"Yes. Still… it's nice to know you like someone."

I shake my head. "I didn't say I liked her; I said I felt sorry for her. There's a difference."

"Heavens," Thompson retorts, smiling. "Is there anyone you *do* like on this case?"

"Yes. I like Mildred Ryder."

He sighs and looks down at the closed diary for a few moments, and then raises his head. "Being as we've got a few minutes, why don't you tell me what it is you don't like about all these people?"

"Why?" I lean forward, resting my elbows on the table. "Is this just an excuse to delay starting work on those names in the diary?"

He smiles. "Yes, and no." He pauses. "You said this was a case that revolved around personalities and, before I get started, I just thought it might be wise to get an idea of what you think of the main characters."

He has a point and, regardless of his motives, taking a few minutes to sum up our potential suspects is a good idea.

"So, tell me what you think about Mrs Hodge," he says.

"She's one of those women who like to tell everyone else how to live their lives," I remark. "She's interfering and bossy."

"You mean she's exactly what I said she was the first time we met her?" he replies. "She's a typical vicar's wife."

"Yes, but it's more than that. There's something fanatical about her as well."

"Fanatical?"

"Yes, and I'm not talking about avid knitting, or manic cake baking."

He chuckles. "You think she'd lose control?"

"I think she might claim to have lost control in certain circumstances, yes."

"Such as, if she'd just murdered someone?"

"Yes… but I think in reality, she knows exactly what she's doing, and that anyone who underestimates her could be in real danger."

He raises his eyebrows for a moment, but doesn't comment. "What about her husband?" he asks eventually. "You think he might have been sleeping with Mildred?"

"I don't know. I doubt he'd have said 'no', given the chance. But I'm not sure Mildred would have slept with him. To be honest, I doubt she'd have slept with anyone – other than Sam, perhaps, in the right circumstances, such as after their marriage, for example. From what we've learned, she just doesn't seem like that kind of girl."

"And yet she was," he muses.

"Was she?"

"She was pregnant, Rufus." He sounds exasperated, which isn't that surprising, really. "Do you still need me to draw you a diagram, even though you've been married for over a week now?"

"No, of course not. But how do we know she was a willing participant?"

His face pales and he frowns. "You mean you think she was raped?"

"Well, if she wasn't willing, then that's the only other conclusion we can draw."

"Are you actually suggesting that the vicar might have raped her?" He sounds even more disbelieving now.

"I'm suggesting that *someone* did… because the more we talk, the more we learn, and the more I think about it, the less I'm inclined to believe that Mildred Ryder would have voluntarily had sex with anyone."

"But the *vicar?*"

"Stop saying that as though vicars aren't also people… Underneath his cassocks, Reverend Hodge is a man, just like you and me."

"I know, but you're talking about rape here, Rufus. Not everyone is a potential rapist. We're not, are we?"

"No, I know… and I'm not saying for certain that it was him. It could have been Norman Wharton, or even someone else that we don't know about yet."

"Are we including Laurence Conroy on your list of suspects?" he asks.

"We're including everyone, except possibly Sam Higgs. I don't think he'd do that."

"No, neither do I." He shakes his head slowly. "But everyone else?"

"Yes. Even the people she named in her diaries. She obviously knew them in some capacity, even if we don't understand what it is yet."

"In which case, I suppose I'd better get on and find out who they all are," he says, standing and looking down at me.

"Yes, and we should also perhaps go over to the Conroy house."

"You want to talk to them again?" he asks. "Because Laurence Conroy won't be there, will he? He's gone back to his base… and possibly over to France by now."

"I know, but I don't want to talk to him – or her, for that matter. I want to carry out a small experiment."

He leans on my desk. "Oh yes?"

"Yes. I want to see how long it takes to get from their house to the place where Mildred was killed, and back again… and whether it's possible to reasonably smoke a cigarette in that time."

"You're thinking of Norman Wharton?"

"Yes… or his wife."

"I thought you liked her?"

"No. I said I felt sorry for her."

"Oh yes, so you did." He stands again. "But if we're talking about rape…"

I shake my head. "We are, but it may not be the rapist who killed her. Mildred was three months pregnant, remember? We're not talking about the act of rape having taken place a few days ago and the man lashing out in remorse, or regret, or even anger. We're talking about the act having taken place a long time ago, and perhaps only recently having been discovered… along with her pregnancy. So, while it could be him, covering his tracks, it could equally be his wife."

"You mean, if she found out what he'd done?"

"Yes."

"But would she kill to protect him? Surely any right-minded woman would be appalled and would hand her husband over to the authorities. They wouldn't commit murder…"

"She might. If she had the right kind of temperament, she might kill to protect herself, or her way of life, or to avoid having to face the fact that her marriage is a sham and having to go home and admit as much to her family."

"So you think it's Mrs Wharton now?" He sounds confused.

"No… I still favour Mrs Hodge. But there is one problem with that."

"Oh?"

"Think about it, Harry… If she was waiting outside the church for the end of choir practice, either ready to ambush Mildred, or because she was the person who Mildred had arranged to meet, how did she manage to be at home when the reverend got back?"

"Because he went back for his sermon," Thompson says reasonably.

"I know. But how did she know he'd do that?"

"She didn't," he replies, slowly, taking in the problem that's been nagging at me for some time.

"No."

"So it can't be her."

I smile, just briefly. "I didn't say that, did I? I think I actually just said that I still favour Mrs Hodge."

"But…?"

"That's where her personality comes in. She's fanatical enough to have taken the chance, to have risked everything to get what she wanted. The fact that her husband was delayed was pure good fortune on her part. I think that – if it was her – she planned on carrying out the murder and getting back as quickly as possible, in the hope that she could make up an excuse about checking the blackout, or putting out the rubbish, or something…"

"That would have been highly dangerous," he mutters, as though he doesn't quite believe me. "Why couldn't it just be one of the men? What's wrong with the theory that one of them raped her – which is bad enough in itself – but somehow managed to persuade her to keep quiet about it…" His face brightens for a moment. "And in that instance, I think Norman Wharton is our most likely candidate, because let's face it, he could have threatened to sack her if she spoke up, couldn't he?"

"Yes… he could," I allow.

"In which case, he'd feel fairly safe, until Mildred found out she was pregnant that is, which we can assume was what her doctor's appointment was about, and then she'd presumably have told him, and possibly have wanted some money from him… and he'd have arranged to meet her and would have killed her to save his marriage, and his reputation." He stops talking, taking a breath. "That scenario works for both the vicar and for Wharton, and probably for a lot of other men in the village. But reputation would matter a lot to both of our leading men… although I prefer Wharton myself."

"Why? Because he's not a 'man of God'?" I borrow his phrase.

"No… because, as I just said, he had the best opportunity to threaten Mildred if she spoke out about being raped… assuming that she was raped, of course."

I nod my head. "Now that we've brought it out into the open, I'm going to treat the rape element as a working hypothesis for the time being, just because it's the only thing that fits with Mildred's personality. But as for one of the men having killed her…"

"You're not convinced, are you?" he interrupts.

"Not entirely."

"Care to tell me why?"

"Of course." I sit back and look up at him. "Think about the way in which she was stabbed. The first wound was quite high up on her abdomen."

"Yes…"

"But the second wound was aimed much lower, as though the murderer intended to kill her unborn child."

"I know… but just killing Mildred would have done that. The unborn child couldn't have survived, and they'd have known that."

"Obviously… but that's what I'm trying to tell you. There was no need for that second wound. There's something about this crime, Harry… something obsessive and cruel and bitter."

"Like a woman wronged?" he suggests.

"Very possibly."

The sound of voices, followed by a peal of laughter, intrudes into our conversation, making it clear that at least some of the men are returning to the office.

"I think that's my cue," Thompson says, picking up the 1939 diary again.

"You're going to enlist some help, are you?" I ask.

"Of course. I think the sooner we can get through these names, the better, don't you?"

"Yes. You have my permission to delegate," I remark and he smiles.

"I wasn't aware I was asking for it."

Chapter Nine

He's spent the whole afternoon in his study, doing paperwork. At least that's what he told me he was doing. Whether he is or not, I don't know… and I'm not sure I care anymore either, not after what he's done.

For myself, I've spent the last couple of hours in our bedroom, lying on the bed, staring at the ceiling, with just a fake headache and his love letter from another woman for company, trying to decide what on earth I'm going to do.

It was bad enough when I thought it was just Annie and Mildred, but to discover there's another one – or maybe more than one – it's too much, especially now I know he was thinking of leaving me. My God… the humiliation! Well, I'm damned if I'm going to let him keep doing this to me. Anyone could find out, and then where would we be? Because let's face it, he's so careless, leaving letters lying around that could incriminate him…

Wait a minute. Maybe that's the answer.

"Could I?" I mutter under my breath.

Killing him is my first and most natural instinct, and I have to admit there would be so much satisfaction in murdering my lying, cheating husband, but then the police would be bound to suspect me, and that would never do. So, maybe incriminating him for my crimes is a better idea. That way he'll pay for what he's done to me, everyone will feel sorry for me, and I'll be free of him; free to start again somewhere else, my conscience clear.

The only problem is, how to go about it?

My head genuinely starts to throb as I run through the possible scenarios, the ways in which I could implicate him, throw the blame in his direction, rather than my own. Thanks to him and his affairs, it's complicated, and I need time…

But then, thinking about it, I have time. I have a few days at least, so there's no need to rush. I can't afford to. I need to make sure I work out my plan properly, so that I don't get it wrong and end up shining too much light on myself.

I turn over and face the closed door, knowing there's no way he'll come up to check whether I'm all right, or if I need anything. He's probably relieved I'm out of the way.

"I'll make you pay," I whisper, resting my head into the pillow and smiling to myself.

———◆———

Thompson comes back into my office, having enlisted the help of Adams and Wells in discovering the identification of the men detailed in Mildred's diaries.

"They're going to go and see the church warden," he says, sitting down in front of me again.

"You did tell them not to reveal why we want to know who those men are, didn't you?" I ask, sitting forward.

"Of course. I may be slow, but I'm not *that* slow."

"You're not slow," I remark and she smiles. "But I do have another job for you."

"Oh yes?"

"Can you see if you can find out who Mildred's doctor was?"

"I can… I'll ring round. There can't be too many GPs in Thames Ditton."

He leaves my room, and I take the opportunity to read through Doctor Wyatt's report, being as this is the first chance I've had since he delivered it this morning. I'm fairly sure he will have told us all the important information, but it's good to make sure, and to check that I'm up to date on everything, which it seems I am, being as I don't learn anything new from reading through the few pages enclosed in the brown file.

Thompson returns a lot more speedily than I'd anticipated, with a smile on his face and a piece of paper in his hand.

"Doctor Fraser," he announces. "He's in St. Leonard's Road."

I get up and go around my desk, putting on my coat and hat. "Let's go and see what he can tell us."

Thompson follows me out to the car, pulling on his own coat as he does so, and we're just in time to see Wells and Adams leaving the station car park, presumably on their way to interview the church warden about Mildred's diary entries.

"It'll be good to get a result on that," I say, nodding in their direction as Thompson and I climb into the car. "Even if only so we can eliminate everyone else."

"You really are convinced you know who it is, aren't you?"

"Yes."

"Even though you can't exactly put your finger on exactly how it was done?"

"Even then… but if I'm wrong, I'll buy you a pint."

He smirks. "You think you can tear yourself away from Amelie for long enough to drink a whole pint?" he says.

I smile across at him, and reply, "I didn't say I'd have one myself, did I?" and he laughs.

"You really have got it bad, haven't you?"

"I certainly have."

The doctor's house is huge, set a little way back from the road, and has a brass plaque to the right of the door, announcing that this is his surgery, with his hours of business shown underneath his name.

"He knows we're coming," Thompson says, knocking on the door, which is answered promptly by a young woman with deep red hair, freckles and pale green eyes, who's wearing a brown business suit, rather than the usual domestic uniform.

"We're here to see Doctor Fraser," I say to her, showing my warrant card.

"Oh yes… the gentlemen from the police." We're not often referred to as 'gentlemen', but I nod my head and step inside the house at her bidding.

The hallway is quite sparse, other than four chairs, which are lined up against the wall beside the door, but then I suppose this is the doctor's place of business as well as his home and, as the woman closes the door, I glance to my left and notice a door, which is marked 'Private', leading I presume to his personal quarters.

"This way," she says, by-passing the half-open door to our left, through which I can see a desk, on top of which is a telephone and a typewriter. The room – which I gather to be her office – looks out over the front of the house, allowing her to see the comings and goings of the doctor's patients. Knocking on the second door, which is closed, she passes straight through and holds it open for Thompson and I to follow, announcing, "It's the police, Doctor," as she does so.

Inside, the room is comfortably furnished, with an examining couch, two chairs, a large book case, and an antique desk, behind which sits a slim, middle-aged man, with steel grey hair and a slightly darker moustache, dressed in a checked tweed jacket, white shirt and brown tie. He stands upon our entry and holds out his hand.

"Doctor Fraser," he says, introducing himself.

"I'm Detective Inspector Stone,' I reply, shaking his hand. "And this is Detective Sergeant Thompson." The doctor shakes Thompson's hand too, going up in my estimation, unlike so many others, who choose to ignore him. "I apologise for interrupting your day."

"Don't worry," he says, indicating the seats in front of his desk, as the door closes behind us, his secretary departing and leaving us in peace. "When Miss Hayward told me you'd phoned, I knew what it was about." He sits down himself, leans his elbows on the desk and stares at me. "This is to do with Mildred Ryder, isn't it?"

"Yes, sir."

He shakes his head. "Such a bad business," he says, his voice soft and quiet. "And such a lovely girl."

"So I gather."

"I heard about what happened to her on the village grapevine, yesterday evening," he adds, explaining himself. "But then, it's hard to keep anything a secret around here."

"Well, I don't think many people knew Mildred was pregnant," I remark, watching his reaction. He blinks a few times, then lowers his head for a moment, before raising it again, his eyes saddened.

"No… I don't think they did," he says.

"She saw you a few days before her death, I understand?"

"Yes… I had Miss Hayward look up my appointments after your telephone call. Mildred came to see me at twelve-thirty last Wednesday."

I nod my head, recalling the entry in her diary, which tallies exactly. "Did she realise she was pregnant before she came here?"

"She suspected," he replies.

"And yet she waited quite some time before coming to see you," I say, almost to myself. "She was three months gone, I believe."

He sighs. "Yes, she was, but that's not unusual, Inspector. We quite often don't see women until they're three, or even four months along. At the risk of giving you more information than you might want or need, a lot of women don't have a regular cycle. So they don't necessarily notice if they miss a period, or even two, or three."

"And if they do have a regular cycle?" I ask, recalling the crosses in Mildred's diary.

The doctor smiles now, as though I'm an errant child, and he's the patient teacher. "Are you married, Inspector?" he asks.

"Yes. Just."

His smile widens. "Then you'll learn that there are all sorts of reasons why a woman's menstrual cycle can become unbalanced, assuming it was ever balanced in the first place, of course."

"Such as?" I'm intrigued now, on several levels.

"Illness, stress, emotional upheaval…" He lets his voice fade.

"So postponing your wedding might be enough?"

He shrugs "I think Mildred was hoping so, yes." He slowly shakes his head. "Obviously she was wrong, in this instance."

"I see. And how did she react when you told her the news?"

"To start with, she just sat there, right where you are, and didn't say a thing. And then she broke down."

"Is that a normal reaction?" I ask, having no knowledge of such things myself.

He smiles. "With unmarried mothers, it can be. Of course, if they're looking to ensnare a young man into marriage, then their response can be markedly different." He raises his eyebrows for a moment, and then continues, "But that wasn't the case with Mildred."

"She told you it wasn't Sam's baby?" I ask.

"Not in so many words," he replies, sitting back in his chair. "What she said was, 'That's it. He'll never want to marry me now,' which made me think it couldn't be Sam's, because I'm fairly sure he'd have jumped at the chance." He hesitates, tilting his head to one side.

"What is it, Doctor?"

"You realise I can't discuss Sam Higgs with you?" he says and I nod my head. "But what I can tell you is that he came to see me early in December, not long after Mildred had asked him to postpone their wedding. He was concerned that there was something wrong with her."

"Why?" I ask. Sam didn't mention this when we spoke to him, and I'm wondering why that might have been.

"Because Mildred wasn't being herself. That's what he said, anyway. He was understandably upset and frustrated about the wedding at the time, but his main concern was with Mildred. He said she seemed distant. He used the word 'remote'."

"I see. And what did you tell him?"

"I suggested that he try to get Mildred to come and see me. I couldn't diagnose her, or even advise them, without seeing her."

"Did she come and see you?"

"Not then, no. The next time I saw her was when she came last Wednesday."

"Oh."

He shrugs his shoulders. "I don't know whether Sam tried to persuade her and failed, or whether he decided to leave it and see what happened."

"And when you say he was upset and frustrated, do you think he'd have done anything... stupid, shall we say?"

"Sam? Good God, no," he exclaims, then pauses, thinking. "Sam loved Mildred very much, Inspector," he says at last. "I don't think I've ever seen a couple so well suited as they were. He wouldn't have cheated on her, if that's what you're thinking, no matter how frustrated he was. And he wouldn't have hurt her either." I can't help smiling as I nod my head, and the doctor smiles back. "You'd worked that out about Sam for yourself, had you?" he asks.

"Well, something along those lines, yes." I sit forward. "So, were you surprised by Mildred's pregnancy?"

"Stunned," he says, narrowing his eyes.

"Have you remembered something?" I ask, recognising the signs.

"Yes," he replies softly, getting up and coming around the desk, standing directly in front of me. "She... she took a while to calm down after I'd given her the news, and then once it became clear that the baby wasn't Sam's, because of her comment about him not wanting to marry her anymore, I stood here, where I am now, and asked her outright who the father was."

"What did she say?" I'm holding my breath in anticipation now.

"She stared at me for ages, and then she shook her head and said she couldn't tell me, and burst into tears again."

I want to swear, loudly, but then I suppose an actual name was too much to hope for. And in any case, I think the doctor would have told us before now, if he'd known.

"Did she say anything at all after that?" I ask.

"Yes. I—I was trying to calm her down," he explains, "and I said to her that she didn't have to tell me, but that she ought to tell the man concerned... whoever he was. She refused to start with, becoming almost hysterical at the prospect, but I reasoned with her, that it was his responsibility. She stopped crying then, rather suddenly, and I'm fairly sure she said, 'It is, isn't it? It's his fault', although it was hard to tell exactly what she was saying, because she only whispered that part, and she was still very upset, but I'm almost certain that was it, and then she got up and left. I followed her out, telling her to come and see me again in a couple of days, but I don't know whether she even heard me. It was like she was in a trance, Inspector."

"I'm going to ask you something now, Doctor," I say, much more seriously. "And I want you to think carefully about your answer. I'm also going to ask you to treat this part of our conversation in the strictest of confidence."

"I'm treating every part of our conversation in the strictest of confidence," he replies, leaning back on his desk and folding his arms.

"Good." I smile up at him. "You knew Mildred Ryder quite well, I take it?"

"Yes. I brought her into this world," he replies.

"So, do you think she's the sort of girl who would have been unfaithful to Sam?"

He shakes his head at once. "Absolutely not," he says, unfolding his arms and pushing his fingers back through his hair. "And, to be honest, that's been worrying me since I heard about her murder. I mean, it was troubling me before, but I'd hoped to be able to see her again, to talk things through with her and find out exactly what had gone on…" His voice fades.

"You think she was raped?" I ask and he blanches.

"That's a strong word, Inspector."

"It's the only word we have. If she didn't give her consent and willingly have sexual relations with whoever the man was, then she was raped. Legally, that is the definition… morally, that is the definition. There's no dressing it up because the consequences might be unpleasant."

"No, I know," he replies, going back around the desk and flopping into his chair. "The problem is that this is a small village and the list of suspects isn't exactly lengthy. And I know them all. It's personal, Inspector, however you look at it."

"I'm aware of that, Doctor. But you can leave the suspects to me. I just need your professional opinion."

"Well, obviously the event itself took place too long ago for me to be medically certain," he says, frowning. "But in terms of Mildred's personality, coupled with her reactions when I told her of her condition, I'd be willing to wager a month's income that she didn't give her consent to whatever took place."

"In other words, it is your view – albeit not a medical one – that Mildred Ryder was raped."

He pauses, lets out a sigh, and then nods his head.

By the time Thompson and I get back to the station, it's nearly five and there's no sign of either Adams or Wells anywhere. The prospect of churning things over and over for the next hour or so doesn't appeal, especially as I don't think we've got anything new to say, despite our visit to the good doctor. All he's really done is confirm my suspicions, but there's not a lot we can do about that tonight.

"I'm going home," I announce, not bothering to take off my hat and coat. "I've had enough today." It's been one of those days, and this is one of those cases… and at the moment, I'm not sure we're getting very far. We're nowhere near close enough to being able to make an arrest, even if I do think I know who's responsible for Mildred's death. Knowing it and proving it are two different things and I'm a long way from being able to prove my theories.

"This wouldn't have anything to do with a need to get back to your wife, would it?" he suggests.

"No comment."

"I don't think you need to comment," he replies, smirking. "It's written all over your face."

"What is?"

"That you should have left here five minutes ago, instead of standing around talking to me," he says. "I'll see you tomorrow, Rufus."

I wish him goodnight and go straight back down the stairs again. My car is parked in the corner, but I can manoeuvre it out of the parking space and I set off home, looking forward to seeing Amelie again after the day I've had, and wondering how she's been faring with the cottage pie. I resolve to myself that I'm going to praise it to the hills, regardless of how it tastes, because I know how much it means to her… and when I've done that, I'm going to take her to bed.

I let myself into the house, which is in darkness, shutting the door behind me and checking that the curtains and blackout are closed before I turn on the light and remove my hat and coat, placing them on the hook behind the door. Taking off my jacket, I leave it over the back of the sofa, calling out a loud, "Hello," to Amelie as I do.

"I'm in here," she replies, her voice coming from the kitchen, and I make my way through, keeping my fingers crossed that this evening goes better than Saturday did – at least in terms of her attempt at cooking, anyway.

I pass through the dining room, where the table is already laid, and follow the lovely smells that are emanating from the kitchen, discovering my beautiful wife, who is standing, leaning with her hip against kitchen sink, looking rather pleased with herself. She's wearing her brown wide-legged trousers and a thick beige sweater, and she looks utterly adorable, as ever. I know men are supposed to find their wives more appealing in tight fitting, more revealing outfits, but for myself, I find this kind of casual attire much more enticing.

Before I even have the chance to walk over to her, however, she takes a couple of steps towards me, and throws her arms around my neck, leaning up and kissing me deeply, her fingers knotting in my hair, her body pressed hard against mine.

After a few minutes, she leans back again, her cheeks flushed, and her breathing uneven.

"What was that for?" I ask, holding onto her waist.

"It was because I've had a good day," she replies, smiling, "and because I love you, of course."

"I'm glad to hear it." I lean down and kiss her.

"Which part?" she asks.

"Both… and I have to say that dinner smells delicious."

She grins, her eyes lighting up. "I think I might actually have cooked something edible," she says, resting her hands on my chest and and looking up into my eyes. "I've just put the cottage pie into the oven, but your mother's recipe says it'll only take half an hour."

"Oh, that's good… I can think of all sorts of things we can do for half an hour."

I lean down and kiss her again, much harder this time, her moans soon filling the room, until she pulls back, chuckling. "There is just one thing…" she says softly.

"Hmm… what's that?" I kiss her neck, working my way up to her ear and she shudders in my arms.

"Could you take the rubbish out first?"

I lean back. "Seriously?"

She nods her head, smiling. "Yes."

"You want me to take the rubbish out? Now?"

"Yes. I've wrapped it up in newspaper, but it's a bit smelly and I don't want it in the house."

I shake my head, still holding her. "And this can't wait until after dinner?"

"No." She breaks free of my grip and goes over to the draining board, picking up a newspaper-wrapped parcel, and bringing it back to me, her nose wrinkled in disgust. "There you go," she says.

"Thanks." I shake my head at her. "You're a tease, you know that, don't you?"

"Well, they say anticipation is half the fun," she replies, her eyes twinkling.

"Do they?" I go over to the back door, flicking off the light before opening it. "Well, whoever 'they' are, they obviously haven't met you, because trust me, the anticipation is killing me."

She laughs out loud as I go outside and down the pathway at the side of the kitchen and bathroom, which leads into the garden, where the dustbin is kept at the end, by the rear gate. I've only taken a few steps, when I regret removing my jacket. It's chilly out here and I quicken my pace, looking up at the starlit sky, then back down again so as not to lose my footing on the path, which is a little uneven.

"What the…?" I stop in my tracks. Even in the moonlight I can see the changes in the garden. I can see that our tiny patch of lawn has disappeared, and been replaced by a pile of earth, all dug over. I frown, holding my breath and then slowly make my way down to the dustbin, depositing the newspaper parcel, before walking back, ignoring the icy wind that's biting through my shirtsleeves.

"Well?" Amelie's voice catches me unawares and I look up and can just about make her out, standing at the corner of the house, by the bathroom wall.

I move closer to her, so I can see her face more clearly.

"Who did this?" I ask, turning back to look at the dug-up garden again.

"I did, of course," she replies, smiling. "What do you think?"

"You did this? By yourself?" She nods her head. "Why?" I ask, trying desperately to stay calm.

"So we can plant vegetables." She gives her answer as though I'm the one being dense around here, even though it's not me who's been digging over frozen ground in early February for no good reason.

"But I still don't understand why."

"Really, Rufus?" Her smile has faded now and she turns, going back into the house. I follow, closing the kitchen door behind us, and switching on the light.

"Yes, really," I say, facing her. "The ground must have been frozen solid. I don't understand why you didn't wait. It's not like you can plant anything outside in February anyway, so why take risks with your health digging it over now, when you could have waited until the weather warms up, or better still, you could have just asked me to do it. You might have hurt yourself."

She shakes her head. "Now you're just being ridiculous."

"Am I?"

"Yes." She glares at me, raising her voice. "Why are you being like this? I have precious little to do around here, and when I actually find something to occupy myself, you try to stop me? Don't you want me to have a life of my own any more, Rufus?"

"Of course I do," I shout, losing my temper. "But I don't understand why you would do something so reckless... so downright stupid."

"Stupid? You're calling *me* stupid?" She opens her mouth to say something else and then snaps it closed again, and before I can comment further, she storms from the room, and within moments, I hear her footsteps echoing up the stairs.

In an instant, I'm jolted back to that evening, just a couple of months ago, when she found out about her guardian's mistress, and more importantly, that I'd known of her existence and hadn't shared that information. At the time, Amelie said she felt she couldn't trust me. She broke off our relationship and ran out of the sitting room in her uncle's house and up the stairs. I can still hear the sound of her footsteps, and I can remember vividly the feeling of my heart shattering in my chest.

I don't pause. I don't hesitate, not even for a second. I take off after her, because I'm not going to let her run from me, not this time, regardless of whether she's upset, or angry. I'll face whatever I have to face, rather than let her run from me. And taking the stairs two at a time, I clatter through our bedroom door, where I find Amelie sitting in the middle of the bed, with her back to me, her shoulders revealing the tension in her body.

"Oh, darling… I'm so sorry." I go straight to her, kneeling up behind her and putting my arms around her. "What have I done to you?" I pull her back into me and cradle her gently. "I'm sorry," I repeat. "Please forgive me." I feel awful. I feel desperate, and I cling to her, like the life-raft that she is.

"W—Why did you say those things?" she mutters, twisting around and looking up at me. She doesn't seem to be angry any more. If anything, she looks disappointed. And I think that's worse.

"Because I'm the one who's stupid," I reply honestly. "Not you. I just wanted to protect you, that's all. Only… only I went about it the wrong way."

She looks up at me. "Don't you see? Can't you understand? It's nothing like I expected it to be… I'm so bored, Rufus…"

"With me?" I can hear the fear in my own voice, and I'll admit she's starting to blur.

"No, not with you. And not with being married to you either, before you ask. But… well, I suppose there was so much going on before the wedding, and prior to that I had my job to keep me busy, and now I can't seem to find anything to do to occupy my time. And when I do, you try and stifle it out of me."

"I'm so sorry, darling," I manage to say through the lump in my throat, my voice cracking. "I never meant to stifle you."

She reaches up, touching my cheek, her eyes searching mine now. "Oh, Rufus," she says eventually. "I'm the one who's sorry." I shake my head, but she stops me, holding my chin. "You're not stifling me," she adds firmly. "I shouldn't have said that. It was wrong of me. You've never tried to stop me from doing anything, and I shouldn't have suggested that you do. And in any case, you're quite right, the ground was really hard, and... and I don't suppose there is anything much we can plant in February." She sighs deeply. "It... it's just that I was so fed up today, and I wanted something to do. I—I thought you'd be pleased."

"Oh God... and now I've spoiled it."

She shakes her head. "No, you haven't. I overreacted. That's all."

She stares into my eyes for what feels like forever, and then leans closer, and closer still, her lips finally brushing against mine. Within seconds, our tongues are clashing, her fingers in my hair and mine in hers, and then she starts to pull on my tie, as I roll her onto her back and reach down to undo the button at the side of her trousers...

I hold her naked body in my arms, still getting my breath back, as is she, our clothes scattered across the bed and around the room, to wherever we threw them.

"As much as I enjoyed that," I murmur, stroking her dishevelled hair, "and as much as it seems I like making up with you, I never want us to argue again. Ever. No amount of making up is worth seeing that disappointed look on your face."

I turn her onto her back again and raise myself above her, nestling into that perfect cradle between her legs. "If you're thinking about saying sorry to me again, then don't," she says, resting her hands on my arms and gazing up at me.

"I wasn't," I reply and she tilts her head to one side, proving that she knows me far too well. "All right, I was. But only after I've told you that I never want to hurt you again. I only ever want to make you happy... that's my job."

She smiles. "You do make me happy, Rufus. Honestly."

She leans up, kissing me and I deepen the kiss, needing her again.

"Oh Christ!" She shifts to one side and I raise my arm, only just managing not to collapse on her.

"What's wrong?"

She moves out from beneath me, and slides off the bed. "The dinner! It'll be ruined."

I roll onto my side, watching as she darts around the room, gathering up her clothes.

"What are you doing?" I ask her, trying not to laugh.

"I'm trying to get dressed," she replies, her underwear getting twisted as she tries to pull it on in a hurry, almost tripping herself up in the process. That's all it takes for me to burst out laughing.

"Why are you bothering?" I ask, sitting up on the edge of the bed and looking up at her.

"Because I need to go downstairs to see if I can rescue our dinner. We've been up here for… how long?"

"About forty-five minutes, I should think."

"Oh no. Really? Forty-five minutes?" She goes to bend down, but I get there first, kneeling before her. "Now, what are *you* doing?" she asks.

"Preventing you from falling over your underwear," I reply. "And worshiping at your feet." I plant a kiss on her flat stomach, then another an inch lower, and another, and another, moving further down each time. She sucks in a sharp breath, her hand on the back of my head.

"Stop!" she cries, breathless, and I pull back, gazing up at her. "If you start that, we'll never have dinner at all."

"And that's a bad thing?" I ask.

"Well, it might be, depending on how burnt the cottage pie is."

"Don't worry. The cottage pie will be fine…" I get to my feet. "Now, about you getting dressed…"

"What about it?"

"Well, who said you had to put your clothes on in order to eat dinner?"

"You want me to eat dinner naked?" She's staring at me now, wide eyed.

"Well, you can if you want… or there's a perfectly good pyjama top of mine lying on your pillow. You could just put that on, couldn't you?"

She looks at me for a moment and then, without saying a word, she reaches over and grabs the pyjama top, shrugging it on. I take a step closer. "Don't do it up on my account," I murmur, my hands resting on her hips.

"And what are you going to be wearing while I'm semi naked?" she asks.

"What do you want me to wear?"

She thinks for a second – no longer – before she walks over to the chest of drawers and bends down, giving me the most perfect view in the world, and opens the bottom drawer, pulling something out, and standing again. She turns, and walks back, her eyes fixed on mine, my pyjama bottoms in her hand.

"These," she whispers, biting her lip.

"Just these?" She nods her head, blushing and I capture her chin with my hand, kissing her just briefly. "If that's what you want, my love."

"It is," she says and does up a single button on the pyjama top she's wearing, leaving the others very temptingly undone, and once I'm dressed in the manner of her choosing, I follow her down the stairs, grateful that we seem to have made up after my stupid comments, although I still feel guilty for having made them in the first place.

"This is fabulous," I tell Amelie, for probably the third time, on only about my fifth mouthful.

"You're not just saying that?" She stares at me from across the table, dragging her eyes up from my bare chest, to my face, a rather absent-minded smile crossing her lips.

"No, I'm not just saying that." I'm really not. Her cottage pie truly is extremely tasty.

"If there's something wrong with it, you can tell me," she says, taking a forkful herself. "I won't take offence, I promise."

"There's nothing wrong with it. Nothing at all. It really is good. It's very good indeed." I reach across the table for her hand, which she places in mine. "Well done, darling."

She gives me the most perfect smile. "Well, you ought to be congratulating your mother, really."

"Why? She didn't cook this. You did."

"I followed her recipe, that's all."

"Stop putting yourself down." I lower my fork to the plate, letting it rest on the side, and focus on her, trying not to be distracted by the way my pyjama top gapes open on her, most revealingly. "Cottage pie is one of my favourite dinners, and that means I know a good one from a bad one… and this is a good one. It's a very good one. You can make this again any time you like."

"Well, I'm not making it tomorrow," she replies.

"You're not?" I'm almost disappointed.

"No. Tomorrow, I'm going to make a stew."

I let out a sigh of satisfaction and lean forward, raising her fingers to my lips, kissing them gently. "Will you marry me?" I say and she giggles.

"I thought you'd never ask," she replies, rather sweetly.

Despite the way our evening ended, when I wake up this morning, my first thoughts and feelings are of guilt and regret over the way I behaved last night. My motives may well have been sound, or even honourable – at least in my own head – but the way I went about delivering my message was nothing short of overbearing and pompous, and as for losing my temper… it was inexcusable. I lie on my side, looking at my beautiful sleeping wife, and I know it's going to take me a while to forgive myself for the things I said, and for raising my voice to her.

I'm aware of time moving on, however, and I lean down and kiss Amelie awake, tracing a delicate line across her lips with my tongue and smiling as she shudders, even though her eyes are still tightly shut.

"Good morning," she murmurs, and my smile becomes a grin.

"I know you'd probably rather I went to make you a cup of tea, but do you think you could forego it this morning, and bathe with me instead?" I plead and she opens her eyes now, gazing up at me.

"You want me to?"

"Of course." It's not something we've done since we returned from our honeymoon, and while I know it's only been a few days, I want to try and recapture some of that magic. No… I *need* to. After the way I spoke to her yesterday, I need to reassure myself that Amelie still loves me as much as I love her.

"Then lead the way," she says, and with one final kiss, I get out of bed and hold out my hand to her.

"Um… we don't have any clothes on," she remarks, staring at me for a moment.

"So? All the curtains are still closed. No-one can see us."

"No, I don't suppose they can," she replies and takes my hand, letting me pull her out of bed and into my arms, where I hold her close to me, kissing her. "We should probably get a move on," she says, when I eventually release her.

"Probably," I reply, caressing her cheek with my fingertips and marvelling that she puts up with me, because I'm not sure I would.

"Are you all right?" she asks, tilting her head.

"Yes."

"You're not, are you?"

"No."

She sits back down on the edge of the bed, pulling me with her.

"Tell me what's wrong," she says softly, her voice soothing my nerves.

"I still feel guilty about yesterday… about the things I said to you."

"Oh, Rufus…" She rests her head on my shoulder and lets out a sigh. "There's no need. We talked about it last night, didn't we?"

"Yes. But the thing is, I still feel awful about it. I was so… so…" I search for the right word.

"Bossy?" she offers, smiling.

"Yes. Bossy." It's the perfect description of my behaviour.

She turns to face me, looking up into my eyes. "So what if you were? I deserved it, and I don't want you to feel guilty," she whispers.

I caress her cheek with my fingertips. "What do you want?"

"I want you to take me downstairs and remind me how much fun a bath can be."

"With pleasure, Mrs Stone." I kiss the tip of her nose, then stand and hold out my hand to her once more, wishing that, in spite of her reassurance, I didn't still feel so ashamed.

*

Breakfast has been a very hurried affair this morning, but that's because we took a lot longer in the bath than either of us anticipated, even though we were restricted to using the rather paltry regulatory amount of water. It was fun sharing it though. So much fun, that Amelie hasn't had time to get dressed yet and is only wearing her dressing gown at the breakfast table, and absolutely nothing else.

"What are you doing today?" I ask her to distract myself from the thought of her nakedness beneath her simple robe, as I gulp down my tea, and then wish I hadn't said that. I don't feel as though I have the right to interfere in what she does now, not having been so tyrannical about the way she passed her time yesterday.

"Once I've got dressed, I'm going to see your mother," she replies, seemingly unaware of my discomfort as she concentrates on spreading a thin layer of butter across her toast.

"You are?"

"Yes." She looks up at me now, smiling. "Don't you remember? I told you, I'm making a stew tonight. Your mother said she'd tell me how to make it, so I telephoned her yesterday and arranged to pop down there this morning, before I go to the butcher's."

"That all sounds very organised."

"Tell me that when I've made the stew," she remarks.

I sit and watch her, wondering to myself whether she told my mother of her plan to dig the garden yesterday, and whether she'll reveal my reaction when I got home. I hope she doesn't, although I wouldn't blame her if she did. I would completely understand her need to talk to someone about what happened, and I suppose my mother is the obvious choice, given that – apart from Amelie – there isn't a soul alive who knows me better. But the thing is, I know my mother quite well too, and that means I know that, if Amelie does tell her what I did last night, and the way I behaved towards her, my mother will make my life a living hell. I'm already in purgatory as it is, re-living my mistakes. I don't need my mother's criticism, no matter how well-deserved it might be. Even so, I'm not going to ask Amelie to keep things to herself. If she wants to talk to my mother, then so be it… I'll deal with the consequences. They'll be well deserved, after all.

"You need to eat up," she says, eyeing my half eaten toast. "You've only got a few minutes until you have to leave."

She's quite right, although I wish I could stay, and I wolf down the last of my breakfast, swallowing my lukewarm tea between mouthfuls.

Amelie comes to the door with me, and I kiss her on the threshold, holding her close to me.

"Have a good day," she says. "And I'll endeavour to make you an edible stew for your dinner tonight."

"I don't care whether it's edible or not," I reply, "just promise you love me."

She doesn't answer me, but leans up and kisses me quickly on the lips. "There. No, off you go, or you'll be late."

It's only as I'm driving into Kingston that it dawns on me that, since we got out of the bath, she's been very matter-of-fact, very efficient, and perhaps less romantic than the last couple of days; there was no suggestion of sitting on my lap over breakfast, even though she was barely dressed. There were no comments about going back to bed. And then I realise that she didn't say she loved me when I asked her, and for some reason, that *really* bothers me.

In the main office, Wells and Adams are talking to Thompson, but I don't feel like joining them. I don't feel like talking to anyone at the moment, and I go straight into my office, hanging up my coat and hat and sitting down in my chair, my elbows resting on the desk, my head on my upturned hands. When I last sat here, yesterday afternoon, everything seemed right and perfect, and now I feel as though I have the weight of the world on my shoulders.

"Is everything all right, Rufus?" Thompson comes into my room, but keeps his voice low and quiet, even though only Adams and Wells, and two other men are present in the outer office.

"Yes, everything's fine," I reply. I know I could tell him what happened. I know he'd listen and probably have some sound advice, but there's only one person I want to talk to at the moment, and she's not here. "What's going on?" I nod toward the outer office, in the hope he'll get the message.

He stares at me for a moment and I know he's not convinced, but he understands me well enough not to push and comes over, sitting in front of me. "Wells and Adams spent most of yesterday afternoon with Clifford Lacey," he says, still looking concerned, but focusing on the business side of our relationship, not the personal one.

"Who's Clifford Lacey?" I ask, sitting forward and taking a breath, trying to concentrate.

"He's the church warden at St. Nicholas'," he replies. "Wells and Adams called round at his house, which is in Church Lane, and explained that they needed him to identify some names from Mildred Ryder's diaries. They didn't go into any more detail than that, even though Mr Lacey was quite inquisitive, evidently."

"I'm sure he was," I muse. "And was he able to help?"

"Yes, he was. He provided surnames for most of the entries, and explained that almost all of them were in the choir, or church congregation. He pointed out that the vicar's name was in there, which none of us had noticed, and there were a few that caused confusion… you know, common names, like Andrew, or David, where Mr Lacey said he couldn't be completely sure who the person was, but we've got about fifteen, I think, who have been positively identified."

"That's good," I remark, without much enthusiasm. "Now I suppose we just need to find their addresses?"

"Yes." Thompson nods his head. "Mr Lacey knew some of them, and tried to guess at others, which wasn't very useful."

"No. I think it's best if we double check all the addresses before we go knocking on the wrong doors."

"I agree," he says, glumly.

"You can leave Adams and Wells doing that, can't you?" I suggest.

"Of course. Why? Are we going somewhere?"

"Yes. We're going to the Conroy house. Remember? I want to try our little experiment."

"Oh yes," he says. "I'll go and speak to Wells, while you put your coat back on."

I glance up to see him looking at me, still with a concerned expression on his face, but he doesn't say any more and simply leaves the room, while I get up and slowly go back over to the door, shrugging on my coat and taking my hat in my hand, before following him out.

Our journey to Thames Ditton has been silent, which I think is because Thompson isn't sure what to say to me, and in a way, I wish he had, because all I've done is think... and that hasn't proved to be very helpful at all, since all I can think about is Amelie, and our morning, and why it felt so different to every other morning so far. I'll admit that we've only shared a few mornings together since becoming husband and wife, but that doesn't mean we haven't developed a few little habits and routines, all of which I thoroughly enjoy, but which today didn't seem to be there.

"We're here," Thompson announces, and I glance out of the window to find he's already parked the car outside the Conroy property.

"Yes."

"Are you sure you're all right?" he asks again.

"Positive," I say and get out of the car.

He follows, even though I can tell he doesn't believe me in the slightest, and comes around to my side of the car, joining me on the pavement.

"As the senior officer – and ex-smoker," he says quietly, "I suppose you're going to be the one who stands here timing things, while I do the running around?"

"Well, walking to start with," I point out. "We have to allow for the fact that the murderer could have been a woman... in this instance, probably Mrs Wharton, and that she was almost certainly wearing high heels."

"You want me to pretend to be wearing high heels?" he jokes, but I've lost my sense of humour today.

"No. Just walk at a reasonable pace. Don't run. When you get to the site of the murder, allow yourself a minute to perform the stabbing, and then walk back."

He nods his head and after I've checked my watch, he sets off, while I stand outside the Conroy's gate and imagine myself lighting and smoking a cigarette – a pastime which I only gave up a couple of months ago.

As I pace up and down, I'm aware of someone watching, and turn to see Mrs Conroy standing at the living room window. She moves away the moment our eyes make contact, but I know she saw me.

"Well?" Thompson says, walking back up to me a few minutes later, and I glance back down at my watch again.

"A few seconds shy of five minutes," I reply.

"Okay. What next?"

"Now, try it running… not at full pelt, because the murderer would probably realise that running too fast would attract attention, but just run at a gentle pace."

"You're too kind," he jests, and sets off again, this time much more quickly than before.

While he's gone, I keep half an eye on the Conroy property, although the lady of the house doesn't return to the living room window at all, and Thompson comes back in three minutes and forty-five seconds.

"It's do-able, isn't it?" he says, barely needing to catch his breath.

"Very," I reply.

"So either of the Whartons could have murdered Mildred during one of their solitary cigarette breaks and not been missed from the party."

"Yes, it looks that way," I muse. "That would mean it would have been one of them that she'd arranged to meet after choir practice, because they wouldn't have had the time to wait around for her."

"No," he says. "But that's perfectly feasible, especially if the man who'd raped her was Wharton."

"Yes. He'd have wanted to keep that quiet and might well have agreed to a clandestine meeting in the churchyard, rather than risk seeing her at his own house, and have his wife overhearing anything untoward."

"The same thing applies to Mrs Wharton," Thompson remarks. "If he'd raped Mildred and she'd found out about it."

I let out a sigh, the web of confusion becoming more tangled with every discovery.

"I don't—"

"Shh," Thompson interrupts and nods towards the Conroy house, and I turn and see Mrs Conroy walking down the path towards us.

"What's going on?" she says, her arms folded across her chest.

"Nothing," I reply.

She tilts her head, and looks at me with a condescending air. "We both know that's not true, Inspector. You've been wandering up and down for the last ten or fifteen minutes, and your sergeant has been dashing backwards and forwards. So something's going on."

"It's just a procedural matter," I say dismissively.

She stares at me, and I stare back, and eventually she backs down, unfolding her arms and leaning on the garden gate. "How's the investigation going?" she asks.

"It's progressing," I lie, because at the moment, I really don't feel as though it is.

"I telephoned Norman yesterday morning," she says quite boldly. "At his office, obviously. But his secretary told me he was busy, which was a pity." I know what he was busy with as well... or rather who, and I wonder for a moment how Susan Conroy would feel about Norman's flirtation with Ethel.

"You could have tried him at home in the evening, couldn't you?" I suggest, simply because I'm intrigued by what response I'll get.

"Good Lord, no," she replies, giving me a disapproving glance before she looks down at the pavement between us. "Lucy might have answered."

"Well, I imagine she might, considering it's her house," I point out.

"Yes, but she always makes things so awkward," she says, with a slightly whining tone to her voice.

"Oh?" I don't say any more, because I have a feeling Susan Conroy is bursting to reveal her story to me anyway, without any prompting on my part.

"Yes," she says, smiling up at me. "You see, before his marriage, Norman and I had a thing together."

"A 'thing'?" I query, acting ignorant.

"An affair," she qualifies, but I continue to stare at her, as though I don't understand. "We were lovers," she says eventually.

"Oh… I see."

"Hmm," she says. "Well, unfortunately Lucy is very tiresome about the whole situation. She's incredibly jealous and childish, and simply won't accept that Norman and I have this rather special friendship as a result of what's gone on in the past."

"And your husband doesn't mind your 'special friendship'?" I ask.

"Laurence understands," she says, and I wonder to myself whether Laurence gets any choice in the matter. It dawns on me then though that maybe Laurence Conroy doesn't know. If I remember rightly, Mrs Wharton explained that Mr Conroy was away at university when his future wife and Mr Wharton were seeing each other, so perhaps he remains blissfully ignorant of their involvement… or maybe he does understand and turns a blind eye. Or perhaps he's less than faithful himself, and can hardly criticise his wife for something he's doing himself… God, I'm getting cynical…

"Well, we must get on," I say, quickly touching the brim of my hat in farewell, and climbing into the car before she can say anything to stop us.

Thompson follows me and starts the engine, pulling away from the kerb, before he says, "She's trouble."

"Only so as you'd notice," I reply.

"If you're asking my opinion – which I know you're not, but I'm going to tell you anyway – there's nothing she'd like more than to resume her relationship with Mr Wharton."

I shrug my shoulders. "Well, now her husband is away on active duty, she might get the opportunity."

"If she hasn't already taken it," he ponders, stopping at the end of the road to wait for a passing lorry. "Wharton doesn't deserve to be married," he says, once we're under way again.

"No, he doesn't," I agree, but then fall silent, wondering whether he's not the only one.

Chapter Ten

I'm really not in the mood for this, but it has to be done…

The monthly parish lunch is a regular feature and most of the time, I look forward to it, because it's something the WI organises and it's nice to feel that I'm giving something back to the local community. It's an event I've attended without fail, for the last five years, ever since it's inception, because not only does it foster a sense of neighbourliness, it also alleviates the boredom of another day spent by myself, and it gets me out of the house for an hour or two. Even so, today, I'd much rather give it a miss. Not that I can, of course, because my absence would be bound to be noticed, being as I'm now on the lunch committee, and the last thing I need is to become the focus of the village gossips.

Today, they're going to be worse than usual, given that Mildred's murder is bound to be the main topic of conversation and I have no doubt that the village busy-bodies will have no shortage of ideas as to who's responsible. I'm sure they'll have come up with their own ludicrous theories as to why she was murdered, and how, and I know it's going to take all my self control not to correct them, or point out the obvious errors in their conjectures. Because there will be errors, trust me. And that's something I suppose I ought to be grateful for… not that I feel particularly grateful for anything at the moment.

I touch up my hair in the mirror, and try not to think about my plan. Well, I don't actually have a plan at the moment, and that's the problem… the more I think about it, the harder it gets to work out exactly how I'm going to incriminate my husband in my crime. I know beyond a shadow of a doubt that I need to, that implicating him is the best solution to all my problems, but finding the best method is proving a lot harder than I thought it would.

Still, I'll think about that later. For now, I need to paint a smile on my face and go to this luncheon. I'll keep an ear open to see what the village thinks is going on, to see if there's anything that might come in useful – although I doubt it – and then I'll come back here and concentrate on my plan once more.

I pick up my handbag from beside the hall table and let myself out of the front door, finding it hard not to smile to myself as I wonder what the gossips would say if they knew the truth.

———◆———

"Back to the station?" Thompson asks, when it becomes clear I'm not going to say anything else. Making comparisons between myself and Norman Wharton isn't helping. And, when all is said and done, while I'm not proud of the way I've behaved I don't think I'm quite in his league.

"No… we need to go and see Mrs Ryder, I'm afraid."

He turns the car onto the High Street. "You're not looking forward to this, are you?" he says.

"Hardly," I reply.

"No…" His voice fades and we continue the drive in silence, pulling up outside Mrs Ryder's house within five minutes.

"I suppose she might be at work," I say, climbing from the car, feeling despondent.

"It's possible. But then we'll just have to come back, won't we?" Thompson is sounding as disheartened as I am now, and I'm perfectly well aware that I'm responsible for that. My own mood is being reflected onto him, but I don't feel as though there's anything I can do about that.

He knocks on the door and we stand together, staring at the wooden panels, a semi-circular stained glass window above, in a decorative floral pattern, both jumping slightly when the door opens to reveal a red-eyed Mrs Ryder. She's still an attractive woman, but she seems to have aged considerably in the last couple of days, which isn't at all surprising.

"Inspector?" she says, her voice faltering.

"Yes, Mrs Ryder."

"You've come about Mildred?"

I nod my head and she steps back, giving us entry to her living room, where I notice a half-drunk cup of tea on the side table, next to the potted plant.

"Can I get you anything?" Mrs Ryder asks, resuming her seat in the chair.

"No, thank you."

"Please sit," she offers, and Thompson and I perch awkwardly on the narrow sofa, which wasn't really made to accommodate two men of our proportions. "I'm supposed to be at work," Mrs Ryder adds unexpectedly, reaching for her tea and taking a sip, "but I can't seem to pull myself together."

"That's understandable," I reply, doing my best to sound sympathetic. I mean, I am sympathetic; I'm just not in the best frame of mind for showing it today.

"Shirley's been covering for me," she continues, as though she hasn't heard me. "I know I ought to be stronger, but..." She lowers her eyes.

I feel even worse now, knowing what we're about to tell her, but I honestly don't see how we can avoid revealing the truth. I doubt there's anything she'll be able to tell us, but I feel that if we delay, there's a chance she'll hear it from someone else.

"I'm afraid I have something to tell you," I begin and she looks up at me, fear crossing her eyes.

"What is it?" she asks.

I take a breath, and then sigh. "I'm sorry, but I have to inform you that Mildred was three months pregnant when she was killed."

For a second or two Mrs Ryder doesn't respond at all, but then her face crumples and she starts to cry, great sobs wracking her body, and for a moment, I consider going to her to see if I can comfort her. But then I realise I have nothing to offer... not in these circumstances. Her grief is simply too profound for anyone to reach her. So, I let her weep, the room filled with the sounds of her anguish.

Eventually, she manages to calm and turns to face us, her eyes filled with anger, rather than sadness, which surprises me.

"Does Sam know?" she says bitterly. "Does he know what he did?"

"He knows, yes, but he denies responsibility."

Her eyes positively flash with rage. "How dare he?" She sits forward in her chair, making me wonder if she's found a new lease of life in her fury, and whether she intends having it out with Sam in person, not that she can, because he'll have already left for the barracks by now. All of a sudden though, she sits back again, deflated. "How could he... I mean, how could *they* be so stupid?" she murmurs and covers her face with her hands. She's not crying now; she seems bewildered and, after a couple of seconds, she lowers her hands again, looking directly at me. "I'm sorry, Inspector, I'm not making much sense, am I?" I don't reply and she continues, "It's just that Mildred assured me they were waiting until they were married. She... she had good reason to, you see..." Her voice fades and she gazes out of the window, avoiding eye contact, I think. Sensing that there's more to come, and that me informing her, again, that Sam had nothing to do with Mildred's condition isn't going to help, I sit in silence and wait, while Thompson shifts in his seat beside me. After less than a minute, Mrs Ryder turns back to face us, her cheeks even paler than they were before. "Mildred was conceived at the end of the last war," she says quietly, "right before Bill was due to be sent to France. Th—there wasn't time to get married, but so many men had gone and not come back... and we both wanted something to remember the other by. We knew it was a risk, but at the time we were young, and we didn't care." She blinks a few times. "I think war does that to people, don't you?" I nod my head and she continues, "Anyway, by the time Bill got out to France, the war was all but over, and he was back home again within a few months, by which time Mildred was already well on the way. I'd written and told him, naturally, and he'd proposed to me in his returning letter." She lowers her eyes again. "I was nearly six months gone when I stood outside that registry office on the arm of my new husband, Inspector, and I thought my mother was going to die of shame... not that Bill and I ever had a moment's regret, you understand. Not one."

"Did Mildred know about this?" I ask.

"Yes. She found out when she was about thirteen. She was a bit shocked at the time, but we didn't talk about it much… not until she and Sam got engaged, and then she vowed she wasn't going to make the same mistake herself, not even if we ended up going to war, which a lot of us thought quite likely, no matter that Mr Chamberlain had been waving bits of paper around just a few months before, and telling us to sleep quietly in our beds… stupid little man." She stops for a second and takes a breath. "That's why this… this pregnancy doesn't make sense…" Her voice fades and I want to tell her that I agree with her. It doesn't make sense, for the very simple reason that it didn't happen like that. But I'm not sure this woman can cope with hearing the whole story yet, not that I know the whole story myself, not in terms of who really is responsible for what happened to Mildred, and I think it's best if Mrs Ryder remains ignorant of the situation until I can tell her everything.

I stand up, making it clear we have nothing further to say. "I'm very sorry, Mrs Ryder… for everything."

She stands too, shaking her head, clearly confused, and leads the way to the front door, opening it. "Thank you for coming to tell me," she replies, which is rather humbling, considering I know how much I've held back.

"Don't think badly of her," I say, because I think it needs saying.

"I don't. Like I say, war makes people do things they wouldn't normally even think about." She sounds so sad, I re-double my resolve to find out who raped Mildred and bring him to justice… no matter who he is.

We're driving along the river before Thompson turns and glances at me. "You decided not to tell her about the rape then?"

"Yes."

"Any reason for that?"

"She'll find out soon enough," I reply. "And being as we can't tell her who's responsible, it seemed cruel to add to her woes…"

"And you think it's all right for her to have misgivings about Mildred and Sam's behaviour, do you?" He sounds cross and I turn in my seat to face him, although he's looking out of the windscreen, concentrating on the road.

"Yes, at the moment, I do. You heard her at the end… she said she doesn't think badly of Mildred, but can you imagine what would happen if we told her Mildred had been raped? She'd be wondering by whom, and how much she'd suffered as a consequence, and why she hadn't noticed any change in Mildred herself… It would be so much worse for her."

"Well, she's going to have to hear about it eventually," he reasons, angrily.

"I know, but at least when she does, we'll be able to tell her who the guilty party is, and hopefully, exactly what happened. There won't be anything for her to mull over and drive herself insane with. And the man will be in custody, so any thoughts she might have of confronting him will come to nothing."

He turns into the station, driving under the archway that leads to the small car park, and pulls up alongside my MG. "I suppose," he says glumly and gets out of the car.

I check my watch and notice that it's nearly a quarter to twelve, before climbing from the car myself.

"Can you manage without me for an hour?" I ask as he walks around the back of the vehicle, heading for the door.

"Yes," he replies, and I wonder if he's relieved at the prospect of my absence, given my foul mood.

"Good." I go straight to my car, looking over the top of it as he stares at me. "I'll be back later."

He nods his head, looking confused, but doesn't reply, and I climb in, starting the engine and reversing out of my parking space.

As I drive back to Molesey, I reason that Amelie should have finished with my mother and the shopping by now, and that we can spend at least half an hour or so talking, because I honestly think I'm going to go mad, if I don't get this off my chest… if I don't tell her how I feel, and how worried – no, scared – I am, since this morning.

I'm in Walton Road within ten minutes, the traffic being light and my right foot being heavy on the accelerator pedal, and am just passing

The Fox public house, when I notice Amelie coming out of School Road, her shopping basket on her arm. She's wearing her navy blue coat and a grey beret on her head, which is bowed down, and she hasn't even glanced in my direction, so I pull over to the side of the road, park the car, and get out, calling to her. She turns, looking around and then her eyes settle on me and although her initial reaction is confusion, a smile quickly forms on her lips, which lightens my leaden heart, and I run across the road to her.

"What are you doing here?" she asks, looking up at me.

I don't reply, not directly anyway, but take her shopping basket from her. "Would you mind if I joined you?"

She tilts her head, still smiling. "Of course not, although I'm not going anywhere exciting... just to the greengrocer's, and the butcher's."

"Then let me walk with you."

She links her arm through mine and we start off down the road, facing into a fairly chilly wind. "Are you going to tell me why you're here?" she asks, after just a few paces.

"To see you," I reply, leaning into her. She looks up and I turn to her, seeing the suspicion in her eyes. "Okay, I'll admit... I've had an absolutely terrible morning."

"Why?" She stops walking, her concern obvious. "What's happened?"

"I can't stop thinking about you."

She frowns. "And that's terrible?"

"It is at the moment, yes."

An old woman walks past, tutting, because we're blocking the pavement, and I pull Amelie aside, closer to the shop window behind us.

"What do you mean?" she says.

"I mean that I still feel guilty about our argument last night. But also... this morning... it was all wrong."

Now she really frowns, to the point where I wonder if she's about to cry. "What was wrong with it?" she says, lowering her voice to a mere whisper. "We had a lovely time in the bath… at least, I thought we did. I thought it was perfect."

"It was," I reply quickly to quell her rising doubt. "That part of the morning was completely perfect. But that's not the part I'm talking about."

"Then I don't understand," she says, leaning back.

"I'm talking about what happened afterwards."

"Afterwards?"

"Yes… you were so detached, so distant over breakfast, and then at the door, when I asked you, you didn't say you loved me."

"Yes I did," she reasons.

"No you didn't. You kissed me and sent me on my way to work."

She shakes her head just slightly, her brow furrowing. "Are you seriously telling me you've come home in the middle of the day because I wasn't quite as talkative as usual over breakfast, and because I didn't say 'I love you' when you asked?"

"Yes. And I know that all makes me sound ridiculously insecure, but the thought of spending another moment in turmoil, worrying about what might be wrong between us was beyond me. Ask Harry… he'll tell you. I've been an absolute bear to work with this morning, and if I'm going to stand a chance of getting anything done today, I knew the only hope I had was to come home and talk it through with you."

She reaches out, placing her flattened palm on my chest. "You need to stop," she says firmly.

"Stop what?"

"All of this. You need to stop feeling guilty about our argument, for one thing."

"Why? I hurt you. I don't like how that makes me feel. And I especially don't like the thought that you ran from me."

"Well, I'm sorry I ran. I shouldn't have done that. It was very childish of me, but you know me well enough to know that I can be childish at times." She smiles up at me, and I try to smile back. "I do understand why you said the things you said," she says calmly, moving closer to me.

"You do?" *I'm* not even sure I understand them, so her statement surprises me.

"Yes. You were trying to protect me, like you always do." Well, that's true enough.

"I know. But I went about it the wrong way. I was overbearing."

"No you weren't. You just didn't express yourself very well, that's all." She leans into me, looking up into my eyes in a very tempting way, forcing me to remember that we're in a public place, as she whispers, "I like being protected by you."

"But not smothered," I say, without thinking.

"You never smother me," she replies, sighing. "You love me."

"Yes, I do. So very much… and I'm sorry."

"I know you're sorry. You've apologised enough and you need to stop that too, and let me apologise for once."

"What on earth for?"

"For this morning," she says. "I'm sorry if you thought I was detached, and I'm especially sorry that I didn't say 'I love you'. I thought I had, but obviously not. The truth is, after we'd finished our bath, I—I… didn't feel all that well…" Her voice fades and I drop the basket to the ground, pulling her into my arms and holding her.

"What's wrong?" I ask. "Why didn't you tell me?"

"Nothing's wrong," she replies, leaning her head on my chest. "I think I'm still just a bit tired and run down, that's all. I feel fine now."

"You need to rest," I tell her, raising her face to mine. "And we need to get to bed earlier."

She leans back, smiling up at me. "I don't think it's the getting to bed that's the issue, do you?" she murmurs.

"No, but I could try being less demanding, and let you get more sleep."

Her face falls. "That's not the problem," she says, biting her bottom lip. "And in any case, I like your demands… although that's not how I see them. And I'm sorry I didn't say I love you when you asked me this morning… I really am. It wasn't consciously done, I promise. I love you so much, Rufus, and I need you all the time. I miss you when you're not with me…" She pauses and looks up into my eyes. "I'm sorry," she mutters. "I'm doing my best."

"Hey…" I cup her face in my hand, the other still holding her close to me. "You're doing an amazing job, but the next time you don't feel well, can you promise to tell me? I've been worried sick all morning…" I stop talking for a moment and decide to be completely honest with her. "Actually, that's not true. I've been absolutely terrified all morning, that I'd done something else wrong, other than hurt you yesterday, that is. I thought I'd done something to lose your love… and if I ever did that, it would break me, Amelie."

I gaze into her eyes and she whispers, "I'm sorry."

"Don't be sorry," I say, brushing my thumb along her bottom lip.

"Then you have to stop being sorry too," she replies, finding her voice.

"Okay… as long as you promise that you're not angry, or upset with me in any way."

She sighs and just stops short of rolling her eyes. "Do you think I could have done what we did last night, and this morning, with quite so much enthusiasm, if I'd been angry or upset with you?"

"No. Probably not."

"There's no 'probably' about it, Inspector."

She's right. There isn't. I know her well enough already to know that she wears her heart on her sleeve. If she'd still been cross with me, there's no way we'd have ended our evening the way we did, and she certainly wouldn't have agreed to bathe with me this morning. She just isn't capable of that kind of pretence.

"So can we stop apologising?" she asks, tilting her head and looking up at me.

"Yes, we can."

She nods her head in satisfaction, and I pull her close to me once more, stroking her hair for a few moments, until she leans back in my arms, looking up at me, a little recovered.

"Now…" she says, her voice a little stronger. "I think it's high time you went back to catching criminals, don't you?"

I smile down at her. "Only after I've helped you with the shopping. You're tired, remember?"

"I'm not that tired." She is. I can hear it in her voice.

"Even so…" I pick up the basket and hold out my arm to her, and without a second's hesitation – I'm pleased to say – she links her hand through and we walk on down the street. "Where to first?" I ask.

"The greengrocer's," she replies. "I'd have gone there straight from your mother's but I neglected to bring a basket… or any money. I'm being so forgetful, I don't know what's the matter with me."

"I think we've already established, haven't we, that you're over tired. Which is why I'm here."

She leans into me. "And I'm very grateful. But are you sure you've got time for this?"

"Positive." I steer us towards the road and wait for a car to pass before we cross to the other side. "And even if I didn't, I'd make time. I told you once, not that long ago, that I would stop time, if I had to, for you."

She looks up into my eyes and sighs, "Yes, you did, didn't you?" and then nestles into me, her head on my shoulder, and we walk on a short distance, arm in arm, until we come to the greengrocer's shop, where I reluctantly let go of Amelie, allowing her to pass through the doorway ahead of me. The owner, a Mr Woods, turns to us as we enter, raising an eyebrow at my presence, but saying nothing.

"What can I get you?" he asks Amelie.

"I need a pound of potatoes," she says quietly, almost as though she's shy of the man, and he turns and starts weighing them, adding one more and tipping them, loose, into the basket.

"And a pound of carrots," Amelie says as he turns back.

He weighs out the carrots, adding them to the potatoes.

"Anything else?" he asks.

"No, I think that's it." Amelie seems uncertain and I recall that she's supposed to be making a stew this evening.

"What about onions?" I suggest and she looks up at me, with a half smile on her lips, before turning back to Mr Woods.

"Do you have a couple of onions?" she asks.

"We do indeed," he replies, giving her a wink, then placing two small onions in the basket and smiling up at me.

"That's everything," Amelie says with confidence and I place the basket on the floor, reaching into my jacket for my wallet. "I've got money," Amelie says quietly. "You gave me some on Saturday, remember?"

"I know, but being as I'm here…" I leave my sentence hanging and lean down, kissing her forehead as I hand the money over to Mr Woods, who's grinning now, looking from me to Amelie and back again, benignly.

Giving back the change, he bids us a warm farewell, and we continue down Walton Road, crossing back over again to get to the butcher's.

"What kind of stew are we having?" I ask Amelie as we approach the shop.

"Your mother said the type of meat didn't really matter," she explains. "And, to be honest, I was rather pleased about that."

"Oh?" I look down at her and she shakes her head, although she's smiling.

"They had me so confused by the time I left," she says.

"About making stew?" I'm confused myself now. I'm not the world's greatest culinary expert, but I've always found stews particularly simple fare.

"About making pastry," she replies and I pull her to a stop.

"Pastry?"

She chuckles. "Yes. We went through the whole process of making the stew, which was really quite straightforward, but then Issa started telling me that the recipe for a meat pie has a similar starting point, and that you can make a stew and then use it to fill a pie, or use leftover stew, if you've got any… which led on to the making of pastry."

"And that was a problem?"

"Yes, because your mother and your aunts couldn't agree on what kind of pastry was best for a meat pie, and then they couldn't agree on how to make it."

"Oh dear…"

"Hello, Inspector!"

I look up at the sound of the male voice that's just beckoned, and am surprised to see the Reverend Hodge and Mr Wharton walking towards us. It's the reverend who's spoken and he has a broad smile plastered on his face.

"Good afternoon," I reply, to be polite.

"I've been visiting with Mr Wharton here," the vicar explains, even though I haven't enquired. "I wanted to make sure he's not been too badly affected by Miss Ryder's death."

That strikes me as particularly odd, considering that, if anyone was going to be 'affected', I would have thought it would have been Mrs Wharton, not her husband… and I'm not sure Mr Wharton would have appreciated a visit from the reverend anyway, being as he's not religious. It seems strange that the man would go all the way over to West Molesey, just to check up on someone who isn't a part of his flock…

"We decided we'd have some lunch together," Wharton adds, which seems equally incongruous.

"Our wives are both at the parish lunch today," the vicar adds. "It's a regular thing and, to be honest, I don't mind in the slightest, being as my wife is a fairly shocking cook." I remember him telling me that yesterday, when Thompson and I visited the vicarage, although he seems to have forgotten himself.

Wharton laughs. "I can't say mine's much better, so any excuse not to go home for lunch at the moment is welcome."

I glare at the two of them, expressionless, noting the exchange of looks between them, before they turn, as one, and stare at Amelie.

"Allow me to introduce my wife," I say, without actually giving her name. To me, it's sufficient that these two men should know her as 'Mrs Stone', and if that seems a trifle possessive, then so be it.

Amelie lets go of me and offers her hand, politely, and the men in front of us step forward, almost grabbing for her, to the point where I take a half step forward myself, while placing an arm around her waist, keeping her close to me. I'm aware of her muscles tensing against me and I tighten my own, just so she knows I'm not letting her go.

Wharton is staring quite openly, his mouth slightly agape. "It's a pleasure to meet you," he croons, and Amelie nods her head. His eyes are alight with desire and I feel my anger rise, in spite of my best efforts to stay calm. The vicar takes his turn, his hand grasping Amelie's, and I struggle not to gasp at the expression on his face, which is one of pure lust. My rising anger threatens to boil over, so before it does, and I end up punching the man, I pull Amelie back slightly.

"I'm afraid we can't stop, gentlemen," I say stiffly.

"Oh, that's a shame," Wharton says, his eyes still fixed on Amelie, although when I glance at Reverend Hodge, I find his silent lechery much more worrisome than his friend's obvious flirtation.

"Well, I'm sure I'll be seeing you both... very soon," I reply, managing to put a soupçon of menace into my voice, sufficient to make them both blanch and return their gaze to me, at least.

"You will?" The reverend says.

"Oh... you can count on it."

Placing my hand on Amelie's elbow, I lead her away, and she looks up at me after we've gone a few yards.

"At least I'm not the only housewife who can't cook," she jokes, her voice sounding a little high pitched and false.

I stop walking and turn to her, cupping her face with my free hand. "I don't care. You have so much more to offer..." I lean down and gently brush my lips against hers, then hold them there, absorbing her into me, until she finally pulls away, glancing first to her left and then her right.

"We're on the street," she says, blushing.

"So what?" I reply, shaking my head. "You're my wife. I'm allowed to kiss you, and in any case, I don't care... unless me kissing you in public makes you feel uncomfortable," I add as an afterthought.

"No, not at all. Although those men did." Her voice drops to a whisper.

"I know."

"The vicar was especially disagreeable. I felt like he was undressing me with his eyes."

I pull her closer, so our bodies are touching. "No-one gets to undress you, except me," I murmur into her ear.

"Good," she breathes back, letting out a sigh. "I'm glad you were here with me."

"I'll always be with you. I'll always keep you safe."

She snuggles into me again, and I turn us, keeping my arm around her, as we continue our walk to the butcher's, our eyes fixed on each other, oblivious to everything and everyone else.

Inside the shop, Amelie studies the various cuts of meat on display. "We had beef yesterday," she muses. "How about mutton?"

"Or we could have rabbit," I suggest, pointing to the display of grey and brown furry creatures hanging upside down behind the counter.

"Rabbit?" She sounds almost afraid and I try not to laugh. "I—I don't think I could skin a rabbit," she says quietly.

"You don't need to, madam." The man behind the counter steps forward, his rotund figure covered with a blue and white striped apron, his red face smiling across at my wife. "We have some already skinned out the back, if you'd like…?"

Amelie glances up at me. "You want rabbit?" she asks.

"Why not?"

"Very well." She turns back to the butcher. "One rabbit, please," she says, then stops and looks back at me again. "Is one enough?"

"One will be fine, darling." I kiss her forehead and give the butcher a nod of my head, whereupon he disappears through a door behind him, returning within moments, carrying a fairly large, skinned rabbit. "Could you portion it for us, please?" I ask and Amelie looks at me. "You don't want to do that, do you?" I check, and she shakes her head quickly.

The butcher grins, but turns away before Amelie notices, and makes quick work of quartering the rabbit, then wraps it in paper and hands it across the counter for Amelie to put into the basket, before I go and pay at the booth to our right, where an older woman is sitting, waiting.

"You realise your mother didn't tell me how to cook rabbit," Amelie says once we're outside again, walking back home, hand in hand.

"Just treat it the same as you would any other meat," I explain. "If you were going to brown the beef, or the mutton, then brown the rabbit, and add the vegetables…"

She nods her head. "Do you think I'll ever get the hang of all this?"

"Of course you will. It just takes practice, that's all."

"Well, I just hope you don't regret your decision," she murmurs.

"In choosing rabbit?" I query.

"No, in marrying me."

I chuckle and grip her hand tighter. "That's one thing I'll never regret."

When we get home, I deposit my hat on the back of the sofa and carry the basket straight through to the kitchen, placing it on the draining board, and then return to Amelie, who's standing in the living room still, staring into space.

"What's wrong, darling?" She looks a little pale and I wonder if she's feeling unwell again.

"Nothing," she replies and I undo the buttons of her coat, easing it from her shoulders and hanging it on the hook behind the door.

"Why don't you sit down for a while?" I suggest.

"I'm fine, Rufus, honestly," she says, coming back to her senses.

"You don't seem fine. You drifted off for a minute then." I rest my hands on her shoulders, gazing at her.

"I know… that's because I've just realised something."

"Oh? What's that?"

"I've just realised how lucky I am." I step closer, moving my hands up and cradling her face instead.

"What's wrong?" I repeat.

"Nothing's wrong… except that I'm grateful for you."

"Grateful?" I query, because that seems like such an odd thing to say.

"Yes." She nods her head, her eyes locking with mine. "Just now, when we met those two men, before we went to the butchers, they looked at me like *I* was a piece of meat… it was uncomfortable."

"I know it was," I reassure her.

"But that's the point," she says quickly, like she's impatient to get her point across. "You knew, maybe even before I did, how nervous those men would make me feel. And that's what makes you so special, because – rather stupidly – I've only just realised how chivalrous you really are. I mean… I've always known it, I suppose, but perhaps I've never appreciated it fully, until now. I've got no experience of other men, you see, or how they behave around women, but I think it's just hit me how lucky I am. And I'm sorry… I'm so sorry I ran from you last night, and that I didn't tell you I how much I love you this morning… because I do, Rufus. I really do love you. P—Please forgive me…"

"There's nothing to forgive… and if I remember rightly, we said we weren't going to keep apologising to each other, didn't we?" She nods her head, just once. "I just want to keep you safe, my love."

"I am safe, because you're here."

I smile down at her. "I'll always be here," I whisper, leaning down and kissing her gently. "But you're wrong about one thing…"

"What's that?"

"I'm the lucky one."

Chapter Eleven

The parish lunch was an idea the WI came up with a few years ago, supposedly as an event for newcomers to the village, to enable them to introduce themselves, and for existing congregation members to socialise… but in reality, there aren't that many newcomers. It's just an excuse for everyone to gossip, and today is certainly no exception. The usual village scandal-mongers are out in force, gathered together in small huddles around the sparse interior of the church hall, whispering none too quietly about the shameful incident that has rocked our sleepy little community.

None of them seem to be aware of Mildred's pregnancy, not from anything I've heard, and I'm not about to alert them, just in case they start asking too many questions about who the father might be.

Today, it's my turn to help clear away the tables and, as I pass around checking to see who's finished, before removing their plates, I overhear Mrs Barlow comment to Miss Simmons that she came to the church hall a different way today, 'to avoid walking anywhere near where it happened.'

"I know," Miss Simmons replies. "My dear, I know exactly how you feel. There might be a policeman still standing there, but I simply cannot bring myself to go anywhere near the place."

I'm so tempted to tell them not to be so stupid. It's not like Mildred's body is still there, after all. She's not going to rise up from the dead and start wailing at them either. But I'm determined to remain as anonymous as possible, and so I pass on, wondering to myself how any of these people manage to cope on a day-to-day basis, with so little between their ears.

I'm carrying a stack of plates through to the kitchen, when I spot Clifford Lacey out of the corner of my eye, looking like he's going to follow me, more's the pity. He's one of the few men who attend these luncheons, mainly because most of men in the congregation are working during the day, and those who aren't probably have better things to do with their time than sit around listening to a group of women gossiping. Personally, I think he likes the gossip, and of course, he'd never say 'no' to a free lunch.

I've always thought of Clifford Lacey as a rather pernickety man. He's probably in his mid-sixties, I suppose, short and rather wiry, with a balding head, and half-moon glasses.

"There's still a policeman in the churchyard," he says, coming into the kitchen behind me, as I expected. "Have you seen him?"

No-one answers, even though there are five of us in here, either clearing plates, washing up, or drying.

"Well," he continues, when it becomes clear none of us is particularly interested, "they didn't come and ask me… you know that, don't you?"

"Were they supposed to?" Mary Norris asks from her place by the sink. She doesn't turn around, but then she doesn't need to for me to hear the smile in her voice, which makes my own lips twitch upwards, and I turn around myself, so that Clifford can't see me stifling a laugh at his pomposity.

"Of course they were," he replies. "It's my responsibility as Church Warden to maintain peace and order in the churchyard."

"Well, you've got a policeman to help now," Mary replies.

"That's not really the point," Clifford replies, sneering at her behind her back. "The point is, they didn't have the courtesy to ask, even though I had two of them with me for a good couple of hours, yesterday afternoon."

We all stop what we're doing and turn to face him.

"You did?" Mary asks, water dripping from her hands onto the floor.

"Yes," he replies, seemingly gratified to have got everyone's attention, at last.

"Why was that?" I ask, intrigued, wondering if perhaps I might learn something to my advantage about the way in which the case is developing. I have more of a vested interest than anyone else, after all.

"Well, I'm not sure I should tell…" he teases, even though we all know he can't help himself. "But I don't suppose it can do any harm." He glances around, like he's checking to make sure no-one else is listening, and then moves a little further into the room. "They came to see me because they wanted me to identify a list of names."

"Names?" Mary queries, sounding disappointed, although I'm still very interested myself.

"Yes. They were all entries in Mildred's diary." He suddenly turns to face me. "Your husband was among them," he says, "along with half the other men in the village."

"Just men?" I ask, even though my heart has just leapt into my mouth, making it quite difficult to speak.

"Yes," he replies, nodding his head sagely.

"Who were the others?" I ask, pretending an interest.

"I'm afraid I'm not at liberty to say." He preens himself, leaning back on his heels and tapping the side of his nose with his forefinger. "But I did wonder if it might mean that Mildred was blackmailing them."

"Blackmail?" Margaret Thorpe almost spits out the word, but then she is prone to overreactions at the best of times.

"Well, can you think of any other reason why the police would be asking?" Clifford says, defensively.

"No, I can't. But then, I don't know whose names were on this list, do I?" she says.

"And I'd like to know what you're implying, Mr Lacey," I add, stepping forward and doing my best to sound offended, while lacing my voice with just sufficient emotion to embarrass the man, and garner sympathy from everyone else in the room. "Are… are you suggesting my husband is being blackmailed?"

Clifford takes a half step closer to me, his face falling. "Oh, my dear," he says, solemnly. "I didn't mean anything… I'm sure there's nothing in it at all." He smiles. "You don't want to go listening to anything I say."

I manage a slight sniffle, just for effect, and take my leave, making my way towards the ladies' toilets, where I shut myself inside a cubicle, trying hard not to laugh out loud.

What a stroke of good fortune! And so soon… Well, who'd have thought?

———◆———

I get back to the station by one-thirty, well aware of the fact that I've been significantly longer than the hour I said I'd be, but not feeling even remotely guilty about that. In fact, I feel so much better than I did earlier, that as I walk through the main office towards my own room, I'm whistling a little tune to myself.

"Sir?" Thompson says, greeting me officially, being as we're not alone, and I notice the surprised look on his face. Given my mood this morning, his confusion is completely understandable.

"Sergeant," I reply, nodding my head towards my office and he follows me in, closing the door and then waiting while I remove my hat and coat, hanging them up, before I sit down behind my desk.

"How are things going?" I ask and he comes over, taking a seat in front of me.

"Fine," he replies. "I've just been using your absence to help Wells and Adams with verifying the addresses of the men from the diary, that's all." He sounds as bewildered as he looks and I decide to put him out of his misery.

"I'm sorry I've been out for so long," I say to begin with, and he shrugs his shoulders, because in reality, I don't have to apologise to him, and we both know that. "I had to go home and see Amelie."

"Is she all right?" His concern is touching, and I smile.

"She's still tired, but she's okay," I reply, deciding against telling him that she was unwell this morning, being as that might have been my fault for overdoing things last night… and in the bath before breakfast. "Th—the problem – the reason I had to go home – it wasn't to do with Amelie," I explain. "It was to do with me."

"So it's you that's ill?" He sits forward. "Don't tell me you're coming down with this flu as well?"

I smile. "No. Physically, I'm perfectly all right."

"Oh…" He stops talking and sits, waiting.

"Amelie and I had an argument last night," I say quickly, just to get the words out. "It was entirely my fault."

He shakes his head now, the beginnings of a smile forming on his lips. "What did you do?" he says, sighing patiently, as though I'm an errant schoolboy.

"I told her off for digging the garden."

"In February?" he queries and I sit back, chuckling.

"That was rather my point actually, but I didn't handle it very well. I was a bit overbearing."

"You? Overbearing?" he mocks. "Surely not."

"I could demote you, you know?"

"I know… but you'd be lost without me… and in any case, I still don't really understand why you and Amelie having an argument meant you had to go home," he says, his brow furrowing.

"Because I needed to make sure she was all right."

"You mean you didn't make it up with her last night?" he queries. "You broke the first rule of a happy marriage and went to bed on an argument?"

"Of course I didn't. I made it up with her straight away, but there was something not quite right about her this morning." That's as much detail as I'm going to give him and he stares at me for a second or two, before he takes a breath and leans back in his chair.

"I know it's still early days, but you're going to have to get used to being a married man, Rufus," he says quietly.

"And what exactly does that mean?"

"It means, you and Amelie are going to argue from time to time."

"God, I hope not."

He smiles. "Well, you are, and my point is, that you can't fall apart every time you do."

"I didn't fall apart." I defend myself, placing my elbows on the desk.

"Can I be the judge of that?" he replies, his face quite serious. "I've known you for a good many years now, and I've never seen you like you were this morning."

I look down at the papers in front of me for a moment, and then return my gaze to him. He's just staring at me, a concerned expression on his face. "I know," I say finally. "That's why I took myself off to find Amelie. I knew there was only one way to straighten myself out."

"And have you?" he asks.

"Yes. Thank you." I sit back again. "And I apologise for this morning."

He shakes his head. "You don't have to apologise," he says, "but next time it happens, you could try talking to me instead."

"Next time?"

He smiles. "Yes, next time. And now, before I start to pine for Julia and you start giving me details as to how you've just spent the last hour or so of your time…"

"As if I would," I interrupt. "I'm not as open as you."

He chuckles. "No, you're not. But if you were, maybe we'd have got to the bottom of your problem a bit sooner."

"Maybe we would," I allow with a nod of my head. "But in any case, there are no details to make you pine for Julia, because I've spent the last hour or so helping my wife with the shopping."

"Shopping?" He's incredulous, staring at me across the table. "Shopping?" he repeats. "You were trying to apologise to your wife, to make up for being an ogre, and you took her *shopping*?"

"I wasn't an ogre. I'm not that bad. And I didn't *take* her shopping," I explain. "I happened to see her walking along Walton Road, and I caught up with her. She was already going shopping herself; I just joined her."

"I see," he says. "Well, I suppose that's more acceptable."

"I'm so glad you approve," I reply sarcastically.

"And you ironed out your problems while shopping?" he asks, perplexed.

"Yes… well, sort of. I think we ironed them out before we even got around to the shopping part, but then something interesting happened…"

"Are you sure you want to tell me this?" He sits forward in anticipation, despite his words.

"Yes, because it's more connected to the case than it is to Amelie and myself… well, mostly."

"Oh yes?" He frowns.

"We met the Reverend Hodge and Norman Wharton," I explain.

"In East Molesey?"

"Yes. They said they were going to lunch together."

"The vicar and Mr Wharton? Together?" He's clearly as surprised as I was.

"I know. I thought it was odd too. The vicar told me he'd been over to Mr Wharton's factory, to see how he was getting on after Mildred's death."

"That doesn't sound right either," Thompson replies, shaking his head. "Wharton doesn't even go to church, so what has his welfare got to do with the vicar?"

"Precisely."

"So what was he playing at? Hodge, I mean."

"I'm not sure, but that's not all of it," I add.

"Oh?"

"No…" I sit forward again. "After we'd been talking for a minute or so, I introduced them to Amelie, and their reactions were… interesting, to put it mildly."

"In what way?" Thompson asks.

"Well, Wharton couldn't take his eyes off of her."

"Your wife is very beautiful, Rufus… you do know that, don't you?" he reasons.

"Of course. But he wasn't just admiring her, he was gawking at her, quite openly, in front of me."

"And he survived?" he jokes.

"Yes… because what he was doing was nothing compared to Reverend Hodge."

"Why? What did he do?"

"Amelie said he made her feel like he was undressing her with his eyes, and I could see what she meant. There was something about him, Harry. There was a kind of hunger on his face… a lecherous hunger. But it was something more than that. He looked… menacing." It's the only word I can think of to adequately describe the vicar's expression.

"Is Amelie all right?" he asks.

"Yes, thanks."

"It's a good thing you were there."

I nod my head in agreement. "This rather confirms our theory," I say aloud.

"Which one?" Thompson remarks. "You have had rather a lot of theories in the last couple of days."

I smile at him. "The theory that the vicar might have raped Mildred."

"Not Wharton?" he suggests and I shake my head.

"I'll grant that Wharton probably had the better means of keeping Mildred quiet, being as he could have threatened her with the sack, but now I've seen Reverend Hodge at close quarters in the company of a beautiful woman, I'm of the opinion that the man probably wouldn't be willing, or even able, to take 'no' for an answer."

"Seriously?"

"Seriously, Harry. You had to be there... you had to see his face..."

"Do you want me to bring him in for questioning?" he asks, going to get up.

"No."

He relaxes back into his seat again. "Why not?"

"We need to make absolutely sure that list of names doesn't amount to anything, before we reveal our hand, because I have the feeling that, once we do, there'll be no turning back... not this time."

"Well, I can lend Wells and Adams a hand," he says, just as the telephone rings on my desk and I pick up the receiver.

Tooley's voice sounds at the other end. "Inspector Stone?" he says, respectfully.

"Yes, Sergeant."

"I have a Mrs Hodge for you," he announces. "She seems upset and wants to speak to you."

"Very well," I reply, raising my eyebrows at Thompson. "Put her through."

I wait, as the line goes dead, and then hear the click as the call is connected.

"Mrs Hodge," I say, and notice Thompson tilting his head to one side and leaning forward. "This is Inspector Stone. How can I help?"

"Oh, thank goodness," she breathes, sounding agitated. "I've been so scared, I didn't know what to do... or who to turn to."

"Try and calm down, and tell me what's happened." I sit back in my chair.

"I—I can't tell you over the phone," she replies. "Do you think you could come over here?"

"Of course," I say, smiling lightly to myself. "When would be convenient?"

"Could you come now? I'm too scared to wait any longer."

"Certainly." I check my watch, which says it's just after two. "We can be there in fifteen minutes."

"Oh… thank you so much, Inspector."

I put down the phone and look up at Thompson, who's staring at me, bemused.

"Well?" he says, impatiently.

"At the risk of sounding like Sherlock Holmes," I reply, standing up, "the game is afoot."

"What on earth does that mean?" Thompson says, following me to the door, where I grab my coat and hat and make my way out to the main office.

"It means we're going to the vicarage," I reply cryptically and he rolls his eyes at me, picking up his own overcoat and fedora, as he passes his desk.

Adams and Wells are sitting together, their heads bowed, and I go over to them.

"Sergeant Thompson and I have to go out," I say to them. "But can you start following up the names on the list?"

"Yes, sir," Wells replies, standing, and showing himself to be one of the few people of my acquaintance who is actually taller than me. "We've just finished cross checking the last of the addresses, as it happens."

"Very good." I look up at him. "Can you pay them all a visit?" I suggest. "And ask them in what capacity they knew Mildred Ryder? I'm fairly sure they'll tell you that the connection was through the church, or the choir, but what we want to know is, did any of them see her outside of those confines."

"Right, sir."

"Try not to raise any suspicions while you're about it, won't you? This is just a routine enquiry."

Wells nods his head and Adams gets to his feet, gathering together all the documents on the desk in front of him.

"Report back here later," Thompson adds, and we leave together.

Thompson parks directly outside the vicarage, fairly close to the front door, which I'm grateful for, as the wind has picked up considerably since my lunchtime walk with Amelie, and it's threatening to rain as well.

We haven't even climbed out of the car, before Mrs Hodge opens the door, a white handkerchief clutched to her nose.

"Please come in," she calls out, glancing around as though keen for us not to be seen, and we follow her inside the house. "I don't know what to do," she says, as soon as the door is closed.

"Well, I suggest you start at the beginning and tell us what's happened."

"Yes," she replies. "Yes, of course."

She indicates the drawing room, holding out her hand, but then leads the way, leaving Thompson and I to fall into step behind her. I don't look at him, nor him at me, and once we're inside the room, I sit down on the sofa, while he remains standing behind me.

Mrs Hodge is already sitting opposite, and I notice that on the table between us, there's an overstuffed brown envelope, which Mrs Hodge is gazing at. She seems to come to her senses, then she sniffles into her handkerchief a couple of times, before she begins her story.

"I—I found this," she says, handing me a blue envelope from her cardigan pocket, which I take from her.

"Where?" I ask.

"In my husband's desk." She stares at me.

"You searched your husband's desk?" I raise my eyebrows, looking down at the letter, but not opening it yet.

"Yes."

"May I ask why?"

"Oh heavens, this is so difficult," she wails, but then adds, "I still can't believe it's happening…"

"What's happening?"

"Well, I—I went to the parish luncheon today," she says, calming slightly, "and Clifford Lacey was there. He's the church warden?" She phrases her words in the form of a question, and I nod my head in understanding before she continues, "He was telling us that he'd had a visit from some policemen yesterday, asking about a list of people whose names were in Mildred's diary… my husband's name being one of them."

"Yes, I know," I reply and her eyes widen slightly, although why it should surprise her that I'm aware of the situation is beyond me, being as I'm in charge of the case.

"Anyway," she says, gathering herself together, "Mr Lacey seemed to be under the impression that your investigations might have something to do with Mildred blackmailing people." She stares at me expectantly, but I don't respond. "Before I continue," she says, "I think it might be wise if you were to read that letter." She nods to the envelope in my hand and I pull out the single sheet of paper, which I notice has been screwed up at some point, and then an attempt made to flatten it out again. I unfold it and scan the neatly printed words, trying not to smile.

"This is dated six months ago," I remark, looking back at Mrs Hodge.

"Yes, I know," she says, "but the thing is…" She stops talking, tears forming in her eyes, and although I'm not convinced by all of her performance so far, I think this part at least is genuine. "The thing is," she continues, "it's not the first time he's done this."

"Your husband has had an affair before?"

"Yes." She nods her head for emphasis. "I actually caught him in the act last time," she says, her voice a little too firm, too gloating, to make her story entirely credible. "They were in his study… on the desk. He and Annie Jennings." She blushes as she speaks. "She's always been a bit promiscuous, that girl, but he promised me that it would never happen again, and I was stupid enough to believe him… it seems this letter just goes to show what a liar he is."

"This isn't from Annie Jennings?" I ask.

"No. The timing doesn't fit," she replies, and I nod my head, replacing the piece of paper in the envelope.

"The thing is, Mrs Hodge, I'm not entirely sure what this letter, or your husband's past misdemeanours have to do with Mildred Ryder?"

"Well, that's because I haven't shown you this."

She leans forward and nudges the brown envelope across the table. I place the blue one beside it and take a look inside, where I discover at least fifty pounds, in folded notes.

"She must have been blackmailing him," Mrs Hodge says, sitting back, almost too triumphantly.

"Who?" I ask.

"Mildred, of course," she replies.

"But why?"

"Well… I assume she must have found out about his affair with whoever this woman is," she says, leaning forward and tapping on the blue envelope repeatedly with her forefinger. "My husband isn't exactly subtle, you know."

While there are a great many things to disbelieve in Mrs Hodge's story, I don't doubt that particular statement, not having seen her husband's reaction to Amelie.

"You think Mildred Ryder somehow discovered that your husband was having an affair with whoever wrote this letter?" I speculate, just for the sake of form. "And that she was blackmailing him?"

"Yes." I seem to be trying Mrs Hodge's patience, but that's all part of the game as far as I'm concerned. "It's the only thing that makes sense."

Not to me, it isn't. I take a few moments, pretending to contemplate the scenario she's presented me with. "You don't think it's possible that he might have been having an affair with Mildred?" I suggest, watching her closely.

She just about manages not to gasp, but her eyes widen in surprise and she hesitates before replying slowly, "I hadn't thought of that."

"Well, you did say he'd done it before," I add.

"Yes, I know…" She seems thoughtful, but before I can respond, Mrs Hodge gets to her feet and comes around the coffee table, sitting down beside me.

"The thing is, Inspector… I—I'm so frightened," she whimpers. "I —I mean, I feel terrible for telling you all of this. It feels like I've betrayed Neville… but what if he decided to kill Mildred, rather than paying her off? I mean, regardless of whether he was having an affair with her, or not… what if I'm living with a murderer?"

That seems a little melodramatic to me, but that appears to be the effect Mrs Hodge is aiming for, as she clutches her handkerchief to her nose and lets out a loud sob, falling back onto he sofa in floods of tears. I turn and look up at Thompson, and immediately wish I hadn't, being as he's struggling not to laugh, which doesn't help the situation in the slightest.

"Where is your husband now, Mrs Hodge?" I ask, getting to my feet.

She stops snivelling and looks up at me. "I—I don't really know," she says, fear etched on her face. "H—He told me he was going to lunch with someone, although I can't remember who… if he even bothered to tell me… and then he said he had some parishioners to call on. But for all I know he could be seeing another of his fancy women." Her face crumples and she starts crying again.

"You need to try and calm down," I say, with as soothing a tone of voice as I can muster. "Your husband will come back soon, I'm sure, and when he does, I need you to telephone me at Kingston police station… preferably without alerting him as to what you're doing."

I bend down, gathering up the letter and envelope of money to take with me.

"Wait a minute," Mrs Hodge says, her tears forgotten as she reaches forward, grabbing my wrist with a surprising amount of strength. "What are you doing?"

"These are evidence," I explain. "I need to take them with me, to have them catalogued. My sergeant can give you a receipt, if you'd like one."

"But…" She pauses, searching for an excuse to keep hold of her precious loot. "But you're missing the point. I—I mean, you can't take them," she says eventually, letting go of me and standing herself. "What will Neville say if he comes back and notices they're not in his desk anymore? He's already killed once…" Her voice drops to a dramatic low whisper, and Thompson coughs behind me.

"Hmm… you have a point," I allow. "I suppose I'd better leave them here. Be sure to put them back exactly as you found them, won't you?"

"Oh, I will, Inspector." She nods her head, taking the envelopes from me and clasping them in her hands. "And thank you so much for coming to see me so promptly. I feel better already."

I don't doubt that. Not for a single moment.

"You were singularly unhelpful," I remark to Thompson on the drive back to the station.

"Sorry," he says, actually sounding contrite for once. "It was just so hard not to laugh."

I glance across at him. "Her performance was comical at times, I'll grant you that."

"It was worthy of the London stage," he replies.

"Hmm… to the point where it was almost believable."

"Surely you didn't think she was telling the truth?" He sounds incredulous.

"No, of course I didn't. But I think, in her underestimation of us, in her belief that we're too stupid to know that she's playing us for fools, she's not only incriminated herself, but she's also inadvertently confirmed that her husband is responsible for Mildred's condition. And that's why, when we get back, I want you to speak to Sergeant Tooley and ask him to arrange to send a couple of men over to the vicarage to keep her under observation. I don't want her to abscond at the first opportunity."

"Well, she'll have to wait for now, at least until her husband comes home and she can report that fact to us."

"Yes, but she's got fifty pounds now, that she didn't have before, being as she rather cleverly insisted I leave it with her, and she's got no reason to hang around for more than a few minutes after we've taken him in for questioning."

"I think it'll be more than 'questioning'," Thompson retorts, frowning. "The man's a rapist."

"I know… but we still have to prove that, and then we have to prove that his wife is a murderer. Don't forget, we have absolutely no concrete evidence against either of them. We're working purely on instinct here."

Thompson chuckles quietly. "I wonder what Mrs Hodge would say if she knew that you'd suspected both her and her husband almost since the very beginning of this case."

"I have no idea," I reply.

"Well, maybe if the interview with her gets boring, we'll tell her and see how she reacts."

I shake my head, twisting in my seat to look at him. "You're warped, you know that, don't you?"

"It's been said before," he remarks, pulling into the car park behind the London Road police station.

I leave Thompson at the foot of the stairs, for him to go and speak with Tooley, while I go on up. The outer office is almost deserted, save for a couple of uniformed officers, who nod their heads towards me in greeting as I pass through on the way into my room, where I remove my hat and coat.

Thompson joins me within a few minutes, explaining that he's spoken with Tooley and given him instructions that the men who carry out the surveillance of the vicar's wife are to follow her if she leaves the house at any time, although they're not to approach her unless she tries to board any buses or trains, in which case, they're to stop her and bring her to the station.

"Very good," I reply, once he's finished speaking.

He sits down opposite me. "He's going to get Beresford on it," he says quietly. "He's only just come back from having the flu today, so it'll be a nice easy job for him… just sitting quietly in a car, watching the front of a house."

I smile and am just about to reply when Wells and Adams appear in my doorway. That's to say Wells appears in the doorway, and the size he is, he fills it, but I can just about make out the shape of PC Adams behind him.

I'm surprised they're back so soon, and I think it must show, because Wells holds his hand up defensively before I've even had a chance to say anything.

"I know we haven't been out for very long," he says, "but there really wasn't much point in going on."

"There wasn't?" I query and he shakes his head, coming further into the room and making space for Adams to follow.

"No, sir," Wells says. "We decided to call it a day after we'd gone through the first four individuals."

"Why not call them 'men', Constable?" I suggest. "That's what they are, after all."

"But that's exactly the point, sir. They're not all men."

"Excuse me?" I sit forward. "I gave explicit instructions that only the men in Miss Ryder's diary should be investigated."

"I know," Wells replies quickly, "and all the people we've been to see have been male." He glances at Adams, and then continues, "But I really don't think they all qualify as men."

"You're going to have to explain yourself," I say, glancing at Thompson, who merely shrugs his shoulders.

"Two of the people we've seen today were only really boys," Wells replies. "One was fourteen, the other a little younger."

"Boys?" I'm confused now.

"Yes. And the other two men were in their sixties," Adams adds, taking up the story.

"Well, I suppose that's not surprising," Thompson remarks. "After all, most of the men of Mildred's age have been called up, or are about to be."

We all nod our heads slowly.

"All four of them knew Miss Ryder through the church, as we expected," Wells continues, "and it looked like we were going to struggle to find the reason for their names being in her diary, until the mother of one of the boys we went to see, asked what we were doing questioning her son. She got a bit cross with us, so we had to explain what it was about… without going into too much detail."

Adams takes a half step forward at this point, one of the diaries in his hand. "I showed her the diary, sir," he says. "Just the page with her son's name on it, and she pointed out that the date in question is his birthday, so we decided to take a risk and showed her a couple of the other pages, and she was able to recognise one of them as being a friend of her son's and he then confirmed that the date beside that lad's name was his birthday too."

"And then the mother remembered that Miss Ryder had sent her son a birthday card," Wells adds. "She said she was like that… thoughtful, you know?"

I nod my head. "I see."

"We'll carry on going through the list, if you want us to, sir," Wells says. "But we thought we should come back here first and let you know what we'd found out."

"No," I tell him, "there's no need to carry on." I look from him to Adams and then to Thompson. "It looks like Mildred was just being kind – as usual."

"It certainly seems that way," Thompson replies.

"And it just confirms what we already know," I add.

He nods his head, although Wells and Adams look a little perplexed. I thank them for their hard work and they leave my office, closing the door behind them.

"I think there's every chance we'll end up working quite late tonight, Harry," I explain once we're alone. "It might be wise if you telephone Julia and warn her."

"You're going to question them both tonight?"

"Probably, although I suppose that all depends on Mrs Hodge, and how she behaves once we've brought the reverend in for questioning. But, in any case, we have no idea what time it will be before the vicar returns home, do we?"

"No, I suppose not."

He gets to his feet and exits the room, leaving me by myself, whereupon I pick up the telephone receiver and wait for the operator to speak. I ask for my own number and, within a minute or so, hear Amelie's voice on the end of the line.

"Hello," I say, relieved to hear her again, even though it's only a few hours since I last saw her.

"Rufus?" I can tell she's surprised. "Has something happened?"

"No, darling. Not really. I just wanted to let you know that I'll probably be a bit late home tonight. I'm not sure how late yet, but things seem to be developing here."

"It's just as well I've made stew for dinner then, isn't it?" she replies. She's trying to sound cheerful, but I can hear something else underlying her voice.

"Are you okay?" I ask.

"Yes. I just miss you, that's all."

"I miss you too," I reply. "And you're sure you've recovered from what happened at lunchtime?"

"At lunchtime?" she queries.

"Yes… our meeting with Reverend Hodge and Norman Wharton. I know that upset you."

"It did, but I'm perfectly all right, Rufus. You were with me."

"And I'm extremely relieved about that."

"Hmm…" she muses. "So am I."

I glance up as Thompson comes back into my room. He sees I'm still on the telephone and goes to leave again, but I wave at him to enter, and he shuts the door and sits down opposite me, waiting, Mildred's diaries in his hand.

"I should probably let you get on," Amelie says. "The sooner you finish, the sooner you can come home."

"I can't wait."

"No, neither can I."

"I love you, darling."

"I love you too." There's a short pause, and then Amelie adds, "Are you alone?"

"No."

She chuckles. "And you just told me that you love me?"

"Of course."

The line falls silent although I can still hear her breathing, and then she says, "Hurry home, Rufus."

"I will. I promise."

"And take care. I need you to come home and give me a cuddle."

"It'll be my pleasure."

I hear her sigh and we end the call.

Glancing up, I notice that Harry is flipping through one of the diaries, stopping every so often on a page, although I doubt very much he's reading anything and, after a few moments, he raises his head and smiles at me.

"I don't know why I'm asking this question, given the stupid grin on your face," he says, "but is everything all right with Amelie now?"

"Yes, it is, thank you."

He nods his head, then puts the diaries down on my table. "I picked these up from Wells on my way back in here," he says, "not that I think we need them anymore."

"No," I reply, picking them up and placing them on my side of the desk. "We'll return them to Mrs Ryder once we've made the formal arrests."

He nods his head. "I'm not looking forward to this evening," he says. "I hate dealing with rapists."

"Well, I think you can assume that Reverend Hodge is highly unlikely to admit to it. I think he'll either deny any sexual relationship with Mildred at all, or he'll say she consented."

He stares at me. "And we can't prove otherwise, can we?"

"No. But that doesn't mean he's going to get away with it. I'll find a way to make it stick."

He frowns. "Any way?"

I stare at him and nod my head. "If I have to, yes."

"Is this because of the way he behaved towards Amelie?" he asks, sitting forward, "because if it is…"

"It's not," I reply, interrupting him. "Well, not entirely. Although I suppose that is a factor."

"What else is it then?" he asks. "Because, while I know you can be unorthodox, you're not normally one for breaking rules."

"In this case, I'll make an exception," I tell him quietly. "I'll break every rule in the book if it gets us a conviction… and that's entirely because of Mildred. I don't think I've ever come across anyone quite so universally loved as Mildred Ryder seems to have been. She didn't deserve to die at all, but she certainly didn't deserve to be left for dead in a freezing churchyard. The very least we owe her is justice, and this time, I'm really not sure I care how we go about getting it."

He nods his head and is just about to open his mouth, when the telephone rings on my desk, it's shrill sound making us both jump.

"Stone," I say into the receiver, holding it to my ear.

"I have Mrs Hodge for you again, sir," Tooley says. "She's insisting on whispering, which is making her quite hard to hear, I'm afraid."

"Don't worry about it, Sergeant. Just put her through."

"Very well, sir."

I wait for a couple of seconds and then hear Mrs Hodge's muttered tones. "Inspector?" she whispers.

"Yes." I speak normally.

"He's home."

"Very well. Can you try and keep him there for the next twenty minutes or so?"

"Y—Yes," she stutters. "But please hurry. I'm scared."

The line goes dead and I hang up, rolling my eyes.

"She's still giving a fine performance, I assume?" Thompson says, standing, and I copy him.

"Oh yes. She's scared, evidently."

"God knows what of," he remarks, opening my office door. "I don't think that woman is capable of fear."

I stop in my tracks and turn to him, my hat in my hand. "Oh, she's capable," I tell him. "Just not in the way you think."

"What do you mean?" he asks, tilting his head.

"That's what this is all about," I explain, placing my hat on my head and shrugging on my coat. "It's Mrs Hodge's fear that has driven the whole case."

"Fear of losing her husband to another woman?" he asks.

"No." I shake my head. "Fear of losing her way of life." We go into the main office, where Thompson collects his own coat and hat. "That letter she showed me made it clear her husband had been contemplating leaving her. Even if he never saw it through for whatever reason, the intent was there."

"Exactly." He turns back to face me. "So, she was scared of losing him."

"No. She doesn't love him enough to worry about that. She's just scared of losing face; of losing her position in society, and having to admit that her marriage is a sham... that terrifies her."

"And she's killed someone, just for that?" He's shocked.

"Yes."

"Seriously?"

"Yes... you wait and see."

We take Wells and Adams with us, telling them to follow in a separate car, just in case the vicar decides to cut up rough, or make a run for it. I doubt that he will, but it's better to be safe than sorry. I'm not in the mood for chasing around the back streets of Thames Ditton in the dark; it's far easier to have a couple of extra men on hand than to be caught short.

In the car, Thompson asks if we're going to be picking up the letter and the money.

"We'll collect the letter, because we need that as evidence, but I'm going to leave Mrs Hodge with the money."

"You are?"

"Oh yes. I want to give her enough rope to hang herself... quite literally."

We pull up outside the vicarage for the second time today, with Adams parking his vehicle immediately behind ours. I instruct him and Wells to wait, while Thompson and I approach the house in the early evening dusk, knocking on the front door, which is answered by the vicar himself.

"Oh, Inspector, it's you," he says, peering out and looking surprised.

I pause, just for a second and then say, "Mr Hodge, we'd like you to accompany us to the police station."

"What on earth for?" he blusters, turning red, his eyes bulging slightly. I've seen fear before many times, and I can recognise it easily these days, so I know I'm staring at a frightened man right now.

"So we can ask you a few questions."

"Why can't you ask me them here?" He folds his arms, making it clear he intends to stand his ground.

"Because I'd rather ask you them at the station," I reply. "And if you refuse to cooperate, I'll have my sergeant arrest you." I move aside just slightly, allowing the reverend to see behind me, to where Adams and Wells are standing and notice his face paling as he glances over my shoulder, and then looks back at me.

"It doesn't look as though you're giving me much choice," he huffs. "I suppose I'd better fetch my coat. It's by the back door."

"My sergeant will come with you," I tell him and he opens his mouth to argue, but then stops, closes it and lets Thompson into the house.

Mrs Hodge appears from the kitchen, coming towards me. "What's going on?" she asks, putting on another sterling performance – although it's for the benefit of her husband this time.

"We're just taking your husband into the station so he can answer some questions," I reply. She nods her head and I lean forward, whispering, "Can you fetch me the letter, please? We may need it."

"Oh… certainly."

She disappears through a door just inside the hallway, returning a few seconds later, with the blue envelope tucked inside her cardigan, and hands it over to me, just as the reverend re-appears from the rear of the house, with Thompson in tow.

"Ready?" I say to the vicar.

He nods his head, not saying a word now.

"When will he be home?" Mrs Hodge asks me.

"That's hard to say, madam," I reply.

"Oh," she says and the vicar takes a step towards her, resting his hand on her shoulder.

"Don't worry, dear," he soothes. "I'll be back before you know it… once these idiots realise they're barking up the wrong tree, that is."

He leans down and kisses her cheek and she gives him a weak smile in return, blinking rapidly, as though she's holding back her emotions.

Turning away from her, Hodge allows himself to be led to our waiting car, more meekly than I'd anticipated, and I give Adams a nod, upon which he and Wells get into their vehicle and drive away, leaving Thompson and myself to deal with the reverend.

"You've got the wrong man, you know," he says as I climb into the back seat beside him and Thompson starts the engine.

"I dare say," I reply, taking a glance down the street to my left when we pull out of the driveway and smiling to myself, as I notice the black Wolesley, parked fifty yards or so further along, two men just about visible in the front seat.

All I have to hope now is that they don't lose sight of Mrs Hodge, because I'm fairly sure she'll make her move soon. Very soon.

Back at the station, Thompson hands the reverend over to Wells, with the instruction to place him in interview room number one, where we leave him to stew while Thompson makes the two of us a cup of tea and we drink it in my office.

"I assume from the fact that we're having our tea in here and not with Reverend Hodge, that you don't intend going easy on him," Thompson remarks, taking a sip from his steaming cup.

I look up at him. "You assume correctly."

"What do you want me to do?" he asks.

"Follow my lead, and whatever I do and say, just go along with it." He nods his head slowly, thoughtfully. "Harry, if you think my methods in this interview are going to bother you, then you can sit this one out."

"No, it's not that," he replies, quickly.

"Then what's wrong?" I ask. "I can tell something is."

"It's just, like I said earlier, I hate dealing with rapists. They tend to bring out the worst in me. I always find myself thinking… 'what if that had been Julia?'. And I know that's all wrong and we're not supposed to make it personal, but somehow I can't help it."

"I understand exactly how you feel," I say. "And if it gets too much, just give me a nudge and we'll take a break."

He agrees and we finish our tea, before making our way to the interview room. We both take a noticeably long breath before I open the door and walk in. Wells is standing just to one side of the door and he steps aside, looking at me, awaiting my instructions as to whether he should stay in the room, or vacate. I nod my head and closes the door behind us, guarding it, his hands behind his back, his presence calming – for me, that is, not for Reverend Hodge, who glances at him, looking worried. With three such large men in a very small room, all facing him, I'm not that surprised.

"What's going on here?" he asks, glancing back at me again as I take a seat opposite him, with Thompson sitting beside me.

"We need to ask you some questions." I repeat my earlier statement and the vicar gazes at me for a moment.

"I know," he says eventually. "You've already told me that. What I want to know is, why here?"

"Well, the nature of our questions means that it's better if they're asked here… where it's more private."

"More private?" he queries.

"Yes."

"Why is privacy so important?" He looks confused, almost sulky.

"Because I'd like for you to tell me about your affairs."

"My affairs?" he repeats again.

"Yes… I mean your mistresses."

His cheeks turn a rather silky grey colour, but he rallies more quickly than I would have expected. "I don't have any mistresses, or any affairs, for that matter," he blusters.

"That's not what we've heard," I say, sitting back in my chair. "We've been given this letter…" I pull the blue envelope from my jacket pocket, watching his face, which has turned almost green now. Removing the letter from inside, I unfold it. "It appears to be from someone who refers to you as 'Poochy', and who calls themselves…" I check signature at the bottom of the other side of the page, "… 'your little teddy bear'." I glance up at him again. "You're not going to try and tell me this was written to you by one of your parishioners, are you?" I look down at the letter again, raising my eyebrows. "Because if you are, I have to say, the content is extremely unusual."

He lets his head rock forward into his hands and groans, "Oh God."

"This... this affair between you and the person who calls themselves 'your teddy bear', it's not your first, is it?" I ask. He doesn't respond, other than to start rocking slightly. "Reverend," I say, raising my voice slightly, forcing him to look up, and enabling me to see the despair in his eyes. "I strongly advise you to start talking, and to tell me exactly what happened between you and Mildred Ryder... because I have to tell you, at the moment, things aren't looking too good for you."

Chapter Twelve

I stand by the closed front door after the inspector and his men have gone, taking Neville with them, waiting for a few minutes, in the still silence, just to be sure that they're not going to come back for some reason, and then I run up the stairs and straight into our bedroom.

I take the small suitcase from the top of the wardrobe and start packing, smiling to myself at the ease with which my plan is falling into shape. I can't believe everything is going so smoothly, but then I suppose, it is my plan, after all, so why shouldn't it work?

I pick up the silver framed photograph from the chest of drawers and turn it over, removing the back and dropping it and the photograph itself onto the bed, an image of myself and Neville on our wedding day, smiling at the camera. Oh, if only I'd known then what I know now...

I don't need any reminders of my wedding, but I will take the frame, which I know to be solid silver and quite valuable. For a moment, I wonder about leaving my wedding and engagement rings, but they will probably fetch a few pounds too, so I hang onto them and close my case, carrying it downstairs and leaving it by the front door, while I go out to the back lobby and collect my hat and coat.

I check that everything is locked and switched off, and make my way through to the front door, putting my hat and coat on the hall table next to my handbag, before pausing, taking a breath, and going into Neville's study, where I open the desk and pull out the envelope of money, checking the contents one last time. It's not enough for me to call myself rich, but it is more than sufficient for me to start again, and I'm sure it won't take me long to find gainful employment... or failing that, a suitably rich husband. After all, it's not like I'll need to worry about divorcing Neville. He'll be hanging from the end of a rope before long...

I must say, it's very satisfying to be able to take my husband's money, after everything he's put me through… all the deceit, the lies, the betrayal. It feels only too right that he should finance the beginning of my new life in Scotland, which is now just a train journey away.

I take a glance around his study, picturing once again, that scene when I caught him in here with Annie Jennings. But then I shake my head. I'm not going to think about that – or him – ever again, and instead I go back into the hallway and place the envelope in my handbag, snapping it shut. As I put on my hat, checking my reflection in the mirror, I chuckle to myself, recalling the inspector's subterfuge in getting me to hand over the letter without Neville seeing it. He seemed to think he was very clever in doing that, but stupid man that is, he forgot about taking the money…

Well, more fool him, because by the time he remembers, the money will be long gone. And so will I.

--------•--------

Reverend Hodge stares at me for what seems like a very long time, and then lets out a loud sigh, before leaning forward and letting his hands fall to the table.

"Very well," he says, sounding resigned. "I'll admit I've strayed a couple of times, but that's not against the law, Inspector."

"Did you 'stray' with Mildred Ryder?" I ask.

He hesitates, and then says, "Yes, I did," his voice a soft whisper, "but you saw her. You saw how beautiful she was. No sane man could resist her… and, in any case, you've met my wife. Surely you can understand. I mean, the contrast is just so great." I raise my eyebrows and he leans even further forward, with a conspiratorial air. "What I'm trying to say is that Eileen enjoys her role as my wife; and she's very good at it, but she has a tendency to go too far, to be too high-handed, too prim and proper, if you get my meaning." He winks at me, but I remain stoney faced and he blushes, but then continues, "She… she forgets, you see, that, under the dog collar, I'm still a man, and that I have a man's needs and desires, just like we all do. But I'm afraid Eileen can be a bit… well, dull, in the bedroom department."

"Dull?" I query.

"Yes. Don't get me wrong, I'm not blaming her. I don't think it's her fault. I think it's just the way she was brought up. That and the fact that she made the assumption that my role within the church would be more important to me than anything else." He smiles. "We had different expectations of marriage, Inspector," he adds, by way of explanation, when I don't respond. "Sometimes young women today just aren't prepared for the realities of life away from their mothers," he adds. "I often have to offer words of advice, when they come to me to arrange their weddings."

"Oh, do you now?" I'm not sure his idea of 'advice' would tally with most people's.

"Yes. I'm sure you understand." He stares at me, and his smile broadens. "Oh, but then, you probably don't, do you?" he says. "Not with a wife like yours."

I'm not sure what he's trying to imply, being as his knowledge of my wife is limited to their five minute meeting in Walton Road, but I do know that he's trying to goad me, and that he's most of the way towards succeeding. There's something distasteful in his tone of voice which makes every muscle in my body tense, my fists clenching involuntarily on the table in front of me.

I'm aware of Thompson sitting forward, right before he says, "Why did you lie to us, Reverend?" and I'm grateful for his intervention, sitting back for a moment, to take a few deep breaths and calm down.

The vicar averts his gaze from me to Sergeant Thompson, his smile fading. "I haven't lied to you," he says, defensively.

"Yes, you have." Thompson flips back through his notebook, in which he's taking down every word of the reverend's statement. "When we first came to see you, you denied having any kind of relationship with Miss Ryder, outside of the choir."

The vicar shakes his head. "What? You wanted me to admit to having an affair with Mildred in front of my wife? She'd already caught me out once, a few years ago, and believe me, Eileen is a very unforgiving woman."

I sit forward myself once more. "Did you know about Miss Ryder's pregnancy?" I ask, taking over the interview again.

"Of course not," Reverend Hodge replies. "I had no idea." The smile returns to his lips. "Mind you," he adds, "judging from how much she enjoyed her time with me, I very much doubt that I'm the only man in the picture for paternity. I certainly don't believe there was nothing going on between Mildred and Sam, however much he might cry innocence… and you could try having a word with Norman Wharton too, while you're about it. I know for a fact that he was more than interested in Mildred."

I stand, my chair scraping on the floor, startling Reverend Hodge, who jumps and only just manages to stop himself from gasping out loud.

"You may be a man of the church," I growl, leaning over the table, "but I don't believe a word you're saying." He opens his mouth. "Shut up." I raise my voice. "Whatever you were going to say, just don't." And he clamps his mouth closed again, clearly disconcerted by the change in my tone.

I turn to Wells.

"Take Reverend Hodge down to the cells, will you?"

Wells steps forward, just as the vicar gets to his feet.

"The cells?" he mutters, stunned by my request. "What for? I mean, I haven't done anything wrong…"

"I'll be the judge of that," I interrupt.

"You can't keep me here." He leans towards me, just as Wells claps a burly hand on his shoulder, pulling him back.

"Yes, I can." I nod at Wells, who steers Reverend Hodge towards the door. "It'll do you good to sit and think for a while. Then perhaps the next time we talk, you'll tell me the truth."

"I have told you the truth," Hodge calls over his shoulder, but Wells is already guiding him from the room.

I sit back down and turn to Thompson. "Thank you for intervening," I say, smiling at him. "I was in danger of losing my temper with him."

"I noticed," he replies, shaking his head and studying his notebook. "Nothing he's said adds up, really, does it?"

"No. One minute he's telling us that he and his wife are trying to start a family, and the next he'd like us to believe she's not being very forthcoming in bed."

"He can't have it both ways," Thompson says.

"That's the problem with lying," I point out. "You need to have a very good memory."

"How long are you going to leave him down in the cells?" Thompson asks.

I shrug my shoulders. "As long as it takes. Certainly long enough for you to get me another cup of tea." I grin at him and he gets to his feet, just as there's a knock on the door and we call out, "Come in," together.

Constable Pearce appears in the doorway, a little out of breath.

"Are you all right?" I ask him.

"Yes, sir. I just came to report to you that PC Beresford and I have picked up Mrs Hodge."

"She's here?" I ask, standing myself now.

"Yes. She's in the other interview room."

"What happened?"

He steps inside the room, closing the door. "I'd already taken a look around when Beresford and I had first arrived at the scene, and had noticed that there were several routes Mrs Hodge could take to get away from the vicarage, so once you drove away from the house, Beresford and I left the car and split up, with him watching the front of the house, and me the rear." He pauses for a second, and then continues, "I suppose it was about ten minutes later that Mrs Hodge came out of the front door. Beresford noticed her, of course, but she didn't go down the driveway. Instead, she went around the side of the house and through the churchyard, almost walking straight into me, as it happened."

"What did you do?" I ask him.

"I hid in a bush," he explains. "And then, when she'd gone past, Beresford came by and we followed her together."

"Where did she go?"

"She carried on down Church Lane, all the way to Speer Road, and then at the end, she crossed over…"

"To the station?" I interrupt and he nods his head.

"We stopped her just as she got to the ticket office, and then I waited with her while Beresford went back for the car. He's with her now," he explains. "She's… she's not very happy."

"I can't imagine she is," I reply. "But you and Beresford have done very well. Very well indeed."

He blushes. "Thank you, sir."

"Are we going to talk to her now?" Thompson asks from behind me and I turn, glancing at the clock on the wall, which tells me that it's five to eight.

I smile at him, and then my smile becomes a grin. "Well, I don't know about you, but I'm tired, and I'd like to go home and see my wife."

"I'm not going to disagree with that," he says, smiling back.

"We'll just go and tell Mrs Hodge our plan, shall we?" I suggest and Thompson chuckles.

"This should be fun," he says, and Pearce opens the door, stepping to one side to allow myself and Thompson to exit, then closing it behind us all.

We go down the corridor to the next door on the left, which I open without knocking, to find Mrs Hodge pacing the floor.

"Sit down," I say harshly.

She stops and glares at me.

"How dare you?" she bellows, walking over and standing just an inch or so from me. Thompson and Beresford take a step nearer and I'm aware of Pearce, right behind me, so close I can hear him breathing. "Who do you think you are?" Mrs Hodge's voice is a shrill wail. "I helped you. I told you—"

"Shut up!" My shout drowns her out and she steps back, stunned into silence. "Thank you," I say, more softly, and then I turn to Beresford. "Please can you take Mrs Hodge down to the cells?" I ask him and he nods his head. "It's too late to begin the interview tonight. We'll make a fresh start in the morning."

"You… You're going to keep me here overnight?" Mrs Hodge is outraged by my statement.

"Yes."

"How dare you?" she shouts, for the second time. "Do you know who I am?"

"I think I have a pretty good idea, yes," I reply, staring down at her.

"You can't treat me like this," she says, as though she hasn't heard me. "If you didn't need to see me until tomorrow, why have you had be brought here now?"

"Because you were about to abscond, Mrs Hodge."

"Abscond?" she scoffs.

"Yes. You were attempting to escape, trying to make a getaway… call it what you will. If I'd waited until tomorrow, I'd have called round at the vicarage and found the nest empty. As it is, I'll know exactly where to find you when I want to talk to you."

"Well, I'm not staying," she says, folding her arms across her chest defiantly.

"It's not optional, Mrs Hodge," I point out. "You're being held here on suspicion of murder." Her eyes widen, but she doesn't comment. "Now, I suggest you spend the night thinking about what you've done, and we'll see you again in the morning."

"I've got no intention of doing any such thing," she says, raising her voice again. "I'm not some flighty little thing, you know, Inspector. I know my rights, and I also know that I'm innocent."

"In that case, you have nothing to fear, do you?"

"This is ridiculous. We both know my husband is the guilty party, not me," she reasons, although there's still an unbecoming harshness to her voice. "You have the evidence… in that letter."

"I have evidence of your husband's adultery; not of murder," I reply, and take a step back, grateful that Pearce seems to have moved out into the corridor, otherwise, I'd have trodden on his feet. "You need to calm down, Mrs Hodge. You need to get some rest, and you need to start telling me the truth… because if you don't, I am going to throw the book at you… and trust me, I will make damn sure it hurts."

I glare at her, until Beresford steps forward, taking hold of her elbow and guiding her from the room, Thompson and I stepping aside to make way for them.

"I don't know about her needing to get some rest," Thompson murmurs as soon as we're alone, "I think we're going to need some too. Tomorrow is going to be interesting."

"That's putting it mildly." I turn to him and we sigh, rolling our eyes and switching off the light as we leave the room.

The aromas that greet me the moment I open my own front door are soothing and inviting, and I quickly take off my coat and hat, throwing my jacket over the back of the sofa and going straight into the kitchen, where Amelie is standing by the sink. She's wearing the same clothes she had on at lunchtime, although I failed to take them in at that point, having been more concerned with other things at the time. Now, I stand for a moment and admire her slim figure, encased in a straight grey skirt, and the thin cream coloured jumper she's wearing on top.

"Hello," I say eventually and she jumps and turns around.

"I didn't hear you come in," she replies, coming over and putting her arms around my neck, as I place my hands on her waist and pull her close, leaning down and kissing her deeply. I feel like she is my first drink of water after days of deprivation in an arid desert, and I slake my thirst for a good five minutes before breaking the kiss.

"I love you," she whispers and I smile, recalling our telephone conversation earlier this evening.

"I love you too, and I'm sorry I'm so late," I murmur.

"If you're going to kiss me like that every time you're late home, I don't think I'll object too much. Although I think I'd rather have you here."

"I know I'd rather be here," I reply, with feeling.

"Has it been a difficult evening?" she asks, leaning back in my arms and looking up at me.

"Yes."

"Do you want to talk about it?" She touches my cheek with her fingers.

"Would you mind if we didn't?" I rest my forehead against hers. "I've got another horrible day to come tomorrow and I'd really rather just forget about work for a few hours."

"In that case," she says, smiling, "why don't you sit down at the table, and I'll bring the dinner through. I can't wait for you can taste my rabbit stew. I think I might have actually done it right…"

Her voice fades and she's about to pull away, but I grab her and hold her close for a little longer. "The stew smells delicious," I admit, then lower my voice and add, "but if I'm being honest, I'd rather take you upstairs and taste you."

"Well, we can do that later," she says softly, her eyes sparkling.

After the day I've had, her words are music to my ears. "I'll hold you to that."

She nods and then takes hold of my arms, turning me around and giving me a gentle nudge in the direction of the dining room. I do as I'm told and go to sit down at the table, where Amelie joins me within a few minutes, carrying a hot casserole dish, her hands protected by a tea towel. She places the dish in front of me, then sits down in her place opposite, smiling at me expectantly, before she removes the lid, and steam wafts upwards, accompanied by the welcoming scent of stewed rabbit.

"I've been looking forward to this all afternoon," I tell her as she dishes up a generous portion onto my plate.

"The smells have been driving me quite mad," she replies, handing me the plate and dishing up her own meal, before we both settle down and start to eat. The rabbit is tender and cooked to perfection, as are the carrots and potatoes. "This is divine," I say after my second mouthful, looking up to find Amelie staring at me, a light smile touching the corners of her lips. She seems pleased with herself and justifiably so.

"This is a recipe I'm going to keep," she replies. "It was actually quite easy to do as well. I'll have to remember to thank your mother." I stop eating and put down my knife and fork. "Is something the matter?" she asks, looking worried.

"No… it's just, there's something I wanted to ask you. I was going to bring it up at lunchtime, when I came home, but we got distracted."

"By meeting those two men?" she suggests and I nod my head. "What did you want to ask?" She puts down her own cutlery now and leans forward slightly.

"I was just wondering whether you mentioned our argument last night to my mother, when you saw her this morning."

Amelie blinks a couple of times and then gets up, coming around to my side of the table and standing beside me. I twist in my seat and she sits down on my lap, her arms around my neck.

"Of course I didn't," she says softly.

"Thank God for that." I let out a sigh of relief. "She'd have made my life a misery."

Amelie chuckles, resting her head against my shoulder. "Why?" she asks.

"For treating you like that," I explain. "She'd definitely have taken your side over mine."

She leans back in my arms, looking into my eyes, serious now. "I'd never share our arguments, or our problems, with anyone else… not that we have any problems, not really. But what happens in our home, between us, is our business and no-one else's."

I feel guilty now. "You… You don't mind that I mentioned it to Harry, do you?" I ask, fearfully.

"Mentioned what?" she asks, leaning back in my arms.

"Our argument. I told him what had happened, when I got back to the office, after lunch."

"And no doubt, you blamed yourself for all of it," she says, frowning.

"Naturally. It was all my fault."

"No, it wasn't."

"Well, either way. You don't mind, do you?"

"No."

"It's just that, I felt I owed him an explanation, considering how foul I'd been all morning."

"Had you really been that bad?" she asks, smiling slightly now.

"Yes."

"Oh dear."

"That's what being out of sorts with you does to me," I explain.

"Then we'd better make sure it doesn't happen too often," she replies. "For Harry's sake, if nothing else."

"Thank you," I say quietly, hoping she'll understand my gratitude as I place my hand behind her head and pull her closer, giving her a soft kiss. "I know you might have wanted to talk to someone too, and that my mother would probably have been the obvious choice, but I'm grateful…"

"I didn't need to talk to anyone but you," she says, interrupting me. "And you did the perfect thing and came home to see me. It… it was as though you knew I needed you."

"Only because I needed you more."

She smiles and kisses me again, and then gets up, going back to her seat.

It doesn't take us long to polish off the stew and afterwards, we adjourn to the living room with a cup of tea to listen to the wireless for a while, leaving the washing-up until the morning. Amelie says it will give her something to do and I recognise that sad tone to her voice again, as we sit side-by-side on the sofa, and she nestles into me.

"How was your afternoon, after I left?" I ask, trying to change the subject.

"Well, I prepared the stew, and then tidied up a bit… and that was about it," she says, her voice a little distant and, if I'm being honest, rather despondent.

"What's the matter, darling?" I ask and she twists around, looking up at me.

"Why do you ask?" she says.

"Because you're not happy, are you?"

She pauses and then slowly shakes her head, letting out a long sigh. "I'm sorry," she whispers and I struggle to hear her over the orchestra that's playing on the wireless.

"Just a minute," I say, and get up, going over and switching it off, before turning round and facing her again. "Why are you sorry?"

"Because married life isn't what I thought it would be," she says, sitting up straight, her hands clasped on her lap, her eyes focused on the fireplace to my right, rather than on me, which I find slightly unsettling. "I—I'm still so tired," she stammers. "And I'm fed up, and so bored. I thought there would be plenty to do. But I seem to manage to get everything done in no time at all... and then the day just drags by."

"You don't regret marrying me, do you?" We may have overcome our most recent difficulties, but there's so much uncertainty in her voice, I feel the need to ask.

"Good God, no," she exclaims and jumps to her feet, throwing herself at me, her arms around my neck. "Please don't think that. I didn't mean for you to think anything like that. I love you. I'm sorry, I—"

"Don't apologise. You have nothing to be sorry for." I take her hand and lead her back to the sofa, where I resume my seat. She goes to sit beside me, but then changes her mind and places her right knee next to my left leg, realising too late the problem of wearing a straight skirt, although she resolves that quite easily by hitching it up, exposing her stocking tops, and then kneeling, astride me. "That's nice," I whisper as she leans down.

"Well, I wanted to make sure you understand that I don't have any regrets," she replies, running her fingers through my hair and kissing me. "None at all."

I place my hands on her behind and pull her closer to me, which makes her squeal and giggle, and that in turn makes me smile.

"I'm sorry," I murmur into her.

"What for?"

"For overreacting, and for being so insecure. I know it's a little out of character, but my only defence is that I miss you, when I'm not with you, much more than I thought possible."

"That's a lovely thing to say. And I don't think you overacted."

"Really?"

"Well, at least you didn't go rushing upstairs."

"No. I'd rather stay and talk to you."

She sighs. "I know I'm not very good at being a housewife," she says, out of nowhere.

"Well, the 'wife' part of that word is the only bit that matters to me, and you're absolutely incredible at that… so as far as I'm concerned, the house can take care of itself."

She giggles again, and then rests her hands on my chest, leaning back. I miss her closeness, but look up into her beautiful face instead. "I'm trying to be serious, Rufus," she says quietly.

"I know you are, but it's only been a few days. You need to give yourself time to adjust." I remember Harry's words and his advice. "I'm here, if you need me."

"I know, but the thing is," she muses, glancing around the room, "it was so much nicer on our honeymoon."

"I'm not going to disagree with you there, my love, but try to bear in mind that it won't always be like this. The timing of this case is pretty awful, and most of the time, my work won't get in the way as much as it has done for the last few days. My hours won't be so erratic and I won't have to work at the weekends either."

She nods her head, then leans forward and rests it against mine, forehead to forehead. I like it when we sit like this. There's something really intimate about it, a closeness that we don't achieve, even by looking at each other.

"I understand that," she says, "but I honestly can't think of anything more boring than being tied to the house, all day, every day."

Reluctantly I break the contact between us and lean back as best I can, allowing for the fact that I'm sitting in the corner of the sofa and grasp her chin in my hand. "You're not tied to anything."

"Except you," she whispers gently.

"No. You're not even tied to me." Her eyes widen in confusion. "You're never tied. That implies an unwillingness. And I would never keep you with me if you didn't want to be here. I love you too much for that."

She moves her hand, touching my cheek with her fingers. "I always want to be here. Right here," she whispers, and then kisses me, intensely. After a few minutes, she leans back and stares at me, our eyes locked. "Just ignore me. I'm sure you're right. I'll get used to things eventually," she murmurs softly.

"I will never ignore you" I tell her. "And if you're really unhappy, why don't you think about volunteering for something. We talked about it before we got married, remember?"

"Oh yes," she says, her face brightening, just slightly. "I'd forgotten about that."

"You could maybe try the WVS, couldn't you?" I suggest.

"I suppose so," she replies, clearly thinking the idea through. "But what would we do about the housework, and the cooking?"

"I'll do as much as I can," I say, resting my hands on her behind again. "And it's not like you'll be volunteering on a full-time basis. It'll just be something to get you out of the house for a few hours a day."

"And it'll mean I'm doing something for the war too," she says, sounding even more enthusiastic now.

"Exactly."

"I'll probably give it a couple of weeks," she reasons, "just so I can learn a few more recipes from your mother first – assuming she and your aunts don't keep confusing me – and I'd like to maybe get more settled into a routine of my own, so I know what hours I can safely volunteer to work, but then I'll definitely look into it." She smiles, biting on her bottom lip. "Thank you," she murmurs.

"What for?"

"For understanding. I feel so much better already, knowing I've got something to look forward to."

"Well, I can't claim that I'll always be able to understand everything, but I'll do my best." I edge forward on the sofa, then stand, holding her in my arms, her legs wrapped around my hips. "And now, I think it's time we went to bed."

"Hmm, so do I." She leans into me, her arms around my shoulders.

"Your stew may have tasted divine, darling, but I know you'll taste so much sweeter."

She giggles and, after she's turned out the light and locked the door, balancing in my arms as she does so, I carry her up the stairs to bed.

Chapter Thirteen

Who does that Inspector Stone think he is?

How dare he lock me up? I mean, does he even know who I am? Does he even realise how well respected I am in the community? He can't just go locking me up like a common criminal.

I sit down on the bench that's supposed to pass for a bed in this God-forsaken place, and gaze up at the barred window. It's dark outside, just as dark as it is in this squalid little cell, and I stare out at the twinkling stars, recollecting how different my life was, just a few short weeks ago, when I lived in ignorance of Neville's affairs. Well, most of them, anyway.

"What happened?" I whisper to myself, blinking back my tears. "What happened to me?"

I married a cheat and a liar. That's what happened to me.

Like a fool, I fell for his stories, I believed his lies, I let him take advantage of me, and now he's ruined everything. Not that his tarts are innocent in all of this. They're just as much to blame as he is, throwing themselves at him. He's only a man, after all. A weak and stupid little man…

What I don't understand though, is why I should have to pay for his mistakes. I'm not responsible for what happened. He is. It's all his fault… well, and his tarts'. And yet it looks like I'm the one who's going to pay the ultimate price.

A smile crosses my face as a thought occurs.

"Well," I whisper almost silently, "that's an idea…"

It might not work, of course, but it's worth a try. And if it fails, the only option I'll have left is to make sure to take him down with me…

Today, I have to leave early.

Thompson and I agreed last night, as I was getting into my car, and he was preparing for his short walk home, that we'd start the first of our interviews at eight, so I have to be away by seven-thirty.

I tried to persuade Amelie to stay in bed, but she's insisted on joining me for breakfast, although at least she hasn't got dressed, which means she's sitting opposite me in her dressing gown again. Unlike yesterday though, there's no underlying tension between us and once we've both buttered our toast, she reaches across the table and takes my hand in hers.

"I think I'll have solved everything by the end of the day," I tell her and she stops eating, putting down her toast on the plate in front of her.

"Really?"

"Yes. Well, to be honest, I've solved it already."

"You know who did it?"

"Yes. They're already in custody."

"Then I don't understand…" She says, leaving her sentence unfinished.

"I don't have any evidence," I explain. "So my only hope is to get the guilty parties to confess."

"Parties?" she repeats. "You mean there are two murderers?"

"No." I hesitate and then take a breath. "Do you remember I told you that the victim was pregnant?" She nods her head. "Well, it seems that she was raped."

"Oh my God. She was raped, and… and then murdered?" she whispers, and I wonder if she's recalling the manner in which Beth Templeton died. Beth was raped and then killed, and it was Amelie who discovered her abused body the following morning in the alleyway beside her guardian's house. We met for the first time a few hours later, and I think it was my need to protect her from what she'd seen, and from anything else that might hurt her, that was my overriding feeling from that first moment. That and love, of course… because I fell in love with her the very second I saw her.

"Yes, but not by the same person," I manage to say, keeping to the point and trying not to let Amelie's mind drift away too much.

Her face pales as a shadow crosses her eyes and her brow furrows. "Let me get this straight," she says, her voice stronger than I would have expected it to be. "The victim was raped, and then murdered, but by two different people?" She looks confused.

"No. I think that the victim was raped and made pregnant, probably in November, and that the murderer found out about it and killed her, to keep her quiet."

"About the rape, or the pregnancy?" she asks quietly, although she's blinking rapidly, clearly affected by my revelation.

"Both," I reply, then squeeze her hand gently. "Are you all right?" I ask. "Has this brought back memories of Beth?"

She looks up at me. "No," she says softly. "It's just that I'm… well, I'm so proud of you," she says, surprising me.

"I hate to disappoint you, darling, but you might not be by the time I've finished this case."

She frowns now. "Why on earth not?"

"Because some of the methods I might have to employ today could be a little…" I search for the right word.

"Unorthodox?"

I shake my head. "No. I have a reputation for that already. Today… Today I think I might have to break a few rules."

She lets out a breath, then gets up and comes to stand beside me, her hand on my shoulder. "Then break them, Rufus," she says firmly. "Do whatever you have to do. Catch whoever did this, and then come home to me."

I put my arms around her waist, my head resting between her breasts, and I cling to her, basking in the last fragment of humanity I'm likely to experience, at least until I come home again tonight.

My drive to work is brief, and I spend it thinking about my parting kiss with Amelie, rather than focusing on the case. She did seem a lot brighter this morning, which I can only put down to our discussion about her joining the WVS in the near future. I can understand that she wants to delay for a while, just so she feels a bit more settled first, but as I said to her yesterday, I will help out as much as I can, and I know it will do her good to get out and make some friends of her own.

When I arrive at the station, Thompson is already there waiting for me, a grim expression on his face.

"I can see you're looking forward to this as much as I am," I remark, walking past him and into my office.

"I haven't slept well," he explains, getting up and following me.

"Thinking about the case?" I ask as I hang up my coat and hat. "Or is there something else wrong?"

"It's mainly the case," he says, "although Julia had a restless night. The baby's moving around a fair bit now, and it decided to keep her awake for an hour or so."

"And she kept you awake in turn?" I ask.

He smiles. "No. I was already awake, but at least that meant I could go and make us both a cup of tea at three o'clock this morning." I shake my head, smiling at the domesticated image of my once carefree friend. "You needn't look so cheerful," he says, smiling back at me. "You've got all of this to look forward to."

"One day," I reply, picking up the files on my desk and thumbing through them. "One day…"

"Hmm…" he muses and then nods to the files. "Who are we seeing first?"

"Mrs Hodge, I think."

"Oh good," he sighs, rolling his eyes. "More histrionics. I'll go and arrange to have her brought up, shall I?"

"If you don't mind." I sit down at my desk. "I'll just go through these."

He nods and leaves the room, while I go over the paperwork, making sure I've got everything fresh in my mind, being as I have absolutely no doubt that both Mrs Hodge and her husband are going to try and run rings around me for the next few hours.

Thompson returns ten minutes later and informs me that Mrs Hodge is waiting in interview room one, and she's not best pleased.

"So there's nothing new there then," he adds, waiting for me by the door. "Shall I have some tea brought in?"

"Has she been given breakfast?" I ask.

"Yes."

"Then skip the tea for now."

He nods and we make our way down the corridor, through the double doors, stopping outside the interview room, where we both take a deep breath, before I open the door.

On the inside, Constable Beresford is standing guard and gives me a brief nod of his head, which I return, letting him know he's to remain exactly where he is, before I turn and look at Mrs Hodge, who is sitting on one of the three chairs surrounding the metal table in the middle of the room.

Her hair is slightly dishevelled and her scant make-up is smudged, but otherwise, she looks the same as she did yesterday evening, her eyes alight and filled with indignation.

"About time too," she says huffily. "I don't know why you felt it necessary to lock me up for the last twelve hours, when we could have dealt with this yesterday evening, and I could have been spared a sleepless night."

I don't respond to her, but walk slowly over to the table, pulling out one of the chairs and sitting down opposite her, waiting a moment for Thompson to take his seat beside me, and then placing the files on the table in front of me.

"Good morning," I say eventually, and she narrows her eyes.

"You know my husband is a rapist?" she says, randomly, blinking rapidly, her hands clasped together, the knuckles almost white. "You know he raped Mildred Ryder?"

I place a deliberately confused frown on my face. "How do you know this?" I ask, not answering her question as to whether or not we are aware of her husband's misdemeanours.

"Because I overheard a conversation between them," she admits, triumphantly.

"Between him and Mildred Ryder?" I play along.

"Yes," she hisses.

"When was this?"

"Let me see…" She pauses, thinking, and looking up at the ceiling for effect, although I'd wager my house that she knows exactly when this conversation took place. "I think it must have been the Wednesday before Mildred was killed," she says at last, looking me in the eye now.

"So, you've known about this all along, and are only telling us now?" I say, sounding cross with her and proving that Mrs Hodge isn't the only one capable of putting on an act.

She blushes, looking away again. "Well, he is still my husband," she says, offering a weak excuse.

"So? I would have thought that would be all the more reason to tell us."

"He's also the vicar," she adds. "Can you imagine the scandal if word got out?"

I glare at her for a moment, in genuine revulsion, but manage to say, "Can you tell me about this conversation?" my voice surprisingly normal.

"Yes," she replies, sitting forward again, clearly keen to get this off of her chest. "Mildred arrived at about four o'clock," she begins, in what sounds to me like a well-rehearsed speech.

"Was your husband expecting her?" I ask, putting her off her stride.

"No. Not that I'm aware of." I nod my head and she continues, "I answered the door, and she asked to see Neville, so I showed her into his study, where he was going over his sermon."

"And you listened in?" I lean back in my seat, raising my eyebrows.

"You have to remember, Inspector, that I'd caught my husband in a compromising position once before," she says, affronted by my remark, as well as my interruption to her flow, I think. "I wasn't about to let him make a fool of me again."

"I see. So, you listened in?" I repeat.

"It's just as well I did," she retorts angrily, "because the very first thing Mildred said was that she was pregnant, and that the baby was Neville's."

"How did that make you feel?" I interrupt again.

"Feel?" She seems surprised.

"Yes. You'd just heard a young woman claim that your husband had fathered her unborn child. How did you feel?"

"Angry," she replies instantly. "And shocked."

"I see. So, what happened next? Did your husband deny it?"

She shakes her head. "No," she replies. "That was what was so odd about it. He didn't say a word. Then I heard Mildred again, saying that what Neville had done to her was wrong; that she'd only gone into the vestry to talk about the Christmas carols they'd been rehearsing at choir practice that evening, and to tell him she thought someone else should have a chance at doing one of the solos... and then he'd turned the conversation round to her wedding – which had still been going ahead as planned at that time, you understand," she adds as an afterthought.

"She said all of this, did she?"

Mrs Hodge nods her head. "Yes. She was crying, but I could hear her saying that she'd thought my husband was just being friendly when he'd asked her how the preparations were going, and whether she was ready for married life." She looks up at me. "Can you believe he said that?" I shrug my shoulders, recalling the comments he made yesterday on the subject, but I remain silent, and she goes on, "Mildred was sobbing by this time, saying how was she supposed to know what he'd meant? How was she supposed to know what he'd do? And that was when my husband spoke for the first time. He seemed to be quite near the door – close enough to make me jump, anyway – and he told her that men have expectations of their brides, and that all he was doing was trying to help her."

"Help her?" I query.

"Yes. He said... he *claimed*, that he just wanted to help, but then Mildred said that what he'd done was wrong... that he had no right to touch her like that, or to force her onto the desk in the way he'd done..." She falls silent for a moment. "Neville asked her to keep her voice down at that point, and then told her that he'd only been trying to prepare her for married life, so it wouldn't be such a shock. Mildred turned on him then, and told him he'd ruined her marriage. She said he was the reason she'd had to postpone it… I can remember her words, Inspector, as clearly as though she'd only just said them, five minutes ago. She said, 'How could I marry someone as good as Sam, knowing I wasn't pure anymore?'." She looks up, with what appear to be genuine tears in her eyes. "That's when I knew," she says softly. "That's when I knew what he'd done. I felt sick to my stomach, but something held me there. Something made me listen to the end of her story."

"And what was the end?" I ask.

"She told him she'd been to the doctor, and that he'd confirmed she was pregnant. She said she'd decided she was going to tell the police about what my husband had done to her. It was her only hope of having any kind of future with Sam… that's what she said. Although quite why she thought Sam would stick by her, once he found out what she'd done, I don't know…"

"What did your husband say?" I ignore her disparaging comment about what Mildred had supposedly 'done', wondering how she thinks being raped could possibly have been the young girl's fault, and continue with my questions.

"He… he offered her money," Mrs Hodge replies, sounding disgusted. It's a sentiment with which I concur, although I'm not sure how genuine she is, so I don't say as much. "He said he'd need a few days to arrange it with the bank, but he begged her to keep quiet. She turned him down flat. She said she didn't want money; she wanted everyone to know what he'd done… especially Sam. As she was talking, I heard her voice getting nearer to the door, so I had to duck into the living room to avoid being seen. The next thing I knew, the front door was slammed shut and Mildred was gone."

I sit for a moment, just looking at her and she holds my gaze with remarkable tenacity. "I still don't understand," I say eventually.

"What don't you understand?" she asks with a fawning, rather condescending tone to her voice.

"Why you didn't tell us any of this yesterday, when you asked us to come and see you, because you were so afraid of your husband? Why didn't you tell us your suspicions then, Mrs Hodge?"

Her eyes flicker for a moment. *You didn't think of that, did you?* I muse to myself. *You haven't got your answer prepared.* Even so, she rallies quickly. "For the very reason that I *was* so scared," she whispers.

"Of your husband?" I decide to play along with her.

"Of course. I explained that. I mean… hasn't it occurred to you that the woman in that letter, the one calling herself his little teddy bear, or whatever it was… hasn't it occurred to you that she might be dead too?"

"How do you work that out?" I frown, doing my best to look bemused.

"Think about it," she says, with mock patience. "In that letter, the woman said that my husband had promised to tell me of their affair, so that they could be together."

"Yes, I know."

"But he never did, did he?" she says.

"Maybe he changed his mind," I reason.

"Or maybe he only said it to her so she'd do what he wanted, and he never had any intention of seeing it through… and when she got too demanding, he did away with her, just like he did away with Mildred, when she became too much trouble." She sits back, with a jubilant expression on her face.

I nod my head very slowly, as though I'm thinking through her idea and coming to a conclusion in her favour.

"We're going to need to speak to your husband about this," I say softly, getting to my feet and picking up the files, neither of which have I opened during the course of our interview.

"Does he know I'm here?" she asks, sounding worried.

"No."

"Please don't tell him." There's a trembling in her voice and, for a moment, I almost admire her. She's good… she's very good.

I nod my head and then turn, going over to the door, with Thompson in my wake. "We'll be back later," I say, looking back at Mrs Hodge and trying not to smile. "I'll arrange to have some tea brought in for you."

She smiles up at me. "Oh, that would be very kind," she simpers and, with a final nod of my head to PC Beresford, Thompson and I leave the room.

"Do you know," Thompson says, once we've arranged to have the Reverend Hodge brought up from the cells, "for a second there, I almost believed her."

"Oh, I believe almost every word of that particular story," I tell him and he looks up at me sharply, from his position outside the interview room, where he's leaning against the wall.

"You do?"

"Yes. I believe that Mildred went to the vicarage that afternoon, that she had a private conversation with the vicar, in which she accused him of rape, and informed him of her pregnancy. I believe he offered her money and that she declined and threatened to come to us… because she loved Sam enough to want to save their relationship, and she hoped that telling the truth and revealing what had been done to her might be her only chance."

"You honestly believe that?"

"It's the only thing that makes sense."

"So, you think the vicar killed her?" he says, shaking his head.

"I didn't say that," I reply. "I said I believed almost all of her story. I think that's how Mrs Hodge found out about Mildred's condition, and her husband's role in it. I also think she's of the opinion that we're stupid enough to fall for her lies, unquestioningly."

"And are we?" he asks.

"No," I reply. "The problem with people like Mrs Hodge, is they're complacent. They let their guard down too quickly."

"They do?"

"Yes." I smile at him as he pushes himself off the wall. "As we were leaving, I glanced back at her. She was staring straight ahead, looking at the wall at the time, but she made the mistake of smiling, just a little too quickly. I saw it. I saw the look in her eyes which told me she thought she'd won…"

Thompson nudges into me. "So you've let her think she has?" he says.

"Yes… for now."

I'm aware that we don't have long before the reverend is brought up and I turn to Thompson. "This is the part we've both been dreading," I tell him, lowering my voice.

"I know," he replies and I let out a long sigh.

"Whatever happens in there, Harry... whatever I do, please don't try and stop me."

He pauses, his brow knitted into a frown, before he slowly nods his head, and we turn as one as the double doors at the other end of the corridor open and the enormous figure of PC Wells appears, with Reverend Hodge a step in front of him, looking diminutive by comparison, but then most people do. He glances up at us, defiance written across his face, and manages a smile.

"Good morning, Inspector," he says, annoying me still further by ignoring Thompson, who's standing a half step behind me now.

"Interview room two, please, Constable," I say to Wells, ignoring the reverend.

Wells opens the door to his left and ushers the vicar inside. We follow them. "Take a seat, sir," the constable says, and then closes the door and steps back into the corner of the room.

Thompson and I take our places in the chairs opposite Reverend Hodge, and I place the files in front of me once more.

"How much longer are you going to keep me here?" the vicar asks, frowning at me.

"As long as it takes," I reply.

"As long as it takes for what?" His frown deepens.

"For you to tell me the truth."

Anger flickers across his eyes. "I've already told you the truth," he blusters.

"No, you haven't." I open the top file and gaze down at it for a moment, even though I don't need to. "Can you tell me about the conversation you had with Mildred Ryder in your study on the Wednesday afternoon before she was killed?" I say, looking up at him halfway through my sentence.

His face has paled significantly, but he purses his lips for a moment and then replies, "I don't know what you're talking about."

"It's quite simple, Reverend," I explain, speaking slowly. "I'm talking about a conversation you had with Mildred Ryder two days before her death, in which she told you that she was pregnant by you, and that she was going to tell the police."

He swallows hard, then licks his lips. "That's nonsense," he says, shaking his head. "What would the girl have had to go to the police about anyway? I—I mean, I've already told you that she and I were having an affair… if you can call it that. And if she was silly enough to get pregnant, then that's hardly my fault, is it? As I said to you yesterday, there's no evidence that her child was even mine, and there's nothing illegal in any of that, Inspector. And certainly nothing for her to come running to you about."

"There is if she didn't consent to having sex with you," I say, hardening my voice and leaning forward.

"Didn't consent?" he mocks. "Let me tell you, she was positively gagging for it."

I nod my head. "Gagging for it?" I repeat slowly, as though the phrase is new to me. "Oh… you mean she was a willing participant?"

"Of course she was," he says mildly. "What do you take me for?" He's let down his guard now. "Just because she changed her mind afterwards, doesn't mean she wasn't more than willing at the time."

"I see," I say, and then lean back, smiling, letting him think I believe him.

"Do you mind me asking how you heard about this conversation?" he asks, relaxing back into his chair.

"Your wife overheard it," I explain. "She told us."

He turns as white as his dog collar. "Dear Lord," he sighs. "I never thought…"

"You never thought what?" I enquire.

"Well, what I mean is, I thought she'd kill me if she ever caught me cheating again. I never thought she'd…"

"Do you admit it?" I ask abruptly, interrupting him and standing at the same time, leaning over the table, intimidating him as best I can.

"A—Admit what?" he stutters, his eyes bulging.

"Do you admit to raping Mildred Ryder in your vestry?"

"I've already explained, it wasn't rape," he replies, lowering his eyes.

I lean in closer, getting within an inch or two of his face. "Did she *really* consent?" I shout through gritted teeth. "Or did she say 'no'? Did she at any time, either before or during the act of intercourse, say 'no' to you?" He raises his eyes, glaring at me. "You do know what 'no' means, don't you?" He continues to stare at me and I stand upright, moving across to the wall, which I lean against, folding my arms, and finally lowering my voice, as I say, "And did you offer her money when you found out she was pregnant?"

"Yes, I did," he replies quietly, "but only because I wanted to help."

I nod my head, as though I'm thinking and then I look up at the ceiling, before I move quickly across the room and grab the back of the reverend's chair, twisting it around and pulling him to his feet by his lapels, then shoving him back hard, slamming him against the wall behind him. "You raped that girl on your desk in your vestry, you made her pregnant and then, when she told you about it, you offered her money to keep her quiet," I growl at him, aware that I'm now taking his weight, that I've lifted him from the floor. "When she refused your offer, you killed her to keep her quiet…"

He shakes his head from side to side, fear written all over his face. "No," he says, pleadingly. "No, I didn't. I didn't kill her."

"But you did rape her." I'm not asking a question, I'm making a statement, and he knows it. "Tell me the truth," I add, before he can comment. "Because if you don't… if you keep lying to me about this, I promise you I will find a way to pin the murder charge on you, whether you're guilty or not… and I won't lose a moment's sleep over it."

There's no more than a few seconds' pause before Reverend Hodge whispers, "Yes," so quietly I'm fairly certain only I will have heard him.

"Say that again… and say it clearly," I tell him.

"Yes… I raped Mildred Ryder," he mutters, loudly enough for everyone in the room to hear. "But I didn't kill her."

I drop him back to the floor, watching as he crumples and then slowly crawls back to his seat, as I walk around the table, resuming my place beside Thompson, who hasn't made a move or said a word throughout the entire interview.

From beneath the top piece of paper in the file, I remove the blue envelope, retrieving the letter from inside and laying it out in front of the reverend, who still seems to be visibly shocked.

"Who is the woman who wrote this?" I ask him.

He stares at me, confused. "Her name is Clara Lyons," he whispers. "And before you ask, I didn't rape her."

I shake my head in exasperation. "I know that," I snap. "I can read. For some reason, the woman was clearly in love with you. What I want to know is, what happened to her. Where is she now? She clearly had expectations of a future with you. I want to know whether you got cold feet?"

"No," he replies simply, deflated now. "I did intend leaving Eileen. I honestly did."

I'm not sure I believe him. It's a habit I've developed whenever a suspect says 'honestly' like that. "So you were lying to me when you told me that you and your wife were trying to start a family?" I say.

He bites his lip, looking embarrassed. "Yes," he says eventually. "Yes, I was."

"Why?"

"Because you were getting awfully close to discovering the truth about me and Mildred, and I wanted to cover my tracks. I thought that if I could get you to believe that Eileen and I were in a close and happy marriage, you'd stop looking…" His voice fades.

"So what happened to Miss Lyons?" I ask. "Is she still in the picture?"

"No. Unfortunately, she had to move away."

"Had to?" I query.

"She wasn't pregnant," he reasons. "But she moved away about four months ago. Just a few weeks before Mildred… and it was such a shame too," he adds wistfully. "Clara was a perfect little thing… absolutely perfect… completely adorable and so very willing…" He stops talking as though he's suddenly remembered where he is and who he's talking to, his face flushing bright red.

"She moved?" I query.

"Yes… well, that's to say, her mother moved house to be closer to her own relatives after the death of her husband. That's how I got to know them, you see?" he says quite reasonably. "I helped the family after the death."

"You have a strange idea of helping," I point out. "But if this girl still lived at home with her mother, was she old enough to be having an intimate relationship with you?"

"She was eighteen," he replies defensively, and then adds, "well, just," as an afterthought. "It was all perfectly legal, I can assure you." He gazes down at the letter before him, letting out a long and wistful sigh of regret, presumably recalling more pleasant times with the young lady in question, while ruing their lost opportunity.

I shake my head, reach across and retrieve the letter, replacing it in its envelope before I put it back into the file and slam the cover shut. Then I turn to Thompson.

"I need to get out of here," I say, standing once more. "Charge him with rape." I nod in the vague direction of the reverend. "Then lock him up and see if you can lose the key."

I wait in the main office for Thompson and Wells to return, then indicate for them to follow me into my office.

"I apologise for that, gentlemen," I say, after Wells has closed the door, the three of us standing in a huddle in the centre of my room.

"For what?" Thompson says, glancing sideways at Wells, and then looking back at me.

"For my little outburst back there, Harry." I decide to use his christian name, despite the presence of a junior officer.

"What outburst would that be?" He turns and looks at Wells directly. "I don't remember any outburst, do you, Constable?"

"None whatsoever, sir," Wells says, his face blank, although I'm almost certain the corners of his mouth are twitching, just slightly.

I stare at the two of them for a moment. "Thank you, gentlemen," I murmur and they both smile.

"Can I get you a cup of tea?" Wells offers.

"That's very kind," I reply, "but I think I'd rather just get the next interview over and done with, wouldn't you?" I turn to Thompson and he nods his head.

"Yes," he says. "And then we can actually put this God-awful case behind us."

I don't bother taking the files with me this time, but accompany Thompson back down the corridor, leaving Wells in the main office. Outside the interview room, I glance at Harry and he smiles, just as I open the door, and step inside, giving Constable Beresford a quick nod of my head. Mrs Hodge looks up sharply from her place at the table, giving the impression that she hasn't moved a muscle in the whole time we've been gone.

"Well?" she says her eyes lighting up, as she leans forward. "Did he confess?"

"Eventually he did, yes," I reply, taking my seat opposite her once more. She lets out a deeply satisfied sigh and smiles complacently. "To rape," I add, and her smile drops.

"To rape?" she queries. "But…"

"And before you ask," I interrupt, "the young lady who wrote that letter… Clara Lyons… she moved away."

"Clara Lyons?" she mutters, clearly surprised. "That little slut. And to think her mother…"

"In spite of sending us on a wild goose chase, you knew she was alive, didn't you?" I say, over the top of her.

"What?" She looks up at me. "What do you mean?"

"I mean, you knew Clara Lyons was alive and well…"

"How could I have known?" she remarks, snidely. "I didn't even know who she was. I had no idea who'd written that letter."

"No, perhaps you didn't," I allow, "but you knew that, whoever it was, they were still alive, for the very simple reason that you hadn't killed them… like you killed Mildred."

"What on earth are you talking about, Inspector?" she shakes her head, putting on a good impression of being astounded by my suggestion. "We both know perfectly well that my husband is the guilty party here."

"He's guilty of rape, Mrs Hodge, but not of murder… and you need to stop playing games with me. I've known that you're the one who was responsible for Mildred's death for a couple of days now. I worked out right from the beginning that you were the kind of woman who would kill, rather than risk your supposed position in society. You'd rather take the life of someone who you consider to be beneath you, than deal with your own problems… problems which you helped to create with your attitude." She's staring at me, open mouthed now, and I lean in closer, as I add, "The thing is, Mrs Hodge, what you failed to appreciate was that Mildred Ryder was better than any of you."

"Better? You're clearly deluded, Inspector, if you think a simple little housemaid can be classed as my 'better'."

For the first time in my life, I'm tempted to strike a woman, even if only to wipe the supercilious, smug smile from her face.

"I'm not even remotely deluded, Mrs Hodge. I'm just saying that Mildred Ryder is someone who I would have considered it a privilege to meet, had I been afforded the pleasure."

"Oh, I see she turned your head as well, did she?" she sneers, glancing down at my hands, which are lying flat on the table.

"No, she didn't. I'm not the type of man who has his head turned. But even if I were, I've only seen her in death, her body cold, her face contorted in pained anguish… and I doubt any man would have his head turned by that sight." I take a breath. "Perhaps it's the years of living with your husband that have made you so bitter. Somehow I doubt it though. I think you were always like this. And that's one of the reasons – just one of them, mind – why I maintain that Miss Ryder is your better."

Her eyes narrow. "You seem to be under the illusion that your opinion matters," she says haughtily. "But then you're very good at forgetting who you are."

"On the contrary, Mrs Hodge, I know exactly who I am. You, on the other hand, seem to think that you're of some importance… and I'm here to tell you that you're not."

"You can't speak to me like that." Her voice becomes shrill, her eyes wide with anger. "I demand to speak to your superior office. Immediately."

I shrug my shoulders and nonchalantly run my finger along the edge of the table. "I'm afraid you're looking at the most senior officer in the building," I reply and give her a very quick, very phoney smile. "Now," I add, "I suggest you stop lying, prevaricating and generally wasting my time, and start telling me the truth. I've already explained, I know you're responsible for Mildred's death. There's no point in pretending anymore… there really isn't."

If she knew how little evidence I have against her, and how much I need this confession, she'd just clam up on me, but as it is, after just a couple of seconds, during which she glares at me in defiance, her demeanour changes, tears form in her eyes and then she visibly deflates in front of me, beaten.

"I wasn't pretending. Not all the time. And I did tell the truth," she whimpers. "At least about the conversation between Mildred and Neville. That much of it was completely true."

"I know," I reply.

"You do?"

"Yes. Believe it or not, we're not as stupid as we look."

She gazes at me for a moment and then shakes her head. "What I didn't tell you was what happened after she left." Sharing in my surprise at the alteration in Mrs Hodge, and her sudden willingness to reveal all, Thompson hurriedly opens his notebook and starts to write, as she continues, "I followed Mildred from the house and caught up with her on the driveway, and we spoke there for a few minutes. She was embarrassed to begin with and denied the conversation had taken place, but I told her I'd overheard it all. She apologised…" She looks up at me now, no longer quite so defeated, it would seem, that conceited expression back in her eyes once more. "Quite rightly of course, considering what she'd done…"

"She'd been raped by your husband, Mrs Hodge," I put in, astounded, and unable to stop myself from commenting this time. "How exactly was that her fault?"

"She shouldn't have put herself in that position, should she?" she retorts, raising her voice. "I don't see how she really thought there was anyone to blame but herself."

"You don't see your husband as being responsible?" I clench my teeth.

"Of course I do. This whole situation is his fault. Why, if it hadn't been for him, none of this would have happened. But he's only being like the rest of his sex, isn't he? You can say what you like, and try to pretend that you're an upstanding gentleman, who'd never stray, and never put a foot wrong, but I'm not that easily fooled. If a woman offered herself to you, you'd do the same as my Neville... and don't bother deny it." She nods her head, as though confirming her point.

"I would not," I reply firmly. "And neither would any other man of my acquaintance."

She sneers and shakes her head as though she feels sorry for me. "Believe that, if you want to," she remarks. "Now, do you want to hear the story, or not?" She sounds as though she's recounting her latest travelling adventures on the continent, not telling me how she went about committing murder, but I take a deep breath, and wave my hand, indicating for her to continue. She nods her head again and says, "Well, I told Mildred I'd meet her after choir practice on Friday so that we could talk some more. I begged her not to be hasty about going to the police, even though she was adamant about it, but I explained that Neville had been unfaithful to me before and that I needed her help... that she'd be doing me a favour, if she'd just wait a couple of days. I— I think she felt so bad about what she'd done, she felt she owed me that much." I don't bother to remark on her interpretation of her husband's actions this time, but just sit quietly and wait. "She agreed eventually that she wouldn't do anything until after we'd spoken again," Mrs Hodge continues.

"So you met her?" I ask, just to provide a break in her monologue, which is starting to make me feel a little sick, especially when I consider that Mildred might well have thought she'd found an ally in Mrs Hodge, when in reality the woman only intended to do her harm.

"Yes," she replies. "I told her to leave after choir practice and then double back and meet me behind the church. Mildred queried that, wondering why we couldn't meet somewhere else, being as Neville quite often took a few minutes over locking up after choir practice, but

I knew it had to be close to the vicarage, so I could get back home, without being missed and without being seen… and somewhere quiet as well. After all, I couldn't risk stabbing her out in the open, could I? Anyone might have seen us together. No…" she muses to herself, "it had to be that way. And even if Neville was still there, I knew he'd either be inside the building, or around the other side of it, locking the door."

"You took a huge risk, Mrs Hodge. Even if your husband did take a while locking the church, how on earth could you expect to kill Mildred and get back to the vicarage before him?"

"I didn't," she says calmly. "Obviously, as I've already said, I knew I needed to get back home quickly, before I was missed. I knew I didn't have long. But you see, when Neville got back from choir practice he used to always go into his study to drop off his hymn book, and then go through to the lobby area at the back of the house to take off his hat and coat… and only then would he come to see where I was. I estimated I had about five minutes to spare. Of course, him forgetting his sermon was a huge bonus… I knew the whole thing was a risk but, as far as I was concerned, it was one worth taking." She stops talking for a moment, as though she's re-living the scene. "Anyway," she adds suddenly, coming back to the story, "Mildred came, exactly as planned and once I was sure we were out of sight, I stabbed her."

She says the words as though they're meaningless, as though her actions didn't end the lives of two people, and alter the course of many others, causing pain and grief to Mildred's mother, her siblings, her fiancé and her friends. To Mrs Hodge, killing Mildred Ryder clearly meant nothing, other than being the means to an end.

"You stabbed her twice?" I query.

"Yes," she says, her lips actually forming into a smile. "The first time was instinctive. It was self defence."

"Self defence?" How can she say that? "Was Mildred armed?"

She shakes her head, smiling in a way that shows she thinks I don't understand, which I don't. "Not self defence in the way that you mean," she parries. "What I mean is, it was self preservation. She was threatening my existence, my future, my very being. I had to stop her."

"So why did you stab her the second time?" I ask.

She stares at me, the half smile dropping from her lips, replaced by a harsh thin line. "Because I wanted to kill the bastard child my husband had seeded inside her," she roars, the ferocity of her hatred taking me by surprise.

I nod at Beresford and he steps forward, placing himself immediately behind Mrs Hodge, just as Thompson gets to his feet.

"Mrs Eileen Hodge," he says, his voice more monotone than I've ever heard it before. "I am charging you with the murder of Mildred Ryder…"

"Tell me he'll hang," she wails, turning to me, pleading. "Tell me they'll hang my husband too."

I stand, looking down at her. "No," I say simply and she starts to sob, showing some real emotion for the first time.

"Why not?" she cries. "This is all his fault. He's to blame…"

"Not entirely," I reply. "He didn't wield the knife, Mrs Hodge. You did. And you alone are responsible for the death of Mildred Ryder. Your husband is responsible for her rape, but unfortunately rape is not a hanging offence. In this case, I wish it was. But I'm going to do everything I can to ensure your husband is sent to prison for the maximum term. And as for you… I will use every little bit of influence I have to ensure you are shown no mercy whatsoever… like you showed none to Mildred, when you left her, in the freezing cold, to bleed to death, alone and terrified."

I give Beresford another nod and, in the company of Thompson, who starts reading Mrs Hodge her rights from the beginning again, they exit the room and I sit back down in the chair, my head in my hands.

Chapter Fourteen

"I didn't do anything wrong!" I call out as they slam the door closed.

"Tell that to the judge," the plain clothed sergeant replies. He sat through the whole of my interview, just jotting down notes and staring at me from time to time, like I was a prize specimen, as though he had any right to judge me.

"It was her own fault!"

This time, there's no response, although I can hear voices talking outside. They're clearly ignoring me.

"Neville is to blame for this! He should be the one hanging, not me!"

I hear a laugh – a man's laugh – and then footsteps moving away from the door and I realise I'm alone.

I'm completely alone.

———◆———

Back in my office, I glance at the clock, quite surprised to see that it's still not yet noon. Not quite, anyway. Can it really be that we've done all of that in less than four hours? It feels like a lot longer to me. But then hearing people tell their darkest, most horrible secrets can have that effect.

I sit at my desk and gaze at the photograph of Amelie, concentrating on her beautiful, calming face, and try not to remember the sight of Mildred Ryder's body, the contorted expression on her lips, the fear in her eyes, the way in which she clutched at her abdomen, presumably in a vain attempt to protect her unborn child… her maternal instincts coming to the fore, even in death… despite the fact that the child was born of a vile act, rather than a loving one.

I have an unsettled feeling in my stomach and, when Thompson knocks on my doorframe a few minutes later, I get to my feet.

"Come on." I march over to the hook behind my door, where I collect my coat and hat. "We're going out."

"We are?" He's surprised.

"Yes."

"What about the case notes… the paperwork?" He follows me into the main office, picking up his own coat and hat on the way.

"They can wait until tomorrow."

We make our way down the stairs and I go to my car, rather than one of the Wolesleys that are parked up.

"You're driving?" Thompson queries, following me.

"Yes."

"Is something wrong?" he asks, sounding worried.

"No… but there are a few loose ends we need to tie up before I can happily put this case to bed."

Thompson lets out a long breath and climbs into the car beside me. "Where are we going then?" he asks.

"The barracks," I reply and reverse out of the parking space.

It's only a short drive, but it's one that we make in silence, because I think Thompson knows my moods well enough to understand when it's better to just stay quiet… and that this is one of those times.

On arrival, a uniformed sergeant stands before us, with a barrier behind him, his tunic pristine, his brass buttons sparkling, and the rifle in his arms sloped at the correct angle.

"Can I help?" he offers, looking into the car with the air of a man who has no intention of being helpful at all.

"I need to speak with Sam Higgs," I reply. "I assume he's a private? He may not be here still, but I'm hoping he is."

The sergeant almost smiles. Almost. "I'm sorry," he says, even though he clearly isn't. "I'm afraid civilians aren't allowed…"

"I'm not a civilian," I remark, before he gets too far into his speech and I reach into my inside pocket, which has the effect of putting the soldier on his guard as he takes a half step back, his rifle now aimed in my direction. "I'm a policeman," I add quickly, half tempted to raise my hands in surrender.

"Step out of the car," he says gruffly.

I obey his instruction and slowly climb from my vehicle, wary of making any sudden moves. "I really am a policeman," I tell him. "My warrant card is in my jacket pocket. You can check it, if you want to."

He pauses for a moment and then steps forward, patting my chest, presumably to ascertain whether I'm carrying a gun, as well as my warrant card.

"Take it out," he says, then adds, "slowly," and I do as he says, handing my identification over to him. He peruses it for a moment and then hands it back. "Who's this man you want to see?" he asks.

"Higgs," I reply.

"Never heard of him."

"Well, I'm not surprised. He only reported here yesterday."

He nods his head. "I'm sorry, but I still can't let you onto the base," he says and I sigh out my frustration.

"I'm investigating a murder," I say, exaggerating slightly, being as the investigation is over.

"And he's a suspect?" the sergeant asks.

"Not exactly, no." I'm getting bored now, as well as frustrated. "Would it be possible to speak with your commanding officer?"

The man narrows his eyes, glances back at my car, and then mumbles, "Wait here," before he turns and disappears into a tiny hut that sits to the right hand side of the gate.

I turn and look at Thompson, who's sitting in the passenger seat of my car still, trying not to laugh, judging by the expression on his face.

The sergeant returns within a couple of minutes. "You can go in," he announces. "Go up the drive, park in front of the main building and you'll be met." And without another word, he raises the barrier and I quickly get back into my car, driving through before he changes his mind.

The man who meets us, almost the moment I've parked the car, is wearing a much more elaborate uniform, with a few medal ribbons dotted across his chest. He's in his early forties, I would say, and beneath his cap, has mid-brown hair, greying at the temples, and after he's introduced himself as Captain Abbott, he explains that he is the colonel's adjutant.

"The colonel is very busy today," he adds as we shake hands, Thompson and I removing our hats. "Is this something I can help with?"

"Very probably," I reply and, as he shows us into the main building, through the large double doors, and up a wide flight of stairs, I explain the situation to him, without going into too much detail.

He guides us into a busy office, where several men and a few women – all wearing khaki uniforms – are sat at desks, typing or writing furiously. We follow, in silence now, ignoring the inquisitive glances of those we pass, and eventually enter through a door on the left, which the captain closes behind us. "This is a sorry business," he says quietly, speaking for the first time since I began giving him the outline of our reason for being here.

"It is indeed," I reply.

"I had no idea Higgs' fiancée had been killed." He shakes his head. "I—I'll arrange to have him brought to you in here," he says, indicating the seats in front of his desk.

"Would you mind being present while we speak with him?" I ask as he turns to leave.

He frowns. "You want me here?"

"If you don't mind."

He shrugs. "I don't mind at all. I'm just intrigued."

"The things I have to tell Sam may well be very difficult for him to hear," I explain. "I'd just like to know that he's got someone here who understands. I appreciate that he may well be sent somewhere else quite soon for training, but at least for the next few days, it may be useful for him to know he's got someone he can talk to, should the need arise."

"What are you going to tell him?" the captain asks, looking concerned now.

"I'd rather not have to say it all twice, if you don't mind." I twist my hat between my hands and he nods his head, indicating that we should feel free to sit and wait for his return, and then he leaves the room.

Sergeant Thompson follows Captain Abbott's unspoken instructions and sits down, but I don't. The painting behind his desk has caught my eye and I take a moment to study the scenic view, of a delightful country church. It's not one that I'm familiar with, but it's very attractive, painted in the evening, with a beautiful sunset filling the sky. There's something familiar about it, or at least about the style of it and I wander over to take a closer look.

"Well, I'll be…" I mutter to myself, smiling as I recognise the signature in the bottom right hand corner.

"What is it?" Thompson asks, keeping his voice down.

"It's one of Aunt Dotty's," I reply.

"Really?" He gets up and comes over, looking more closely at the painting himself. "She painted this?"

"Yes. That's her signature." I nod to the bottom corner of the frame, just as the door opens and the captain comes back in.

"Private Higgs will be here in a few minutes," he says. "I've sent someone to fetch him." He closes the door and turns, looking up for the first time, and then he smiles. "Oh… I see you're admiring my painting."

"Yes," I reply, feeling a little self conscious for having intruded, and Thompson and I both move back around to the other side of his desk, taking the seats Abbott offered prior to vacating the room.

"I know the artist," he says, sounding a bit smug, as he sits down opposite us, twisting in his chair and looking up at the picture, before turning back to us again. "Well," he adds, "that's a bit of an exaggeration. I don't know her personally, although I have met her a few times. But my father knows her well… and knew her husband even better."

"Oh yes?" I ask, playing dumb – at least for the time being.

"Before he retired, my father was at the Foreign Office," he explains, clasping his hands together in front of him, "and through his dealings there, he got to know a man called Sir Samuel Lytle. He was a really big cheese out in the Far East, although he returned to London several years ago, I believe, and settled down to a peaceful life of retirement with his wife, Dorothy." He pauses for a moment. "Anyway, when I got married back in '35, this arrived out of the blue, literally just a few days before the wedding." He turns again, admiring the painting. "I have no idea how Dorothy found out the date, unless she'd been talking to my mother, of course, but this is the church where Jane and I were married. It was a perfect present, and when the war's over and we can go back to our house in Oxford, we'll hang it back there, above the fireplace in the drawing room again. Our flat in London is too small, I'm afraid… but neither of us wanted to leave it behind…" He turns back and smiles at us, looking embarrassed perhaps.

I nod my head and decide to come clean. "Dorothy Lytle is my aunt," I tell him and his mouth drops open.

"Excuse me?" he mutters, stunned.

"Lady Dorothy Lytle… she's my aunt. She's my mother's sister."

"Good Lord," he exclaims. "Why on earth didn't you says something? Preferably before I called your uncle a big cheese?"

I smile at him. "Because I think that's a fairly good description of Uncle Sam. I think he'd have liked it too."

"We were all sorry to hear about his death," the captain says, lowering his voice.

"Thank you," I reply. "And I'm pleased you brought the painting with you. Dotty will be thrilled when I tell her."

"Do you see much of her?" he asks.

"Oh yes," I reply. "She only lives around the corner from my wife and I." I stop speaking, enjoying saying 'my wife', yet again.

"Then please will you send her my regards?" the captain says. "I'm Ralph Abbott, and my father's name is Bernard. I'm sure she'll remember him."

I smile at him again. "I'm pretty sure she'll remember you," I remark. "She's like that."

He smiles back. "Yes, she is, isn't she?"

We're interrupted by a sharp knocking on the door and the captain sits up abruptly.

"Come in!" he barks, his demeanour changing completely. He's an officer again now.

Thompson and I both turn, and then stand as the door opens behind us, admitting Sam Higgs, who looks very different in the khaki uniform of a private, his hair trimmed a little shorter beneath his sloped cap.

"Inspector?" he looks at me, puzzled, but then remembers himself and salutes the captain, who salutes him back, as the door is closed softly and invisibly, behind him.

"Come and sit down," the captain says to Sam, before moving to the side of the room to fetch a third chair, which he places at the end of his desk.

Sam obeys, looking nervously from myself to the captain, and back again as he removes his cap, clutching it in his clasped hands. "Has something happened?" he asks me.

"Yes, Sam… it has."

"You know who did it, don't you? You know who killed Milly?"

"Yes. We do." I put my hat down on the captain's desk and lean forward, resting my elbows on my knees, looking directly at Sam. "But that's not really why we're here."

"It's not?" Sam looks even more confused now. "In that case, I don't understand."

"We're here because I wanted you to know how she came to be pregnant," I tell him, and the captain coughs rather pointedly. I want to ask him not to, but I don't. Instead I keep my eyes focused on Sam.

"We all know how that happened," he says, although I notice there's no bitterness in his voice now. He simply sounds resigned. And very, very sad.

"Do we?" I query.

"Of course we do," he replies. "Unless you're here to tell me it was an immaculate conception, or whatever it is they call it."

"No, I'm not here to tell you that," I say, patiently.

"In that case, I think it's fair to say that Mildred was having an affair – or at least a fling – with someone…" He eyes me closely. "And you know who, don't you?"

I shake my head. "She wasn't having an affair, or a fling," I tell him and then add, "and she wasn't unfaithful to you, not in the way you think," before he can interrupt.

"Oh come off it, Inspector," he cries, getting to his feet, and wringing his cap between his hands.

"Sit down, Private," the captain says, without raising his voice in the slightest. "I think you should listen to what the inspector has to say."

Sam turns, as though to argue, but then remembers the consequences of doing so, and sits back down meekly. "Go on then," he says, truculently, narrowing his eyes, "you explain it to me."

I take a breath, knowing I can't dress this up in any way that's going to make it easier for him to hear, and that being the case, I may as well just say it. "Mildred was raped."

Sam gasps, drops his cap to the floor, and clamps his hands over his mouth. "Oh my God," he mutters, shaking his head at the same time. "Oh my God… no."

I get to my feet and move forward, standing right in front of him. "I'm sorry, Sam… Reverend Hodge forced himself on her in the vestry one evening after choir practice."

"Reverend… Reverend Hodge?" he says, his face contorting, and then crumpling as tears start to fall. "Reverend Hodge?"

"Yes," I confirm, as he holds up both of his hands, rather like a child, giving me no choice but to take them, to let him ground himself, and to comfort him in the only way I can.

"He… he raped her?"

"Yes. He's confessed to it, and is now in police custody. I wanted to come and tell you, because I didn't want you to go to war thinking badly of her. I didn't want you to hate her. She didn't deserve your hatred. She was faithful to you, Sam, insofar as she was allowed to be."

He looks up at me, tears streaming down his cheeks. "Is that why she postponed the wedding?"

"Because of the rape? Yes. She didn't know about the pregnancy then. She didn't find out about that until a couple of days before she died. She was ashamed of what had been done to her, you see."

"Ashamed?" he whispers, pulling his hands from mine and pushing them back through his short hair, his despair obvious. "What did she have to be ashamed of?" He shakes his head. "It wasn't her fault... none of it was her fault." He stops talking, catches his breath and then starts again. "Why didn't she just tell me?" he says. "I'd have listened. I mean, obviously I'd have been angry, but with him, not her. It—It wouldn't have made any difference between us... not to me. Not if I'd known the truth."

"I know, Sam." It's true. I honestly do believe that, if Mildred had told him, they'd have been able to work things out. They seem like the kind of couple who would have got through anything, as long as they were together. If only she'd seen that... If only the shame hadn't been too much.

"Did he kill her?" he asks, interrupting my train of thought.

"No."

"No?" He frowns at me. "Then who did?"

"His wife killed her... to keep her quiet. I think – rightly or wrongly – that Mildred thought she could live with the rape, and maybe come to terms with it. I think she postponed your wedding, rather than cancelling it, in the hope that she could do just that... find a way of accepting what he'd done to her, and of telling you about it, in the hope that you'd forgive her."

"There was nothing to forgive." He raises his voice, rounding on me.

"I know, Sam," I say soothingly. "I'm just trying to give you my interpretation of events, based on conversations Mildred had with people we've interviewed. That's all. I don't think she wanted things to be over between you for good. But finding out she was pregnant was too much for her. In her eyes, that meant losing you, because once you found out she was expecting another man's child, you'd never be able to accept what had happened, and she couldn't face that... So, she went to Reverend Hodge and told him she was going to report him to the police."

"For the rape?" Sam queries, much calmer now.

"Yes. She thought it was her only chance of keeping you. Unfortunately, Mrs Hodge overheard their conversation, and in her desperation to keep Mildred quiet, she killed her."

He looks at me for a full minute and then slowly lets his head fall into his hands, his shoulders shaking as he weeps. I step back and resume my seat, and the three of us sit in silence, listening to the sound of the broken young man beside us, sobbing for the woman he loved, more than anything in the world, who's been so cruelly taken from him.

"What will happen to them?" he asks eventually and we all turn to face him again. He's red-eyed and slightly out of breath.

"Mrs Hodge will almost certainly hang," I explain. "And I'll do everything possible to ensure that she does…"

"And him?' he asks. "The vicar?"

"I'm going to make it my personal mission to ensure that he doesn't see daylight for a very, very long time."

Sam nods his head slowly and then gets to his feet, picking up his cap from the floor, before holding out his hand to me. I stand, offering my own and we shake hands. "Thank you for coming to tell me," he says.

"I had to," I reply and he nods.

I'm about to let go of him, when he tightens his grip on my hand, halting me. "Just so you know, Inspector," he says quietly, "I was really sorry I said all those things about Milly. I went and sat in my room after you'd left that day, and thought everything through and I realised that, even if she had cheated, as long as she'd still wanted to be with me, I'd have forgiven her…" His voice fades for a moment, but then he continues, "I wish she'd come to me. I wish she'd told me what he'd done to her. I'd have married her anyway and told the world the baby was mine, if that was what she wanted. She… she was too good for me, you see."

I sigh deeply, rather moved by the young man who's standing in front of me.

"No, she wasn't, Sam. You were right for each other. And she loved you."

"Thank you for saying that," he whispers, looking embarrassed, even though I'm not. It needed to be said.

"Take care of yourself, Sam," I say with considerable feeling.

"I'll try, sir," he says, blinking back yet more tears.

"You've got your whole life ahead of you," I add, keeping hold of his hand still. "Remember that."

He nods again. "I will."

I finally release him and, picking up my hat, make my way over to the door, with Thompson following behind. I'm just about to put my hand on the door knob when Sam calls me back, by name.

"Just one more thing," he adds, and takes a step nearer.

"Yes?"

"You said you came here because you didn't want me to hate Milly?"

"Yes."

He shakes his head. "I didn't. I never hated her. She just wasn't the sort of girl anyone could hate."

I nod and open the door, stepping outside, where Thompson joins me.

Back in the car, we both take a long, slow breath.

"He's a remarkable young man," Thompson says, shaking his head, staring out through the windscreen.

"Yes. Very." I follow his gaze and we sit in silence for a moment.

"What are you thinking?" he asks eventually.

I turn to him. "I'm not sure that I am."

"Yes, you are," he replies. "I know that look."

I shrug my shoulders. "Well, I suppose if I'm thinking anything, it's that I feel inadequate."

"Inadequate? How on earth do you work that out? You practically solved the case on day one, had the culprits in custody by the end of day three and their confessions by lunchtime on day four. For a case with no evidence, I'd say that's pretty good going."

"It would be, if I was talking about the case."

"What are you talking about then?" he asks.

"Forgiveness," I reply.

"Forgiveness?" he echoes. "In what context?"

"This context." I turn to look at him. "Up until half an hour ago, Sam believed Mildred had been unfaithful to him, because it was the

285

only logical explanation for her pregnancy – at least as far as he was concerned."

"And?"

"And he was not only willing to forgive her, but also to contemplate the idea of having married her and passing her child off as his own."

"And?" he repeats. "I'm not sure I see your point. I admire his generosity, obviously, but…"

"I'm thinking about the contrast," I point out. "Between him and me."

"You mean when Victoria cheated on you?" he asks. "With me?" he adds, even though it doesn't need saying.

"Yes. Let's face it, not only did I break off our engagement the very next day – quite brutally, I might add – but I cut you out of my life for six years."

He nods his head. "That was different though," he reasons.

"How?"

"Because you weren't really in love with her, were you?"

"No," I reply immediately. "No, I wasn't."

"If Amelie cheated, things would be very different indeed," he says and my blood runs cold, just at the thought.

"If Amelie cheated…" I echo, my voice a mere whisper.

He holds out his hand. "I'm not saying she would," he says quickly. "In fact, you two are so in love, I doubt it would ever cross her mind, but I imagine your reaction would be the polar opposite to what it was with Victoria."

"Yes, it would." I can't say any more, but I know… because I told him this the other day, in a fit of pique, that if Amelie did ever cheat, I'd want to understand… I'd want to know why. What I'd do about it after that, I don't know. I think it would depend on her answers. "Could you forgive Julia?" I ask eventually, because I know he's waiting for me to speak.

"It would take a long time, but yes, I think I probably could," he says. "Obviously we have Christopher and the baby to think about, which I suppose makes a difference, but I love her. I'd want to work it out."

He sighs. "I certainly wouldn't throw away our relationship on a whim."

"Like I did, you mean?"

"Once again," he sighs, "you weren't in love with Victoria… and she'd hurt your pride more than anything else."

"I know."

"Look, I'm not saying it would be easy to forgive Julia, but if she did ever cheat on me – and I seriously hope she never does – then I'd want to try and make things right again." I nod my head, a little surprised. "That shocked you, didn't it?" he says.

"Yes, it did." I start the engine.

"Maybe I've finally grown up," he admits.

"You? Grown up?"

"I know… it's a ridiculous idea, isn't it? Forget I ever said that."

We both chuckle, lightening the somewhat sombre mood in the car, and I start driving, although I don't go back to the station, and instead head towards Thames Ditton.

"What are we doing here?" Thompson asks as we drive into the village.

"We've got a couple more people to see," I explain, turning into Queen's Road.

"Mrs Ryder?" he queries.

"Yes. She deserves to know."

Thompson nods his head as I park the car and we both climb out together, with him getting to the door ahead of me.

Mrs Ryder answers his knock quickly. "Inspector?" she says enquiringly, presumably surprised by our third visit in as many days.

We step inside the house at her invitation, and tell her the same story we've just told Sam, watching in silence as she breaks down in front of us.

"The vicar?" she says, shaking her head. "The vicar raped my daughter?"

"Yes. I'm very sorry."

"I should… I should have noticed," she says, wringing her lace handkerchief between her hands. "I saw she was upset, but I thought that was about the wedding… I never thought to query why she was calling it off in the first place." She purses her lips. "I was so blind…"

"It wasn't your fault, Mrs Ryder," I reason. "Reverend Hodge used his influence over Mildred to enforce her silence. It was only after she went to Doctor Fraser and found out that she was pregnant that she decided to confront the vicar. The doctor suggested she should inform the man responsible, you see."

"Did the doctor know about the rape?" she asks, shocked.

"No," I reply quickly. "No, he had no idea. He was just talking to her in terms of getting the man to accept his responsibilities, that was all. But it obviously made Mildred realise that what the vicar had done was wrong, and that she didn't owe him her silence."

"There are some truly wicked people in this world," Mrs Ryder says thoughtfully.

"Yes, there are."

"Mildred didn't deserve any of it," she adds. "And neither did Sam. They were so happy together, and they should have been allowed to get on with their lives… not have that man… that man…" She stops speaking, her anger and tears getting the better of her.

She sniffles into her handkerchief again, and then looks up at me.

"Thank you, Inspector," she says. "You've been so very kind and considerate to us."

"I really haven't done anything, Mrs Ryder."

She gets up from her seat. "Oh, but you have," she says, blinking rapidly. "You've got justice for Mildred… and now that we don't have her anymore, that's what matters. We need to know that the people who did this to her won't get away with it."

"They won't, Mrs Ryder. I can promise you that."

She manages a half smile as she shows us to the door.

Outside, we climb into the car, although neither of us says anything. For myself, I'm feeling a little humbled, and I start the engine, pulling away from the kerb and turning left at the end of the road.

"Where are we going now?" Thompson asks.

"We're going to see the Whartons. He should be home from work by now."

"The Whartons? Why them?" he queries.

"Because Mrs Wharton has spent the last four days absolutely convinced her husband is guilty."

"Of murder?"

"No, of adultery. She was certain he was sleeping with Mildred Ryder. Surely you picked up on that?"

"And we're going to do what?" he asks, not really replying to my question.

"Explain to her that he wasn't. She deserves to know that, at least. And who knows, it might help them…"

He nudges into me, even though I'm driving. "Marriage really has turned you into an old romantic," he says and I can hear the grin on his face, even though I can't see him, because I'm concentrating on the road.

"I don't know about that," I reply, turning into the High Street.

"Really?"

"Well, I'm not that old."

He chuckles. "But you are romantic?"

I don't reply, but simply tilt my head first one way and then the other, in a kind of non-committal acceptance, which makes him laugh out loud.

It's Mr Wharton who answers the door, still wearing his jacket and holding his hat in his hand, and making it clear from his impatience and haughtiness, that he's only just got in from work, and that our visit is most unwelcome.

"I really am sorry to disturb you," I say, putting my foot inside the door, just so he can't slam it in my face. "Perhaps we could come inside for a few minutes?"

He pauses, for a moment and then reluctantly steps aside, letting us enter, and then shows us into the drawing room, where Mrs Wharton is sitting by the fire, a glass of something that looks remarkably like a gin and tonic, nestled in her hand. She startles on our entry and gets to her feet, placing her glass on the table beside the sofa.

"I didn't hear you come in," she says.

"I'm sorry to disturb your evening," I reply, waiting for Mr Wharton to join us, which he does, minus his hat, going over to his wife and standing beside her, although not too close. "It's just that we thought we'd come and tell you that the case is concluded."

Mrs Wharton seems to visibly sag before us. "You mean… you mean, you know?" she says, and I wonder for a second if she's going to faint.

"Yes. We've got the culprits in custody, and they've confessed to their crimes, which is why I'm able to tell you about it."

"Culprits?" Mr Wharton queries, picking up on that, rather than the confessions.

"Yes. You see, there are two people involved in Mildred's death, one more directly than the other."

"How do you mean?" Mrs Wharton's voice is shaky.

"Unfortunately, a few months before she was killed, Mildred was raped…"

"Oh, my God." Mrs Wharton flops down into the sofa, stunned.

"So that's how she got pregnant?" her husband says, ignoring her.

"Yes."

"And who raped her?" he asks.

"Reverend Hodge. It seems that his wife found out about it and, in order to protect her position in society, she killed Mildred."

"To protect her position?" Mr Wharton echoes.

"Yes."

"Bloody hell," he whispers, just as Mrs Wharton gets to her feet again, linking her arm through her husband's.

"I'm so relieved," she says, looking up at him. "It's been a living hell for the last four days… simply a living hell."

"Why?" he turns to face her.

"Because I thought it was you," she replies, and he takes a step back, releasing himself from her grip.

"You thought I'd killed our maid? Are you mad?"

She shakes her head. "No… I didn't think you'd killed her."

"You thought I'd raped her then, did you?" He sounds angry now.

"Of course not. I didn't know she'd been raped until two minutes ago…"

"Then what did you think?" he thunders.

"I thought you were having an affair with her." Mrs Wharton raises her own voice now. "You've done it before, Norman. We both know that… and I saw the way you used to look at her. I know you promised you'd never do it again, but I thought…"

"I promised, didn't I?" Wharton says and for a moment I think back to the way he was talking to Ethel, and the way he looked at Amelie, wondering to myself how much his promises are worth. Very little, I imagine.

"Yes," she replies, "and I'm sorry I doubted you."

He shakes his head and then they both turn to face us, as though they've suddenly remembered we're still in the room. "We'll leave you to it," I say quietly.

"I'll show you out," Wharton offers and for once, I don't decline.

When we get to the front door, Wharton looks like he's going to follow us outside into the dark evening chill, but keeps one foot inside his hallway, the other on the top step.

"That comment of my wife's," he says in a jokey, man-to-man tone. "I'm sorry about that."

"No need to apologise."

"I did have a brief affair," he continues. "It was a couple of years after we were married, when things were at their most trying financially… and unfortunately, Lucy came to my office to surprise me one lunchtime, and caught me with Brenda… one of the girls from the factory."

"One of the girls from the factory?" I repeat, raising my eyebrows, and he has the decency to look ashamed, both of us clearly recalling his encounter with Ethel. "And you promised not to stray again, did you?" I remind him.

"Well, yes, I did…"

"And did you mean it?" I ask.

"Of course I did." He's offended now.

"Really?"

He chuckles, in a sort of embarrassed fashion. "I know what you're thinking, but there's no harm in looking, Inspector. We all do that, don't we?"

"No," I reply, completely straight faced. "No, we don't."

I'm getting fairly sick of being judged by other men's standards and I turn to walk away, just as Wharton grabs me by the arm. I'm aware of Thompson standing right beside me, but I just glare at the connection Wharton has created, until he's wise enough to release me.

"Don't you judge me," he hisses. "You don't have the right."

I hesitate for a moment and then decide I have nothing to lose, so I may as well say what's on my mind. "How long have you been married" I ask him and he frowns, clearly perplexed by my question.

"I don't know," he replies, revealingly. "Eight years, I suppose. There or thereabouts."

I nod my head. "So I'll assume, in spite of your transgression, that you can still remember your vows. Because I think you'll find you promised to love and cherish your wife… to worship her, in fact… until you were parted by death. And if you're so much as looking elsewhere, then you're not doing that, are you?" He doesn't respond, but looks at me, rather sheepishly. "I'm not judging you, Mr Wharton," I say more softly, although I've just noticed Mrs Wharton has come out of the drawing room and is standing a few paces behind him, listening intently. "How you conduct yourself is entirely your business, and no-one else's. But I can tell you that, when you marry the woman you claim to love, she's entitled to expect something more from you than a ring on her finger, and the use of your surname." I put my hat back on my head. "Good day to you, sir."

Walking down the footpath towards the car, Thompson leans into me and whispers, "Nice speech."

I turn to him and murmur, "Oh, be quiet," and we get back into the car together.

Amelie must have been looking out for me, because she actually greets me at the door, a smile on her face, and rests her hands on my shoulders as I hold onto her, inhaling her scent, breathing her in.

"Is it over?" she whispers.

"Yes… it's over." Well, it is bar the paperwork, but Thompson and I decided that could wait until tomorrow and I dropped him off at home, before driving myself back here.

"Thank goodness." She steps aside and I enter the house, turning on the lights and removing my coat and hat, which Amelie takes from me and hangs up on the hook by the front door.

"What are we having for dinner?" I ask as she turns back to me. I'm hoping that, whatever it is, it won't be ready for at least an hour or so. Because I've got plans…

"I have absolutely no idea," she replies, surprising me, and smiling so broadly that I can't help but laugh. "What's so funny?" she says.

"For someone who's been so tense and anxious about what to cook, and how to cook it, ever since we got back from our honeymoon, you seem very relaxed all of a sudden."

Her smile widens even further. "That's because I decided I'd had enough of being anxious all the time. I felt so much better this morning, and being as I now have a plan for the future, I thought I'd have a relaxing day," she says.

"Well, I'm glad to hear it." I rest my hands on her hips and gaze down at her, as she bites her bottom lip and looks up at me.

"The only problem is, we don't have anything to eat."

"Nothing?" I tease. "I find that hard to believe."

"Well, we do have some bread and eggs," she says quietly, thinking, "and there's some bacon in the larder…"

"Well, bacon and eggs sounds like the perfect supper."

"It sounds more like breakfast to me," she says, shaking her head.

"Breakfast, supper… who cares." I shrug my shoulders and she moves closer, resting her head on my chest.

"How would you feel about cooking?" she asks in a low whisper. "I mean… I know I haven't done much all day, and you've been working really hard, but I wondered how you'd feel about cooking us something and telling me about your case at the same time?"

"That sounds wonderful," I tell her, my immediate plans forgotten. They can wait for now, the idea of cooking and talking, and just being with my adorable and happy wife is more than enough for me. So, taking her hand, I lead her through to the kitchen, removing my jacket when we reach the dining room and placing it over the back of one of the chairs.

"How has it been?" she asks, fetching the eggs and bacon from the larder.

"Well, we got the confessions much more easily than I thought we would," I explain, placing the frying pan on the stove top.

"And did you have to break the rules?" She comes and stands beside me, looking up into my eyes.

I tilt my head to one side. "I may have fractured them… just a little bit." I hold my thumb and forefinger about half an inch apart, and she leans into me.

"How?" she asks.

"I threatened the man who raped the victim, in order to get him to confess."

"In what way?" Her brow furrows and I put down the knife I'm holding and turn to her, clasping her face between my two hands.

"I told him that, if he didn't tell me the truth, I would pin the murder charge on him anyway… even though I knew he wasn't guilty of it. I might also have been holding him up by his lapels at the time," I add.

"Would you have done that?" She's wide-eyed now. "I mean, would you have framed him for something he didn't do?"

"Framed him?" I chuckle, leaning down and kissing her forehead. "You've been reading too many detective novels."

"I borrow yours," she replies smartly. "Now stop prevaricating and answer the question. Would you have framed him?"

"Yes. I would. I'm sorry if that shocks you."

She hesitates for a moment, then whispers, "Don't be sorry," and puts her arms around my waist, leaning into me. I let go of her face and stroke her hair instead. "I assume he confessed?" she says eventually.

"Yes… to the rape."

"But he didn't murder her?"

"No, his wife did."

She leans back. "It was a woman?"

I nod my head. "I'm afraid to say it was."

"What was her motive?" she asks.

I let out a sigh. "She did it to protect her status in society, to keep up appearances."

Amelie's face falls and she frowns. "Sorry?" she says, confused. "Is that even a motive?"

"It's an unusual one, I'll grant you, but this woman seemed to think that being a vicar's wife gave her some kind of social superiority, and she wasn't about to let that go, just because her husband had…"

"Wait a minute," Amelie interrupts, stepping away from me, her face darkening. "Are you telling me that the rapist was a vicar?"

"Yes."

"Oh, good God," she says, with feeling, pushing her fingers back through her hair, and messing it up in the process, right before her face pales and she stares at me. "Do you mean it was that vicar we met the other day? The one who made me feel so uncomfortable?"

She leans back against the sink, in shock. "Yes." She starts to tremble and I go straight to her, pulling her into my arms. "Don't be afraid," I whisper. "You were perfectly safe… I promise."

"I know," she murmurs, even though I can hear the emotion building in her voice. "I know I was safe. You were there."

We stand for a while, just like that, holding onto each other, until eventually, I lean away and look down at her. "Shall I make a start on this supper?" I suggest. She nods her head, smiling, and I kiss the tip of her nose, before turning back to the stove and switching on the gas.

It doesn't take long to rustle up some bacon and eggs, and while I'm doing that, Amelie makes a pot of tea and lays the table, taking through the bread and butter at the same time.

Sitting opposite each other, as usual, we tuck into our feast and Amelie smiles at me.

"I'm so glad I married you," she says, swallowing down a mouthful of bacon.

"Why's that?" I ask.

"Because you know how to cook," she replies, teasing.

I nod my head. "Is that the only reason?"

"No, but at the moment, it seems like the most important one. I'm so hungry, I could eat a horse."

"Well, I'm not much good with cooking horse, so you'll have to settle for bacon and eggs for tonight."

She chuckles and cuts into her egg yolk and I settle back into my chair, feeling properly relaxed for the first time since we came back from the South Downs on Saturday lunchtime. Hopefully, I'll have a quiet few days now, and Amelie and I can spend some time together.

"If you got the confessions so easily," Amelie says, putting down her knife and fork and pouring the tea into our cups, "what have you been doing for the rest of the day? Did you have to finish up the paperwork and things?"

"Ordinarily we would have done, yes, but in this instance, we had a few people to go and see."

"Oh yes?" She passes me my tea cup.

"Thank you, darling." I smile across at her and she smiles back.

"Who did you have to go and see?" she asks.

"The victim's fiancé for one," I explain, taking a slice of bread. "He joined the army just a couple of days ago, so I had to argue my way into the barracks first, and then I ended up meeting with a captain, who it turned out was a friend of Dotty's."

"Really?" She smiles.

"Yes, really."

"But you met the fiancé in the end?"

I nod my head. "Yes."

"Why did you want to see him?" she asks.

"Well, it was partly to explain about who had killed Mildred."

"Was her name Mildred?"

"Yes, although her fiancé called her Milly."

Amelie smiles at me. "That's nice," she says softly, tilting her head. "Were they very much in love?" She sounds sad now.

"Yes. That's really why I went to see him. I—I felt he deserved to know that Mildred hadn't cheated on him. Do you remember, we talked about it?"

"I do, although I also remember being confused about the whole thing," she replies.

"Well," I explain, "Sam – he's the fiancé – he was extremely angry when we told him that Mildred was pregnant. He accused her of seeing another man behind his back… and his language was rather choice, to put it mildly. He wasn't very kind about her."

"I suppose, in the circumstances that's understandable," she reasons and I feel myself frowning, involuntarily.

I take a moment, before continuing, "I—I wanted him to know that, although she was pregnant, she hadn't consented. I didn't want him to go to France – or wherever they end up sending him – and not know the truth."

"That's very sweet of you, Rufus," she says.

"I just didn't want him to think badly of her… but as it turned out, he'd already forgiven her."

Amelie pauses for a moment, taking in what I've said. "You mean, he forgave her, before he knew what had happened to her? He forgave her, thinking she'd been unfaithful?" I nod my head and she sighs, saying, "Well, I don't think I could do that," and I carefully put down my knife and fork, and look at her.

"You couldn't?" I ask, desperately wanting to know… to understand.

"No." She shakes her head, quite firmly. "If you… if you did that… with another woman, I don't think I could forgive you." She stops talking, as though she's thinking it through. "I mean, I'd love to sit here and say that I could be as generous as that young man, and that I could forgive and forget, but I honestly don't think I could. The trust would be gone, wouldn't it? And without that, where would we be?"

She blinks a few times, and I wonder if she's about to cry. She doesn't, but I reach over and take her hand in mine anyway.

"Don't get upset," I murmur. "You don't need to worry about it, because it'll never happen. I'll never do anything to hurt you."

She smiles, her eyes twinkling with what I know to be unshed tears, and she whispers, "I don't need to ask you whether you could forgive me," she says, "I already know the answer to that."

"You do?"

She frowns, just for a moment. "Of course I do. I know you could never forgive me either… You couldn't forgive Victoria, so I know you'd never forgive me."

I look down at our joined hands, but I obviously delay my reply for a moment too long, because Amelie pulls her hand away from mine.

"Rufus?" she whispers and I look up at her. The tears are brimming now.

"Don't cry," I urge, but she shakes her head and, pushing her chair back from the table with a loud scrape, she jumps to her feet and bolts for the door. Unfortunately for her, she has to pass me on the way and I grab her arm, pulling her back. "Don't you dare," I say to her, getting to my feet and looking down at her. "Don't you dare run away from me again."

"But…" she mumbles, as she blinks and two tears fall onto her cheeks.

"But what?" I let go of her arm, moving my hands to her face, cupping her chin and holding her, staring into her eyes.

"But I thought I meant more to you than Victoria."

I smile, shaking my head. "Of course you do," I reason. "You mean everything."

"And yet, you… you wouldn't mind if I… if I went to bed with another man?"

I frown. "Did I say that?"

She thinks for a moment. "Well… no, I suppose not," she allows.

"If you went to bed with another man, I'd be devastated… completely devastated. It would finish me, I think. But that isn't the point here, is it? The point is, could I forgive you?"

"And what's the answer?" She blinks again, more tears falling, and I wipe them away with my thumbs.

"The answer is, that it would depend."

"On what?"

"On the reason why you did it."

She sighs and shakes her head. "I don't understand," she mumbles, and I step closer, my feet either side of hers, so our bodies are fused, melded together.

"If you slept with another man because… I don't know… because you were curious about how it would feel to be with someone else, or because you just met someone and you simply fell head over heels in love with them, and realised I wasn't the man for you after all, then no, I don't think I could forgive you. As you said earlier, that would be a betrayal of our trust. You would have broken the bond between us, and I don't think I'd be strong enough to mend it. Maybe that's a failing on my part, I don't know, but I really don't think I could put something like that behind me."

"Then you do feel the same way as I do," she says, sounding a little stronger.

"In that set of circumstances, yes, I think I do. However, if you slept with another man because of something I'd done…"

"Do you mean like revenge, because you did it first, or something like that?" she asks, tilting her head to one side.

"No, darling. Because I'd never do it."

"Well, neither would I," she says forcefully.

I brush my thumb along her bottom lip and rest my forehead against hers. "I know… I know… but we're talking hypothetically here, and I want to explain this to you, because you seem to be in some doubt."

She sighs and pauses, and eventually whispers, "Go on then."

"What I meant was, if you slept with another man because I… because I wasn't paying you enough attention, or because I'd stopped telling you every single day how much I love you – and meaning it – or because you stopped feeling loved by me, or because you felt second best for any reason… if you slept with another man because I was neglecting you and not doing my job as your husband… then maybe… just maybe, I could forgive you, because it wouldn't be your fault. It would be mine." I kiss her lips. "If you ever felt the need to seek attention and affection from another man, then I would be responsible for that." I kiss her again. "I'd have failed you."

"You never fail me," she says, her voice catching with emotion. "Never. You never neglect me, or make me feel second best, and you always make me feel loved. You always make time for me, even when you're busy… I know that." She reaches up and touches my cheek with

299

her fingertips. "This is your case talking," she whispers. "You see so much lying, so much cheating, so much wickedness, but none of that is ever going to happen to us. I promise." She gulps down her tears. "We don't need to talk about this, Rufus, because I don't want anyone but you."

"And I don't want anyone but you," I echo and she smiles. "You'll never have to look to someone else to make you happy, or to make you feel loved," I whisper, leaning down and kissing her deeply. "Because there is no-one in the world who could love you more than I do."

Without another word, I bend down and lift her into my arms and, leaving our half-eaten supper on the table, I carry her through the house and up the stairs, to our bedroom, closing the door quietly behind us.

The End

The Rufus Stone Detective Stories will continue in Book 5,
The Peacock, due out in Autumn/Winter 2021.

Printed in Great Britain
by Amazon

31532212R00175